MADELINE BAKER

Winner of the *Romantic Times* Reviewers' Choice Award For Best Indian Series!

"Lovers of Indian Romance have a special place on their bookshelves for Madeline Baker!"
—*Romantic Times*

Critical acclaim for Madeline Baker's previous bestsellers:

COMANCHE FLAME

"Another Baker triumph! Powerful, passionate, and action-packed, it will keep readers on the edge of their seats!"
—Romantic Times

PRAIRIE HEAT

"A smoldering tale of revenge and passion as only Madeline Baker can write...without doubt one of her best!"
—Romantic Times

A WHISPER IN THE WIND

"Fresh, powerful and exciting, a time-travel novel taut with raw primal tension and rich in Indian history and tradition!"
—Romantic Times

FORBIDDEN FIRES

"Madeline Baker is synonymous with tender western romances, and *FORBIDDEN FIRES* should not be missed!"
—Romantic Times

LACEY'S WAY

"A breathlessly fast-paced romance!"
—Romantic Times

RENEGADE HEART

"Madeline Baker's latest Indian romance has all the elements she is famous for: a lover's triangle, seething passion, greedy villains and jealous rivals."
—Romantic Times

LOVE FOREVERMORE

"Madeline Baker fans will be thrilled with her latest, best romance!"
—Romantic Times

SAVAGE DESIRE

"Carrie, what's wrong?"

"Everything," she sobbed, her voice muffled by the heavy buffalo robe. "I love you, and you don't love me. I want you, and you keep pushing me away. I can't help it if I'm not pretty, like Red. I —"

"Carrie!" Morgan threw the covers aside and swept her into his arms, hugging her close. "You don't love me, honey. You don't even know me."

"I do too."

"And I do want you, Carrie. You know I do. But it isn't right. You're a beautiful woman. The only reason I push you away is because I don't want to hurt you. You're so damn young, you don't understand how it is, how people would look at you if they saw us together."

"I don't care," she said, sniffing back her tears. "I'm not asking you to marry me, just love me!"

MIDNIGHT FIRE

MADELINE BAKER

LEISURE BOOKS   **NEW YORK CITY**

A LEISURE BOOK®

September 1992

Published by

Dorchester Publishing Co., Inc.
276 Fifth Avenue
New York, NY 10001

Copyright © 1992 by Madeline Baker

Cover Art by Pino

Printed in the United States of America.

With love to my "Little Sister," Karen Amarillas, who is destined to be one of our great historical authors. I can't wait to see *Snow Angel* in print!

Prologue

New Mexico, 1846

She paced back and forth, her fingers worrying a lock of hair as she waited for him, knowing he would come to her as he had almost every night for the past eight months.

"Hurry, Jonnie," she whispered. "Please hurry."

She was afraid. For the first time in her life, she was afraid to face her father's wrath. What could she say? How could she explain? He'd never forgive her for what she'd done. Never.

She whirled around at the sound of footsteps entering the barn, and felt a rush of relief so intense it was almost painful when she saw Jonnie silhouetted in the doorway.

With a sob, she flew into his arms, sighing with pleasure as his arms enfolded her. She could face anything so long as he was there beside her.

"What is it?" he asked, seeing the worry in her eyes. "What is wrong?"

"Oh, Jonnie, I'm . . ." She couldn't say the word.

He said it for her. "Pregnant." He felt the weight of the world settle on his shoulders as she nodded. He had never intended for this to happen. He'd told himself to leave the ranch before it was too late. But each day he fell more deeply in love with her, and it grew harder to leave, harder to keep from touching her, until, in the end, his desire had overcome his self-control and he had made her his. And then leaving became impossible.

"Oh, Jonnie, what are we going to do? You know how my father hates Indians. *All* Indians. He'll never let us get married. Never!"

Jonnie grunted in soft agreement. Harrison Slade would never let a dirty redskin marry his only child.

"We'll run away," she said, smiling brightly. "Yes, that's what we'll do."

"No. I am not ashamed of what we have done. I love you."

Tears glistened in her eyes. "My father has a terrible temper. He'll kill you."

Jonnie sighed heavily. The thought had crossed his mind the first time he had dared to touch her, but he would not run away. He was a man, a warrior, and a warrior did not run away from his responsibilities.

"I will meet you here tomorrow night," he promised solemnly. "We will go to your father together and ask for his permission to marry."

"And when he refuses?"

"Then we will go to my people." He took her face in his hands and kissed her gently, tenderly. "Until tomorrow night."

"Tomorrow night," she whispered, and left the barn with her head high and her heart full of hope.

Chapter 1

Galveston, Texas
March 1874

He was dying and he didn't care. But the pain weakened him, sickened him. He stared at the long-handled knife embedded in his rib cage and felt the vomit rise in his throat. Damn Kylie. The man had the tenacity of a bulldog and the tracking skills of a Cheyenne Dog Soldier.

Uttering a low groan, he closed his eyes and waited for death, sweet welcome death that would release him from the pain that pulsed through him with every beat of his heart.

His hand groped for the bottle at his side. His eyes still closed, he opened his mouth and let the last few drops of whiskey dribble onto his tongue and then, abruptly, he tossed the empty bottle away.

He hadn't failed at everything, he mused ruefully. He'd been a damned good drunk! He'd bought the best Kentucky bourbon when he could afford it, had begged for beer when he was broke, enduring the jeers and ridicule of his betters for the promise of just one drink.

How about a rain dance, Chief?

He'd cheerfully obliged, making up the steps as he went along, but they didn't know that. He'd danced, he'd let them call him names: dirty redskin, drunken Injun, no-account half-breed. He'd been called all those things and worse, but he didn't care because he was afraid they were all true.

A low groan escaped his lips as a fresh wave of pain swept through him. They were right. They were all right. He was nothing but a worthless half-breed born on the wrong side of the blanket, deserted by his father before he was born, despised by his mother because he was a constant reminder of the man who had abandoned her.

But it didn't matter now. None of it mattered now. He'd killed Lou Kylie's kid brother, and Kylie had killed him and it was all over now. No more looking over his shoulder, wondering when Kylie would strike. It was all behind him and there was nothing left but death.

He smiled faintly. At least he'd die outside, where his spirit could fly free. The Navajo believed that the spirits of those who died indoors were forever doomed to remain inside. The body might be removed and buried, but the ghost remained.

He didn't believe such nonsense, of course, couldn't even remember where he'd heard such superstitious hokum. But he was glad to be outside nevertheless.

He felt a sense of euphoria as he drifted into a land of quiet darkness, felt himself slipping down, down, into nothingness. . . .

Chapter 2

Carolyn Chandler darted between two buildings and hurried down the dark alley, one hand holding up her long russet-colored skirts as she ran blindly through the night. She had to get away before it was too late, away from Roger Brockton, away from her father.

Despair followed her down the alley. Her father had sheltered and pampered her all her life, giving her everything she had ever needed, everything she had ever asked for, until now.

Earlier that night, she had listened to her father in stunned disbelief as he informed her she was to marry Roger Brockton the following Sunday at noon.

She'd stared at him blankly, certain he didn't mean it, praying that it was some kind of horrible joke. Not only was Roger Brockton more than twice her age, he was two inches shorter than she was and almost as round as a barrel.

She had begged her father to reconsider, and

when that failed, she had resorted to tears. But for the first time in her life, even that surefire ruse had failed her. She had begged for an explanation, but none had been forthcoming. She would marry Roger Brockton the following Sunday at noon, her father had warned, or she would find herself locked away in the convent in New Orleans.

Carolyn dashed the tears from her eyes. She simply could not marry Mr. Brockton. And being shut up in a convent, deprived of pretty clothes and servants and most of all, her freedom, was simply too awful to contemplate. So she was taking the only course left to her. She was running away, running just as fast as she could.

She was halfway down the alley now. Dark brick buildings rose on both sides. Raucous laughter and the notes of a tinny piano wafted on the salty air, and she realized she was in the alley behind one of the brothels.

The thought spurred her onward and she ran faster. A little cry of alarm erupted from her throat as her foot struck something hard, and then she fell, bruising her hands on the hard-packed ground.

She lay still for a moment, the breath knocked from her body, her hands stinging. And then, to her horror, she realized she was sprawled across a body.

Carolyn scrambled quickly to her feet, her insides churning as she stared at the man lying on his back in the dirt. A knife protruded from his right side, and his shirt was wet with blood. She glanced around, holding one hand at her throat.

He'd been attacked and robbed, she thought, or, more likely, killed in a drunken brawl, for he reeked of cheap whiskey. And blood.

Gathering her skirts, Carolyn stepped around the body, her heart set on escape. And then she heard a low moan.

He wasn't dead.

Carolyn hesitated, then took another step. She had to get away before daylight, had to find a place to hide. The injured man would have to take care of himself.

But the man groaned again, the sound raw with pain and tinged with despair, and she knew she couldn't just leave him lying there on the ground.

Heaving a sigh of resignation, Carolyn knelt beside him, her gaze shying away from the blade's narrow haft.

She was trying to decide how best to help him when his eyelids flickered open and she found herself staring into a pair of deep gray eyes.

"Just lie still," she murmured. "I'll help you."

"No." His voice was gruff and edged with pain. "Let me die."

Carolyn blinked, startled by his request. Surely she had misunderstood him. "Do you live near here?" she asked.

The man nodded.

"I'll take you home."

"No . . . just . . . leave me alone."

Carolyn glanced over her shoulder as her mind worked furiously. It was almost midnight. She had to find a place to hide until she could find a way out of town, someplace where her father would never think to look for her. What better place to hide than in the home of this stranger?

"Please, tell me where you live," she said urgently. "I need a place to stay."

He stared at her thoughtfully. The ground was hard, cold, and damp. Perhaps it would be better to die in his own bed, after all. "If I take you there, will you let me die?"

His speech was slow and slurred, whether from drink or pain she couldn't say. Probably both, she decided.

Carolyn nodded. "Yes, but please, let's hurry."

He stared at her for a long moment. Then, gathering what little strength he had left, he took hold of the knife and jerked it from his flesh. A great gush of blood bubbled from the wound.

Choking back the urge to vomit, Carolyn pulled the white silk scarf from her hair, folded it into a neat square, and placed it over his wound. Lifting the man's hand, she pressed it over the makeshift bandage to hold it in place.

"Help me up," he murmured, and reached for her hand.

He was a tall man, big through the chest and shoulders, and it was all she could do to support his weight. It was fortunate he didn't live far from the alley, Carolyn thought as they reached the front door.

She wrinkled her nose with distaste when they entered the place. It was little more than a shack built of clapboard and tar paper. An oil lamp dangled from a wire affixed to a beam in the ceiling, illuminating the dingy interior. There was little furniture in the main room. A broken-down sofa and a cane-backed chair were placed against one wall. An ancient cast-iron stove stood in the far corner, an empty woodbox beside it.

The man gestured toward a half-open door. "In there."

Carolyn nodded as she helped him through a narrow doorway into a small bedroom with an iron cot topped by a lumpy mattress and a worn sheet that might have once been white. The stub of a candle stood on a wooden crate beside the cot. The whole place smelled musty and dirty.

She helped the man to the bed, and saw his face go pale as he dropped down on the mattress and closed his eyes. Lighting the candle, she saw that her scarf was soaked with blood, and she wondered how he could possibly still be alive. Surely he would be dead soon. The thought frightened her. She did not want to spend the night in this awful place with a dead man.

She was staring at him, wondering what to do, when she heard the front door open and a woman's voice calling, "Morgan? Morgan, are you here?"

Fearful of being caught in such a disreputable place with a wounded man, Carolyn's gaze darted anxiously around the room, looking for another way out, but there was only the one door, and a tiny window set in the far wall that was too small to accommodate her.

"Morgan?"

Carolyn looked up as a voluptuous redhead, clad in a skin-tight green skirt and flimsy low-cut yellow blouse, entered the bedroom.

"Who are you?" the redhead asked, her voice registering her obvious surprise at finding another woman in the house.

"Who are you?" Carolyn retorted, piqued by the woman's unfriendly tone.

The woman frowned at Carolyn and then, seeing the man lying on the cot, flew to his side. "Morgan!" She turned to glare at Carolyn. "What have you done to him?"

"I haven't done anything," Carolyn said quickly. "I found him lying in an alley with a knife in his side."

"He's lost a great deal of blood," the redhead remarked. She glanced over her shoulder at Carolyn. "Will you stay with him while I go for help?"

"Yes, but, please, don't tell anyone I'm here."

"How can I?" the woman retorted irritably. "I don't even know who you are." She studied Carolyn through suspicious brown eyes. "Are you sure you've never seen Morgan before, never been here before?"

"Quite sure. You have no need to be jealous."

The redhead nodded, then left the room.

Carolyn breathed a sigh of relief as she heard the front door open and close. She glanced at the man, Morgan. He had good taste in women, if you ignored the skimpy skirt and blouse. The redhead was tall and beautiful and amply endowed, everything Carolyn had always wanted to be.

Carolyn stared at her reflection in the narrow window. She was short, plain, and a trifle plump. "Baby fat," her father had always said. But she wasn't a baby anymore. She was seventeen and she'd resigned herself to the fact that she'd never be tall or beautiful or voluptuous. Her hair was an ordinary shade of brown, and while her features were pleasant enough, she knew she'd never be toasted as a beauty. Her eyes were her best feature. Large and green beneath delicately arched brows, they were fringed by thick dark lashes.

A low groan drew her attention to the man on the bed. His hair was long and black, and a beard covered the lower half of his face. His skin was dark, and she decided he was probably one of the Mexicans who worked on the docks. His clothes were worn, covered with a thin layer of grime. He was just another drunk, she thought derisively, in a town full of drunks. She wondered what the red-headed woman saw in him.

Morgan opened his eyes and stared at the girl standing beside the bed. "Who are you?" he asked groggily.

"Don't you remember? I found you in the alley. I brought you home."

He nodded faintly, then glanced down at his right side. Blood covered his shirt and had soaked the scarf that had been placed over the wound. It hurt to breathe, and he wondered how much longer he had to live, how much longer he'd have to endure the pain of his wound, the pain of living.

He lifted his gaze to the woman. She was staring at him as if he were some kind of oddity, her expression a benign mixture of curiosity and pity.

"Can I get you anything?" Carolyn asked, disconcerted by his unblinking stare. His eyes were a deep, dark gray, almost black in the dim light of the bedside candle.

"Whiskey."

Carolyn glanced around the bleak room. "Where?"

"Under the bed."

Grimacing, she peered under the rickety cot and found a bottle of cheap bourbon. Uncorking the bottle, she placed her free hand under the man's head and held the flask to his lips. He drank deeply, swallowing the fiery liquid as if it were water.

"You disapprove," he remarked as she took her hand from the back of his head and placed the bottle on the crate.

Carolyn shrugged. "Why should I care if you drink yourself to death?"

A wry grin touched his lips. "You've got that right, miss," he muttered, thinking that if he'd been sober, Kylie would never have been able to sneak up on him. "Drink was the death of me."

"You're not dead yet."

"But you promised to let me die. I'd think you'd let me go peacefully instead of nagging me about the evils of demon rum when I'm about to reap the consequences."

Carolyn frowned at him. "Why are you so eager to die?"

"Maybe 'cause I've got nothing to live for."

She was about to assure him that everyone had something to live for when she heard the front door open, and then the redhead entered the room, followed by a large woman with long gray braids.

Carolyn blinked in surprise. She had supposed the redhead was going for a doctor, but the gray-haired woman looked like an Indian.

Anger flared in the man's deep gray eyes when he saw the old woman. "What is *she* doing here?" he demanded.

Carolyn took a step back, grateful that his anger wasn't directed at her.

"I brought her here," the redhead stated in a no-nonsense tone. "You need help."

"Get the hell out of here, Red, and take these two meddlers with you."

"Don't be silly, Morgan. I'm not going to let you bleed to death. I'm surprised you're still alive with all the blood you've lost."

The Indian woman paid no attention to the argument going on between Morgan and the red-haired woman. Crossing the room, she opened the window, then moved to stand beside the bed.

Lifting her arms, she began to sing of all the things in the world, declaring them to be as perfect as when they had first been made. She praised the heavens and the wind, the clouds and the rain, lightning and the rainbow, the moon and the sun and the stars, the earth, the mountains and the corn and all things that grew in the earth.

Her words closed around Morgan, and though he understood only a few words of her language, he knew she was singing a healing song that had been taught her by an old Navajo shaman. Her voice was low, slightly husky, and strangely soothing.

Once, she had told him that certain songs were

25

sung over the sick to place the sick person in a perfect world, so that a new and perfect life would come to him and he would be reborn into a state of wholeness. She had said that the song told of how all things were made in pairs, to help each other, as the heavens helped the earth with the rain.

Yellow Sage had taught him the song long ago, but he had forgotten all of it save for one verse.

> *Now the Mother Earth,*
> *And the Father Sky,*
> *Meeting, joining one another,*
> *Helpmates ever, they.*
> *All is beautiful.*
> *All is beautiful.*
> *All is beautiful, indeed.*

Yellow Sage had taught him other things as well. He'd learned that the Navajo believed that First-Man was made from white corn, and that First-Woman had been made from yellow corn. White was the color of the east, yellow the color of the west.

He had been eager, almost desperate, to learn of his father's people. Yellow Sage had taught him willingly, somehow sensing his need to know about his Indian heritage, his need to feel a bond with the father he had never known, however slim and intangible that bond might be.

When she'd finished singing, Yellow Sage opened her bag and laid out her nostrums, sterilized a pair of scissors. Next, she removed the sodden scarf and eased Morgan out of his shirt, exposing the wound.

When she reached down to touch him, he batted her hands away. He was in pain, weary in body and spirit, and he wanted only to be left alone.

"You will have to hold him," Yellow Sage ordered curtly.

Red immediately took hold of Morgan's right arm, then stared at Carolyn expectantly.

With great reluctance, Carolyn took hold of his left arm and held it down while the Indian woman began to wash the blood from the ugly, ragged wound.

Morgan swore under his breath, cursing the fact that he was too weak to make them leave him alone. Every touch was agony and he wanted only to die, to drift away into blessed oblivion and forget he had ever been born. The whole thing had been a mistake, anyway. His parents should never have met. Hell, they never would have met at all if his father hadn't gone to work for Harrison Slade, but one thing had led to another, and Slade's daughter had fallen in love with the Navajo wrangler, and Morgan was the result. Supposedly, Morgan's father had promised to marry his mother once he learned she was pregnant, but he'd hightailed it out of town instead.

Morgan bit back a groan as the old Indian woman swabbed his side with some foul-smelling concoction, then rinsed the wound with warm water. Though her hands were gentle, each touch brought fresh waves of torment. He looked up, his gaze settling on the dark-haired girl holding down his left arm as Yellow Sage began stitching the ragged cut in his side. Who was she, this girl with eyes the color of new grass and hair as soft and brown as freshly turned earth?

He clenched his teeth as the needle pierced his flesh. He saw the green-eyed girl's face turn fish-belly white as she watched Yellow Sage sew up the wound. What had Green Eyes been doing prowling around in the alley behind the Golden Grotto? And why the hell hadn't she just left him alone? Oh, yes, he remembered, she needed a place to stay.

The answer raised more questions. She had the look of someone accustomed to money, servants, and three meals a day. Her dress was of dark rus-set-colored silk, the scarf she had placed over his wound was finely woven, expensive, as were the boots on her feet and the gold heart-shaped locket she wore on a narrow black ribbon around her neck.

He closed his eyes as Yellow Sage finished stitch-ing the wound. She smeared one of her pungent salves over his side, then wrapped a length of clean linen securely around his middle.

"Will he live?" Red asked anxiously.

Morgan held his breath as he waited for the old woman's reply. Earlier, he had wanted to die, but not now, not now . . .

"His life is in the hands of the Great Spirit," Yellow Sage remarked fatalistically. "If it is his time to meet his Creator, he will die. If not . . ."

Red nodded, and then looked over at Carolyn. "Are you staying the night?"

"Yes."

Red grunted softly. "Well, I have to go. I've been gone too long already." Bending over the bed, she kissed Morgan on the cheek, then hurried out of the room.

"He will be very sick," the old woman told Carolyn as she gathered her things. "There will be a fever. You must mix one of these with water and make him drink it," she said, handing Carolyn some small paper packets. "You must make him drink water, lots of water. And keep him still so he does not reopen the wound."

Yellow Sage gazed at Carolyn. "Can you do it?"

Carolyn nodded, afraid that if she said no, the old woman might send her away. And she had nowhere to go.

"I will come back tomorrow," Yellow Sage promised, and tucking her bag under her arm, she left the room.

Chapter 3

Carolyn let out a long sigh as she gazed at her surroundings. The small room was littered with several empty whiskey bottles in one corner, and a white shirt, looking none too clean, hung from a hook on the wall.

Carolyn wrapped her arms around her body, suddenly aware of the cold. It was drizzling outside. She could hear raindrops falling on the roof. She glanced at the bed, and shrugged when she saw there was only a single blanket, and that it covered the man called Morgan. It was just as well, she thought, certain she'd rather freeze to death than let that filthy blanket touch her. It was probably crawling with vermin.

Tiptoeing from the bedroom, she went into what she supposed was the parlor and sank down on the sofa. It sagged beneath her, squeaking loudly, but she was suddenly too tired to care. Her encounter with her father, combined with the events of the night, had left her emotionally drained.

Tucking one hand beneath her cheek, she curled up on the dilapidated sofa and closed her eyes, praying there were no bugs lurking under the cushions.

It seemed as though she had just closed her eyes when she heard a harsh cry. Alarmed, Carolyn sat up, her heart beating wildly as she stared into the darkness, momentarily disoriented.

A second cry reached her ears, and she recalled with startling clarity where she was. Rising, she hurried into the bedroom. The candle on the crate had gone out, and she fumbled for the box of sulfur matches, struck one on the rough wood, and lit a fresh candle.

Morgan was tossing restlessly on the narrow cot. In the dim light of the candle, she could see that his face was sheened with perspiration.

Moving quickly, Carolyn poured a glass of water from a clay pitcher and added one of the old woman's powders.

"Here," she said, lifting his head. "Drink this."

"No."

"Drink this," Carolyn repeated firmly and placed the glass to his lips.

"Go 'way," he mumbled. "Leave me alone."

"This will make you feel better," Carolyn said patiently.

Stubbornly, he shook his head.

Exasperated, Carolyn glared at him. Then, her lips compressed in a narrow line, she placed her knee behind his back to hold him upright while she pinched his nose with the thumb and forefinger of her free hand. When he opened his mouth

31

to breathe, she tilted the glass upward.

Carolyn grinned triumphantly as most of the medicated water went down his throat. Lowering him onto the bed, she took a corner of the sheet and wiped his mouth.

Morgan glared at her, but even that small act of defiance required more strength than he possessed and he closed his eyes as pain swallowed him up again.

Carolyn gazed down at him with pity. His heavy beard and moustache were inky black against his pale skin. Sweat glistened on his brow and dampened the grimy sheet that covered him.

Pulling a handkerchief from her skirt pocket, she soaked it with water and wiped the perspiration from his face and neck. Then, reluctantly, she drew back the blanket, revealing a broad chest lightly covered with curly black hair. For a moment, she could only gaze at the expanse of flesh she had uncovered. Never in her seventeen years had she seen a man's naked chest, but she was sure this one was magnificent.

With a shake of her head, she dipped the kerchief in water again and began to sponge the perspiration from his shoulders and torso, trying not stare at him. He was sick and she was caring for him and there was nothing more to it than that. But the curly black hair beneath her hand was soft and springy, tickling her palm, curling around her fingers.

Again and again, she dipped the cloth into the cool water and wiped his face and chest, hoping to bring down the fever that burned through him.

If only she could give him a bath, which he needed badly. He smelled of old sweat and whiskey, and she wondered when he'd bathed last. Not for several days, she guessed, and wrinkled her nose with distaste. She'd never gone a day in her life without bathing at least once. His bedding could use a good scrubbing, too, although she doubted that all the soap in the world could make that sheet white again. It was beyond her comprehension how he could live in such filth.

After an hour, his fever seemed to have abated a little, and Carolyn returned to the sofa in the parlor. But, tired as she was, she couldn't sleep. Instead, she lay wide awake, wondering about Red and her relationship to Morgan, wondering who Morgan was, and who had stabbed him, and why. Wondering if he would live, wondering why she cared. He was the most disreputable-looking man she had ever seen.

She woke, shivering. Hugging herself, Carolyn went into the bedroom to check on Morgan. He was asleep, shivering even more violently than she was.

Crossing the room, she took the shirt from the wall hook and slipped it on over her dress. Moving to the bed, she stared at Morgan for several seconds. Then, with a sigh, she slipped under the covers and drew him close.

The warmth between them increased almost immediately, and Carolyn closed her eyes, grateful for his body heat.

She was almost asleep when she heard the front

door open, the sound of hurried footsteps, and then Red's shocked voice.

"What the hell is going on here?"

"Nothing," Carolyn said, feeling her cheeks blossom with color. "He was cold."

"I'll bet," Red retorted sarcastically.

Carolyn made a low sound of disgust as she sat up. "I don't make it a habit of jumping into bed with men I don't even know," Carolyn replied indignantly. "Especially men who smell like the inside of a whiskey bottle!"

Low masculine laughter rumbled behind her, and Carolyn felt her cheeks grow even hotter as she realized that Morgan was no longer asleep.

She jumped out of the bed as though she had discovered a sidewinder coiled beneath the sheet.

Red glared at Carolyn, her fists on her hips, her eyes narrowed. "So, you were just trying to keep him warm. Hah!" She turned her gaze to Morgan. "And you, you swine, I guess you're going to tell me that nothing happened between you."

Morgan shook his head. "Nothing happened, Red," he assured her. "I don't have the strength, or the inclination." He tried to sit up, and groaned as he fell back against the grimy pillow. "I need a drink."

"What he needs is a bath and a shave and a decent meal," Carolyn remarked, speaking to the redhead. "Is there any way you could bring us some food and some blankets?" She glanced over her shoulder at Morgan. "And some soap?"

A faint grin touched Red's lips. "I guess so. Do you have any money?"

"No."

Red looked skeptical. The other woman had money written all over her. Why, her dress alone cost more than Red made in a month at the Golden Grotto. And the gold locket at her throat had cost plenty, too, as had the diamond earbobs she wore.

"I've got a couple dollars," Morgan murmured. "Take it and buy what she asked for. And bring me a bottle, too."

"Why can't she go?" Red asked crossly. "I just got here."

Carolyn shook her head. "I can't go out. I . . . I'm hiding from someone. They mustn't find me."

"Oh, all right, I'll go," Red decided. "But you'd better not be in that bed when I get back."

Her hips swaying seductively, Red crossed the room to the cot. Reaching under the covers, she slipped her hand into Morgan's pants pocket and withdrew a few crumpled bills. She grinned at Carolyn, her expression smug, and then left the room.

Carolyn turned to face Morgan, about to give him a piece of her mind, when she saw he was perspiring heavily again. Her anger forgotten, she took up her handkerchief, dipped it in the pitcher, and began to sponge the sweat from his face.

"Feels good," he murmured. "You're a regular little angel of mercy, aren't you?"

"Hardly," Carolyn retorted. "I wouldn't be here if I had anywhere else to go."

"What are you running away from?"

"That's none of your business."

He nodded, too sick to argue. His side throbbed

35

mercilessly, his mouth tasted like the inside of an old boot, but, more than anything, he needed a drink. Just one drink to ease the pain. One drink to get him through the day. He closed his eyes as he began to tremble convulsively.

"What is it?" Carolyn asked. "What's wrong?"

"I need a drink." He was shaking violently now as chills and fever wracked his body. Not knowing what else to do, Carolyn sat on the edge of the bed and put her arms around him, holding him close, as though he were a child.

Morgan snuggled against her, seeking the warmth of her body, finding comfort in her nearness. She was soft and she smelled faintly of lilacs. He'd never known a woman who smelled so good. His mother had smelled of whiskey, Red smelled of cheap perfume and lust, but this woman smelled of flowers and sunshine, of good food and soft beds and easy living. He wondered again who she was and who she was hiding from.

His eyelids grew heavy and he closed his eyes, thinking how nice it was to be held in her arms. It reminded him of the way his mother had once held him, before her affection had turned to indifference, and then to resentment. His mother . . .

She hadn't always smelled of whiskey. When he'd been very little, she'd smelled of rosewater. She'd loved him then. Late at night, when she was finished working, she would come to him and hold him. Sometimes she told him fairy tales. And sometimes she just held him in her arms and cried, but she would never tell him what caused her tears. He didn't remember exactly when it began, but gradually she held him less and less. She didn't cry anymore, and the scent of rosewater grew fainter and fainter until the smell of cheap whiskey became her perfume....

When he woke, his fever was down and he was naked beneath a scratchy woolen blanket. There was a basin of water beside the bed, together with a clean cloth, a bar of scented soap, and his razor.

There was no sign of the woman with the beautiful green eyes. Had she gone? Who could blame her?

His nostrils flared as the rich aroma of beef stew drifted into the room. She was still here, he thought. Red couldn't even boil water.

A wry grin twisted Morgan's lips. Funny, he hadn't pictured Green Eyes as the domestic type. He'd figured her for a spoiled rich girl, one accustomed to being waited on hand and foot.

He struggled to sit up as he heard her footsteps.

"I've brought you something to eat," Carolyn said as she entered the room. "Are you hungry?"

Morgan shrugged. "I'd rather have a drink."

"This is better for you."

"You make it?"

"No. The Indian woman brought it over a little while ago. She examined you while you were asleep."

Morgan grunted softly. "She undress me, too?"

"Well, I didn't do it!" Carolyn exclaimed, shocked that he would even think such a thing.

"Where's Red?"

"She had to leave. Something about an engagement."

Morgan grunted. Trey Corrigan must be in town,

he thought. Aside from himself, Corrigan was the only man Red would give up her afternoons for. Corrigan was young and rich, and Red was misguided enough to hope he would marry her, but Morgan knew there was no chance of that. Wealthy young men didn't marry whores, not even pretty ones.

"Shall I feed you?" Carolyn asked.

"I can do it." He sat up, wincing as pain darted along his side.

He watched Green Eyes as she spread a towel across his hips, careful not to touch him in any way. Her cheeks were flushed when she handed him the blue enamel bowl.

He ate slowly, the spoon feeling heavy in his hand. The stew was rich and warm and he ate it all, dismayed to find that the simple act of eating left him utterly weary.

Handing her the bowl, he rested his head against the pillow. "You gonna give me a bath?" he asked, gesturing at the basin.

"If I have to."

"All of me?"

Color washed into her cheeks again. "No. You'll have to ... ah ... you know, do some parts yourself."

"Yeah?" he drawled. "What parts might that be?"

She stared at him, mute, as the flush in her cheeks spread down her neck. "I ... you ..." She lifted her shoulders and let them fall. "You know," she said, her voice barely a whisper.

Morgan grinned faintly. He wished suddenly

that he felt better so he could tease her a little more. As it was, all he wanted to do was sleep. But first he needed a drink. Bad. "Did Red bring me a bottle?"

"Yes." Her disapproval was strong in that single word.

"Where is it?"

Carolyn frowned, disgusted by the eagerness in his voice. "On the floor. There."

He reached for it immediately, ignoring the pain that lanced through his entire right side as he reached for the flask. Whiskey was the answer to pain. It was the answer to everything.

He could feel her censure as he uncorked the bottle and took a long pull, and then another. The liquor was prime, and he knew that Red had filched it from Danny Monroe's private stock at the Grotto. The whiskey was as smooth as silk as it flowed down his throat, easing the gnawing ache in his side, quieting his trembling hands.

Sighing with pleasure, he took one more drink, then corked the bottle and placed it on the crate beside the bed, feeling better than he had in days. Whiskey, he mused. It had never let him down.

Feeling pleasantly drowsy, his pain momentarily forgotten, Morgan gazed at the green-eyed girl standing beside his bed. "You ever gonna tell me your name?" he asked, but he was asleep before she had time to respond.

Chapter 4

Red stabbed a finger in Carolyn's direction. "You're her!" she exclaimed, her voice rising with excitement. "Carolyn Chandler, the missing heiress. Why, it's all over town, how you ran away from home."

Carolyn stared at the redhead. "I . . . I don't know what you mean," she stammered, alarmed that the other woman knew who she was.

"Don't give me that. You fit the description perfectly. Brown hair, green eyes, red dress."

Dismay settled over Carolyn's shoulders like a heavy shroud. If everyone was looking for her, she'd never get away.

Red stared at Carolyn, a frown creasing her brow. "What I want to know is why? Why would you run away from that gorgeous house and that rich old man?"

"It's none of your business. You didn't tell anyone I was here, did you?"

"Not yet, but I'm going to. Why, there's a thousand-dollar reward for information regarding your whereabouts."

"Oh, please, you mustn't!" Carolyn threw a beseeching glance at Morgan. "Don't let her tell my father where I am, please."

Morgan frowned. He had the granddaddy of all hangovers and all he wanted to do was sleep. His side was still as sore as a boil, but with enough whiskey, he could stand the pain. What he couldn't stand was these two women screeching at each other.

"Leave her be, Red," he muttered.

"Are you crazy?" Red exclaimed, her fists on her hips. "Do you realize what we could buy with a thousand dollars?"

"Better booze."

"Booze! Is that all you ever think about?"

Morgan nodded solemnly. His eyelids were getting heavier by the minute. "Just leave her be, at least for now. I need her here to look after me."

"I'll look after you," Red purred seductively.

"You're a working girl, remember?"

"With a thousand dollars, I could afford to quit."

"She saved my life," Morgan said flatly. "Not that I wanted her to, but she did. I owe her something for that."

Red's shoulders sagged. "But ..."

"Not now, Red," he murmured groggily. "Got to sleep. We'll talk later ..."

Red glared at Carolyn, then shook her head. "I'm not sure his life's worth a thousand dollars, but I'll keep your secret, at least for another couple of days."

41

"Thank you," Carolyn said stiffly. "I'll make it up to you when I can."

Red's face lit up. "Yeah? You got money of your own?"

"A little, but I can't get to it right now."

"I can wait," Red said. "But not too long."

Carolyn sighed heavily as she watched Red leave the room, wondering if the woman would really keep her secret. A thousand dollars *was* a lot of money, especially to a woman in Red's line of work.

Carolyn stared at the man sleeping on the narrow cot, wondering again about the relationship between Red and Morgan. Were they lovers, or just friends?

A faint grin tugged at the corners of Carolyn's mouth. Red didn't look like the kind of woman who would waste her time with a man who was just a friend. Carolyn didn't know much about such things, of course, but she'd overheard enough in her seventeen years to realize what Red did for a living.

With an irritated shake of her head, Carolyn put Red from her mind and studied Morgan. He looked a little better each day. Some of the color had returned to his face and he seemed to be in pretty good shape, all things considered. The Indian woman stopped by each day to check his wound, which was healing nicely. His fever was up and down, but gradually getting lower. In a day or two, he'd be well enough to get out of bed, and Carolyn would have to be on her way.

She should have left before this, but Morgan

needed her. It was a curious feeling, being needed. No one had ever needed her before. Her father loved her, but he didn't need her. He had his work and his friends to keep him busy, and only spent time with his daughter at meals and on Sundays, leaving Carolyn to her own devices the rest of the week. Carolyn saw more of Grady, the butler, and Mrs. McMahon, the cook, than her own father.

Still, her days had never been empty. On Mondays she took piano lessons, on Tuesdays she plied her needle, making pillowslips and doilies for her hope chest. On Wednesdays she accompanied Mrs. McMahon into town to buy groceries for the week; on Thursdays she joined several of her friends to study the works of William Shakespeare. And on Fridays and Saturdays she entertained at home, or spent a quiet evening reading, losing herself in the tragic story of Romeo and Juliet, laughing at the antics of Puck in *A Midsummer Night's Dream*.

Carolyn frowned thoughtfully, wondering if Morgan even knew who Shakespeare was. And then, for no particular reason, she found herself wondering what Morgan would look like without that dreadful beard. Cocking her head to one side, she tried to imagine him in a black frock coat and fashionable cravat. His hair was as black as midnight, his skin dark brown. His nose was straight, rather sharp. His mouth, what she could see of it, was wide and sensual. He had prominent cheekbones, straight black brows, and lashes that were ridiculously long for so masculine a man.

Carolyn felt a faint blush warm her cheeks. She had never spent so much time studying a man's appearance before. And this man was a stranger to her. For all she knew, he could be a common thief, a smuggler, a murderer!

She laughed softly as her imagination began to run wild. Surely if he was a murderer, Red would not be consorting with him. Then again, maybe she would. Maybe she was a murderer, too....

"Enough!" Carolyn said aloud. She was being ridiculous. Being cooped up in this dingy little shack was beginning to get on her nerves. She needed something to do with her hands, something to occupy her mind. She glanced around the room, then grinned. What was she hoping to find? The latest copy of *Godey's*? Or perhaps a long-neglected book of poetry gathering dust under the bed beside one of Morgan's old whiskey bottles?

Going into the parlor, she noticed a broom in the corner beside the stove. She looked at it speculatively for a moment. She had never swept a floor in her life, but if ever a floor needed sweeping, this one did.

And how hard could sweeping be? Mrs. Miller, the housekeeper, did it all the time. Taking up the broom, Carolyn began to sweep the floor. Moving dust around had little to recommend it, she mused, and the floor, stained and warped as it was, didn't look much better for her efforts.

Carolyn cast a baleful eye toward the stove. There was an item that really needed a good scouring, she mused. Too bad Mrs. Miller wasn't here to do it.

Finding a rag, Carolyn began to wash the stove top. Scrubbing away what looked like years of crusted grime took considerably more effort than sweeping the floor, and she was perspiring heavily by the time she finished.

She whirled around at the sound of footsteps, and glared at Morgan as he began to chuckle softly.

"Well," he murmured, "this is a sight I never thought to see."

"I was bored," Carolyn muttered sullenly. Her hands were filthy and she wiped them on the makeshift apron she'd tied over her skirt. "What are you doing out of bed?"

"*I* was bored. Think you could make me a cup of coffee?"

"I don't know how."

Morgan grunted softly. Hand pressed against his injured side, he crossed the floor to the stove, lifted the lid from the battered coffee pot, and peered inside. "Looks like there's enough left from breakfast for two cups," he remarked. "Do you want some?"

"Yes, please."

He chuckled again, amused by her polite answer as he added fresh wood to the fire in the grate.

Moving carefully, he sat down on the dilapidated sofa, his gaze moving over Carolyn. Scrubbing the stove had left her face flushed with exertion and her hands stained with grime. She looked more like a little girl playing house than an heiress. A few wisps of hair, as brown as the coffee in the pot, had managed to escape her customary coronet. Her dress, made of russet-colored silk and cut in the latest style, had probably cost more than everything he had ever owned. The slippers on her feet were of kidskin, dyed to match her dress.

"Why are you staring at me?" Carolyn asked.

"I was just wondering why you're running away."

Carolyn hesitated a moment, and then shrugged. What difference would it make if he knew? "My father wants me to marry an old friend of his."

"And you don't want to marry this guy?"

"No."

Morgan nodded. "So where are you headed?"

"To Nebraska. My brother lives in Ogallala."

"That's a long way from here, especially for a chit of a girl traveling alone."

"I'll get there."

"How?"

"I don't know, but I will."

Morgan eyed the heavy gold locket at her throat. It was real, he had no doubt of that. And those earbobs, they'd fetch quite a price down on the waterfront. For a moment, he considered turning the runaway over to her father and collecting the reward. A thousand dollars was a hefty sum, but even as the thought crossed his mind, he knew he wouldn't do it. She'd saved his life, for what it was worth, and he wouldn't betray her. But he might be persuaded to take her to Ogallala in exchange for her jewelry and whatever cash she could lay her hands on.

Morgan scratched his jaw thoughtfully. Taking her to Ogalalla would solve her problem, and maybe one of his. Not that he'd ever thought of Red as a problem, but lately she'd been getting too possessive, too demanding. She'd hinted several times that she'd like to be more than friends, but he wasn't ready for that. Hell, he'd never be ready for that. And he didn't want to be around when she realized that Trey Corrigan wasn't going to marry her. He couldn't go through all that again, the disappointment, the anger, the tears. And he could always count on Danny Monroe to give him a job if he decided to come back to Galveston.

But the best reason for cutting out of Texas was to put some distance between himself and Lou Kylie, because as sure as summer followed spring, Kylie would be looking to cut out his heart if he discovered that Morgan was still alive. And Morgan wasn't ready to face that knife again. Not now, not ever.

Morgan gestured toward the stove. "That coffee should be hot now. Think you could pour me a cup?"

Carolyn nodded. She took two blue enamel cups from the small cupboard beside the stove, filled them with coffee, and handed one to Morgan before taking a seat in the lumpy chair next to the sofa.

"Your father will be watching the stage office and the docks," he remarked.

Carolyn shrugged. "I guess so."

"You could strike out on your own He wouldn't be expecting that."

"I don't know the way," Carolyn replied, and it occurred to her that there were a lot of things she hadn't taken into consideration when she decided to run away.

"I do."

"You!" Carolyn exclaimed. "Why, you're so drunk most of the time, you probably couldn't find your way out of Galveston."

"I can get you to Nebraska."

Carolyn stared at Morgan thoughtfully. Maybe he *could* get her there. Traveling by stage or boat was out of the question. Her father would have every ordinary means of transportation watched. Morgan had the right idea. She would have to find her own way to Nebraska. And perhaps he could get her there. He looked big enough, and strong enough, to protect her along the way, assuming he could stay sober long enough to find his way out of Texas. But could she trust him? What if he got her out in the middle of nowhere and they got lost?

Oh, but it was unthinkable. She couldn't travel cross country alone with a man. It simply wasn't done. Her reputation would be in shreds.

She was about to refuse his offer when she remembered why she was running away. The thought of spending the rest of her life married to Roger Brockton made the loss of her reputation seem inconsequential. "What do you want in exchange for taking me to my brother?"

"Your locket and those diamond earbobs, and whatever else you've got that's worth anything."

Carolyn lifted a hand to her locket. It had been a gift from her father; the earbobs had belonged to her mother. She felt a keen sense of regret at the thought of parting with the diamonds, and then she squared her shoulders. "How soon can we leave?"

"Not for a couple of days. I'll have to see about getting us some trail gear. Bedrolls, supplies, stuff like that. You'll need something else to wear." He looked at her expectantly. "Do we have a deal?"

"Yes."

He held out his hand, and after a moment, Carolyn took it. His palm was rough, callused; his hand was large, almost twice the size of her own, and very warm. An odd flutter stirred in the pit of her stomach as Morgan's fingers closed over hers and she felt suddenly warm all over, as if the heat from his body had been transferred to her own.

"Done!" he said.

"Done," Carolyn agreed, and quickly withdrew her hand from his.

She finished her coffee and carried the empty cup to the dry sink, conscious of his unwavering gaze on her back.

What on earth had she gotten herself into?

Chapter 5

"Pants!" Carolyn exclaimed in horror. "I can't wear pants." She looked at Morgan as if he'd gone crazy. "And I won't wear that ugly plaid shirt, either, or those awful boots."

Morgan sighed impatiently. "Listen, Carolyn—"

"That's Miss Chandler to you, and don't you forget it."

"Pardon me, *Miss* Chandler, but you can't go riding across the country in a silk dress. It isn't practical."

"I'm a lady. Ladies wear dresses. And hats. And gloves."

"We aren't going to a tea party, Miss Chandler. We're going to be crossing some pretty rough country, Indian country, and it'll be a good deal safer for you if you dress and act like a man while we're on the trail."

Carolyn frowned at him. She couldn't wear pants. Why, her father would be scandalized! She bit down on her lower lip. If it weren't for her father, she wouldn't be running away.

Carolyn held out her hand as if waiting for Morgan to cut if off. "Very well, I'll wear them."

"Good."

"You'll have to leave the room while I change."

"What? Oh, yeah, sure."

Carolyn waited until he'd left the shack before she removed her dress, ruffled petticoats, chemise, slippers, and lace-trimmed pantalets. She was glad she wasn't wearing a corset. Imagine having to ask Morgan to unlace her! Her cheeks flushed at the very idea.

She gazed with distaste at the rough denim pants, the scratchy wool shirt, the worn boots. Lifting the pants, she discovered a set of longjohns. These, at least, were new. She felt a twinge of gratitude as she pulled them on, knowing she'd never have been able to tolerate them if someone else had worn them first. It was bad enough to wear a hand-me-down shirt and pants. She'd never worn anything in her life that hadn't been purchased exclusively for her own use.

The clothing fit surprisingly well, though the shirt was a little large and the pants a little tight. The boots, however, were a perfect fit.

She wished fleetingly for a mirror so she could see how she looked, and then decided she really didn't want to know.

She was folding her dress and underthings when the front door swung open.

"You decent yet?" Morgan called.

"Yes, come in."

A wry grin curled Morgan's lips as his gaze went

over Carolyn from head to toe. She didn't look like a fine lady now, he mused. More like a cowboy down on his luck, which was exactly the image he had in mind. The big floppy hat he'd bought her would hide her hair and shade her face. And the poncho would cover everything else.

Carolyn blushed hotly. It was embarrassing, letting a man see her dressed like this. How could she even think of going out in public? What if she saw someone she knew? Why, she'd die of mortification.

"Morgan?"

Carolyn groaned inwardly as Red swept into the room. She was wearing a bright pink dress with a fitted bodice and a ruffled skirt. Her cheeks were rosy with paint, her eyes dark with kohl.

"Morgan, I . . ." Red burst out laughing when she saw Carolyn.

"That's enough, Red," Morgan chided, choking back a grin of his own.

"But she looks so strange!"

"It's how I want her to look. Stop it now, hear?"

"Sorry." Red pursed her lips, then slid a glance at Carolyn. "Sorry, I didn't mean to laugh."

Carolyn nodded curtly, her cheeks hotter than the fires of Hades.

"When are you leaving?" Red asked, gazing up at Morgan.

"Right now."

"So soon? How long will you be gone?"

Morgan shrugged. "As long as it takes."

"I'll miss you."

"Yeah."

"Take me with you."

"Don't be silly. This is business."

"I'm in business."

Morgan laughed softly as he caressed Red's cheek. "Yeah, but this isn't *that* kind of business."

Red swayed against him, her expression pouting and seductive. "Can't we even say goodbye properly? I'm sure she wouldn't mind giving us a few minutes alone."

"Not at all," Carolyn said. Taking up her bundle of clothing, she started toward the door.

"Not now, Red," Morgan said firmly. He placed his hands on Red's shoulders and put her away from him. "I want to get an early start, before there's a lot of people on the street. The fewer witnesses we have, the better. And remember, you don't know anything about Miss Chandler, or where she's gone." He gazed at Red intently, then lowered his voice so only she could hear. "And if anybody asks about me, I was stabbed to death in that alley. Okay?"

Red nodded. "You can trust me, Morgan. You know that," she replied solemnly, and lifted her face for his kiss.

Carolyn had stopped at the front door when she realized that Morgan wasn't going to indulge in a long goodbye. Now, she couldn't help watching as Morgan drew the redhead toward him, his eyes closing as he slanted his mouth over Red's. Red swayed against him, her arms going around his neck, moaning softly as the kiss lengthened.

Feeling as though she were intruding on something much more intimate than a hasty farewell, Carolyn looked away. She'd never been kissed by anyone who wasn't family. What was it like, she wondered, being kissed like that, being held like that?

"Ready, Miss Chandler?"

"Yes."

"Let's go, then. Take care of yourself, Red. And remember, not a word."

"Goodbye, Red," Carolyn said quietly.

"Don't call me that. My name's Annie." The red-head sent a last, heartfelt look at Morgan; then, blinking back a tear, she left the shack.

"I thought her name was Red," Carolyn remarked, puzzled.

"It's my nickname for her," Morgan muttered. "No one else calls her that."

Carolyn followed Morgan outside, only to stare aghast at the pack mule and the two saddled horses standing ground-reined near the door.

"What's the matter?" Morgan asked. "Haven't you ever seen a horse before?"

"Of course, but ... these aren't for us, are they? I mean ... I thought we'd take a carriage."

"A carriage?" He stared at her as if she weren't too bright. "You want to cross hundreds of miles of rough country bouncing around in a carriage?"

"Yes ... no ... I don't know, I mean ..." She broke off in confusion.

"You *can* ride a horse, can't you?"

Carolyn lowered her head, refusing to meet his eyes. "No."

Morgan swore under his breath. "You don't cook, you can't make coffee. What *can* you do?"

"I do needlepoint very nicely," Carolyn snapped, angered by the disdain in his voice.

"Needlepoint! Listen, Miss Chandler, I think you'd better high-tail it back to your old man and live the life you're suited for. You won't last five minutes once we leave town."

"I will too!" Carolyn exclaimed, stung by his derision. "It isn't my fault I was raised to be a lady."

"Well, I can't think of anything that'll get you killed on the trail quicker. Forget it, the deal's off."

"No, please, you've got to take me to my brother. I don't have anywhere else to go. He'll pay you whatever you ask."

"Yeah?" Morgan asked, interested in spite of himself. "He rich?"

"Of course. He's my brother."

"Of course," Morgan muttered dryly. "He's her brother. All right." He took up the reins to the horse he'd chosen for her. "This is a horse. This is the front—"

"You don't have to treat me like an idiot," Carolyn snapped.

"Sorry. Most horses like to be mounted from this side. Put your left foot in the stirrup and swing your other leg over the saddle."

"It's a long way up, isn't it?" Carolyn remarked, thinking she'd never seen such a tall horse.

"I picked this one for you because she's barely fifteen hands high. Here, I'll give you a boost."

"Mr. Morgan, please," Carolyn protested as she felt his hands at her waist, but it was too late. He'd already lifted her into the saddle.

"Just Morgan, Miss Chandler."

"You mustn't touch me so intimately."

"Intimately! You call that intimate?"

"A gentleman never touches a lady's person."

"I'm no gentleman. Now, take up the reins. You pull the left one when you want to go left, and the right one when you want to go right. Pulling straight back will make her stop."

"Are you sure?" She clung to the saddle horn with both hands.

"I'm sure."

Carolyn stared at Morgan. She felt most peculiar, sitting astride the horse. She didn't know much about being an equestrian, but she knew that ladies rode sidesaddle. Straddling a horse was most unseemly. It was a little heady, being so high off the ground, and more than a little frightening.

"You gonna be all right up there?" Morgan asked dubiously.

Carolyn nodded. Letting go of the saddle horn, she picked up the reins, wondering how two thin strips of leather could possibly control such a large animal. "Does she have a name?"

Morgan grinned. "Her name's Whiskey."

"You're not serious!"

Morgan shrugged. "That's her name. I bought her from the bartender at the Grotto."

"Whiskey," Carolyn murmured, stroking the

mare's neck. "Maybe we can think of something else."

Morgan snorted as he swung aboard a big gray gelding and took up the reins to the pack mule.

It was going to be a long trip, he mused ruefully. Very long indeed.

Chapter 6

The first day on the trail was the worst day of Carolyn's life. Morgan rode steadily onward, apparently not bothered by the long hours in the saddle, the heat, the dust, the smell of a sweaty horse, or the fact that she had never ridden before.

He paused briefly at noon, offering her a piece of dried meat that looked and tasted like old shoe leather, and a drink of lukewarm water from his canteen. She would have complained, longed to complain, but she held her tongue for fear he'd turn right around and take her back to Galveston.

They rode all afternoon, pausing now and then to rest the horses. Morgan never seemed to worry about whether *she* needed rest, and apparently he never needed any. Carolyn glared at his back, hating him, hating the heat, the perspiration that trickled down her neck and pooled between her breasts. Her thighs were sore, her back and shoulders ached, and her derriere...well, that part of her anatomy didn't even bear thinking about. She was certain she'd never be able to sit down again, assuming she could summon the strength to get off her horse.

At dusk, Morgan drew rein in a sheltered grove of trees. After removing the pack from the mule, he unsaddled his horse and began to rub it down with a handful of grass.

He frowned when he caught Carolyn staring at him. "See to your horse," he said curtly.

"Me?"

"You rode it, didn't you?"

"Yes, but I thought you'd . . . never mind." Grimacing, she flipped the stirrup over the saddle the way she'd seen Morgan do and began fumbling with the cinch, but no matter how hard she tugged on the thick leather strap, she couldn't loosen it.

"For crying out loud," Morgan muttered. "Get out of the way. I'll do it."

"Good."

"Spoiled brat."

"I am not."

"Like hell. Move over, and I'll show you how it's done."

Carolyn watched, her mouth set in a sullen line, as he loosened the cinch and pulled the rigging from the mare.

"Grab a handful of grass and rub her down until she's dry. You always take care of your horse first thing when we stop at night."

"But I'm hungry. And tired."

"She's tired, too. She's been carrying you all day, and without her, you'd be afoot. And I'm pretty sure you wouldn't take to walking any more than you take to riding. Trust me, riding's easier."

Muttering under her breath, Carolyn snatched up a handful of grass and began to rub it over the mare's hide. Curiously, after the first minute or so, she found she rather enjoyed the task.

Morgan grinned at her over the back of the pack mule. "The old cowboys have a saying: 'The outside of a horse is good for the inside of a man.' I reckon it applies to women, too."

Carolyn scowled at him even though what he'd said was true.

"Spread your bedroll under that tree," Morgan directed. "I'll build a fire and fix us some grub."

Carolyn nodded, too weary to speak. She winced as she picked up her bedroll, and uttered a soft moan of pain as she bent over to spread the ground sheet. Every muscle and joint in her body ached, and her legs were trembling so badly she knew she would fall down if she didn't sit down soon. So she sat, then groaned again as her backside touched the hard ground.

She hardly tasted her dinner. Indeed, she wasn't even sure what she was eating, so badly did she hurt.

Morgan seemed unaware of her discomfort. When dinner was over, he quickly washed the dishes and the frying pan, then sank down on his bedroll, a cigar in one hand and a bottle of whiskey in the other.

Carolyn eyed the flask with distaste. "I'd rather you didn't drink that."

"I'd rather you'd mind your own business."

"I think it is my business, since I'm paying for the trip."

"Sorry, Miss Chandler. I'll stay dry during the day, but I've got to have a drink at night."

"I should think you'd want to keep your wits about you."

"I don't plan to drink myself into a stupor," he assured her. "It helps me relax, that's all."

"Yes, you were certainly relaxed when I found you in that alley."

Morgan scowled at her. Why'd she have to remind him of that? He'd put it all behind him when they rode out of town: meeting Kylie in the alley, Red's increasingly ardent advances, everything.

"Maybe you should take a swig," he suggested. "Might help you loosen up a little."

"I'm fine, thank you."

Morgan grunted, then tilted the bottle to his mouth and took a long swallow. He'd gotten plenty of cash money for her gold locket and earbobs, enough to outfit them and keep them in food and booze until they reached her brother. And he'd bought plenty of whiskey, good whiskey, to keep him company on the trip. And if little Miss Goody Two Shoes didn't like it, that was just too bad. He liked his booze, and he didn't intend to give it up for her or anyone else.

He watched her crawl into her bedroll, and heard a low groan of pain as she drew the top blanket up to her chin.

"You all right?" he asked gruffly.

"Fine."

"You don't sound fine." He gazed at her thoughtfully, and then grinned. She'd never been on a horse before, he reminded himself. No doubt she was hurting. All over.

He took another drink, corked the bottle, and stood up. Chuckling softly, he approached her bedroll and hunkered down on his heels beside her.

"Roll over," he said.

She stared up at him through eyes as dark and green as the Pacific. "Why?"

"Just do it. I'm not going to hurt you."

Carolyn eyed him suspiciously for a moment, then rolled over onto her stomach, her head resting on her arms, her whole body tensing as he drew back the blanket.

"Relax," he said gently. "I'm going to rub your back, that's all."

"But—"

"I know, I know. A gentleman never touches a lady's person."

"That's right," Carolyn said. "And I don't think you should . . ." Her voice trailed off as strong fingers began to knead the soreness from her back and shoulders. As his thumbs made little circles over her shoulder blades, she closed her eyes, certain she had never felt anything so wonderful in her life.

His hands moved up to her neck, his fingertips gently massaging the nape; then his callused hands slowly worked their way down her arms, performing their subtle magic.

Carolyn made a half-hearted protest when he began to massage her legs, then sighed with pleasure when she felt his hands moving expertly over her denim-clad calves, easing away the soreness, the tension. She never thought to object when he took her left foot in his hand and began to rub it gently.

She was asleep in minutes.

Morgan sat back on his heels, staring at Carolyn Chandler. She was too young for him, too short, too plump, but he felt a sudden desire sweep over him, heightened by the whiskey. It occurred to him that, in the future, he should probably keep his hands to himself.

Chapter 7

Carolyn woke with a groan, wondering why the bed was so hard and why she was so cold. Then she remembered where she was.

With a grimace, she drew the blanket closer around her shoulders. She was cold and stiff and her whole body ached, whether from spending the night on the hard ground or from the long hours she'd spent in the saddle the day before she couldn't say. She knew only that it hurt to move.

"About time you woke up."

Carolyn looked over her shoulder to where Morgan sat cross-legged on his bedroll. "What time is it?" she asked groggily.

"After seven."

"In the morning!" she exclaimed. Why, she rarely got up before nine. "How long have you been up?"

"Since six. Want some coffee?"

"I'd rather have tea."

He stared at her as if she'd asked for poison.

"Sorry, all we've got is coffee."

"Very well." She looked at him expectantly, waiting for him to bring it to her.

"It's on the coals, Miss Chandler. Help yourself."

"Oh." Wincing, Carolyn stood up. With one hand pressed against her aching back, she hobbled to the fire, feeling a hundred years old. Conscious of being watched by Morgan, she reached for the blackened coffee pot and filled the tin cup he had put out for her. "Is there any cream?"

Morgan chuckled. "Afraid not."

"Sugar?" she asked hopefully.

"In the sack."

Carolyn picked up the bag he indicated and peered inside. There was no spoon and she was tired of asking him for help, so she took a little sugar in her hand and sprinkled it in her cup. The coffee was strong and bitter, even with sugar in it.

"Not what you're used to, is it?" Morgan asked sardonically.

"No," she admitted.

"Well, you'd best get used to it. There won't be many fancy meals while we're on the trail. No soft beds. No tea."

"I'll be fine," Carolyn said, but she didn't believe it. She was already doubting the wisdom of this trip. Morgan was a stranger to her. This morning he looked like a Barbary pirate, what with his unkempt long black hair and the heavy growth of beard along his jaw and upper lip. She could easily imagine him standing on board ship, a cutlass in his teeth and a scantily clad damsel at his feet.

Except for the red kerchief around his neck, he was dressed all in black from his hat to his boots, and she thought that it suited him perfectly.

Carolyn stared into her coffee cup. Perhaps she should go back home, back where she belonged. At least she knew what was expected of her there, and Roger Brockton would not expect her to do anything as unladylike as ride a horse, or wash dishes, or cook. She'd have a big house of her own, servants to wait on her, pretty clothes to wear.

But then she thought of Roger Brockton. He was almost as old as her father. What if he wanted children? She shuddered at the thought of sharing her bed with an old man, a man she didn't love, a man who barely came up to her chin.

She slid a gaze at Morgan. He might be a drunkard, he might be as poor as Job's donkey, but he was so . . . so masculine. She remembered the way Red had looked at Morgan, the way she had pressed her body to his when they kissed. What had it been like, being kissed by a man who was tall and darkly handsome, who radiated virility the way heat radiated from a fire?

"Want some breakfast, Miss Chandler?"

"What? Oh, yes, please," she replied.

"Bacon and biscuits all right?"

She nodded, knowing better than to object since he was doing the cooking.

"Come here and watch me. I don't intend to do all the work on this trip."

"I don't see why not," Carolyn retorted. "I'm paying you for your services."

"You're paying me to take you to your brother.

That doesn't include waiting on you hand and foot."

Sullen-faced, Carolyn knelt beside Morgan and watched while he sliced the bacon and mixed up a batch of baking powder biscuits. It looked easy enough, she thought, but she really didn't care to learn.

They ate in silence. Carolyn was constantly aware of Morgan as he sat beside her. It made her self-conscious, knowing he was watching her while she ate, no doubt criticizing her every move. She noticed he ate with single-minded purpose.

Morgan drained his coffee cup, then sat staring at her, his expression bemused. "Do you always eat so slow?"

"I beg your pardon?"

"I said, do you always eat so slow?"

"Food should be enjoyed, not wolfed down in a single gulp."

Morgan grunted, fascinated by the tiny bites she took, by the way she held her fork, by the way she drank from her cup, as though it were made of fine china instead of tin.

"I'll go saddle the horses and load the mule while you finish up," he muttered.

Carolyn nodded. Was he going to criticize everything she did? It wasn't her fault she couldn't cook, or that she'd never ridden a horse.

She slid a glance at Morgan as he saddled her horse. His muscles rippled beneath the cheap cotton shirt he wore, holding her gaze. He was a big man, tall and broad-shouldered. And she had no business being with him. A lady did not go gallivanting across the countryside in a man's company unless she had a chaperon. Her father would be scandalized.

Carolyn frowned. It was her father's fault that she was out here. She could not understand his behavior, could not begin to imagine why he wanted her to marry Roger Brockton.

"Miss Chandler?"

She glanced over her shoulder, suddenly aware that Morgan was calling her name.

"There's a creek beyond that rise. Think you could wash up the dishes?"

"Why, yes, I guess so."

"Good. How about filling those canteens, too?"

"Very well."

Grumbling under her breath, Carolyn gathered up their dirty dishes and utensils, as well as the canteens, and made her way to the shallow creek. Kneeling beside the water, she filled the canteens and washed their few dishes, vowing she would never stoop to such menial labor again once she reached her brother's home. Jordan was a rich man in his own right. Perhaps he could find her a suitable husband, someone who understood a lady's needs and respected a lady's limitations.

"Ready yet?"

"No, I need to . . . to . . ." Carolyn's cheeks flamed with embarrassment. How could she tell this man she needed to relieve herself?

Morgan stared at her for a moment, obviously puzzled, and then he grinned impudently. "Over there," he suggested. "Behind that bush."

Carolyn nodded, too mortified to speak. What

was she doing in this wilderness? She stayed behind the bush longer than was necessary, overcome with embarrassment. No lady ever alluded
to such a personal need, let alone attended to it
while a man, a *stranger*, waited only a few yards
away.

"You ever coming out of there?" Morgan called,
wondering what the devil was taking her so long.

Cheeks flushed, Carolyn emerged from behind
the bush, refusing to meet his gaze. She would
never get over the humiliation. Never.

"You ready now?" he asked, suppressed laughter evident in his voice.

Carolyn glared at him. "Yes," she answered
curtly.

"It's about time. Here." He thrust her horse's
reins into her hand, then swung agilely into the
saddle, only to look at her in wry amusement as
she struggled to mount her horse.

"I can't help it if I never learned to ride," she
snapped, annoyed by his amusement at her expense.

"I didn't say anything."

"You were thinking it, though!" Carolyn accused. With a great effort, she managed to get her
left foot in the stirrup and swing her right leg over
the saddle. It was humiliating, having him watch
her, and even more embarrassing to have to wear
pants that clearly outlined her legs and derriere,
leaving little to the imagination, making her feel
positively indecent.

Swallowing a grin, Morgan clucked to his horse.
He'd never seen a more helpless female in his life.

* * *

Lost in thought, Carolyn was hardly aware of the miles slipping by. She hadn't seen her brother, Jordan, in over five years. She'd never even met his wife, Diana. Now that she was on her way, Carolyn wondered if her brother would be glad to see her.

Jordan was eight years her senior, and though she'd always adored him, they'd never been truly close. Jordan wrote home twice a year, on her father's birthday and at Christmas, bringing them up to date on his family, telling them about Ogallala, about how it was growing bigger every year, occasionally writing about Indian attacks in outlying areas.

Indians. Carolyn shuddered. She hadn't thought about the possibility of running into Indians when she decided to go to Nebraska. What if they were attacked? What if she was killed? Worse, what if Morgan was killed and she was taken alive? Tortured? Raped?

She thrust the horrible thought from her mind, refusing to dwell on it. Morgan was probably more of a threat than any Indian. Why hadn't she left him in that alley? Why had she decided to make this ill-advised journey? Why did her father want her to marry Roger Brockton?

She lifted a hand to her temple. No wonder she had a headache.

Carolyn let out a shriek as her horse shied sideways. She tumbled to the ground, landing hard on her backside.

She heard Morgan mutter, "What the hell..."

as he reined his horse to a halt, then sat there staring down at her, a bemused expression on his swarthy face.

"You all right?" he asked.

"I guess so," Carolyn replied, one hand rubbing her bruised behind.

Morgan swung out of the saddle and offered her his hand. "What happened?"

"I don't know." Carolyn put her hand in Morgan's and he pulled her to her feet, his gaze darting from side to side. "I reckon something spooked her."

"I guess so," Carolyn replied, glancing around. "But what? I don't see anything."

Morgan shrugged. "Beats me. Mares are like women. Unpredictable."

Carolyn made a low sound of disgust as she snatched up the reins and put her foot in the stirrup. "Unpredictable," she muttered. "Hah!"

"Don't move," Morgan said quietly.

"What?"

"Don't move. I see what spooked your horse."

"You do? What?"

"Rattlesnake. Over there."

Carolyn followed his gaze. The snake was coiled in the shade of a spindly cactus. "Why isn't it moving?"

"I think it's dead," Morgan remarked. Gun drawn, he walked toward the rattler. Satisfied that the snake was dead, he holstered his Colt. "I guess your mare smelled it. Horses don't like snakes."

Carolyn patted her mare's neck. She had never been particularly fond of horses, but anything smart enough to dislike snakes couldn't be all bad.

Carolyn was about to put her foot into the stirrup when she felt hands encircle her waist.

She turned to face him, ready to tell him she didn't need his help, but the words died in her throat when she found herself staring into his eyes, deep, dark eyes as gray as a storm-tossed sky. His lashes were thick and black, and she noticed again how long they were. There were tiny lines at the corners of his eyes, and a faint white scar just below his hairline.

She felt an odd stirring in the pit of her stomach as Morgan gazed down at her, his expression unfathomable. His nearness made her uncomfortable, and she lowered her gaze to his mouth, felt a sudden heat suffuse her as she wondered what it would be like to feel his lips on hers. She was acutely aware of his hands, still on her waist, of the rough stubble that shadowed his jaw, making him look dangerous and somehow desirable.

Morgan frowned, surprised by the attraction that hummed between them, by the quick surge of desire that had caught him completely off guard. It was even more surprising because she wasn't his type at all. He liked tall, buxom blondes or redheads, not short, plump brunettes.

He gazed into her eyes, those green eyes that sometimes haunted his dreams. Abruptly, he lifted her into the saddle and turned away. He'd better get her to Nebraska quick, he thought, before he did something they'd both regret.

Moving toward his own horse, he told himself that what he'd felt for her didn't mean a thing. It was just that he hadn't had a woman in a long while. In the last few months he hadn't taken anything to bed except a bottle.

Swinging into the saddle, he took up the reins of the pack horse and headed north, all thought of a green-eyed woman disappearing as he contemplated bedding down that night with a cozy fire and a bottle of prime Kentucky bourbon.

Whiskey, he thought with a grin. It kept you warm and it didn't talk back.

Chapter 8

Carolyn snuggled deeper into the blanket around her shoulders. The night had turned cold, and she watched as Morgan tossed an armful of wood on the fire, then made his way back to his bedroll and sat down, his hand searching for the bottle he'd been drinking from since dinner.

. "Don't you think you've had enough?" Carolyn asked.

Morgan shook his head. "Not yet." He took another long pull on the bottle and wiped his mouth with the back of his hand. "Want some?"

"No, thank you."

"Too good to drink with me?" he challenged. His voice was thick, the words slurred.

"No, I just don't drink spirits."

"Especially with me," Morgan muttered. He snorted disdainfully. "White women. Always think you're better than everybody else."

"What on earth are you talking about?"

"White women. They're all alike. Won't give a

man the time of day once they find out."

"Find out what?"

He turned to stare at her, his face hard, his eyes glinting like shards of broken glass. Carolyn shivered as a sudden chill skittered down her spine, a chill that had nothing to do with the cool breeze that whispered out of the hills and ruffled the tall grass.

"It's late," Carolyn said curtly. "I'm going to sleep." She detested his drinking, and yet, even though it seemed he drank a lot, he'd never gotten really drunk. But there was always a first time, and the thought frightened her.

Morgan grunted, then tilted the bottle to his mouth again. Another drink, maybe two, and all the ghosts would be gone.

He gazed into the darkness, trying not to remember how his mother had looked that night with the blood running down her legs and death hiding in her eyes. But the memory was clear, so damn clear. He could almost smell the blood and hear her voice cursing him even as he held her, dying, in his arms. . . .

A high-pitched scream shattered the midnight silence. Morgan sat up, his hand reaching for his gun, his eyes probing the darkness.

He swore under his breath as a second cry followed on the heels of the first. "What the hell," he muttered, rolling to his feet.

Then he realized that the hoarse cry had come from Carolyn. Glancing across the fire, he saw that she was thrashing around in her blankets, apparently in the grip of a nightmare.

Slipping his gun into the waistband of his pants, he skirted the firepit and dropped down on his haunches beside her. "Miss Chandler?"

He shook her shoulder gently as another anguished sob rose in her throat. "Miss Chandler. Carolyn, wake up."

She woke with a start, still trapped in the mists of her nightmare. Her eyes went wide with fear when she saw him crouching beside her. "No!" she screamed. "No, no, leave me alone!"

"Carolyn, it's me, Morgan. You're having a bad dream."

She blinked up at him, her heart pounding wildly. She'd been dreaming of Indians, dreaming that they had captured her, that they were going to torture her and scalp her and leave her for dead.

"You all right now?" he asked gruffly.

"Yes," she lied, and rolling onto her side, she curled into a ball and began to cry. What was she doing out here, alone with this man? She missed her father. She missed her own bed, a decent meal, a hot bath. She'd never felt so alone, so confused. And the dream, it had been so real. What if it was a premonition? What if she was going to die a horrible death at the hands of bloodthirsty savages?

Fresh tears coursed down her cheeks. Morgan was right. She should have stayed home where she belonged. Instead, she was out in the middle of the Texas wilderness with a drunken stranger.

With an exasperated shake of his head, Morgan stood up. Women! No wonder he'd turned to booze. He was heading back to his own blankets when a heart-wrenching sob reached his ears.

Muttering an oath, he retraced his steps to Carolyn's side. He hesitated a moment, wondering if he was doing the right thing, and then he gathered her into his arms, blanket and all. With a sigh, he sat down on a log, his arms holding her close.

Carolyn went tense all over, fear of Morgan stronger now than the fading images of her nightmare. Did he mean to attack her?

Then she felt his hand in her hair. His touch was hesitant, unsure, and yet strangely soothing, and after a moment, she felt the tension drain out of her limbs. It felt good to be held against his chest. The arm that circled her waist was firm and strong, making her feel safe and protected. And his hand, moving in her hair ... she closed her eyes, surrendering to the subtle magic of his touch. No one had ever held her like this before.

As the last images of her nightmare faded, Carolyn became startlingly aware of Morgan's arms around her, and equally aware of the fact that it was most improper for her to be sitting in his lap. His coarse wool shirt felt rough against her cheek, and she could smell the whiskey on his breath, reminding her that he was nothing but a drunk, a stranger she had hired to guide her to Nebraska.

Morgan felt the change in her, the subtle withdrawal. Wordlessly, he stood up and carried her back to her bedroll. Carefully, as though she were made of eggs, he tucked her in, then turned on his heel and disappeared into the darkness.

* * *

She couldn't face him in the morning. She had behaved like a child, crying in the dark because of a bad dream. What must he think of her now? It was bad enough that he thought she was spoiled rotten, now he would think her a crybaby, too.

"Think you could make breakfast this morning?" he called, and Carolyn nodded, still refusing to meet his gaze.

She thought about her father's house as she sliced the bacon. At home, she'd still be in bed. Mrs. McMahon would bring her a cup of hot cocoa and a pastry, and later, if she was still hungry, she would breakfast on fluffy scrambled eggs and fresh ham and fried potatoes.

She uttered a small cry of pain as the knife sliced into her thumb. Morgan was beside her almost immediately, reaching for her hand to examine the cut.

"Damn, girl, you'd best watch what you're doing before you take off a finger or two."

"I was watching," she retorted, her gaze riveted to the blood oozing onto her palm. It was warm and very red.

"Yeah." He poured warm water from the coffee pot over her thumb, then wrapped the cut with a strip of muslin pulled from one of his saddlebags. "Damn, can't you do anything right?"

Carolyn looked up at him, two huge tears forming in her eyes.

Morgan swore under his breath. Her eyes, misted with tears, were a deep sea green. Feeling awkward and foolish, he patted her shoulder. "I'm sorry," he muttered gruffly. "I'll fix breakfast."

"I'll do it."

"I don't care for blood in my bacon," he warned, but his voice was kind, and there was a twinkle in his eye.

"I'll be careful," she promised, and returned to the task of fixing breakfast, determined to prove that she wasn't entirely helpless.

Later, she watched Morgan while he ate, trying to judge by his expression what he thought of her culinary efforts, meager as they were.

"Not bad," he remarked as he put his plate aside. "A little more practice, and you might turn into a passable cook."

She blinked at him, her heart swelling with pride and gratitude. It was the first compliment, if it *was* a compliment, that he'd ever given her.

A short time later, they were riding again. Carolyn watched Morgan. He rode as if he were a part of the horse, moving easily in the saddle. She couldn't help but envy the way he rode and wondered how long it took to perfect such horsemanship. Years, surely, she thought, and hoped she'd never have to ride a horse again once they reached Ogallala.

At noon they came to a small pool surrounded by lacy cottonwoods. Dismounting, Carolyn gazed longingly at the water while Morgan let the horses drink. When he led the animals away from the waterhole, she pulled off her boots, rolled up her pants and longjohns, and waded into the pond, closing her eyes with pleasure as the cool water lapped against her bare legs.

Glancing up, she saw Morgan frowning at her.

"Do you wanna take a bath?"

"Could I?"

"If you make it a quick one. Waterholes like this are frequent stops for Indians."

"Indians." Carolyn shuddered, but the prospect of being clean was stronger than her fear of attack from an unseen enemy.

Emerging from the water, she began to unbraid her hair, eager to wash away the layers of dust. "You're not going to watch me, are you?" she asked when she saw Morgan staring at her.

"No. I'll be over there. Make it quick."

Carolyn waited until he was out of sight behind some scrub brush, and then quickly undressed and slid into the water.

She began to shiver as the cold penetrated her skin. She'd never bathed in cold water before, never washed without a bar of perfumed soap. At home, she had a beautiful enamel tub and people to fill it with warm water and bubbles. She had fluffy white towels to dry off with, scented undergarments and clean clothes to wear. But for this moment, she was blissfully content just to rinse the trail dust from her hair and skin.

A muffled cough drew her attention to the shore, and she saw Morgan standing there.

"What are you doing here?" she demanded, crossing her arms over her breasts even though the water covered her from the shoulders down.

Morgan held out his hand, revealing a thick chunk of yellow soap. "I thought you might need this."

"Oh. Thank you. Just leave it there."

Morgan nodded, but he didn't move. She looked beautiful. Her hair swirled around her shoulders like a cloud of dark chocolate silk, her skin glistened with drops of water, her eyes were the color of sun-kissed emeralds.

He let his gaze meet hers, and saw her cheeks turn scarlet as she realized that he stood between her and her clothes. He knew the exact moment when she realized what he was thinking. She took a step backward, even though she had nowhere to go, and he saw the sudden fear in her eyes and in the slight tremor of her shoulders.

Surprised at the unexpected longing that engulfed him, he dropped the soap on the ground and turned away. He hadn't wanted a woman in months, he mused. And he didn't want this one, either. But he couldn't forget the way she looked, standing there in the water, as if she were a mythical water goddess just emerging from the sea, unspoiled and untouched.

Morgan made a sound of disgust low in his throat as he squatted on his heels and rolled a cigarette. He sounded like a love-sick school boy, he thought irritably, and then he grinned. There were plenty of girls waiting at the Grotto back in Galveston, he mused. Hell, maybe he'd even give in and make love to Red. Whatever he decided, he could put his lust on hold until then.

Carolyn rode beside Morgan, her gaze straight ahead. She wasn't sure what she'd read in his eyes that afternoon by the pool, but whatever it had been, it had left her feeling nervous and ill at ease, as though she were standing on the edge of a precipice where one wrong step would send her plunging toward disaster.

Even more unsettling was the fact that he was drinking again, taking long swallows from a bottle of bourbon he had pulled from one of his saddlebags. He hadn't shaved in two days; there was a dark growth of bristles on his jaw, a brooding expression on his swarthy face.

With every mile that passed, Carolyn grew more aware of the folly of running away from home. But she couldn't go back now. She couldn't face her father and admit she'd started to run away and then lacked the courage to go on. She couldn't face the humiliation.

Most of all, she could not marry Roger Brockton.

Carolyn patted her horse's neck, finding comfort in touching something warm and alive. She wished she could talk to her mother, ask her advice. It wasn't fair that Deborah Chandler had died so young. Never before had Carolyn missed her mother quite as much as she did now, or needed her advice so urgently.

"Oh, Mama," she murmured. "I wish you were here."

"What?"

Carolyn shook her head.. "Nothing."

"If you're missin' your ma, I can take you home."

"No," Carolyn answered, her voice low and tinged with sadness. "She's . . . she's gone."

Morgan grunted softly. "How long?"

"Since I was thirteen." Carolyn slid a glance at Morgan. "Is your mother still alive?"

"No." He took another pull from the bottle, then slipped it back into his saddlebag.

"I'm sorry."

"Don't be."

"Aren't you?"

Morgan shrugged, as if it didn't really matter.

"My mother was a wonderful woman," Carolyn remarked. "She was tall and slender, with beautiful black hair and dark green eyes. She could sing and play the violin, and she wrote poetry."

Carolyn looked at Morgan expectantly, waiting for him to tell her about his own mother, suddenly curious about his parents, his childhood.

A muscle twitched in Morgan's jaw, and then, in a voice that was cold and flat, he said, "My mother was a whore."

Carolyn's eyes grew wide. "I...I'm..." She looked up at him, her cheeks flushed with embarrassment, her eyes filled with sympathy.

Morgan gave a sharp tug on the reins. "We'll camp here tonight," he said curtly and swung from the saddle, effectively ending their conversation.

The heavy silence between them lasted through dinner. Carolyn's gaze kept straying in Morgan's direction, and she wished she could think of something to say to him, something to ease the pain she'd detected in his voice, but nothing came to mind. *I'm sorry* seemed inadequate, and everything else sounded trite or condescending, and in the end she said nothing. But she could not help wondering if he'd been born in a house of ill repute, if he'd grown up among prostitutes, if he knew who his father was.

They were sitting next to the fire when Morgan turned to face her, his gaze cold and direct. She knew immediately that he'd been aware of her covert glances, that he knew exactly what she'd been thinking. A slow flush burned her cheeks, and she was suddenly ashamed of herself for being so curious about something that was none of her business, something that was obviously painful.

"My father was a Navajo," Morgan said. "I never knew him. The way my mother told it, they fell in love and he promised to marry her when she told him she was pregnant, but he hightailed it out of the territory instead. Her father was a tough old bird, and he despised Indians. I could never figure out why the old man hired my father in the first place."

"Is your grandfather still alive?"

"Yeah. He's got a place in Wyoming. Anyway, when the old man found out my mother was pregnant, he called her a slut for letting an Indian touch her and threatened to send her to a convent to repent of her sins. I guess she didn't care much for that idea, because she ran away from home. She took to whorin' to support me after I was born because nobody else would hire a seventeen-year-old girl with a half-breed brat. She used to laugh about it sometimes. Said her father had accused her of being a light skirt, and it turned out he was right."

"My father threatened to send me to a convent

in New Orleans," Carolyn remarked quietly. "That's why I ran away."

Morgan grunted softly. "I guess all parents make mistakes of one kind or another." He stared at her, one black brow arching inquisitively. "You're not running away to work in a brothel, are you?" he asked bluntly, thinking he'd like to be her first customer.

"Of course not," Carolyn replied indignantly, and then she blushed and looked away. "That's what Red is, isn't she? She's a...a..."She couldn't bring herself to say the word.

"A whore? Yeah."

"Have you known her long?"

Morgan let out a heavy sigh. "We grew up together."

"She loves you, doesn't she?"

He hesitated a moment, his eyes hooded, and then he nodded.

"Do you love her?"

"In a way."

"Are you going to marry her?"

Morgan looked at Carolyn as if she'd lost her mind. "Marry Red!" he exclaimed. "Hell, no."

"But ..."

Morgan shook his head. "I don't have any plans to get married," he muttered, "but if I was ever to tie the knot, it sure wouldn't be to a whore. I've had enough of them to last me my whole life."

Carolyn had nothing to say to that, no words to ease the anger in his voice, or the faraway hurt she'd seen in his eyes. Murmuring a quick good night, she sought her blankets, her heart heavy with regret for the unhappy childhood he'd had, for the decision her own father had made that had brought her here, to this place.

With a sigh, she closed her eyes, praying that, somehow, everything would work out.

Chapter 9

Carolyn was almost asleep when she sat bolt upright, her eyes growing wide. He was an Indian! She glanced across the dwindling flames. Morgan was still sitting there, taking slow sips from a whiskey bottle.

He was an Indian.

"Something wrong?"

Carolyn stared at his back, wondering how he knew she was awake. She hadn't made a sound. "No. Yes."

"Well, which is it?" His voice was thick, the words slurred, and she wondered if he was drunk. The thought frightened her. He drank a little every night, but it never seemed to affect him.

"Nothing's wrong. Good night."

Morgan grunted in reply. He didn't have to look over his shoulder to know she was staring at him. He could feel her silent castigation as he took another drink, could almost hear her thoughts. *No-good drunken Injun. Worthless half-breed.* He tried to be angry with her, but it was no use. She was right, damn her.

Eyes hard, he swung around to face her. He was feeling mean, filled with self-loathing for what he was, for what he'd become, and he wanted to punish himself, to see the scorn in her eyes. Carolyn Chandler was a good girl, a lady, untouched and innocent, and he knew he'd never have a woman like her. Never.

Maybe he should go home and marry Red, he thought bleakly. They were two of a kind. But once, just once, he'd like to make love to a woman who hadn't warmed a hundred other beds, a woman whose love would be fresh and unfeigned.

Carolyn began to shiver all over as Morgan continued to stare at her. His eyes, as dark as the sky before a storm, were unfathomable. His face was set in hard lines, his mouth turned down in a mocking grin. She wanted to look away, to pull the blanket over her head and hide, but she couldn't seem to move, couldn't seem to draw her gaze from his.

Slowly, deliberately, Morgan put the bottle aside and stood up. Swaying slightly, he walked toward her, his intent clearly visible in his dark-eyed stare.

Carolyn shook her head. "No. Don't."

"Don't what?" he asked sardonically. "I haven't done anything yet."

"Please," Carolyn begged. He loomed tall and menacing in the darkness. The dim glow of the dying campfire outlined his silhouette in shimmering shades of orange and red, as if he were emerging from the flames of hell.

"Please?" His voice mocked her fear. "Please what?"

"Leave me alone."

"I haven't touched you."

He was beside her now, towering over her. His skin was dark, his hair black and long. *Indian*. The word screamed in the back of Carolyn's mind. Was this why he had agreed to guide her to Nebraska, so he could defile her in the wilderness and bury her body where it would never be found?

Her breath caught in her throat as he knelt beside her. One hand, big and brown and callused, reached out to stroke the curve of her cheek, then to comb through a lock of her hair, loosened from its braid.

Carolyn recoiled from his touch, all the color draining from her face as his hand moved to the back of her head, imprisoning her in his grasp. She could feel his fingers biting into her scalp, and then he was leaning toward her, blotting everything else from her sight.

He was going to kiss her. The thought chilled her blood and filled her with a nameless terror. Overcome with panic, she raised both hands to his chest and pushed as hard as she could. He tumbled backward with an oath, and she scrambled to her feet and ran blindly toward the fire, thinking to grab a piece of wood for use as a weapon.

In her haste, she tripped over a rock and went sprawling into the fire.

Carolyn screamed as her hands skidded across

the hot coals, and screamed again as sparks exploded in her face.

With a strangled cry, Morgan raced toward Carolyn. Grabbing her by the shoulder, he yanked her out of the fire, his hands putting out the tiny flames that were licking at her clothes.

"Leave me alone!" Carolyn struggled wildly to free herself from his hold, more frightened of him than she was of the fire.

"Stop it, you little fool!" Morgan wrapped his arms around her to hold her still. She continued to struggle for a moment, and then she went limp, her head lolling back on his arm.

Morgan scooped Carolyn into his arms, suddenly stone-cold sober as he carried her to her blankets. Gently he laid her down, then examined her hands. The left one looked the worst. The palm was burned, how badly he couldn't say.

Cursing softly, he pulled a strip of clean muslin from one of his saddlebags. Dipping the cloth in the water from his canteen, he began to wash the dirt and ashes from her hands and face. When that was done, he smeared some of Yellow Sage's healing salve over Carolyn's hands, glad he'd had the foresight to bring some of the smelly stuff along. He also dabbed a little on Carolyn's cheek where one of the sparks had singed her delicate skin.

After bandaging her hands, he pulled off her Levi's and the bottoms of her longjohns and examined her legs, trying not to notice the smooth ivory-colored skin, the decidedly feminine contours of her hips and thighs. The layers of cloth had protected her legs, and Morgan breathed a sigh of relief, thinking it would have been a shame to mar such beauty.

He was tucking the blanket around her shoulders when she regained consciousness. The fear in her eyes hit him like a physical blow, and he quickly stood up, backing away from her so she'd know he didn't mean her any harm.

"You're all right," he said. "You got burned a little, but I don't think it's serious."

Carolyn stared at him for a moment, then studied the bandages on her hands.

"Get some rest," Morgan said gruffly, and turned away, unable to bear the pain etched in her face, the silent accusation he read in her eyes.

Carolyn swallowed hard. "Are your hands all right?" she asked, and wondered why she should care.

Morgan nodded curtly. His hands hadn't been badly burned, but they hurt like sin. It was, he thought ruefully, no more than he deserved.

"Get some rest," he said again, and walked into the shadows. Once out of sight, he squatted down on his heels, the pain in his own hands forgotten as he watched Carolyn Chandler cry herself to sleep.

Carolyn woke slowly, feeling as if she hadn't slept at all. Overhead, the sky was clear and blue. The scent of fresh-brewed coffee drifted through the air. In the distance, she heard a bird singing cheerfully.

How nice to be a bird, she mused, free to fly

wherever you wished. She stared at the bandages on her hands, wondering what damage had been done, and if she'd be horribly scarred. Maybe she'd have to wear gloves the rest of her life.

She glanced up at the sound of footsteps and saw Morgan walking toward her.

"How are you feeling this morning?" he asked.

Carolyn shrugged.

"Are you hungry? I made some breakfast."

Carolyn shook her head. She *was* hungry, but she couldn't eat with her hands all bandaged up, and she didn't want him to feed her. She never wanted him to come near her again.

"How about some coffee?"

"I'm not hungry," Carolyn insisted, and then her stomach rumbled loudly.

"You should eat," Morgan remarked.

Ignoring her protests, he helped her sit up, propping her back against one of the saddles. Filling a plate, he sat beside her and fed her as though she were a child. She refused to meet his gaze, refused to thank him.

"Why don't you get some shut-eye?" he suggested. "You probably don't feel much like riding today."

Carolyn nodded curtly. Slipping under her blanket, she rolled onto her side and closed her eyes. But she couldn't sleep. She kept remembering the way Morgan had looked at her the night before, his eyes dark with some emotion she was afraid to examine too closely. She remembered the awful fear that had engulfed her when she stumbled into the fire, the pain that had shot through her hands as the hot coals seared her tender flesh, Morgan's anguished cry as he dragged her to safety.

From beneath the veil of her lashes, she watched as he gathered the dirty dishes, and saw him wince as he lifted the coffee pot and set it on the coals to warm. His hands were hurting, too, she thought. She heard him curse softly as he washed the dishes and put them away. She supposed he had saved her life. If her hair had caught on fire, she might have died. But then, none of it would have happened if he'd left her alone, if he hadn't been drinking.

She hated him, she thought, but she couldn't stop watching him. Unaware of her gaze, he stripped off his shirt and began to wash with water he'd heated in the coffee pot. His back was broad and solid looking, his chest was lightly furred with curling black hair. His stomach was hard and flat, ridged with muscle, and she felt a peculiar tightening in her own belly as she remembered how firm his body was. She had touched him often when she nursed him back in Galveston, more often than necessary, perhaps, but she'd been unable to help herself. He was such a beautiful man.

Dismayed by her thoughts, she closed her eyes, only to open them again moments later. He was sitting beside the fire, staring at his hands, flexing his fingers. She hoped he was hurting, she thought callously, and then, irrationally, she hoped he wasn't.

Eventually she dozed off, and when she woke again, it was late afternoon. Sitting up, she saw Morgan squatting on his heels, his head bent over his left hand. She felt a sudden queasiness in her stomach as he pulled the knife from the sheath on his belt and slid the point into a large waxy-looking blister on the palm of his left hand. A clear watery substance oozed in the wake of the blade.

Feeling Carolyn's gaze, Morgan looked up and their eyes met. A muscle twitched in his jaw as he stared at her, remembering what had happened the night before. She was remembering, too. He could read the fear in her guarded expression.

Sheathing his knife, he stood up and walked toward her, cursing under his breath as she drew the blanket around her shoulders as if to ward him off.

"Miss Chandler . . . Carolyn, I'm sorry about last night. It won't happen again."

Carolyn licked lips gone suddenly dry. She'd never had cause to be afraid of a man before, never known anything but kindness and deference from the men she associated with. But she was afraid of this man, afraid of his strength, afraid of the emotions he aroused in her.

Morgan swore softly. "I'm sorry," he said again. "Do your hands hurt?"

"A little."

Moving slowly so as not to frighten her, Morgan knelt beside Carolyn. Removing the bandages, he gently wiped away the salve that covered the burns. Her left hand was red and blistered; the right one seemed to be only a little singed around the edges.

"I'm going to drain those blisters," Morgan explained as he drew his knife.

Carolyn nodded, her expression solemn. "Will it hurt?"

"No."

Morgan held out his hand and Carolyn placed her left hand in his, palm up, noticing again how large his hand was compared to hers. She wondered why she wasn't afraid of him anymore.

Very gently, Morgan folded his fingers around Carolyn's hand to hold it in place. Her hand was warm in his, her green eyes bright as she watched him.

Carolyn swallowed hard as the point of the blade pierced her skin, releasing a stream of colorless fluid.

"Am I hurting you?" Morgan asked, his voice husky.

"No."

He looked up, his gaze meeting hers for several taut moments. Then he directed his attention to the other blister on her hand, acutely aware of the trust in her eyes, of the way her hair tumbled over her shoulders in a riot of earth brown curls. He wondered suddenly why he had ever thought her plain.

He put his knife away, smeared more of Yellow Sage's ointment on Carolyn's palms, and wrapped her hands in strips of clean muslin. And all the while he was aware of her green-eyed gaze watching him.

He stood abruptly, needing a drink badly, just one drink to still his hands and calm his nerves. Just one drink. He moved swiftly toward his saddlebags and withdrew a bottle.

Then he saw her eyes again, watching him warily as he uncorked the bottle and lifted it to his lips. "Just one drink," he promised. "I need it."

She didn't say anything, just continued to watch him, her eyes luminous in her pale face.

"I need it," he said again.

"Why?"

"Because it's all I've got," he said brusquely, and turning on his heel, he walked away, leaving her sitting there feeling sad and alone.

Chapter 10

Carolyn let out a long sigh. Ten days had passed since she'd burned her hands and it seemed like ten years. She was weary of long hours in the saddle, of a never-ending diet of bacon and beans and coffee without cream, of sleeping on the ground, of being dusty and tired.

Strangely, she was not tired of Morgan. She was a little wary of him, perhaps, and she admitted to being more than a little frightened of him when he was drinking, but she wasn't tired of him.

Despite everything, he was taking good care of her, making sure she had enough to eat, looking after her horse. He hardly spoke to her, though, and she noticed that he kept his distance now that her hands were better, making sure he never touched her.

It made her feel like an outcast, a pariah. She needed someone to talk to. The country was beautiful, if wild and rugged, and she wanted to be able to share her sense of wonder in the land. She wanted someone to share a sunset with, someone who would listen and understand how small she felt when she gazed at the vast blue vault of the sky. But she didn't know how to breech the silence between them, nor did she fully understand it.

Carolyn pulled her hat lower in an effort to block the bright spring sunshine from her eyes. She wished Morgan would stop, if only for a few minutes, so she could stretch her legs. She wished she'd stayed home where she belonged, but she'd gone too far to turn back now.

There was a stream ahead, and she felt a flutter of relief when Morgan reined his big gray gelding toward it. She dismounted when he did, then hurried toward the water. Removing her boots and stockings, she plunged her feet into the stream, sighing as the coolness covered her ankles.

Morgan squatted on his heels beside her. Removing his kerchief, he dipped it in the water and wiped his face and the back of his neck.

"We'll camp here," he remarked tersely, and without waiting for a reply, he rose to his feet and began unsaddling the horses.

They had fallen into a kind of routine. After they cared for their horses, Morgan gathered wood for a fire while Carolyn prepared supper. Her cooking hadn't improved much. She often scorched the meat and burned the beans, but Morgan insisted she keep at it. He didn't like cooking any better than she did and was willing to eat whatever turned up on his plate.

Now, after a quick meal of roast rabbit, they sat on opposite sides of the dwindling fire. Carolyn gazed at Morgan, wondering what he was thinking. Was he sorry he'd agreed to take her to Nebraska? Was he missing Red? She wondered about his past, imagining all kinds of things, and finally the questions evolved from thoughts to words.

"Where were you born?" she asked.

Morgan glared at her. "What difference does it make?"

"None, I . . . I just wondered."

Morgan shrugged. "I don't really know where I was born. My mother moved around a lot when I was young. The first place I remember was a rather elegant house of ill repute in New Mexico. I spent a lot of time locked in one of the back rooms to keep me out of my mother's hair while she was working. I guess I was about sixteen when the place burned down, and my mother decided to move to Arizona. They'd struck gold in La Paz, and she thought she'd cash in on it the best way she knew how."

"Where did you meet Red?"

"In La Paz."

"Was she . . . did she . . . ?"

"Not then. Red was fifteen at the time and worked downstairs serving drinks. She made pretty good money and even managed to save a little. When she turned sixteen, I tried to get her to leave before Mozelle talked her into becoming one of the upstairs girls, but it was too late. Red had fallen in love with one of the customers by then, and one night she took him upstairs."

Morgan grunted softly. "The man was no good, but Red couldn't see it. She said he loved her and was going to marry her. She was heartbroken when she found out he already had a wife and a couple of kids. She swore she'd never fall in love again, and that she'd make all men pay for what he'd done to her."

Carolyn shook her head, feeling a sudden wave of sympathy for Red and a surge of gratitude for her own childhood, which had been happy and carefree until her mother passed away.

"She loves you, though," Carolyn remarked.

"I know."

"Hasn't she ever wanted to do anything else?"

"She got married once, but it only lasted a couple of years. I don't think she loved the guy, I think she just wanted to be respectable for a change. I guess maybe it was too late by then."

"What about you? Have you always worked in ... in those kinds of places?"

"Not always." Morgan stared into the distance. He'd tried to go straight after his mother died. Fresh out of jail, he'd tried to find a decent job, but there weren't a lot of openings for a half-breed with a prison record, so he left Arizona. It had been hard, leaving Red. She was the only real friend he'd ever had, but he needed a change, so he'd kissed her goodbye, and headed for New Mexico, and then Colorado. But it was the same story wherever he went. Nobody wanted to hire a half-breed for anything except mucking stables. He'd learned some things along the way, like how to deal from the bottom and how to quick-draw a Colt, and when he got tired of drifting, he went to work dealing for the house in a Denver saloon. That was where Red's letter had caught up with him. Her marriage was over by then and she'd been feeling pretty low. She'd taken it into her head to go to Texas, so he had quit Denver and gone with her to make sure she didn't get into any trouble along the way.

"Why do you drink so much?"

The sound of Carolyn's voice brought him back to the present. "What?"

"I said, why do you drink so much?"

"Why do you ask so many questions?"

Carolyn shrugged. "How else can I find out about you?"

"You don't need to know any more about me than you know now."

"Do you have a job?"

Morgan stared at Carolyn in exasperation. "Yes, I have a job, Miss Chandler. I work at the Grotto, making sure the customers behave themselves. And when I'm very good, Danny slips me a bottle of his best bourbon and lets me spend the night."

"With Red?" The question slipped out of its own accord.

"No." One black eyebrow lifted in wry amusement. "You don't believe me?"

"I thought . . . I mean, it's obvious she loves you, so I just thought . . ." Flustered, Carolyn clasped her hands in her lap and bowed her head, sorry she'd said a word.

"I know what you thought. But we're just good friends."

For some reason, Carolyn suddenly felt like smiling.

"What about you, Miss Chandler? Were you born in Texas?"

"No. In New York. We came here after my mother died."

"Have you always been rich?"

"What an ill-bred question."

"Not as personal as some I've been asked lately."

"Touché, Mr. Morgan."

"Just Morgan. And you didn't answer my question."

"Yes, we've always been rich. My father inherited a great deal of money from his father and went into banking. He's been very successful."

"I guess you had maids and a butler and all that stuff."

"Yes."

Morgan grunted. "That's what I figured. It explains why you're so helpless."

"I am not helpless!"

"Darn close."

She wanted to argue, to scream that there were lots of things she could do, but nothing came to mind, so she changed the subject. "What's your last name?"

"Morgan."

"What's your first name, then?"

"Morgan."

Carolyn stared at him, annoyed by his stubbornness. "Why won't you tell me?"

"Because you don't need to know." He raised his arms over his head, stretching, and then stood up. "Gonna be another long day in the saddle tomorrow. Why don't you turn in while I check on the horses?"

"Very well," Carolyn agreed. She crawled under her blankets and pulled them up to her chin, only to lie awake staring at the vast star-studded sky. It was beautiful out here. The weather was warm, the skies were clear, and she might have enjoyed being out in the wilderness if she had someone along to do all the hard work. Her hands were rough and chapped from washing the dishes and gathering firewood and currying her horse. Her skin, once pampered and protected from the sun, was no longer the color of cream. Instead, it was tanned a light golden brown.

Carolyn let out a long sigh. She missed wearing pretty clothes. Her plaid shirt and denim pants were secondhand and ugly, and so were her boots. She'd never been pretty, but at least her clothes had been stylish and well-made, giving her a sense of being fashionable if not beautiful. Now she felt like a trail hand, and probably smelled like one, too. No doubt her skin would be the color of saddle leather and her legs as bowed as a fiddle by the time she reached her destination.

She was feeling good and sorry for herself when she heard Morgan return to the fire. Her self-pity forgotten, she stared at him through the veil of her lashes. He sat cross-legged on the ground, bottle in hand, gazing into the flames. The firelight cast his face in bronze, and she studied his profile, the square jaw, the high cheekbones, the long, straight nose. He was handsome, she thought. Handsome and secretive. What was he hiding from her? Why wouldn't he tell her his last name?

He was a puzzle, Carolyn mused, but one she intended to solve before they reached Ogallala.

Chapter 11

The first sign of trouble appeared in the form of a wagon track. Carolyn was puzzled by Morgan's concern. After all, what harm could there be in a wagon? When she questioned him, he refused to answer, just told her to stay close. Though she didn't know what he was afraid of, she felt the fear building within her as they rode northward.

Morgan rode warily now, his gaze constantly sweeping the horizon, his hand never far from his rifle. Not only was he more cautious, but he was drinking less in the evening now, and that fact alone caused Carolyn concern. What was he afraid of? Why wouldn't he tell her what was wrong?

They had left the tree-lined river they'd been following and now were crossing a desolate stretch of ground marked by shallow arroyos and high-walled canyons.

Even the land was intimidating, Carolyn thought as she glanced around. Spiny cactus, sharp rocks, and thorny bushes dotted the land, as unfriendly and dangerous as the wildlife Morgan said inhabited this part of Texas. But it wasn't animals Carolyn was afraid of. It was Indians. The Comanche also occupied this part of Texas, raiding outlying settlements, stealing cattle and horses, killing any whites who happened to cross their path.

Morgan told her bits and pieces of what he knew about the Comanche. The name itself, taken from the Ute word *Komantcia*, meant "anyone who wants to fight me all the time." Morgan told her the Spaniards picked up the word from the Utes, and the Americans took it from the Spaniards. In sign language, the Comanche were known as the Snake People. Before the arrival of the horse, the Comanche used dogs to draw their travois. They called the horses God-dogs, Morgan said. And, of course, horses were more practical than dogs. A horse could eat grass and the bark of trees, its flesh could be eaten when food was scarce, and its skin could provide shelter and robes. But best of all, the horse allowed the Comanche to run down and kill the buffalo on the open plains, and to carry the meat back to camp. Some men loved their horses more than their wives, and killing a man's favorite horse was akin to murder.

She glanced at Morgan. He was Indian. Perhaps, out here in this forsaken country, his Indian blood would be an asset. Perhaps the Comanches wouldn't hurt one of their own kind ... but then, Morgan wasn't a Comanche, he was a Navajo. Did Indians regard other tribes as friendly or hostile?

Feeling suddenly vulnerable, she urged her horse closer to his.

Morgan slid a glance in Carolyn's direction. Her expression was as easy to read as the tracks of the coyote he'd seen earlier that day. She was afraid, afraid of him, afraid of the unknown. But he was the lesser evil of the two, the only protection she had. He wondered if she was ready to turn back yet, ready to admit she'd made a mistake in leaving Galveston.

"We can always go back," he remarked quietly.

She hesitated for only a moment, then shook her head. "No, I can't."

"Suit yourself," he muttered, and then, suddenly, it was too late to turn back.

Carolyn drew in a sharp breath when she saw them, seven men who appeared out of the nearest arroyo, riding hard in their direction. She threw a frantic glance in Morgan's direction, saw the defeat in his eyes, and knew they were doomed to die in the wilderness.

They were surrounded in moments. Morgan was knocked from his horse, his weapons taken, his hands tied behind his back. One of the desperadoes dropped a loop around his chest and snugged it tight.

Carolyn watched in horror, wondering what they would do to Morgan, until the men turned toward her. In that instant, as all eyes focused on her, her worry for Morgan vanished. Whatever they did to him would be nothing compared to what was about to happen to her.

The men spoke among themselves, their voices

low, their eyes hot as they leered at her. They were a disreputable lot, their clothing stained with mud and grime, their boots worn, their hair unkempt. But there was nothing old or ill-kept about the rifles aimed in her direction.

Morgan had not moved since the bandits tied his hands behind his back. His first instinct had been to make a grab for his rifle, but such a move would have meant certain death for him, and maybe for Carolyn, as well, although he figured she'd rather be dead than mauled by seven Comancheros. He could see the lust in their eyes as they stared at Carolyn. They weren't really seeing her, he knew; all they saw was a woman, vulnerable, there for the taking.

He licked the blood from his lip and stood up. "I wouldn't hurt her if I were you," he said calmly, loudly.

The outlaw nearest Morgan backhanded him across the mouth. "Shut up," he ordered brusquely. "We will deal with you later."

"Let him speak, Rafael."

"But, Jornado . . ."

The outlaw leader looked at Morgan expectantly. "You have something to say, *hombre*?"

"She's rich," Morgan said. "Her daddy will pay handsomely to have her back in one piece."

Rich! All eyes swung toward Morgan, lust momentarily replaced by greed.

"How rich?" Jornado demanded brusquely.

"Her father owns the bank in Galveston. She's a runaway. I was taking her back for the reward."

He heard Carolyn's surprised gasp and silenced her with a glance.

Jornado studied Morgan thoughtfully. Captured women were customarily used by the men, then sold into one of the brothels south of the border, but if what this man said was true, the girl's worth lay in Galveston, not Mexico.

Morgan kept his expression impassive as Jornado's eyes bored into his. All he was doing was buying time, he thought bleakly. They'd kill him for sure sooner or later, but if they thought Carolyn was valuable to them, they might leave her alone. Hell, she might even get back home in one piece.

He tried to appear nonchalant as he returned the outlaw's gaze. Jornado was short and squat, with massive shoulders and legs like tree trunks. His hair was black and greasy, his eyes were brown, wary, and intelligent. He wore a .45 Colt strapped to his right hip, and his hand caressed the smooth walnut gunbutt as he weighed the risk of returning Carolyn to her father against the reward.

"How much is she worth?" the outlaw asked after a while.

"Twenty thousand dollars."

Jornado whistled under his breath.

"She's a virgin," Morgan remarked. "Her father might not pay as much for damaged goods."

A murmur of low-voiced protests rose from the other Comancheros, but their complaints were silenced at a curt word from their leader.

"We will go to Galveston," Jornado decided. "We will see if what this half-breed says is true.

If it is, we will claim the reward. If not ..." His eyes moved over Carolyn in a long, lazy assessment, and then he grinned. "If not, we will still have our reward."

"And what of him, *jefe?*" A tall, bow-legged outlaw jerked a thumb in Morgan's direction.

The outlaw leader shrugged. "He is of no consequence, Cashero. Kill him or not, as you wish, but do it later. Let us find a place to camp for the night."

Morgan felt his insides tighten with dread as Rafael took up the end of the rope around his neck, then swung aboard his horse and urged the gelding into a walk.

Carolyn cried out in protest as one of the Comancheros tied her hands together. She looked at Morgan for help, but he couldn't help her now. His own hands were tied behind his back, and there was a rope around his chest. And even as she watched, Rafael was urging his horse to go faster, forcing Morgan to run to keep up. *Oh Lord*, she thought hopelessly, *why didn't I stay home where I belong?*

They rode until dusk. Carolyn was numb by then, numb with fear, numb from the hard ride. And Morgan ... she glanced at him now, surprised that he was still alive. Rafael had forced him to run for several miles, and then, when Morgan fell, the outlaw had dragged him until he got bored with the game and he and another outlaw had thrown Morgan over the back of a horse, securing his hands and feet beneath the animal's belly.

The outlaws ignored her as they went about setting up camp, building a fire, roasting the rabbits they had killed earlier in the day.

For a moment, Carolyn stood where they'd left her; then, summoning what little courage she possessed, she went to Morgan. He was lying on his side near a clump of mesquite. His eyes were closed; his face was badly scratched, and his shirt and pants were in tatters. There were long scratches on his forearms, and his knees were bruised and bloody. But he was still breathing.

Though her hands were bound, Carolyn reached out and brushed a lock of hair from Morgan's brow. Her touch woke him instantly and she found herself gazing into his eyes, smoky gray eyes filled with pain and a hint of despair.

"Sorry," he muttered.

"For what?"

"I thought I could get you to Ogallala. I should have known better. I've never done anything right in my life."

Carolyn blinked at him, wanting him to explain, to delve into his past so that she might discover why there was always a hint of sadness in his eyes. But just then Rafael grabbed her by the arm and forced her toward the fire where he demanded that she pour him a cup of coffee.

She did so reluctantly, her whole being filled with resentment. She was so tired of being told what to do. Her father, Morgan, and now this brigand. Oh, to be a man, she thought enviously; to be able to have control of her own life, and tell others what to do.

Rafael reached for the cup, his grin a mile wide, his gray eyes drilling into her own. He looked so smug, so arrogant. No doubt he thought she was afraid of him, that she'd do whatever he said without question...and he was right. The thought filled her with such self-contempt she almost choked on it. Then, hardly aware of what she was doing, she hurled the contents of the cup in his face.

It was a toss-up as to who was more surprised by her actions, Rafael or Carolyn. The outlaw loosed a string of obscenities as he clawed at his eyes, and then he grabbed Carolyn by the arm and slapped her across the face, hard. She gasped with pain, her eyes filling with tears.

She drew in a sharp breath as Rafael raised his hand to strike her again, then felt her knees go weak with relief when Jornado stepped between them.

"Enough, Rafael. Leave the girl alone."

"She threw coffee in my face!"

Jornado shrugged. "You'll recover, *hombre*. Go relieve Vicente."

Rafael glared at Jornado, then, muttering an oath, he walked away.

"Go sit down, girl, and don't do anything to call attention to yourself," Jornado warned. "My men haven't had a woman in a long time, *comprende*?"

With a nod, Carolyn hurried toward Morgan.

"You all right?" he asked.

"Y...yes." But she wasn't all right. She was scared, more scared than she'd ever been in her life, and she began to shiver uncontrollably.

Morgan cursed softly as he struggled to sit up. He hurt everywhere. "Come here," he said quietly. "Sit close to me."

She did as he asked, pressing against his side, wishing his hands were free so he could hold her. She needed to be held, to be comforted. She wanted him to tell her that everything would be all right, even if it was a lie.

"I don't guess you've ever held a gun," Morgan remarked as he glanced around the camp.

"No."

Morgan nodded. It had been a foolish hope. He watched the outlaws settle down for the night. One of them had a bottle and Morgan licked his lips. He needed a drink. Just one drink to ease the ache from his punished flesh. He saw Rafael standing in the shadows, a rifle in the crook of his arm. Cashero stood at the opposite end of the camp, his thumbs hooked in his gunbelt. The others were crawling into their bedrolls. The leader, Jornado, was sitting by the fire smoking a long black cigar.

"Carolyn," Morgan whispered. "I'm going to lie down with my back toward you. See if you can untie my hands."

"All right." She sat cross-legged, her head falling forward, her hair shielding her hands as she struggled with the knots. Whoever had tied them had done a good job. She bit down on her lip as she concentrated on what she was doing.

Morgan kept an eye on Rafael and Cashero. They were standing together, drinking coffee.

"I can't do it," Carolyn complained, her voice

filled with discouragement. "The knots are too tight."

"Dammit, keep trying."

"Oh, all right," she hissed, and attacked the knots with renewed vigor.

It took twenty minutes, but she finally managed to loosen the rope binding his wrists. Another few minutes and his hands were free.

Morgan bit back a groan as the blood flowed into his hands again. So, he mused, his hands were untied. Now what?

He let his gaze wander around the camp. Jornado had turned in for the night. Rafael was sitting on his haunches near the fire, waiting for the coffee to warm up. Cashero was checking on the horses.

Morgan frowned. He needed a distraction of some kind. "Carolyn," he whispered. "I want you to go over to the fire and flirt with Rafael."

Her head jerked up and she looked at him as if he were crazy. "I will not!"

"Just do as I say, dammit. I don't have time to argue."

"What are you going to do?"

"I'm going to try and get us out of here."

"How?"

"I'm not sure yet. Just go over by the fire. Flirt with Rafael. You know how to flirt, don't you?"

"Of course," she retorted.

Morgan heaved a sigh of resignation. She was lying, and they both knew it. "Just bat those big green eyes at him and smile. Tell him you're sorry you threw coffee in his face. Ask him about himself. Tell him the rope is hurting your wrists. Maybe he'll cut you loose. After a few minutes, tell him you need to take a . . . that you need to relieve yourself."

Color washed into Carolyn's cheeks. "I can't say that!"

"Just do it. I want you to get him away from the others."

Bracing herself, Carolyn stood up and walked over to the fire. Rafael glared at her, and she took a deep breath. *Pretend you find him attractive,* she told herself as she neared the fire. *Smile.*

"I . . . I'm cold," Carolyn said. "Do you mind if I sit by the fire?"

Rafael shrugged, and Carolyn took a deep breath. So far, so good. "I'm sorry I threw coffee at you," she said, forcing the words from her mouth. "I was scared."

Rafael grunted. "Just don't do it again."

"I won't." She sat down beside him, her mind whirling as she searched for something to say. "Are you from Texas?"

"Why?"

"I was just curious. I was born in New York. Have you ever been there?"

"Not hardly. I was born in El Paso. Never been east of the Missouri."

"Are you married?"

"No."

Carolyn smiled at him. "A handsome man like you, not married?" she gushed. "I find that hard to believe."

Rafael smiled. Always it was the same. Women found him irresistible. Even this plump little *gringa* couldn't keep her eyes off him.

Carolyn flexed her fingers, hoping her expression looked woebegone. "My wrists are awfully sore. Do you think you could untie me?"

"Maybe for a few minutes," he agreed, and cut her hands loose.

Carolyn rubbed her chafed wrists, her cheeks growing warm as she summoned the nerve for what she was about to say. "I...I need to...ah ...be alone for a minute."

Rafael grinned. "Sure, come on."

Her face burning with embarrassment, Carolyn stood up and walked into the shadows. She could hear Rafael's footsteps echoing her own.

"I...you aren't gong to watch me, are you?"

"No." He turned his back to her. "But make it quick."

Morgan moved noiselessly toward the picket line, a good stout stick in his hand. Cashero was stroking the neck of one of the horses. The man never knew what hit him.

Morgan stifled a groan as he reached down to relieve the outlaw of his gun. Then, moving like a cat through cream, he made his way into the shadows. He could hear Rafael's voice, softly wheedling, as he tried to persuade Carolyn to kiss him, just once.

Scowling, Morgan ghosted up behind Rafael. A single blow to the back of the head with Cashero's gun rendered the outlaw unconscious.

"Come on," Morgan urged, reaching for Carolyn's hand. "We haven't got all night."

Hearts pounding, they skirted the sleeping ban-

dits. In minutes, they were mounted and riding
north at a breakneck gallop, driving the Comancheros horses ahead of them. Carolyn was grateful the outlaws hadn't unsaddled the horses.
Morgan had told her it was a precaution in case
they were attacked by Indians or other outlaws in
the middle of the night. Whatever the reason, she
knew she'd never have been able to stay on Whiskey's back without a saddle.

They rode until dawn, finding shelter in a narrow canyon watered by a small underground
spring. A few cottonwood trees grew alongside a
shallow pool, and there was graze for the horses.

Utterly weary, Morgan and Carolyn spread their
blankets beneath the trees, and were asleep before
the sun had topped the canyon wall.

Chapter 12

Carolyn woke with a start, the last remnants of a nightmare fading as she stared at the sun shining overhead. A faint breeze stirred the leaves of the trees, a bird lifted its voice in song. In the distance, she could see the horses and the pack mule standing close together, grazing on the short grass that grew near a shallow waterhole.

She let out a long sigh as the memory of her nightmare returned. Outlaws had been chasing her through a dark forest, their hands reaching out for her, their eyes filled with lust as they called to her, begging her to stop, swearing when she kept running, running for safety, searching for someone who wasn't there. And then arms had reached for her, strong arms that had held her close and frightened all the demons away....

She turned her head to gaze at Morgan, sleeping peacefully beside her. He didn't look like a knight in shining armor. He didn't act like any of the heroes she'd read about. But he had managed to get her away from the Comancheros.

She studied his profile, aware that she'd done it often of late. His face was scratched, discolored by bruises; his arms, too, were bruised where he'd been dragged across the rough ground. In sleep, he looked almost benign. She found herself wondering again why he drank so much, why he always seemed so sad. She was puzzled by his relationship with Red. It was obvious that Red loved him, and he had said he loved her, and then claimed they were only good friends.

Morgan moaned softly in his sleep. A muscle twitched in his jaw, his right hand balled into a tight fist, and she heard him swear softly.

Bad dreams, she thought. It seemed he had his share, too.

He moaned again, and she heard him whisper, "Sorry . . . so sorry."

The pain in his voice tugged at Carolyn's heart. She wondered what demons haunted his past, what ghosts walked in his dreams.

Pleased to have an excuse to touch him, she placed her hand on his shoulder and shook him gently. "Morgan."

He woke instantly, his hand reaching for his gun, and then, seeing her, he relaxed. "What's wrong?"

"You were dreaming."

Pain flickered in the back of his eyes and then was gone. "Was I?"

Carolyn nodded, wishing he'd tell her what troubled him, wishing she could share her own bad dreams with him. Perhaps if they talked about the things that caused them such anguish, it would make them seem harmless. But one look in his eyes told her he wasn't going to tell her anything.

Morgan groaned as he rolled to his feet. Every muscle in his body ached, and for a moment he just stood there, getting acquainted with the pain. He felt like an old, old man as he made his way to the waterhole. The Comancheros' horses snorted at his approach, scattering as he walked through their midst. He'd have to unsaddle them soon, he thought, but not now.

With an effort, he removed his tattered shirt, pants, and boots and lowered himself into the water. Closing his eyes, he rested his head against the edge of the pool.

A faint gasp told him that Carolyn had followed him to the waterhole. He looked up at her through half-closed eyes and saw her lower lip tremble as she stared at his chest. Looking down, he saw what had upset her. His torso was black and blue, crisscrossed with scratches and dried blood.

"No need to be alarmed, Miss Chandler. It's not as bad as it looks."

"But it must hurt dreadfully."

"A little," he admitted.

"More than a little, or I miss my guess."

Morgan shrugged. "I've been hurt a lot worse."

An image of Morgan lying in a dark alley, a knife stuck in his side, flashed through Carolyn's mind. "Yes," she replied solemnly. "I know."

"I think we'll lay up here today if you don't mind."

"All right." She glanced at the pile of clothing near her feet, and felt her heart turn a somersault as she realized he was naked. "I . . . I'll go fix breakfast," she said, and quickly turned away.

She gathered wood for a fire, found some matches in one of Morgan's saddlebags, filled the coffee pot with water and a handful of Arbuckles, and all the while her gaze kept straying toward the waterhole, toward broad, sun-bronzed shoulders and a black-thatched head.

She heard a splash as he stepped from the pool, and though she told herself not to look at him, she couldn't resist one quick covert glance in his direction. Tall and bronze and beautiful, he was. His shoulders were wide, his back smooth, his buttocks small and firm, his legs long and well-muscled.

When he started to dress, she turned her gaze to the task at hand, dismayed to discover the bacon was very close to being burned, thanks to her wandering eyes.

She heard his footsteps, and felt her cheeks grow pink as he stared at the overcooked bacon.

"That's a mite well done, don't you think?" he mused aloud.

"I like it that way," Carolyn retorted.

He grunted softly as he sat down beside the fire. "Coffee ready yet?"

"Yes." She found a cup and filled it, realizing only then that it had boiled far too long.

Morgan lifted one black brow in her direction. "Like your coffee well done, too, I see."

She would have snatched the cup from his hand, but he was too fast for her. "Hold on, now," he

121

admonished, holding the cup out of her reach. "I was just joshing."

"No, you weren't."

"Okay, I wasn't. What were you thinking about, to let the bacon burn like that?"

Carolyn glared at him. What, indeed?

"Nothing," she replied, ladling a spoonful of beans and bacon onto his plate. "Eat your breakfast."

"Yes, ma'am."

It was awful, the worst meal they'd had on the trail. Morgan ate without comment, his dark eyes settling on her face now and again. She refused to look at him, refused to admit he seemed to grow more and more handsome with each passing day. It was only her imagination. That, and the fact that he was the first man she'd ever spent any time with, the first man she'd ever been alone with. The first man she'd ever been remotely attracted to. But none of that mattered. He was a drunk and a half-breed, and when they reached Ogallala, she'd never see him again.

When he finished eating, she gathered up the dishes and carried them to the waterhole to wash while he unsaddled the horses and unloaded the pack mule. She chided herself for her earlier foolishness. He was just a man. There was nothing special about him, nothing out of the ordinary about those marvelous shoulders and long, long legs. His back was just a back, and his ... She jerked her thoughts from his anatomy and concentrated on scrubbing the frying pan. He was just a man, after all, and not a very nice one, at that.

When she got back to camp, Morgan was asleep again, his head resting on one arm. She gazed at him for a moment and then smiled. She could bathe while he slept.

The water was colder than she'd hoped, but Carolyn thought she'd have braved an ice-bound river to be clean again. She washed herself thoroughly, twice, and then washed and rinsed her hair. She sent a cautious glance at Morgan, making sure he was still asleep before she stepped, shivering, from the water.

She dressed quickly, then sat in the sun, combing the tangles from her hair, her thoughts drifting toward home. She wondered what her father was doing, if he missed her, if he'd changed his mind about her marrying Mr. Brockton. Perhaps, when she reached Ogallala, she'd write to her father and see if he still felt the same.

And perhaps she wouldn't. What if he still wanted her to marry Roger Brockton? She tried to think what she'd do when she reached Ogallala. Once the shock of her unexpected visit passed and Jordan made her welcome, how would she keep him from notifying their father of her whereabouts? And if she did manage to convince Jordan to keep it a secret, what was she going to do in Ogallala? She didn't fancy the idea of living with her brother and his wife forever, even if they'd have her. She wanted a life of her own, a place of her own. Her biggest problem, once she convinced Jordan to keep her presence in Ogallala a secret, would be money. She couldn't wire the bank in Galveston because then her father would know where she was. Perhaps she could borrow some money from Jordan. Maybe she could find a job. Perhaps she'd even get married ...

"You look like you just swallowed a handful of sour berries."

Carolyn whirled around to find Morgan propped up on one elbow, his dark eyes regarding her curiously.

"Is something wrong?"

"No," Carolyn said. "I was just thinking about what I was going to do with the rest of my life."

"Reach any decisions?"

"Not really. I'd like to have a place of my own, be my own boss. I'm so tired of always having someone telling me what to do. My father, my teachers. I want to live my own life, make my own mistakes."

"That's pretty radical thinking for a girl your age."

"Is it? Well, maybe it is, but I don't care. No one tells *you* what to do because you're a man."

"Yeah," Morgan said flatly. "And look how well I turned out."

Carolyn shook her head. "You don't understand. I've always had people preaching at me, telling me how to sit, how to talk, how to behave. My mother, my father, my teachers, Mrs. McMahon."

"At least they care enough to take an interest in you and in what you're doing."

"That's easy for you to say. You've always been allowed to make your own decisions, your own mistakes. No one tries to do your thinking for you."

"Maybe somebody should. Maybe I wouldn't

have made such a mess of my life if I'd had a father to help me, or a mother who cared ..." He broke off abruptly, his expression suddenly guarded, his eyes opaque. "I'm going for a walk," he said curtly.

Carolyn saw the pain that flickered in his eyes as he stood up, and then he was walking swiftly away, past the waterhole, toward the far side of the canyon.

A mother who cared ...

Carolyn stared at his retreating figure. She thought of her own mother, kind, loving, caring, more concerned for her family's happiness than her own. And then she thought of what Morgan had told her of his mother, of the pain in his voice, the shame in his eyes. *My mother was a whore.* That was all he'd said. She realized now that those few words spoke volumes.

He was gone a long time. Carolyn had dinner cooking when he returned. His face was closed against her, his eyes like dark fire, warning her to keep silent or suffer the consequences.

They ate in silence, Morgan eating hurriedly, hardly tasting the food, Carolyn covertly watching Morgan, wondering about his past. Was that why he drank, because of the terrible unhappiness in his childhood?

She took his dish to wash, filled his cup with coffee, and all the while questions chased themselves through her mind, questions only he could answer if she could find the nerve to ask them.

He swallowed his coffee in several quick gulps, then pulled a bottle from his saddlebags. Carolyn started to object, but he quelled her protest with a sharp glance. Going to her bedroll, she sat on the top blanket and began to brush her hair, conscious of the man sitting across from her, conscious of every time he lifted the bottle to his lips.

Morgan drank sullenly, hoping to blot out the ugly ghosts that haunted him. He watched Carolyn as she brushed her hair, longing to bury his hands in it, to lift it to his lips and breathe in the scent of woman, to bury himself in her sweetness and forget, if only for a moment, what a worthless creature he was. But she wasn't for him. Not now. Not ever.

But he couldn't stop watching her. Her hair was beautiful, long and dark, as brown as the earth. Her eyes were green, long-lashed, innocent. Her skin was the color of honey. He swore softly and took another drink. Why didn't she go to bed? He let his gaze slide down her plump little body, and his imagination went wild as he thought of all that warm feminine flesh that was so inviting and so out of reach.

"Morgan?"

Her voice, soft as velvet, reached out to him through the darkness.

"What?" His voice was gruff, filled with liquor and longing and a yearning for something he'd never had.

"It might help if you talked about it."

"About what?" he replied obtusely.

"About whatever it is that's eating away at you."

"Nothing's eating at me, *Miss* Chandler. Go to sleep."

"I'm not tired."

"Go to sleep anyway."

"You're just like everybody else," Carolyn retorted petulantly. "Always trying to tell me what to do."

"Maybe that's because you so badly need looking after."

"I do not!"

He tilted the bottle upward and took a long swallow. "You're so young," he muttered. "So damn young. You don't know anything about...anything."

"And you know so much," Carolyn retorted. "Where'd you get your education? In the back room of a brothel?"

She saw the rage flare in his eyes, the hurt, the resignation. "I'm sorry," she said quickly. "I shouldn't have said that."

"Forget it. You can learn a lot about life in a good whorehouse. I know I did."

He was hurting deep inside. Carolyn saw the pain in his eyes, heard it in the weary sadness of his voice, and she knew she had never felt the kind of pain he was feeling. He gazed into the distance, the bottle in his hand temporarily forgotten. She had the feeling he had forgotten about her, too.

"You can learn a lot," he said again. "I learned that love could be bought and sold, that everything had a price. My mother thought so, too. She thought she could buy her freedom, but it never happened. No matter how many men she took to her room, she could never save enough money to buy her way out of that place."

He shook his head, his expression bleak. "She

almost put that kind of life behind her once. We were in some little town in Arizona. I guess I was ten or eleven at the time. Anyway, she met a guy who seemed a decent sort and she fell in love with him. I guess Frank loved her, too, because they started talking about getting married. She figured it was safe to tell him about me after they set the date, but she was wrong. Once he learned she had a half-breed son, she never saw him again.

"I left her a couple of times when I got older, but I always went back. She looked old the last time, really old. I couldn't stand to see her living like that anymore, so I robbed the bank in La Paz and gave her the money and told her to get the hell out of that place. Only by then, she didn't wanna go. She said it was too late."

He laughed softly, bitterly. "I spent five years in jail for robbing that bank, and when I got out, I headed straight for Mozelle's. My mother wouldn't let me in her room until I threatened to break the door down, and when I saw her, I knew why."

He raked a hand through his hair, his eyes filled with an aching grief that tugged at Carolyn's heart. "She was pregnant and she didn't want me to know. She didn't want the baby, either. Said she was too old. Hell, she was only thirty-four, but she went to some Gypsy woman who was supposed to have some kind of potion that would get rid of the baby. But whatever the stuff was, it didn't work, so my mother took a knitting needle and . . ."

He let out a long sigh. "She got rid of the baby all right, and then she bled to death in my arms." He shook his head. "She blamed me. With her last breath, she blamed me for everything. Said it was my fault my father had left her. My fault Frank had left her. My fault she'd become a whore."

He looked down at the bottle in his hand. "Hell," he muttered. "Maybe she was right."

Carolyn lifted a hand to her cheek, surprised to find she was crying.

"Stop it," he said gruffly. "I don't want anybody cryin' for me."

But her tears kept coming. She knew why he drank now, and she wept for the miserable life he'd lived, for all the hurt he'd endured, for the loss of her own mother.

Morgan swore under his breath. And then he reached for her. Carolyn went willingly into his arms, snuggling against him as she rested her head on his shoulder. *He* was comforting *her*, she thought, confused, when she should be comforting him. She had never heard such a wretched story in her life, and she wondered how a mother, any mother, could say such terrible things to her son. Did the woman have no compassion, no inkling of the remorse and guilt that would haunt her son for the rest of his life?

She felt Morgan's hand move in her hair, his touch light, achingly tender. He murmured her name, his breath warm against her cheek, and she looked up into his eyes, wanting to tell him how sorry she was, to tell him his mother had been wrong, that it wasn't his fault. But the words died in her throat. His eyes, as gray as a winter sky, were blazing into her own, and she knew he was going to kiss her.

It never occurred to her to object. Her eyelids fluttered down, her head tilted back, offering him easy access to her lips. She heard him groan softly, and then his mouth closed over hers.

His kiss was hard and demanding and tasted of whiskey. Its effect was immediate and totally unexpected. Fire shot through her from head to toe, heating her blood, draining the strength from her limbs so that she sagged against him, mindless, helpless, drowning in a sea of sweet emotions that ranged from euphoria to delight to surrender.

His voice was hoarse as he murmured her name, his hands like molten lava, trailing flames wherever he touched her. Had Red felt like this? Had anyone else ever felt like this?

His fingertips caressed the curve of her cheek, then his hand curled around the back of her neck and he kissed her again, his tongue delving into her mouth, and she felt as if she were drowning in honey, warm sweet honey.

Unknowing, she pressed against him, her body responding to his touch, instinctively seeking the fulfillment that only he could give. She touched her tongue to his, and heard him groan as if in pain. And then he was pushing her away.

"What is it?" Carolyn asked, dazed. "What's wrong?"

Morgan stared at her, his hands balled into tight fists, his breath coming in ragged gasps. He was a lot of things, he thought bleakly, and most of them weren't very nice. But he'd never taken advantage of an innocent girl before, and he wasn't about to start now.

"Morgan . . . ?" She gazed up at him, her eyes still hazy with passion.

"Go to sleep," he said brusquely.

"But . . ."

"You shouldn't be out here with me! Dammit, what made you agree to this fool idea in the first place?"

"*You* did."

"Miss Chandler . . . Carolyn, go to sleep before I do something we'll both regret."

She stared up at him for a moment, not understanding, and then she gasped. "You . . . I'm not . . . whatever gave you the idea that . . ." She broke off as words failed her. Did he think she was like Red? Oh, but what else could he think, the way she'd melted in his arms?

Humiliated, she crawled into her bedroll and pulled the cover over her head. Perhaps she should have stayed in Galveston. Perhaps she should have married Roger Brockton . . . She shuddered as she thought of allowing Roger Brockton to share her bed. But she felt no such horror when she thought of Morgan lying beside her, and her cheeks grew hot as she remembered the touch of his hands in her hair, the rough velvet of his tongue sliding against her own.

She shook her head, hoping to dispel the images, but his touch had branded her and she fell asleep wondering what would have happened if he hadn't pushed her away.

Chapter 13

She couldn't face him the next day. She woke before dawn and went for a long walk, needing to put some distance between them while she tried to sort out her feelings. She had no experience with men. Was her reaction to Morgan normal? Would she have reacted to any man's kisses as she had to his, melting like butter left too long in the sun? Was she more like Red than she cared to believe?

She stooped to pick a blade of grass and twirled it between her fingers. If only her mother had talked to her about life, about the differences between men and women. There was so much she didn't know, so much she wanted to know. But she'd had no one to talk to. Asking her father had been out of the question. Once, she'd tried to talk to Mrs. McMahon, but the woman had been shocked. She had admonished Carolyn to put such shameful thoughts from her mind, declaring that no decent young lady should even think about such things, let alone speak of them aloud.

With a sigh, Carolyn sat down on a flat rock and gazed into the distance. The canyon was quiet beneath a canopy of blue. She saw a gray squirrel scamper up a tree, saw a couple of birds dusting their feathers. A fat green lizard rested in the shade of a spiny shrub.

It was peaceful here, Carolyn mused. Peaceful and beautiful. Had it been like this in the Garden of Eden before the serpent came and spoiled it all? Would Adam and Eve have lived forever in the Garden if Eve hadn't let her curiosity get the best of her?

She propped her elbows on her knees and rested her chin in her hands. The sun was warm on her back, and her eyelids grew heavy. She was almost asleep when she heard footsteps. It could only be Morgan, and she realized that the moment she had been dreading had come. She'd have to face him now, see the scorn in his eyes.

"What's the idea of wandering off?" he asked, coming to stand in front of her.

"I . . . I just wanted to take a walk."

"It isn't safe to be roaming around out here alone."

"There's no one here but us." She could feel him watching her, but she refused to look up.

"There are plenty of wild animals running around," he said. "Mountain lions, wolves, bears."

"Here?" she asked skeptically.

"Well, maybe not right here," he admitted, and she heard the smile in his voice. "But it's still not a good idea for you to take off by yourself."

"I won't do it again."

He grunted softly. "Look at me."

Carolyn shook her head. She couldn't face him, not after last night.

"Miss Chandler, look at me."

He had called her Carolyn the night before, she thought irritably, or had he forgotten?

"What's the matter?"

Carolyn shrugged. "Nothing. Why?"

"I thought maybe you were mad at me because of last night."

She stared at him, not knowing what to say. How could she be angry with him? What had happened was as much her fault as his. She could have said no.

"Well, anyway, I'm sorry for what happened. I guess maybe I'd had a little too much to drink."

Pain shot through Carolyn, sharper than a knife. She had thought he wanted her, had been foolish enough to think he even found her a little bit desirable. But it had only been the whiskey. Any woman would have done as well. Humiliation washed over her, but she covered it with anger.

Throwing the blade of grass away, Carolyn rose abruptly to her feet. "Apology accepted. Please don't let it happen again."

She was angry now, he thought, surprised. Her cheeks were rosy, her green eyes glinting like glass in the sun. Breasts heaving, she glared up at him and he had a sudden desire to grab her and kiss her again. He'd been drunk last night, but not so drunk that he couldn't remember how good she'd felt in his arms.

As if reading his thoughts, Carolyn took a step

backward, her arms crossing over her chest. She didn't look angry now, he noticed, only young and afraid.

Morgan swore softly. She was as vulnerable as a newborn kitten, as lovely as the wildflowers growing at her feet.

But she was not for him. He shoved his hands in his pockets to keep from reaching out for her.

"I'm hungry," he said curtly. "How about fixing some breakfast?" Without waiting for an answer, he turned on his heel and headed back the way he'd come.

Carolyn stared after him. She knew very little about men, and less about passion, but she would have sworn that she'd seen a flicker of desire lurking in his fathomless gray eyes, if only for a moment. The thought pleased her more than it should have.

They left the canyon after breakfast. As soon as he'd finished eating, Morgan saddled their horses and loaded the pack mule. He waited impatiently for Carolyn to roll up her blankets and mount her horse, and then he rode ahead without a backward glance. He was angry with her, she realized, but for the life of her, she couldn't figure out why. What did *he* have to be angry about?

She was still pondering Morgan's mood when she saw the Indians riding toward them. There were twelve or fifteen warriors, all grotesquely painted.

She turned toward Morgan as the clammy hand of fear curled around her insides. She shuddered when she saw her own anxiety mirrored in the depths of his eyes.

Morgan watched the Indians approach, chilled by their fierce demeanor, their arrogance. They were painted for war, and his first instinct was to make a run for it, but that course seemed like suicide. Sitting there waiting to be attacked seemed almost as foolish, but something warned him not to run.

"Easy," he said. "Let's just sit tight."

"Shouldn't we make a run for it?" Carolyn asked, her gaze darting wildly from side to side.

"To where? Just sit tight."

She swallowed hard, more frightened than she'd ever been in her life. Even the Comancheros had not aroused such gut-wrenching fear. They had been dirty and ill-bred, but at least they'd had a thin veneer of civilization. But these were Indians, savages. Their hair, as shiny and black as obsidian, was worn in long braids and adorned with feathers and bits of fur. Their skin was dark reddish-brown, painted with grotesque designs and symbols. They wore loincloths and buckskin leggings. Necklaces made of animal teeth circled their necks. They carried bows and arrows and lances decorated with buffalo tails and bits of hair. Human hair, Carolyn thought bleakly. Taken from murdered white women and children.

She was trembling violently now, and she threw an urgent look in Morgan's direction, silently beseeching him to save them. But he only sat there, his hands well away from his guns, while the Indians surrounded them.

And then his hands were lashed together and it was too late to do anything but pray.

Carolyn pulled away as one of the Indians reached out to remove her hat, his expression one of surprise when he discovered that she was not a boy, but a young woman. She screamed when the warrior pulled the pins from her hair.

"Be quiet," Morgan admonished. "They aren't going to hurt you."

"How do you know?"

"You'll just have to trust me. They're curious, that's all. They probably haven't seen very many white women, especially dressed in men's clothes."

Carolyn nodded, then gave a little squeak as another warrior reached out to brush his fingers over her skin. A third warrior squeezed her breast, as if to make sure she was really a woman.

Indignant, Carolyn slapped him, then felt the blood drain from her face as she realized what she'd done. But the warrior grinned at her, the expression ludicrous beneath the hideous paint on his face. He spoke to his companions and they all laughed. Then one of the warriors took up Whiskey's reins while another took the reins to Morgan's big gray gelding.

Dear Lord, Carolyn thought. *What now?*

They rode all that day. She'd thought Morgan was a hard taskmaster when it came to riding, but the Indians put him to shame. They rode hard and fast, stopping for only moments to let their horses rest, then moving on at the same breakneck pace.

She was bone weary when the Indians finally

drew rein for the night. Quickly and efficiently, they built a small fire and huddled around it, talking in soft tones as they ate strips of dried meat pulled from their saddlebags.

No one paid any attention to Carolyn, so she walked into the shadows, attending to a personal need that had been plaguing her for hours. She thought briefly of trying to sneak away, but that seemed foolish. She couldn't get to her horse without being seen, and trying to get away on foot was out of the question.

When she returned to the fire, she saw that Morgan was sitting apart from the warriors. He held a strip of dried meat in his bound hands. For a moment she just stood there, and then she went to sit beside Morgan.

"Want a bite?" he asked, offering her the jerky.

She eyed it with the enthusiasm of a woman contemplating a scorpion. "What is it?"

"Jerked venison. It's not bad."

Carolyn shook her head, wondering how he could eat at all. She was too frightened to think of food, especially food that looked as disgusting as what Morgan was chewing on.

She glanced up, startled, as one of the warriors offered her a drink from something that looked suspiciously like an intestine. Repulsed, she shook her head, then watched in horror as Morgan took a long swallow.

"You'd best take a drink. You aren't likely to be served tea in a china cup out here."

She longed to refuse, but she was far too thirsty to be picky. The water was cool, refreshing, and she tried not to think about the container that held it. She smiled her thanks when she'd had enough. The warrior returned her smile, then walked back to his companions.

"Are you sure you don't want some of this?" Morgan asked.

Carolyn eyed the jerky dubiously for a moment, and then bit off a piece. It was like eating shoe leather, but it did take the edge off her hunger.

"What are they going to do to us?" she asked.

"Whatever they want," Morgan replied; then, seeing the fear in her eyes, he added, "I don't think they mean us any harm."

"You don't *think* they mean us any harm? Don't you know? You're one of them."

"I'm a Navajo," he reminded her with a wry grin. "I don't know what tribe these guys belong to, but they aren't Navajo. Sioux, maybe, or Cheyenne."

"What difference does it make?" Carolyn remarked glumly. "They'll probably kill us and take our scalps. I'll never get to Ogallala now. Oh, I should have stayed home and married Mr. Brockton."

"Maybe so," Morgan muttered. "Damn, I wish I had a drink."

He looked longingly toward the pack mule, and frowned when he saw two Indians going through their supplies, tossing out his extra shirt, exclaiming over Carolyn's lacy underwear, examining his shaving brush and razor, laughing at Carolyn's ruffled pantalets.

The other warriors gathered around, curious to

see the white man's belongings, amused by the strange clothing, until one of the warriors discovered the whiskey.

With a whoop, he held the bottle over his head. "*Minne-wakan!*" he exclaimed, and everything else was forgotten as they uncorked the bottle and passed it around.

Carolyn looked anxiously at Morgan. Everyone knew that Indians couldn't hold their liquor, that they became wild and unpredictable when intoxicated.

"Just sit tight," Morgan said quietly. "Maybe they'll all get drunk and pass out."

"And maybe they'll start looking for some entertainment," Carolyn said tremulously. "And we'll be it."

Morgan shrugged, hoping his casual attitude would help to calm Carolyn's nerves, but inwardly he was just as uneasy as she was.

It was a worry that was well-founded. The Indians had emptied two bottles and were working on a third when one of them decided he needed a little feminine companionship.

Carolyn screamed as the warrior pulled her to her feet and began to run his hands over her body. Other warriors quickly gathered around, urging their friend on as they continued to pass the bottle back and forth.

Morgan felt his gut tighten with dread as he gazed around the camp. Some of the Indians had passed out, a few were sitting by the fire, too liquored up to move, but the seven warriors gathered around Carolyn were feeling rambunctious as hell.

She screamed again as the warrior holding her removed her poncho and began to unfasten her shirt. Morgan didn't understand what the warrior was saying, but the look on the Indian's face was the same in any language, and Morgan let out a long sigh of resignation, knowing he couldn't just sit there and let them rape Carolyn; knowing, too, that he had little to gain but his own death by interfering.

Carolyn twisted away from the warrior who was trying to disrobe her. Eyes wild with fright, she began to kick and scratch at the Indians as they closed the circle around her. Instinctively, she kicked one of the Indians between the legs, suddenly glad for the ugly boots she was wearing when the man howled in pain and limped away. The other Indians laughed, and then they reached for her again, clawing at her hair, pulling at her clothes, ripping the shirt from her body, then tugging at the long white underwear.

She screamed for Morgan, tears of panic and fright coursing down her cheeks. Then, somehow, he was there beside her, a knife clasped in his bound hands, his lips drawn back in an ugly snarl.

There was a sudden silence as the Indians drew back, their attention focused on Morgan. They weren't laughing now, and Carolyn wondered how it was possible for men who had been drunk a moment ago to have sobered up so quickly.

The Indians gathered together, conversing rapidly, occasionally gesturing in their captives' direction.

Carolyn stood beside Morgan, shaking visibly as

she wondered what the savages were saying, what they would do next.

A warrior with a single black feather in his hair stepped toward them, and Morgan dropped into a crouch, his body shielding Carolyn's, the knife thrust out in front of him.

It was a brave thing to do, Carolyn thought, but what good was one man, one weapon, against so many?

Black Feather laughed softly as he drew his own knife. With his free hand, he gestured for Morgan to come closer.

"Morgan, don't!" Carolyn cried, knowing he would be killed. How could he possibly win when his hands were still tied together?

"Stay out of this," he warned, and took a step forward.

Black Feather grinned as he, too, took a step forward, his knife hand weaving from side to side. Morgan stood his ground, his gaze focused on the warrior's face as he waited for him to make the first move.

The watching Indians cheered their companion, urging him on, and he lunged forward, his knife reaching for Morgan's belly. Morgan let him come, closer, closer, and then he struck out with his own blade, cutting a long, shallow furrow in Black Feather's left forearm.

The sight of his own blood infuriated the warrior, and he lunged forward a second time, his blade slashing wildly.

Morgan grunted as Black Feather's knife sliced into his right side, but before the warrior could drive the blade home, Morgan pivoted on his heel and slammed his locked fists down on the back of Black Feather's neck. The man fell in his tracks, the knife tumbling from his hand.

With an oath, Morgan took a step back, his breath coming in short, hard gasps as he faced the remaining warriors, his knife poised to strike, blood oozing from the gash in his side.

A tall warrior stepped forward, his hands lifted in a gesture of peace. "Enough."

Morgan took a wary step backward. "You speak English?"

"*Chikala,*" the warrior replied. "Little."

Morgan pointed at Carolyn. "She is my woman."

The warrior nodded. "Put down your weapon."

"No."

"You hurt."

"I'm fine."

"No more *kicizapi* . . . no more . . . fight."

"All right by me," Morgan said. Still holding the knife in front of him, he pressed his elbow against the wound in his side. "Just let us go."

The warrior shook his head. "No more fight. No touch woman."

"What do you want with us?"

"You learn me speak *wasicun tapi.* White man's tongue."

"Why?"

"Many whites come our land. I need learn white man's tongue. You help me, then I let you go."

"And if I refuse?"

143

The warrior grinned. "You hurt. You no fight us all."

With a sigh, Morgan dropped his knife, wondering if he'd just made the biggest mistake of his life. Behind him, he heard Carolyn's sigh of dismay as the Indian picked up the knife and slid it into his belt.

The warrior looked at Carolyn, then pointed at the wound in Morgan's side. "You fix," he told her.

Carolyn watched as the Indians carried Black Feather to the fire. The whiskey was beginning to take effect, and after covering the unconscious warrior, the others rolled into their sleeping robes, all but two who remained awake to keep watch.

Carolyn looked at Morgan, waiting for him to tell her what to do, but he was sitting down, his left leg drawn up to his chest, his forehead resting on his knee. A dark stain was spreading over his shirt.

"You fix," she muttered as she made her way to their packs and rummaged for the ointment Yellow Sage had sent along. She found it lying on the ground next to the jumbled pile of her extra clothing.

Grimacing, she picked up the salve, then searched inside Morgan's saddlebag for a length of cloth to use as a bandage. She frowned when she discovered the cloth was wrapped around a bottle of whiskey the Indians had overlooked. Her first thought was to empty the contents into the dirt. She did not approve of whiskey for any purpose, but Morgan looked as if he might benefit from a drink or two.

"Here," she said, returning to his side. "Drink this."

He looked at her as if she'd just offered him a million dollars; then, uncorking the bottle, he took a long drink, sighed heavily, and took another.

"You don't have much luck where knives are concerned, do you?" Carolyn muttered as she lifted his shirt to get a better look at the wound.

"Not lately." He shook his head as he saw the color drain from her face. "I'd do it if I could."

And she would have let him if his hands were free, she thought guiltily. But he'd been wounded defending her. The least she could do was bandage the wound. "Never mind, I'll do it."

He was in no mood to argue, but he doubted that she was going to do him much good. Her hand was shaking like a reed in the wind as she began to wipe the blood from his side, and her face was fishbelly white.

"You're not going to faint on me, are you?"

"No."

He nudged her arm with the bottle. "Here, pour a little of this over it."

"Won't that hurt?"

"Likely. But do it anyway. And try to save a little."

Carolyn nodded. Her hand was decidedly unsteady as she lifted the bottle and dribbled whiskey over the ugly gash in his side. Morgan swore, his whole body tensing with pain as the liquor seared his flesh. Grabbing the bottle from her hand, he lifted it to his mouth and took several long swallows. Miraculously, the lines of pain disappeared from his face. His body relaxed and he sank slowly to the ground.

Carolyn stared at him, uncertain if he was asleep or unconscious; then, taking her lower lip between her teeth, she wiped away the last of the blood and bandaged the wound as best she could. And then, utterly exhausted, she stretched out beside him and went to sleep.

Chapter 14

Most of the Indians had hangovers the next day. One by one, they went to the stream and plunged into the cold water. None of them seemed interested in food, but they offered Morgan and Carolyn pemmican and water for breakfast.

Carolyn was surprised to find pemmican rather tasty. "It's good," she mused. "What's it made from?"

"Dried buffalo meat, sun-dried wild berries, and tallow. The whites call it Indian bread. The stuff's supposed to last forever."

It was almost afternoon before the Indians felt like traveling. Without the hideous war paint, they weren't nearly as frightening. Carolyn was relieved to see that they had repacked her clothes and belongings in her saddlebag.

She watched as Morgan swung aboard his gelding, squealed in alarm as one of the warriors lifted her onto Whiskey's back, and then they were riding across the plains, surrounded by Indians.

"Where are they taking us?" she asked, but Morgan just shrugged.

"Beats the hell out of me," he muttered. He glanced at Black Feather, who was riding beside him. The warrior grinned good-naturedly, apparently not carrying a grudge over their fight the night before.

Late in the afternoon, three of the warriors broke away from the main group.

At dusk, they made camp alongside a shallow stream flanked by cottonwoods. A short time later, the three warriors returned with fresh meat, which was roasted over a fire of buffalo chips.

Carolyn's stomach growled loudly as the scent of roasting venison filled the air. It bothered her that her hands were still tied. It was frightening, knowing she was completely helpless, and that Morgan would be powerless to protect her if the Indians decided to attack her.

But apparently they harbored no such thoughts. After offering their captives something to eat, and checking to make sure their hands were securely bound, the Indians ignored them. Gathering around the fire, the warriors talked and laughed. Occasionally one stood up, apparently telling a story, and there was a lot of shouting and loud laughter as the listeners reacted to the tale.

Gradually Carolyn began to relax. It was obvious they weren't going to bother her, at least not tonight. Her eyelids grew heavy, and she rested her head on Morgan's shoulder.

"Why don't you put your head in my lap and go to sleep?" he suggested.

It was terribly improper, and terribly tempting, and after a moment, she did as he suggested, grateful for his nearness, and his kindness.

She fell asleep almost immediately, and that night there were no bad dreams.

Morgan had a low fever the next day, but other than that he seemed to be fine. The Indians had allowed Carolyn to spread some of Yellow Sage's salve over the wound, and there was no sign of infection. She was surprised that the wound didn't hurt more than it did, and then she realized he was drinking to ease the pain. She'd thought the Indians had downed it all, but Morgan still had two bottles of the stuff. After that first night, the Indians hadn't touched the whiskey. Indeed, they stared at Morgan with something that looked suspiciously like pity each time he reached for the bottle.

They'd had little time alone in the past three days. The warrior who wanted to learn English was ever at Morgan's side, asking him questions, wanting to know more about the whites, why they thought as they did, why they had no honor, why they felt they had the right to trespass on land that had belonged to the Indians for longer than the oldest warrior could remember.

Carolyn was surprised to find she was jealous of the time Morgan spent with the Indian, whose full name was White-Eagle-That-Soars-in-the-Sky. She tried to understand why she was jealous and decided it was because, for the first time in her life, she had someone all to herself, someone who, for the time being at least, could devote all his time to her. Her father had never had time for her. Mrs. McMahon had always been busy with the house. Grady, the butler, had been too old to have anything in common with a young girl. But Morgan...he had nothing but time. And if he didn't really want to be with her, at least she'd had his undivided attention since they left Galveston.

Carolyn was beginning to think they were going to ride across the plains forever when they reached a wide green valley watered by a lazy river. Nestled in the valley were perhaps a hundred Indian lodges.

Looking at the encampment from a distance, Carolyn thought it looked quiet, almost picturesque. A vast horse herd grazed peacefully on the far side of the river. Tall trees grew along the sloping hillsides. She could see women and children playing along the shore. Downriver, she could see several men and boys engaged in a horse race. Long tendrils of blue-gray smoke curled skyward, rising from conical-shaped tipis and outdoor cookfires.

She reined her horse closer to Morgan's as they neared the village. Their hands were no longer bound, and the Indians had treated them kindly so far, but she could not suppress the growing knot of fear in her stomach. Everyone knew that Indians were unpredictable. No telling what might lie in store for them now that they had reached their destination.

She felt Morgan's hand on her arm. Turning to

face him, she saw that he was smiling at her, his dark gray eyes warmly reassuring.

"They aren't going to hurt us," he said. "Remember that, and try not to be afraid."

Carolyn nodded, and immediately forgot his words of reassurance as what seemed like hundreds of Indians suddenly swarmed around them, pointing at her and Morgan, speaking in a language that sounded more like grunts and groans than any form of conversation. She looked out at a sea of copper-hued faces and felt whatever courage she possessed dwindling to nothing. These were Godless savages. They killed indiscriminately, then scalped their helpless victims. They burned and raped and caused terror wherever they went.

She turned frightened eyes on Morgan, silently begging him to do something before it was too late, before she was defiled and scalped and her body left to rot on the plains.

"Carolyn, it's all right."

She stared at him, uncomprehending, hardly able to hear him for the fierce pounding of her heart.

Dismounting, Morgan lifted her from her horse and took her in his arms. She immediately buried her face in his shoulder, her body trembling convulsively.

"Hey," he said softly. "Relax. I won't let them hurt you."

His hand was stroking her hair, gently, tenderly. She felt the strength of his arms, the hard comfort of his chest. She could hear the Indians talking among themselves, their voices growing faint as they walked away, returning to their own lodges, until only White Eagle remained.

"This your lodge," the warrior said. Indicating the nearest tipi. "No leave here."

Morgan nodded, then, taking Carolyn by the hand, ducked inside.

It was a good-sized lodge. A small pit had been dug in the center of the floor, a pair of buffalo robes were spread out near the back wall.

"Home sweet home," Morgan remarked.

"How long will we have to stay here?"

"I don't know. I guess long enough for me to teach White Eagle whatever he wants to learn."

"That could take months."

"I don't think so. He knows quite a bit of our language now."

Carolyn nodded, but she didn't believe White Eagle for a minute. She was certain that, once the Indian had learned what he wanted, he would kill them both.

Two large tears welled in her eyes. She would never see Jordan now, never see her father or her home again. Even marriage to Mr. Brockton would have been better than this.

Morgan bit back an impatient oath when he saw the tears in her eyes. She was just a kid, after all, he reminded himself. She'd been spoiled and sheltered all her life. Maybe she had every right to be afraid. Hell, he was a little afraid himself.

Grabbing Carolyn by the hand, he drew her into his arms and held her close. He wasn't good at this sort of thing, he mused ruefully. He wasn't used to dealing with sweet young girls. He was accustomed to dealing with women who'd lost their dreams and their innocence long ago, women who knew how to take care of themselves. Women like Red, and his mother.

He felt the old anger, the old hurt, rise up within him, and wondered why his mother's rejection of him still had the power to cause such pain. It had happened a long time ago. He was a man now, fully grown. He didn't need mothering now. Maybe he never had.

Carolyn sighed as she pressed her face to his shoulder, and he felt his body stir at her nearness. She felt good in his arms, soft and pliable. She smelled of perspiration and trail dust, but over it all was her own unique scent. The scent of woman.

He hadn't had a woman in a long time and he drew her closer, his need pressing against her belly. She made a little cry of protest and wriggled against him, trying to twist from his grasp, but he only held her tighter, her resistance firing his desire. It would be so easy to throw her down on one of the buffalo robes and ease the ache in his loins. So easy...

Perhaps if she'd kept fighting, he would have taken her by force, satisfying some deep-seated primal urge to prove his male superiority, to conquer and possess that which he desired. But she went suddenly quiet in his embrace, her head falling back over his arm, her luminous green eyes gazing up at him, filled with trust and innocence, and the first faint stirrings of passion.

Passion, not love. He would not take her, would

not awaken her to the pleasures of the flesh simply to satisfy his own lust. To do so would make Carolyn no better than his mother, and prove that he was no better than the men who had bought his mother's love for a few measly dollars when he could not buy it at all.

With an oath, he pushed her away, hating her for being young and beautiful and beyond his reach, hating himself for wanting her.

He saw the confusion in her eyes, and he turned away, his hands shaking, his head hurting. His steps were stiff as he made his way to his gear. Dropping to his knees, he rummaged around in his saddlebags, cursing under his breath until he had a bottle in his hand. He threw back his head and took a long drink, shuddering as the fiery liquor blazed a path to his belly, making him forget everything but the sweet promise of oblivion.

Carolyn stood in the center of the lodge, her arms wrapped around her waist, watching Morgan as he drank. She saw the tension drain out of him, saw the old hurt fade from his eyes. One more drink, and he stretched out on one of the buffalo robes and closed his eyes. In minutes, he was asleep.

Her gaze caressed him while he slept, and she wished there was something she could do to soothe the ache in his heart, to erase the bitter memories from his past. She wondered if he had ever been in love. He had made no mention of a woman except for Red. And he'd said she was only a good friend.

Carolyn sat staring at him for a long while,

thinking of the horrible childhood he'd had, wondering if she would ever see her brother or her father again, wondering what it would be like to have Morgan hold her in his arms all night long.

She was still wondering when sleep wrapped her in its embrace.

Chapter 15

He woke with a low groan. His mouth tasted like ashes and there was a steady pounding in his head. He reached automatically for the bottle beside him, and cursed when he found it empty. He needed a drink bad.

Rolling out of his blankets, he crawled across the floor and fumbled inside his saddlebags, searching for the other bottle. Just one drink, he thought, a little of the hair of the dog, and he'd feel better.

He tilted the bottle to his mouth and let the liquor slide down his throat. Just one bottle left. He'd have to teach White Eagle English in a hurry, he thought with a grin, or he'd be out of booze.

Putting the bottle aside, he found himself staring into Carolyn's luminous green eyes.

"Is that your breakfast?" she asked sarcastically.

"Maybe."

"Well, that's fine for you, but what about me?"

"What about you?"

"I'm hungry. It must be after noon."

Morgan grunted. He was rarely hungry when he woke up, but then, he was usually hung over. Rising, he swayed unsteadily for a moment, then headed for the doorway. "I'll go see if I can round you up something to eat."

"White Eagle told us to stay here."

"Well, I can't let you starve to death."

"I'm not starving," she said, ashamed of her earlier bad temper. She gestured at the two empty bowls next to the firepit. "They must have brought them this morning while we were sleeping. I ate mine." Her cheeks turned rosy. "And yours."

Morgan chuckled softly, thinking how pretty she looked with her hair tousled around her shoulders and her cheeks bright with color. Her eyes were clear and green, like pools of water after the first spring rain.

And he wanted her. In spite of everything, he wanted her. He took a step forward, refusing to think of the consequences, wanting only to hold her close, to lose himself in her sweet innocence....

"Morgan?" White Eagle's voice shattered the moment, and then the warrior stepped into the lodge. "My woman has food waiting."

"Thanks."

"Thanx?"

"Thanks. Thank you. It's an expression of gratitude."

"Ah. *Pilamaya.*" White Eagle nodded. "Come. Eat."

* * *

Carolyn sat in the shade cast by a tall tree. It was mid-afternoon and she could see Morgan and White Eagle walking beside the river. They'd been down there for over three hours, sometimes walking, sometimes sitting on the riverbank. Occasionally she heard White Eagle's laughter as he mispronounced one of the white man's words.

After a while, she let her gaze wander toward the village. Indian women could be seen moving from lodge to lodge, visiting friends. Others were bent over outside cookfires, and still others knelt on the ground, scraping the meat and fat from hides of some kind. Probably deer, Carolyn thought, as they seemed too small to be buffalo hides and too large for rabbit. Little girls trailed at their mothers' heels, copying whatever their mothers did, while little boys played with small bows and arrows or wrestled in the dirt like frisky puppies. She saw old men and women nodding in the sun. Downriver, a group of young men were showing off their equestrian skills.

Carolyn watched them for a long time, mesmerized by their horsemanship. They rode bareback, sometimes standing up, sometimes sitting forward, sometimes backward. They hung over the sides of their horses and plucked a bit of fur from the ground while riding at full gallop, or jumped off the horse while it was running and then jumped back on. She shook her head, awed by their skill and their fearlessness.

She turned her attention back to Morgan and

White Eagle. She was bored. Everyone had something to do except her.

Rising, she walked down to the river and sat beside Morgan. Taking off her boots and socks, she dangled her feet in the water.

It took her only a moment to realize that not only was Morgan teaching White Eagle to speak better English, White Eagle was teaching Morgan to speak Lakota.

"Are you hungry?" Morgan said.

"Are you hungry?" White Eagle repeated, and then said the phrase in Lakota. "*Loyacin hwo?*"

"*Loyacin hwo?*" Morgan said. "Have you had enough to eat?"

"Have you had enough to eat? *Ota wayata hwo?*"

Carolyn listened to the alternating languages, wondering which man was learning the most. Lying back on the grass, she closed her eyes as they began to recite numbers.

"One," Morgan said, holding up one finger.

"One," White Eagle repeated, holding up one finger. "*Wanji.*"

"*Wanji,*" Morgan repeated, then held up two fingers. "Two."

"Two," White Eagle said, raising two fingers. "*Nunpa.*"

"*Nunpa.* Three . . ."

Something was tickling her cheek. She batted it away with her hand, but it came back, sliding across her cheek and down the side of her neck.

Opening her eyes, Carolyn saw Morgan leaning over her, a blade of grass in his hand.

"Wake up, sleepy head."

He brushed the blade of grass across her lips, then lowered his head toward hers, blotting out everything but his face. Carolyn gazed deep into his eyes, his beautiful gray eyes, her insides fluttering. He was going to kiss her. And even as the thought crossed her mind, his lips were slanting across hers.

Carolyn closed her eyes, reveling in the feel of his lips on hers. She longed to put her arms around his neck and to draw him close, but she was afraid he would pull away from her as he had so often in the past.

His kiss deepened, his tongue lightly caressing her lower lip. She groaned softly, her arms reaching for him, her hips arching upward. She needed to touch him, to be touched by him. But it was the wrong thing to do. As soon as her arms went round his neck, he drew away.

Carolyn stared up at him, her lips bereft, her heart beating fast. "Morgan . . ."

He shook his head. In one graceful fluid movement, he stood up and turned his back to her. A long shudder convulsed him, and then he was walking away, toward the river.

Morgan hunkered down on his heels at the water's edge, his hands braced on his knees as he took several deep breaths. He hadn't meant to kiss Carolyn, but she looked so pretty lying against the grass, with her hair spread over her shoulders and the sun dancing across her face. Her lips, slightly parted, had been a temptation he couldn't resist. He had felt his body's quick response the moment his lips touched hers, and then she had awakened, like the princess in a fairy tale. But he wasn't a prince and never would be. He was nothing but a worthless half-breed, not fit for decent women. But he wanted her. Dear Lord, how he wanted her!

"Morgan?" She was standing behind him, so close he could almost smell the sun in her hair. Her voice was soft, tinged with confusion at his rejection, slightly pleading. It cut him to the quick.

"Go back to the lodge, Miss Chandler. I'll be there in a few minutes."

Carolyn stared at his back, bewildered by his gruff tone. She was no expert where men were concerned, but he seemed to like kissing her. She certainly liked kissing him. Why did he always push her away?

He stood abruptly and whirled around to face her, his jaw taut, his eyes blazing with desire. Before she could speak, he grabbed her by the shoulders and pulled her body against his, and then he was kissing her. It was a hard, brutal kiss. His lips ground against hers with such force that she tasted blood, and then his tongue forced its way between her lips, plundering the inside of her mouth. She was shocked by the intimacy of it, and when she began to struggle, he grabbed both her hands in one of his, then locked his other hand around the back of her head, holding her immobile as he continued to brutalize her mouth. There was no tenderness in this kiss, no hint of affection or regard for her feelings.

She heard the blood pounding in her ears as the kiss went on and on. His scent filled her nostrils, she could taste only him, see only him. The strength went out of her legs, her blood turned to fire, and then she was kissing him back, pressing her body against his.

She stood staring up at him for several seconds before she realized he had let her go.

"Is that what you want, *Miss* Chandler?" he asked roughly. He stared at her for one timeless moment, his breathing ragged, his hands clenched at his sides. then he turned on his heel and left her standing there.

Carolyn stared after him, her lips bruised, the taste of blood like brass in her mouth, her ears ringing with his words: *Is that what you want, Miss Chandler? Is that what you want . . . ?*

To her shame and horror, the answer was yes.

Chapter 16

He was avoiding her again. Carolyn told herself it
was for the best. It was obvious she displeased
him, that he found her undesirable and unattrac-
tive. Every time he touched her, he pushed her
away. She told herself it didn't matter, that she
was going to make a new life for herself in Ogallala. And no matter how much she was attracted
to Morgan, he would never fit into her way of life.
He was handsome, but crude. So handsome, but
he drank too much. After their encounter at the
river, she had returned to their lodge to find him
sitting cross-legged on his bed, drinking steadily.

She had turned on her heel and left him there.
Now almost two weeks had passed and they were
still avoiding each other, which was no easy task
when you shared a one-room tipi. They spoke to
each other only when necessary. Morgan left the
lodge immediately after breakfast and didn't return until dinner. Carolyn couldn't help but wonder what he did all day. Sometimes she strolled

through the village, looking for him, but usually he was nowhere to be seen. She would have swallowed her pride and asked where he was, but, except for White Eagle, none of the Indians spoke English. And White Eagle seemed to be gone whenever Morgan was absent.

Now, walking through the village, Carolyn felt like a stranger in an alien land. The Indians looked at her as she passed by, their expressions friendly and curious. A few smiled at her, a few spoke to her.

"*Hinhanni waste,*" called an old woman whose hair was as gray as iron. "Good morning."

"*Hou ke che wa?*" called another woman. "How are you?"

"*Tnau wau an,*" Carolyn replied. "Very well."

And she smiled at the woman, wishing she could speak the language better, grateful that she understood the little that she did.

She envied the women. They were always busy, cooking, sewing, tending their children, gathering wood and water, digging for roots, looking for nuts and berries, tanning hides, making jerky and pemmican, while she had little to do to occupy her time. White Eagle's wife, Sunrise Woman, brought food and water to their lodge twice a day, so the only thing Carolyn had to do was gather wood for the fire, and that was hardly enough to fill a whole day. She missed reading. She missed shopping. She missed visiting with her friends. She missed Morgan . . .

Her heart skipped a beat when she saw him a short distance away. He was standing between

164

White Eagle and another warrior, laughing at something White Eagle had said. It was a rare thing, to see Morgan laugh. It erased the hard lines from his face and made him look almost boyish and carefree. He turned to listen to what the other warrior was saying, then smiled, and she felt her heart skip a beat. He was handsome, the most handsome man she had ever known.

Carolyn was so enthralled with watching Morgan laugh that it took her a moment to realize he was no longer wearing pants, shirt, and boots, but buckskin leggings, a sleeveless vest, and moccasins. His skin was as dark as that of the Indians, his hair as black and almost as long. Only the color of his eyes kept him from looking like a Lakota warrior.

She knew he was half Indian, of course. He had told her so. At first, it had caused her some concern, but then, as she'd gotten to know him better, it had ceased to matter. He might be part Navajo, but he had been raised as a white man, not a savage.

But now, seeing how easily he blended in with the other two warriors, she felt a slight sense of apprehension. The Indians hadn't done anything to make her feel uncomfortable or unwelcome, but they *were* different. They believed in heathen gods, they participated in barbaric rituals, they believed that the grass and the trees and the mountains were alive and had spirits. The whites thought the Indians were all savages, and while she no longer believed that was true, she realized there was a great cultural gulf between red man and white man, a gulf that was wider than the Pacific and more difficult to cross.

In spite of the day's warmth, Carolyn shivered. She didn't belong here, and she was suddenly homesick for her own people, for her father, for familiar food and surroundings.

Gradually she became aware of the fact that Morgan was watching her, and then he was walking toward her, his strides long and filled with a kind of self-assurance she had never noticed before.

"What is it?" he asked. "What's wrong?"

"I don't belong here. I want to go home."

He understood immediately. Carolyn saw the sympathy in his eyes, in the softening of his expression as he took her by the hand and led her toward their lodge.

His unexpected concern was her undoing and she was crying when they entered the tipi.

Wordlessly, he took her in his arms and held her while she cried. She wept because she was homesick, because he was suddenly gentle after weeks of silent rejection. She felt his hand move in her hair, heard him whisper her name, and his quiet show of affection made the tears flow faster.

Morgan sighed heavily as he stroked Carolyn's hair. He knew how she felt. Lord, he'd been homesick his whole life, yearning for a home he'd never had, for love and acceptance, for a life that wasn't filled with ugliness and rejection.

"I'll take you home as soon as I can, Carolyn," he promised. "It can't be right away, but I'll take you home."

"When?"

"I don't know," he hedged, too big a coward to tell her that they weren't leaving now because he didn't want to leave, wasn't ready to leave. He liked it here. He liked the Indians, liked their way of life. The Sioux didn't treat him like he was dirt. They respected him for his willingness to accept Lakota ways without question or derision. For the first time in his life, his Navajo blood was not cause for rejection or ridicule, and no one cared that he was a half-breed.

Carolyn stood in the circle of his arms until her sobs lessened and her tears dried on her cheeks. It was so pleasant to be held, to feel the strength of Morgan's arms, to know she wasn't alone after all. He did care. Surely he had to care at least a little to hold her so tenderly, to so readily understand how she felt.

She drew back a little so she could see his face, and frowned. "You like it here," she said accusingly. "That's why we can't go home now. You want to stay."

"Carolyn..."

"Don't you?"

"Yeah, I wanna stay."

"Why?"

"Because I *do* like it here. I don't know how to explain it, but I belong here. I feel like these are my people. I hear the drums at night, and..." He broke off, embarrassed. It sounded so corny to say that the drums were like the beat of his own heart, that the language, though vastly different from what little Navajo he knew, seemed familiar. He

167

was drawn to the Lakota way of life and he couldn't explain why, because Lakota beliefs and Navajo beliefs were almost as far apart as the ways of the whites and the Indians.

Carolyn stared at him, trying to comprehend what he was saying, and not saying. In a way, she could understand why Morgan liked it here. Lakota men were proud, arrogant. They spent their days hunting, riding, gambling, repairing their weapons, telling old war stories. She supposed that, for a man like Morgan, it held a vast appeal when compared to his old way of life. If he wanted to stay here, that was fine with her, so long as he took her home first.

Morgan cleared his throat. "White Eagle has been teaching me how to be a warrior. In another few weeks, I'll be adopted into the tribe."

"Another few weeks!" she exclaimed angrily. "I want to go home now."

"I know, but this is something I've got to do and I may never get another chance."

"You could take me to Ogallala first," she retorted. "You promised to take me to my brother, remember? I *paid* you to take me to my brother!"

"I know."

"Oh, you! You're . . ." She searched her mind for a word bad enough to call him, and stamped her foot when nothing vile enough came to mind. "Damn you, Morgan, I'll never forgive you for this. Never!"

Twisting out of his embrace, she ran out of the lodge, running blindly through the village toward the river. Fresh tears coursed down her cheeks as she railed at Fate for the sudden turn of events. He wanted to be a warrior! Hah, that was rich! He was nothing but a drunkard!

Her tears fell faster, and she cried because he wouldn't take her home, because he drank too much ... because she was beginning to love him.

She ran until her side ached and she was out of breath. Dropping to her knees, she buried her face in her hands and rocked back and forth, wondering what she was going to do. Being an Indian might be loads of fun for a man, but as far as she could tell, it was nothing but hard work for a woman. The women did everything but the hunting. They cooked and cleaned and made new clothing, cared for the children, gathered wood and water, planted gardens and cared for them, tanned hides, jerked meat, and did a hundred other chores.

So far, White Eagle's woman had taken care of Carolyn's and Morgan's needs, but how long would she be happy to do the work for two lodges? How long did it take for a man to become a warrior?

She heard footsteps in the tall grass behind her and dashed the tears from her eyes. She didn't want Morgan to know she'd been crying again.

She lifted her head and squared her shoulders, determined not to forgive him for his treachery no matter what he said or did. He had promised to take her home, and now he had gone back on his word and there was no excuse for it as far as she was concerned. No excuse at all.

She turned around, determined to tell him so. Only it wasn't Morgan standing there.

The Indian was tall and lean. His face was painted black, his naked chest also painted black. His hair was roached, and his scalp painted red. He held a war club and a bow in his left hand, and a quiver of arrows was slung over his shoulder.

He was the most frightening thing she had ever seen. Frozen with fear, Carolyn stared at him as he took a step toward her, grinning broadly. His teeth were very white against his blackened face. And then he was reaching for her, his right hand closing over her shoulder, dragging her to her feet.

The touch of his hand galvanized her to action, and she began to struggle against him, shrieking with pain as he released her long enough to slap her across the face, hard.

He said something to her, his voice gruff and cruel, and then he grabbed her around the waist, lifted her over his shoulder and carried her downriver.

Carolyn pummeled his back with her fists, tears of fear and frustration welling in her eyes.

Moments later, he flung her, face down, over the back of his pony, vaulted up behind her, and raced away, heading downriver.

Morgan left the lodge thirty minutes after Carolyn. He figured that would give her time enough to sulk, time to get used to the idea of staying in the village until he'd accomplished his goal.

It shouldn't take long. He was learning to speak Lakota almost as fast as White Eagle was learning to speak English. For the past few days, White Eagle had been teaching him how to hunt and

track, how to use a bow and arrow, how to find
water and food on the trackless plains. It all came
easy to Morgan, and he didn't know if it was because of his Navajo blood or just because he
wanted so badly to learn. He had great respect for
White Eagle. The man carried himself with pride
and dignity and self-assurance, qualities Morgan
had long admired and coveted.

He walked downriver, pleased with his newfound ability to distinguish Carolyn's tracks from
all the others, to determine which way she had
gone even when he couldn't find her footprints. It
gave him a sense of pride and confidence to know
that he could read trail sign, and that, if necessary,
he could survive off the land.

He felt a vague sense of unease as he continued
to follow Carolyn's trail, surprised that she had
run so far from the village. Didn't she realize it
wasn't safe for her to go wandering off alone?

He began to walk faster, his gaze scanning the
ground. The trail suddenly became clear and easy
to follow as the ground grew softer. He saw where
she had slowed in her flight, where she had knelt
in the dirt . . . where a large man had come up behind her.

Heart pounding, Morgan read the signs of a
struggle, saw the deep imprints of moccasined
feet, and knew that the man had carried Carolyn
away.

He was running now, his gaze sweeping the
ground, his voice hoarse as he murmured, "No,
no," over and over again.

He was breathing heavily when he came to the

place where the man had mounted his horse. The horse's tracks went south, toward Crow territory.

He stood there for a moment, head hanging while he caught his breath, and then he turned and ran back toward the village.

It was all his fault. Dammit, he should have taken her away from here when he'd had the chance. He'd never be a warrior, not in a million years. Who was he trying to kid? He'd left Carolyn alone for weeks while he played Indian, pretending he was as brave as White Eagle and the others, pretending he could change what he was. Hell, he *knew* what he was.

He was out of breath when he reached his lodge. Ducking inside, he went to his saddlebags and reached for the bottle, his last bottle. Hell, it really was time to get back to civilization.

He took a long drink, hoping to steady his nerves. He couldn't go after Carolyn alone. He'd have to ask for help. He wiped the back of his hand over his mouth and corked the bottle. He was wasting time. Every minute that passed took Carolyn further away.

He was about to leave the lodge when he heard White Eagle call his name.

"Yeah, in here," Morgan said.

"The Fox Soldiers are having a dance tonight," White Eagle said. "Would you and your woman ..." His voice trailed off as he saw the bottle in Morgan's hand, the wild look in his eyes. "What is wrong?"

"She's gone. Carolyn's gone."

White Eagle frowned. "Gone where?"

Morgan lifted his free hand and let it fall. "I don't know. The Crow took her."

"And you stand there drinking *minne-wakan* while your woman's life is in danger? What kind of man are you?"

Morgan shook his head. "I don't know," he muttered under his breath. "I wish to hell I did."

"Have I been wasting my time, trying to teach you the way of a Lakota warrior?" White Eagle asked angrily. He grabbed the bottle from Morgan's hand and emptied the contents into the dirt. "You will not find your courage in a bottle of crazy water, nor will you find your woman alive if we do not hurry."

Morgan glared at White Eagle, then stared at the wet stain on the ground. His last bottle . . .

"Are you coming with me?" White Eagle asked, his voice filled with contempt. "Or will you stay here and lick the white man's firewater from the dirt?"

Shame washed through Morgan, stronger, more humiliating than anything he had ever known. He saw the scorn in White Eagle's eyes, the contempt, the disdain. A warrior's first priority was the safety of his family. A man, a *warrior*, found his courage within himself. If necessary, he sacrificed his own life to save the lives of the People.

Drawing himself up to his full height, Morgan said, "I'm coming," and followed White Eagle out of the lodge.

In less than ten minutes, a dozen warriors were mounted and ready to ride.

Chapter 17

She was cold and hungry and frightened, so frightened. The world passed by in a blur as the Indian raced his pony across the plains, stopping for only minutes at a time. He held her face down across his mount's withers, his hand firm on her back. She marveled that she didn't break in two from the strain.

Day turned to night, and still he rode, slower now. She wondered where he was taking her, why he had abducted her, if she would ever see her father, or Morgan, again.

It was full dark when the Indian drew his horse to a stop. Yanking her from the back of his horse, the Indian threw her to the ground, his finger pointing at her in a gesture that clearly told her to stay put.

Shivering, her arms wrapped around her body, Carolyn sat on the hard, cold ground, her gaze never leaving the Indian as she waited to see what he would do next.

He spoke to her in a harsh tongue, but she shook her head, unable to understand what he wanted, and he slapped her hard twice, then pushed her down on the ground and tied her hands behind her back.

Squatting on his heels, he took a long drink from a deerskin bladder, then pulled a hunk of jerky from a pouch around his neck and began to eat.

Carolyn's mouth filled with saliva and her stomach rumbled loudly, but the Indian ignored her. Swallowing the last of the jerky, he drew a blanket around his shoulders and sat staring at her, his eyes dark with malevolence.

She was going to die. She knew it suddenly, clearly, and without doubt. He had not kidnapped her for pleasure or ransom, but for revenge. His dark eyes glittered with hatred as his hand caressed the knife on his belt, and then he smiled, a cruel, bitter smile that promised pain, hours of pain, before she died.

She closed her eyes, unable to bear the loathing in his eyes. A cold wind picked up out of the north and she shivered uncontrollably.

She was going to die.

She tried to pray, but all she could say was "Please, please, please," over and over again.

Hours passed. She was numb from the cold, from the paralyzing fear that held her in its grip as she tried to imagine what the morning would bring.

A coyote howled, its voice sounding dangerously close, and she opened her eyes. She could see the Indian's horse standing hip-shot a short distance away. The Indian was still sitting up, his head resting on his knees. He was breathing deeply, evenly.

He was asleep! For the first time, hope fluttered in Carolyn's breast. Perhaps she could get away. Moving slowly, quietly, she sat up, rolled to her knees, then stood up. Step by slow step, she moved toward the horse, wondering how she'd be able to mount with her hands tied behind her back. She looked for something to stand on, then screamed as she felt the Indian's hand close around her arm.

He spoke to her, his voice angry, and then he hit her, once, twice, three times. She felt herself falling, saw the ground rising to meet her, and then there was only darkness. . . .

Pain, nothing but pain. Carolyn tried to lift her hand to rub her aching jaw, but her hand wouldn't move. She realized two things simultaneously: she hurt all over, and her arms and legs were spread-eagled. It hurt to breathe, and she knew that the Indian must have kicked her several times after she passed out.

Panic raced through her. She opened her eyes to find her captor squatting on his heels beside her, a long-bladed knife in his hand. He laughed when she tugged against the ropes that bound her hands and feet to stakes driven into the ground, and laughed again as he placed the tip of the blade under her chin.

She began to shiver spasmodically as he moved the knife over her body, making circles on her stomach, drawing diagonal lines across her breasts and thighs.

She shook her head, her eyes pleading with him. "No, no," she murmured. "Please, I've done nothing to you."

The Indian stared at her, his dark eyes filled with hatred and contempt as he ripped away her shirt, then slashed her long white undershirt to ribbons, not caring that the blade pierced the skin of her shoulder.

Carolyn stared at the blood, her blood, in horror. She was going to die. Now. Tonight. Horribly.

She stared up at the night sky and thought about clouds and rain and the sound of thunder rolling across the skies.

She felt the knife bite into her skin as the Indian cut away her pants, but her mind refused to accept the pain. Instead, she thought about Morgan, whose eyes were as dark as the sky above, whose touch was like the sun, whose kisses made her heart thunder and her blood sizzle. Her captor yanked off her drawers, and she closed her eyes, withdrawing into herself, shutting out the fear and the pain....

Morgan crouched in the dark beside White Eagle, his hand caressing the knife at his side as he watched the Crow cut away Carolyn's clothing. Her skin shimmered like ivory silk in the campfire's rosy glow. A narrow ribbon of red glistened on her shoulder, a bright splotch of crimson stained her left leg.

A muscle worked in Morgan's jaw as he ran his

thumb over the blade of his knife, hardly aware when the blade sliced into his flesh. He glanced down at the blood oozing from his thumb and smiled coldly. There would be a lot of blood shed this night. Crow blood.

At White Eagle's signal, the Lakota warriors began to creep forward, moving like silent shadows. Too late, the Crow realized he was surrounded. Too late, he sprang to his feet.

Unmindful of the danger, Morgan stood up and lunged toward the Crow. Knocking the knife from the Indian's hand, he drew back his arm and drove his fist into the warrior's face, let out a howl of delight as he felt the Indian's nose break and felt the warm tide of blood splash over his hand.

The Indian fell backward, reached for his knife, and sprang to his feet, the blade darting left and right like the tongue of a serpent, but Morgan was too outraged to be cautious. He plowed forward, his own knife reaching for the Crow's belly, penetrating skin and muscle, driving deep, deeper, until the Crow sank to his knees, his eyes dark with pain, and then empty of feeling, of life.

Morgan yanked his knife from the Indian's body and raised it over his head, a shrill cry of victory erupting from his throat.

He heard White Eagle's victory cry mingle with his own, and heard the other warriors cheer. He savored the moment, reveling in the approbation of the Lakota warriors, in the pride of having defended what was his. Then he hurried to Carolyn's side and cut her free.

"Carolyn." He gathered her into his arms and

held her close. "Carolyn?"

She stared at him, unseeing, her face as pale as the moon, her beautiful green eyes devoid of expression.

"Carrie! My God, Carrie!" He shook her, frightened by her stillness, her silence.

He heard White Eagle and the others making camp. Two of the warriors were dragging the Crow's body into the darkness.

"Take this," White Eagle said, handing Morgan a blanket.

"Pilamaya," Morgan murmured absently. He wrapped Carolyn in the blanket, then drew her to his chest and rocked her back and forth, his hand stroking her hair, his face dark with anguish as he gazed at her, his heart aching for what she had suffered. And it was all his fault. If he'd only taken her to Ogallala sooner, none of this would have happened.

The Lakota warriors turned in for the night, and still Morgan sat rocking Carolyn, whispering to her softly, promising to take her home if she'd only look at him, scream at him, recognize him.

"Carrie, Carrie," he murmured. "Look at me, darlin'. You're all right, Carrie. It's all over. He's dead. He can't hurt you anymore." He shook her, then shook her again. "Carrie, please, look at me. I'm Morgan, remember? Tell me you hate me, that I drink too much, that it's all my fault, but please, just look at me!"

A voice. Words. They hummed around her head like bees, annoying, persistent. She would have swatted them away, but it was too much trouble.

And then she heard his name. Morgan.

She looked for him in her own private world, but he wasn't there, only the sound of his voice calling to her, begging her to look at him.

It was hard, returning to his world. Pain awaited her there, pain of the flesh, fear of the unknown. But he was there, too, and she loved him.

"Carolyn?" Hope soared in Morgan's heart as she blinked at him, her expression no longer blank. She recognized him! Dear Lord, she recognized him. "Thank God," he murmured, and hugged her to him.

Carolyn cried out as his arms tightened around her, and he released her immediately. "What's wrong?"

"It hurts," she complained softly.

Morgan swore under his breath as he held her, careful not to hold her too tight, as he quietly cursed the man who had abused her.

Later, when he felt he could let her go, he wiped the blood from her shoulder and thigh, bound her ribs with what was left of her long underwear, dressed her in his buckskin shirt, then covered her with the blanket.

"Stay with me," she said, fearful of being alone.

"I will." He sat beside her through the night, holding her hand in his, never taking his eyes from her face. He spoke to her quietly when bad dreams haunted her, pleased beyond words when she called for him, and when the sound of his voice soothed her.

* * *

Carolyn woke with the dawn, her mind still filled with the last vestiges of a horrible nightmare. And then, as she turned her head and saw Morgan sleeping beside her, she knew it hadn't been a nightmare at all.

Her hand explored the bandage swathed around her middle, then she lifted her hand to her face. Her jaw was sore and swollen, as was her left eye.

But she was still alive, and she had Morgan to thank for that. She turned to face him again and saw that he was awake and watching her, his expression solemn.

"How do you feel this morning?" he asked.

"Sore," she replied.

He nodded and sat up, the blanket falling away to reveal the broad expanse of his chest. It was then that Carolyn realized she was wearing Morgan's shirt and nothing else.

She watched him stand up, her eyes drawn to the width of his shoulders, to the hard wall of his sun-bronzed chest and the play of muscles in his arms as he stretched, his hands reaching for the sky.

She was suddenly aware that they were not alone. She heard White Eagle's voice, and then the voices of others as the Lakota began breaking camp. They were in Crow country and eager to be on their way home.

Morgan helped her to her feet, and she glanced around, wondering what had become of the Indian who had kidnapped her. She looked at Morgan, a question in her eyes, and then looked away. The Indian was dead, and Morgan had killed him. She knew it as surely as she knew her own name.

Morgan lifted her to the back of his horse, swung up behind her, and urged the horse into a lope. She rested her back against his chest, feeling its hardness and warmth. His left arm curled around her waist, holding her tight against him, and she placed her hand over his forearm, feeling his strength beneath her fingertips.

He had killed a man because of her.

Tears came, silently welling in her eyes and coursing down her cheeks.

Carolyn sat beside the fire, her hands folded in her lap, her lower lip caught between her teeth as she watched Morgan pace the lodge, his steps unsteady, his hands balled into tight fists.

They had returned to the village the day before. He had promised to take her home immediately, but traveling was out of the question now. He was in no condition to make a long trip across the plains. He needed a drink, and needed it badly, but there was none to be had.

A shudder passed through him, and Carolyn looked away, her heart aching for him. She had not realized how dependent he had been on whiskey, or how painful it would be for him when it was gone.

She heard him swear a vile oath, and when she looked up, he was huddled on his sleeping robe, shivering violently.

Crossing the lodge, Carolyn sat down beside him and drew his head into her lap and stroked his brow. His skin was cold and damp, and she could feel him shaking uncontrollably.

"Just one drink," he whispered. "Dammit, all I need is just one drink."

"I know."

"Damn!"

"It'll be all right," she murmured reassuringly.

"Go away."

"Don't be silly."

He clenched his fists, willing himself to stop shaking so that he could sit up. When he did so, he glared at her. "Get the hell away from me. I don't want you here."

"Morgan, I'm not leaving, so why don't you just lie down and try to get some rest?"

"Dammit, Carolyn, at least let me keep a little of my pride."

She looked at him in exasperation. "Pride? Is that what this is all about? Your pride?"

"I admit I don't have much, but you might let me keep what little I've got left."

"You're sick, Morgan. I won't leave you here alone, and I won't think the less of you when it's over."

He cursed softly, but he didn't pull away when she put her hand on his shoulder and encouraged him to lie down again. With his head in her lap, he closed his eyes, shuddering violently as his body cried out for that which it had depended on so long.

It was a time for truth, he thought bleakly; time to stop kidding himself. Oh, he'd told people he was a drunk, and sometimes he drank a hell of a lot, but he'd always believed he could quit whenever it suited him. He'd told himself that he drank because he liked it, not because he needed it. But he couldn't lie to himself any longer, and the truth filled him with shame and disgust.

White Eagle stopped by later that evening, bringing food for Carolyn and a bowl of beef broth for Morgan. But Morgan pushed it away, the smell making him sick to his stomach. Carolyn offered him water instead, and he gulped it down, then lay back, breathing heavily.

Toward morning, he fell into a deep sleep, his head cradled in her lap, his hand clasping hers.

Carolyn watched him sleep, surprised by the strong maternal instinct he aroused in her. She wanted to soothe him, to protect him, to heal the deep inner scars that caused him such pain.

Sitting there, her hand in his, she realized that she had fallen in love with Morgan. She wanted nothing more than his happiness, and if he thought he could find it here, in this place, then she would stay as long as necessary, because she also realized that, once they reached Ogallala, he would return to Texas, and to Red, and she would never see him again.

But for now, in this place, she would be his woman. She would watch him become a warrior. And then she would let him go.

It occurred to her suddenly that she had grown up. Somewhere out there on the plains, when she had looked death in the face, she had grown up.

Surprisingly, the thought did not make her happy.

Chapter 18

He felt like the devil. His head hurt, his pride hurt. Through all the ghastly hours when he'd shivered and been sick in mind and body, Carolyn had been there. Night and day, she'd taken care of him, comforting him with the sound of her voice when he was cold and afraid, helping him outside when he needed to relieve himself, holding his head when he had the dry heaves. Damn, he'd felt as helpless as a baby, felt what little pride he had left shrivel up and die like a worm on hot coals.

He sat up, surprised to find himself alone in the lodge. He was wondering where Carolyn had gone when she stepped inside, her hair damp, her skin glowing.

She smiled shyly. "Hi."

"Hi, yourself. Where've you been?"

"Taking a bath." She smiled uncertainly, then pirouetted before him. "Do I look all right?"

She looked better than all right. She was beautiful. "Where'd you get the dress?"

"Sunrise Woman gave it to me." A faint blush rose in Carolyn's cheeks as she slid her hands down her waist. "I think I've lost some weight."

Morgan nodded. She had lost weight. The doeskin dress was soft and pliable and molded itself to every curve. Ankle-length moccasins hugged her feet, and a shell necklace circled her neck.

"Is that what you're gonna wear home?" he asked gruffly.

"Home?"

"To Ogallala. We're leaving this afternoon."

"No."

"No?"

"You said you wanted to be a warrior, and that you might not get another chance."

"I promised to take you to Ogallala and that's what I'm going to do."

"Why are you suddenly so anxious to leave?" she demanded suspiciously. "Can't wait to get rid of me? Or maybe you just can't wait to ride into the nearest town, and the nearest saloon!"

Morgan closed his eyes, the thought of a drink making him almost light-headed. Just one drink, what could it hurt?

"I wouldn't think whiskey would be so appealing after all you've been through," Carolyn mused.

"It isn't," he lied. "Do you really want to stay here?"

"Yes."

"All right. But if I'm going to be a warrior, you'll have to behave like a warrior's wife. No more letting Sunrise Woman do all the work."

Carolyn nodded. "She's already started teaching

me how to cook, and tomorrow she's going to show me how to make moccasins."

Morgan grinned. "Well, here's to the new you, and the new me. Let's see who cries Uncle first."

Carolyn snuggled deeper into her blankets. Two months had passed and her whole life had turned upside down. She spent long hours with Sunrise Woman, learning how to cook and sew. Though Sunrise Woman didn't speak English, the two of them managed to communicate quite well. For the first time in her life, Carolyn went to bed each night feeling a sense of accomplishment. She was no longer helpless, totally dependent on others. To her surprise, she discovered she enjoyed taking care of Morgan, enjoyed doing things for herself. She liked cooking and sewing. She didn't even mind gathering wood and water. And looking for nuts and roots and herbs with the other women was actually fun!

But most satisfying of all was the change in Morgan. He had changed in the past weeks, changed from a man who felt worthless into a man who knew who he was, a man who took pride in himself. He laughed more, he smiled more. He was at ease with the warriors, no longer an outsider, but a part of the group. He rode with a new self-assurance, he had mastered the bow and the lance, he could hunt and track with the best of them. Often, without thinking, he spoke to her in the Lakota tongue.

Surprisingly, she was beginning to pick up a few words of the Indian tongue herself. *Han waste* was

Lakota for Good night; *Ota wayata he?* meant Have you enough to eat?

She was learning proper tipi etiquette as well. If the door to a lodge was open, people were welcome to enter, but if the flap was closed, a visitor was expected to announce himself and wait to be asked inside. Men went to the right when entering a tipi; a woman entered behind her husband and went to the left. Visitors never passed between the fire and anyone in the lodge. When invited to a feast, guests were expected to bring their own bowls and spoons and to eat all they were given. When the host cleaned his pipe, it was a signal for everyone to go home.

She stared at the small patch of sky visible through the smokehole. The tipi itself was a special place, symbolizing the way the Lakota viewed the world. The floor represented the earth, the walls the sky, the tipi poles depicted the trails from the earth to the Spirit World. Sweetgrass, cedar, or sage were burned in a special place in the rear of the lodge in the belief that the fragrant smoke would carry the prayers of the people to the spirits above. It reminded Carolyn of her grandmother, who had burned candles before a small wooden statue of the Blessed Virgin.

She had learned a lot about the Lakota; she wished she knew as much about the man who shared her lodge. He had become a warrior, and she was his woman in every way but one.

Carolyn tossed restlessly, wishing she had the courage to go to him, to crawl under his blankets and rest her head on his shoulder, to ask him to hold her and to kiss her. Living with Morgan in such close quarters, sleeping only a foot apart, had awakened a restlessness within her, a tension she did not fully understand. She had only to look at him and her stomach quivered and her heart pounded. He was tall and dark and, oh, so breathtakingly handsome. Sometimes, seeing him dressed in nothing but a clout and moccasins, she longed to reach out and touch him, to let her fingertips trail across his chest, to caress his hard muscular arms, to kiss the hollow of his throat. But, of course, she didn't.

She heard him enter the lodge and she watched surreptitiously as he undressed, then slid under his blankets. Maybe tonight, she thought, maybe tonight she would go to him. She thought of a dozen things to say, but they all sounded silly, foolish, pleading, and in the end she said nothing at all.

Morgan sat outside, enjoying the solitude, enjoying the warmth of the sun on his bare shoulders. He was happy here, he mused, at peace for the first time in his life. Only one thing marred his happiness, and that was Carolyn. He wanted her, wanted her as he wanted food to eat and whiskey to drink...ah, whiskey. It was like Carolyn, he mused, warm and tempting and dangerous. He had promised himself that he would never drink again. It was a form of slavery, being chained to a habit he couldn't break, hadn't wanted to break, until now. No more whiskey, no more losing his dignity and his identity in the bottom of a bottle.

He was a warrior now. He wore an eagle feather in his hair, a red dot painted on it to show he had killed a man in battle. Now only one thing was left: to seek a vision. And when that was done, he would take Carolyn to Ogallala, and then he would try to make something of himself, his life.

Carolyn . . . No matter how he changed himself or his life, she would always be out of his reach. Because one thing he couldn't change was his heritage. He was a half-breed, and nothing he did could alter that fact.

That night, they were invited to White Eagle's lodge to listen while Sunrise Woman's ancient grandmother recited the story of how the Lakota were created.

"It was long ago," she began, her voice soft and strangely hypnotic. "There were people on the earth, but Wakan Tanka was not happy with them. They were lazy and wicked, and so he sent a water monster to cause a great rain to fall upon our mother, the earth. It rained for many days. People climbed on high rocks to escape the water, but soon the rocks were covered and all the people were killed except one young girl who was carried away by the great spotted eagle, Wanblee Galeshka. The eagle carried the girl to the highest pinnacle of the Paha Sapa and there, on the top of the world, the woman and the eagle had children together.

"When the waters went away, Wanblee Galeshka helped the woman and her children down the mountain and told them to become Lakota Oyate, a great nation."

There was a murmur of approval as the story ended.

"You see," White Eagle explained to the children gathered in the lodge, "our people are descended from the eagle, and that is good. The eagle is the wisest of birds. He is Wakan Tanka's messenger." White Eagle touched the feather in his hair. "That is why we wear Wanblee Galeshka's plume."

Morgan lifted a hand to the feather in his own hair, intrigued by the tale, and by its similarity to the story of Noah and the Flood.

There was a dance later that evening. Morgan sat with White Eagle, pretending to listen as the warrior related how he had killed three Crow warriors in his first battle, but all his attention was focused on Carolyn. She was wearing a new dress, one she had made herself, and she looked more lovely than he had ever seen her. Long fringe dangled from the sleeves, swaying gracefully when she moved. Her moccasins were decorated with blue and yellow quills, and she wore a yellow choker at her neck. Her hair fell in soft waves around her shoulders, the part daubed with vermilion.

Morgan glanced at White Eagle as the Indian poked him in the ribs. "Are you listening to what I say?"

Morgan shook his head. "No. Sorry."

"You are staring at your woman as if you would like to carry her into the shadows."

"Yes."

White Eagle grinned. "The fire still burns."

Morgan nodded. "It burns, my friend."

"Then go, and let her put it out."

"Yeah." Rising to his feet, Morgan walked around the dance circle until he came to where Carolyn sat with Sunrise Woman.

Taking Carolyn by the arm, he drew her to her feet and guided her into the moon-dappled shadows near the river.

Finding a secluded place, he took her in his arms and kissed her. He had expected her to resist, to argue, to struggle, but she returned his kiss with a fire to match his own, her body straining to be close to his as her arms went around his neck.

Startled, he drew back to gaze into her eyes, and then he kissed her again, deeply, kissed her as though he were a damned soul and she his only hope of salvation.

Slowly they sank to their knees, their mouths still fused together. Carolyn felt her heart soar as Morgan crushed her to him. At last, she thought happily, at last! Moaning with pleasure, she drew him down on the damp grass and stretched out beside him, molding her hips to his, wanting to be closer, closer.

Morgan groaned low in his throat as Carolyn pressed against him, her nearness the sweetest kind of torture. His hand slid over her ribcage, down her hip, and up again, the need rising within him, engulfing him, tempting him until he drew away and sat up, his head cradled in his hands. Damn! Before they'd come here, he hadn't thought he was good enough for her, and now, curse his newfound sense of honor and decency, he discovered he couldn't take advantage of her, couldn't rob her of her virginity simply to satisfy his own longing. She was a maiden, and the Lakota held the virtue of their women in high regard. A warrior, a true warrior, did not defile a woman of the People; he vented his lust on captive women, or remained celibate.

"Morgan?"

He felt her hand on his arm, and the touch of her fingertips seared his skin like a living flame. "Don't."

"Why do you always push me away?" she asked softly. "Do I displease you so much?"

"You must know that's not true."

"Then why? Why won't you hold me?"

"Because it tears me apart inside. Because ..." He swore under his breath. Why was life so complicated? Why couldn't he just make love to her and forget it? He wanted her more than life itself, wanted her because she was young and innocent, because he'd never made love to a woman who hadn't had a hundred other men before him. But he couldn't tell her that.

"Morgan?"

"I don't want you to be like Red and my mother." He paused, his eyes dark with pain and confusion. "I don't want to ruin your life."

Carolyn slid her hand up his arm, lightly caressing the rock-hard muscles that quivered beneath her fingertips. "You won't ruin my life. Please, just hold me, kiss me. Please, Morgan."

"I can't. I can't hold you and kiss you and then stop. Don't you understand?"

She shook her head, her deep green eyes luminous in the moonlight. Why was he making it so difficult?

"Carolyn, I'm not made of stone. I can't just kiss you and then let you go. It's too painful."

"Then don't let go."

"You don't know what you're saying...what you're asking."

"Then show me."

"I can't. I'm a half-breed, Miss Chandler. Decent women don't associate with men like me."

"I don't care."

"I do. Besides," he lied, "I like women with a little experience." A low groan rose in his throat as her eyes filled with tears. Rejection, that was what she was feeling, and he ached for her. But she was too young, too innocent, and he knew he'd never be able to live with himself if he took advantage of her now. Better to hurt her with words, let her think he didn't care, than ruin her life.

Carolyn turned her back to him as the tears came faster. It was true! He didn't want her. Maybe no man would ever want her. No, that wasn't true. Mr. Brockton wanted her. He wanted her enough to marry her.

And suddenly being Mrs. Brockton didn't seem nearly as bad as it once had. When they left here, she'd go on to Ogallala and visit with her brother, and while she was there, she'd send a wire to her father and tell him to set the date. And Jordan could take her home.

Wordlessly she rose to her feet and smoothed the front of her dress. Then, wiping the tears from her eyes, she started walking back to the village.

She didn't need a man like Morgan. Who was he, anyway? Just a half-breed with no ambition. Once they left the Indian camp, he'd probably go back to Danny Miller's place. He'd work at night and drink all day and probably be dead before he was thirty.

Morgan watched her walk away, feeling more wretched than he ever had in his life. But it was for the best. She deserved a man who had roots, a decent family, a respectable past. No matter that he'd found a new sense of pride and self-worth in the last few months, no matter that he had vowed to give up the booze and get a decent job, he was still a half-breed. He'd never be accepted by her friends and family.

He let out a long sigh, wondering when he'd started to love her, and how he would ever let her go.

Chapter 19

He sat alone on a high mountain, clad only in a brief elkskin clout and moccasins. A broad slash of white paint adorned his left cheek, and a red lightning bolt was emblazoned on his chest.

Lifting his arms high above his head, Morgan gazed up at the sun and cried to Wakan Tanka for a vision.

Three days he'd been here, with nothing to eat or drink. Three days and two lonely nights. Nights filled with an immense silence as he gazed up at the moon and the stars, his heart crying for a vision.

He'd felt a little foolish at first, standing atop a windswept mountain offering tobacco to the earth and the sky and the four directions, but gradually he'd been drawn into the magic of it, the mystery. And now he wanted a vision with every fiber of his being, felt his life would be incomplete without a medicine dream to sustain him and give him courage.

He'd never been a praying man, never been particularly religious. Nor had he ever been able to accept the God his mother believed in. But now, as he prayed for strength and courage, he knew he was being heard, that there was Someone listening, Someone who cared what happened to Morgan Slade.

Earlier, he had offered a pinch of tobacco to Man Above, to Mother Earth, to the four directions. He had offered his hunger, his thirst, and when that failed to produce a vision, he had drawn his knife and pierced his flesh, offering his blood as a token of his sincerity, a symbol of his desire. The Lakota were big on symbolism, from the way they lived to the way warriors decorated their war ponies. A red handprint on the horse's shoulder or rump was called a blood mark. This was the highest honor a warrior could receive. An upside-down handprint meant the warrior was going on a do-or-die mission. If a handprint was incomplete, it was an oath of vengeance for the dead. A red circle painted around a horse's nose was believed to give the animal a keen sense of smell; a red or white line painted around the eye was to improve its eyesight. Battle scars on a horse were circled with red paint as symbols of honor.

Red, Morgan mused, for blood. Each day, he had offered his blood to the gods, and now, three days later, he was still waiting for a sign.

He stared at the sun, his arms raised to the sky, his mind focused on that which he desired. Time lost all meaning, and his hunger was forgotten. There was a gust of cold wind, and then, as he watched, dark gray clouds swirled overhead, shrouding the sun, stealing its light and its warmth. Lightning sizzled across the lowering skies, thunder rolled across the heavens, and then he saw a warrior on a dark horse emerge from the midst of the clouds. The warrior wore a black wolf-skin clout, nothing more. A slash of white paint adorned his left cheek, a red lightning bolt was emblazoned across his chest. For a moment, the warrior paused, his dark eyes boring into Morgan's with such intensity it was almost tangible. And then, slowly, the warrior rode toward the west, and as he rode, the clouds began to fade and a double rainbow appeared above Morgan's head, the colors bright and clear.

Mesmerized, Morgan watched the ghost warrior ride across the now-cloudless sky until he disappeared into the sunset.

Exhausted, Morgan sank to the ground, his head between his knees, as he murmured a quiet prayer of thanksgiving.

Then he started down the mountain, his destination the lodge of the *wicasa wakan* where he would be told what his vision meant.

Keeper-of-the-Wind listened intently as Morgan related what he had seen on the mountain top. Occasionally the aged medicine man nodded; once he grunted softly. When Morgan had finished speaking, Keeper-of-the-Wind bowed his head, his eyes closed in meditation.

Morgan sat patiently, his gaze wandering over the lodge and its contents. Many bundles hung from the lodgepoles, along with an assortment of pipes and eagle feathers. A long blond scalp adorned a war shield. There were bowls filled with herbs and sweet grass, a feathered lance, a war club made out of the leg bone of a deer.

As the minutes went by, Morgan studied the old man sitting across from him. Keeper-of-the-Wind had hair the color of iron, skin like wrinkled brown paper, a nose as sharp as a blade. He wore a white buffalo robe around his shrunken shoulders and a single white eagle feather in his hair.

"Ah," the medicine man said softly. "I have seen the meaning of your vision, my son. The clouds represent your past, which has been filled with darkness and doubts. The warrior on the dark horse is the man you have become since you came to us, a man who will conquer whatever obstacles arise in his future. And the rainbow, it signifies that which you desire. Hereafter, you shall be called Rides a Dark Horse. Your medicine will be as powerful as the lightning, so long as you do not stray from the path of the warrior on the dark horse."

"And will I obtain that which I desire?"

"If you are worthy, then yes, it shall be yours."

Morgan nodded slowly. Rising to his feet, he bowed his head in the old man's direction and left the lodge, his expression thoughtful. Rides a Dark Horse, he mused. It was a fine name, a strong name, one he would prize and respect.

Crossing the village, he saw Carolyn outside their lodge. She was bent over a kettle, stirring. In the distance, fading but still visible, he could see a rainbow.

He continued on to White Eagle's lodge. White Eagle listened carefully as Morgan told him of his vision and of Keeper-of-the-Wind's interpretation of it.

"Rides a Dark Horse," White Eagle murmured. "It is a fine name, a strong name. Tonight I will give a feast to honor your new name. It is customary for you to present the medicine man with a gift. I have a fine white mare. She is yours to give."

"*Pilamaya*, my brother."

The feast started at dusk. Sunrise Woman and her friends had prepared huge quantities of food, and the whole tribe turned out to celebrate, for it was a great day when a new warrior was added to the People.

Carolyn sat with the women, hardly tasting her food. She couldn't keep her eyes off Morgan. He wore a black wolfskin clout that reached to his knees and a pair of moccasins beaded in black and yellow. Wide copper bands circled his biceps, a slash of white paint adorned his left cheek, and a lightning bolt crossed his chest from his left shoulder to his waist. The firelight cast his profile in bronze, and the sight of him took her breath away. He was handsome, magnificent, virile. Desirable.

She felt a catch in her heart. She wanted him and he didn't want her. She blinked back a tear, chiding herself for her lack of pride.

Glancing up, Carolyn saw one of the women staring at Morgan, her dark eyes aglow with admiration and desire. Jealousy knifed through Carolyn's heart, so intense it was almost painful.

Someday, he'd find a woman who pleased him, a woman to love. She was thankful she would not be there to see it.

During a lull in the feasting, White Eagle stepped into the circle, his chest puffed with pride as he motioned for Morgan to join him.

"Three moons ago, I brought this *wasicun* to our lodges so that he could teach me to speak the white man's tongue. He has become a good friend, and I am proud to call him brother to the Lakota. He has received a powerful vision, and from this time forward he shall be known as Rides a Dark Horse."

White Eagle clasped Morgan's forearm in a firm grip. "Welcome to our lodges, Rides a Dark Horse. May Wakan Tanka always smile upon you, and give you many strong sons and beautiful daughters."

"*Pilamaya*," Morgan said, his throat clogged with emotion. "*Pilamaya*."

White Eagle smiled broadly, then clapped Morgan on the shoulder. "You will always be one of us now, Rides a Dark Horse. One day you may have to leave our lodges, but you will always be welcome here."

Morgan nodded, too choked to speak. He belonged. For the first time in his life, he belonged. It was a good feeling.

The feasting went on for hours. Morgan sat beside White Eagle as the dancing began. There were dances for the maidens only, dances for married couples, for those who were courting, for the warriors. Morgan hesitated when White Eagle tugged on his arm, inviting him to dance with the men.

And then, impulsively, he stood up and entered the circle. At first his steps were awkward and unsure, but gradually he let the beat of the drum penetrate his heart and soul and direct his steps. Dancing around the fire, he was filled with a sense of belonging, of power. This was who he was, who he had always been.

Carolyn watched Morgan, hardly breathing as he danced with the men. He was fascinating, forbidding, intriguing. His skin glowed like burnished bronze, his expression was intense. His steps were graceful, masculine, exuding strength and self-confidence.

Gradually all the other warriors left the circle until Rides a Dark Horse danced alone, his body moving to the changing beat of the drum, his steps intricate as he circled the fire, his blood burning within him as he acknowledged who he was, who he had always longed to be.

Unshed tears welled in Carolyn's throat. She had never seen anything so beautiful, or loved him so much.

Quietly, she left the circle and walked into the darkness, her heart overflowing with pride for what Morgan had become. And mingled with that pride was a growing sense of loss. Like a mother who raises her child and then must let him go, she knew that she had lost Morgan forever. He belonged here, with these people. He would take her to Ogallala and leave her with Jordan, and she would never see him again.

She blinked back her tears at the sound of his footsteps, and then he was standing behind her, motionless as the rocks, silent as the stars.

"You have a fine new name," she said at last.

"Yes."

"White Eagle is very proud of you."

"Carolyn . . ."

"It's cold. I think I'll go back to the fire."

He wanted her. No matter that she could never be his, no matter that he was wrong for her, he wanted her as he had never wanted another woman. He wanted to hold her and touch her, hear her laugh, see her smile, watch her eyes glow with passion. He wanted to walk with her in the morning sun, and make love to her in the quiet of the night.

"Carrie." His hands closed over her shoulders and he drew her back against him. "Sweet, so sweet."

He nuzzled the side of her neck, and Carolyn felt her blood turn to honey and her bones to water. His nearness, the sound of his voice, the touch of his lips, all conspired to drain the strength from her limbs, and she swayed against him, longing for him, and knowing he would not give her what she yearned for.

"Carrie, I'm sorry."

From deep inside she summoned the strength to pull away. "I'm going now."

He didn't try to stop her. Hands hanging limp at his sides, he watched her walk away.

Letting her go was the hardest thing he'd ever done. And yet, it was for the best. "For the best," he muttered as he walked along the river. She was young, too young. She thought she was in love with him, but she didn't realize what the consequences would be if she let him make love to her. One day she'd find a decent man to marry, and then she'd be torn with guilt and regret for the loss of her virginity. She'd hate him then, hate him for taking advantage of her, for stealing that which should rightfully have belonged to her husband.

It was for the best. He said the words aloud again, hoping to ease the ache in his heart and cool the fire in his blood.

Pausing beneath a tree, Morgan closed his eyes. His mind filled with images of Carrie: Carrie sweeping the floor of his dismal shack; Carrie clad in a faded shirt and Levi's, looking young and vulnerable and desirable; Carrie bathing in the river; Carrie innocently tempting him with a look, a touch; Carrie comforting him when he was sick, injured. Carrie, Carrie.

He cursed softly as he turned and started walking upriver. He'd sworn never to drink again, but now he wished he could lose himself in a sea of alcohol, drown his desire in whiskey.

The village was quiet when he returned, the campfire almost out. A dog growled as Morgan made his way to his lodge, and he scowled at the beast, wondering how he'd manage to sleep, with Carrie lying only a foot away.

The inside of the lodge was warm and dark. He could make out Carolyn's form under her blankets, and the twin talons of passion and desire rose up within him, their claws slashing at his self-control. She was there and she wanted him. All he had to do was take her.

He stared at her for a long time, his hands clenched at his sides, his palms damp, as desire warred with honor. He thought of how much he loved her, of the fact that, once he left her with her brother in Ogallala, he'd never see her again. This was the only time they'd have to make love. He told himself that it was what he wanted, what *she* wanted. But in the end, none of that mattered. She was not his wife. She was a maiden. Under Lakota law, he was sworn to protect her from men like himself.

He took a long breath, let it out slowly, then turned toward the door. He couldn't sleep here tonight, not knowing she was within arm's reach. He was just a man, after all, not a stone saint, and there was only so much a man could endure.

He was about to step outside when he heard the sound of her tears. He hesitated a moment, certain that leaving was the right thing to do, but unable to leave her there, crying alone, in the dark.

Padding quietly across the floor, he knelt beside her. "Carolyn? Carrie, what's wrong?"

"Everything," she sobbed, her voice muffled by the heavy buffalo robe. "I love you, and you don't love me. I want you, and you keep pushing me away. I can't help it if I'm not pretty, like Red. I—"

"Carrie!" He threw the covers aside and swept her into his arms, hugging her close. "You don't love me, honey. You don't even know me."

"I do too."

"And I do want you, Carrie. You know I do. But it isn't right. You're a beautiful young woman. Yes, beautiful," he repeated when she started to protest. "And the only reason I push you away is because I don't want to hurt you. You're so young, so damn young, you don't know, you don't understand how it is, how people would look at you if they saw us together."

"I don't care," she said, sniffing back her tears. "I'm not asking you to marry me, just love me. Please, Morgan."

She sat quietly in his embrace, tense from head to foot as she waited for his answer. She had done the unthinkable; she had begged him to make love to her, and now she felt naked, vulnerable. What if he refused? How could she bear it?

"Are you sure, Carrie?" he asked, his voice thick.

"Yes." And suddenly she was sure. She wanted Morgan to hold her, to show her what it meant to be a woman, before she gave up all her hopes and dreams and settled down to being a proper young matron. Surely she was entitled to one night of happiness. And even if she wasn't, she was going to take it. "Yes," she said again.

He put her away from him and gazed deep into her eyes. "If I make love to you now, and you're willing, we'll be married according to Lakota custom. Does that bother you?"

Carolyn shook her head slowly.

"Of course, the marriage won't be legally binding once we leave here. No court in the land will recognize it. I'm not sure it's even legal for an Indian to marry a white woman."

"It doesn't matter."

"It matters to me. You're not a tramp, and I

don't want to treat you like one. For this night, in this place, you'll be my wife.''

Her heart was racing like a runaway train as she gazed into the depths of his eyes. His wife. For this night, she would be his wife according to Lakota custom. The wonder of it could not be measured.

"Will you be my wife, Carrie?"

"Yes," she replied breathlessly. "Oh, yes."

She smiled, her tears forgotten, her heart singing as he cupped her face in his hands and kissed her, gently, tenderly.

"Tonight I will be Rides a Dark Horse," he said softly, "and you will be my woman."

"Yes." She leaned toward him, lifting her face for his kiss, sighing with pleasure as his mouth closed over hers in sweet possession, his tongue boldly exploring until she was quivering with desire. Her hands wandered over his arms and back and chest, familiarizing themselves with the contours of the man who was, for this night, her husband. There was no softness in him, only hard muscular flesh, the perfect complement to her own soft curves.

She felt no fear, no apprehension, as he stretched out beside her on the soft buffalo robes. His kisses chased away all doubt. She was his wife, and she wanted him with every fiber of her being, every beat of her heart.

She waited impatiently while he shed his clout, her eyes lovingly caressing him. He was beautiful, so beautiful, from the crown of his head to the soles of his feet. She loved his broad shoulders, the muscles corded in his arms and legs, his flat belly ridged with muscle.

She sighed with pleasure when he drew her close, unprepared for the exquisite sensation of skin against skin. He was warm, solid, everything she had longed for.

Morgan held her close, his lips nuzzling her cheek, as he let out a long, shuddering sigh. He hadn't been prepared for the soul-shattering effect of holding her against him. She was soft and warm, the embodiment of everything beautiful and desirable.

He shuddered as she kissed him, her arms holding him close, her body pressed to his. He let his hands slide over her thigh, afraid to go too fast, wanting to make her first time something she would remember favorably. But it wasn't going to be easy. He'd waited so long, but he held himself in check, concentrating on Carrie as he caressed her. Her skin was like smooth satin beneath his fingertips, her breasts full and sweet. She moaned softly, pressing against him, her hands clutching him close as desire spiraled through her. A low groan emerged from his lips as he rose over her, unable to wait any longer, wanting to make her his for now. For always.

He gazed deep into her eyes, loving the way she looked back at him, her expression drowsy with passion, a faint smile on her lips as she drew him close.

Murmuring her name, he buried his face in her

neck, felt himself surrounded by her warmth. She gave a little cry of pain as the delicate membrane tore, and then they were moving together, two halves of the same whole soaring upward, ever upward....

Chapter 20

Carolyn woke slowly, still smiling as the last images of her dream faded into memory. It had been so wonderful. In her dream, Morgan had made love to her, his touch so gentle, so tender, it had brought tears to her eyes. And just before the dream ended, he had whispered that he loved her, his voice husky and low, so low, but she had heard the words, and they warmed her heart.

Abruptly she became aware of the fact that she wasn't alone in bed. Rolling over, she found Morgan lying on his back beside her, one arm flung over his head.

So it hadn't been a dream after all.

Carolyn studied the man beside her, vividly remembering the pleasure he had brought her the night before. Remembering, too, that she'd had to beg him to make love to her. Would he be sorry this morning? Would he wake up and stare at her with disgust?

She couldn't face him, not now. Rolling out of

the blankets, she dressed quickly and hastened from the lodge, heading for the river. She needed to bathe, and to think.

Finding a secluded spot a good way from the village, she slipped out of her dress and waded into the chill water, vigorously scrubbing her body as she recalled the night past. Surely no man had ever made love to a woman so tenderly! She had felt loved, cherished. Was it possible he cared for her? Perhaps she had not been dreaming; perhaps he *had* whispered that he loved her.

The thought brought a wistful smile to her lips. She didn't care if he was a half-breed, she wouldn't have cared if he was a wild Indian, she loved him. How could she even think of marrying Mr. Brockton now? What good were position and money and a place in society if you weren't married to the man you loved?

She whirled around at the sound of footsteps, and quickly folded her arms over her breasts when she saw Morgan standing on the shore, a lazy smile playing over his lips as he gazed at her.

"Mornin'," he drawled. "Mind if I join you?"

Carolyn shook her head, unable to speak, then turned her back as he began to peel off his leggings. It was too soon, she thought, her mind whirling with confusion. She wasn't ready to see him nude in the full light of day. In spite of all that had happened the night before, she hadn't really *seen* him, and she wasn't ready now. She needed time, time to sort her feelings, to come to grips with what had happened between them. She knew she should be mortified by what she'd done; instead, she felt shy and insecure one moment and happy and excited the next. Her heart was pounding as if she had run a great distance.

She heard a splash, and then he was in the water beside her, his dark eyes searching hers.

"Are you all right?" he asked.

Carolyn nodded, her gaze drawn to his bare torso, to the fine mat of curly black hair that covered his chest, tapering down, down, to disappear beneath the water.

"Carrie?"

"What?" she blurted, embarrassed because she'd been staring at him so blatantly, and because she wanted him to make love to her again.

"It's all right, Carrie. It's normal for you to be curious, especially after last night."

She nodded, the heat rising in her cheeks as she lowered her lashes.

She was so young, he thought with dismay, so young. Was she regretting last night? He had no experience with nice girls, no idea what she might be thinking or feeling. Was she happy? Sad? Disappointed? Probably the latter, he mused, since she couldn't bear to look at him. Making love to her had seemed so right last night, but now . . . He let out a long sigh. Nothing had really changed. He wanted her, but he was no good for her. Hell, until they'd come here, he hadn't been any good for himself, either.

He was about to turn away when she raised her gaze to his, her green eyes bright and shining. He searched her expression for some sign that she was sorry for what had happened, but he saw only con-

tentment and a hint of something he was reluctant
to believe.

He gazed down at her for several moments, admiring the way the morning sun danced in her
hair, the way the water lovingly caressed the
smooth contours of her slender shoulders. She
stood with her arms crossed over her breasts, her
cheeks rosy with embarrassment, and his heart
swelled with emotion even as he reminded himself
that there could be no lasting relationship between them. What had happened the night before
could not happen again.

But even as he vowed not to touch her, his hands
were reaching for her and he was drawing her
close, burying his face in the damp silk of her hair,
kissing the wildly beating pulse in her throat. He
told himself he would let her go if she said no, but
she only sighed and pressed herself against him,
the warmth of her body like a living flame against
his chest, and he was lost.

Lifting her into his arms, he carried her toward
the shore, intending to take her back to the lodge,
but the fire wouldn't wait. Laying her on the grassy
bank near the water's edge, he stretched out beside
her, his gaze moving over her face. Slowly he
leaned toward her and licked the drops of water
from her neck, her shoulders, the curve of her
breast.

Carrie sighed as she surrendered to his touch,
everything else forgotten but the man bending
over her. She gazed into his eyes and knew he
found her beautiful, desirable. Her lips parted beneath his, sharing his breath as they kissed. She

heard his voice murmur her name, and then he was speaking to her in soft Lakota, and though she could not understand the words, she had no trouble comprehending their meaning. He was telling her he loved her. For a moment, she wondered why he spoke to her in Lakota, and then it no longer mattered, nothing mattered but the man in her arms. . . .

The next few days were the happiest Carolyn had ever known. She sang as she did her chores, her gaze ever drawn toward the tall, handsome man who shared her lodge and filled her heart with joy. She was jealous of every moment he spent away from her, and lived only for the hours they spent together alone in the lodge. All doubts, all fears, were put away, and she knew that she would be happy to spend the rest of her days with the Lakota if it meant she could share her nights in Morgan's arms. He was Rides a Dark Horse, and she was his woman, and content to be so.

Sometimes in the evening they took walks along the river, pausing to watch as the deer came down to the water to drink. Standing there with her hand in his, she knew a kind of inner peace and happiness that made her heart swell with tenderness.

One night she heard the high, trilling notes of a flute. When she asked Morgan what it meant, he told her that one of the warriors was serenading the maiden of his choice. It was powerful medicine, Morgan said. There were many kinds of flutes, but the most effective was the Big Twisted

Flute made of cedar and decorated with the likeness of a horse, which was considered the most ardent of all animals. Such flutes were crafted by a shaman who had dreamed of the Buffalo. It was believed that these flutes possessed so much power that a girl upon hearing it would leave her tipi to follow the music, and a woman who was touched with such a flute would become so entranced she would follow her lover anywhere.

Carrie smiled at such a romantic notion and then put it from her mind. But the next evening after supper, Morgan pulled a Big Twisted Flute from inside his shirt and began to play, his deep gray eyes moving softly over her face as the lilting, sweetly haunting notes of the flute filled the lodge.

Carrie felt tears well in her eyes as the music embraced her, telling her ever so softly that she was loved beyond words.

He was still watching her when he finished playing, his eyes filled with the words he couldn't seem to say.

Carrie moved to sit beside Morgan. Placing her head on his shoulder, she gazed up into his eyes.

"It works," she said, her voice husky with emotion. "I'd follow you anywhere."

"Carrie . . ."

"I know," she whispered, lifting her face for his kiss. "I know."

She had put all thought of going to Ogallala out of her mind, happily resigning herself to spending the rest of her life with the Lakota, and learning their ways and language. Then, in the space of an hour, everything changed.

She was sitting outside the lodge, trying very hard to make pemmican the way she'd seen Sunrise Woman do it, when she glanced up and saw a white man riding into the village. Carolyn stared at him curiously, wondering who he was that he dared ride so boldly into the Lakota camp.

He was leading a pack mule, and as he dismounted from his horse, the Indians swarmed around him carrying pelts and furs and other items. Carrie realized then that he had come to trade with the Lakota.

She watched for an hour, smiling as she listened to the women haggle with the trader. She laughed when one of them threatened to hit him over the head with a rock if he didn't meet her terms.

When she saw Morgan approach the trader, a sudden heaviness fell upon her heart as the trader drew a bottle of whiskey from one of his packs. Time seemed to hang suspended as she watched Morgan stare at the bottle. Finally, with a curt shake of his head, he turned away, and Carrie let out a sigh of relief.

She smiled up at him as he came to sit beside her.

"You weren't worried, were you?" he asked.

"No, I . . . yes," she admitted sheepishly.

"Don't be. I've given it up for good."

She was about to say she was sorry for doubting him when she saw the trader coming toward them. He was a big man with stringy hair and a pock-marked face. His pale brown eyes moved over her in a long, appraising glance, as though she were a piece of merchandise he hoped to sell.

"How much do you want for the squaw?" he asked Morgan.

"She's no squaw," Morgan said curtly. "And she's not for sale at any price."

"Everything has a price," the trader retorted. "What do you want for her? Rifles? Whiskey? I got lots of whiskey. Enough to warm you through the winter."

Morgan rose slowly to his feet, his hand resting on the knife sheathed at his side. "She's not for sale. Now get the hell out of here."

"Sure, sure," the man said, his gaze riveted on the knife. "I don't want no trouble. I just thought—"

"I know what you thought," Morgan snapped. "Now get out of here."

Nodding vigorously, the trader turned and walked away.

Morgan stared after him, wondering who he hated more, the trader for insulting Carrie, or himself for what he'd done to her. What else could the man think, seeing Carrie living with a half-breed? And it would be the same wherever they went.

"Get your stuff together," Morgan said curtly. "We're leaving this afternoon."

"This afternoon? Why?"

"Because I said so."

Carrie stared up at him, puzzled by his tone. "I don't want to leave," she said, thinking he'd be glad to know she wanted to stay with him, with the Lakota.

"I don't give a damn what you want," he said,

217

his dark eyes blazing with anger. "We're leaving."

He didn't give her a chance to argue, or try to talk him out of it. He'd been wrong to touch her in the first place. He'd known it then, he knew it now. He would not taint her with his presence any longer than necessary. He'd take her home where she belonged.

"In an hour," he said, and left before he changed his mind.

It was in her mind to call him back, to beg him to reconsider, but from somewhere deep inside a pride she didn't know she possessed stilled her tongue. If he didn't want her, so be it. If he didn't think he was good enough for her, maybe he wasn't. And if he didn't love her enough to face whatever the future held together, then she didn't want him, either!

It was for the best, Morgan thought as he walked toward White Eagle's lodge to say goodbye. In his mind, he knew it was true; all he had to do now was convince his heart.

Carolyn stared at Morgan's back as they rode out of the valley. Their leave-taking had been hurried, as if he couldn't wait to be on his way and get her off his hands. Did he hate her now? Did he think her no better than Red and his mother? Had she forever shamed herself in his eyes? Why wouldn't he look at her, speak to her? She had never felt so alone.

Morgan rode steadily onward, acutely aware of the girl riding behind him. He could feel her gaze on his back, the silent accusation in her eyes.

Guilt stabbed at his heart, sharper than a blade, more deadly than rattlesnake venom. He had wanted her, wanted her desperately, and so he had rattled off a few words about her being his wife to ease his conscience. Not that he hadn't meant what he said. For the last three days, she *had* been his wife, his woman.

He had loved her as gently as he had ever loved a woman. But it changed nothing. He was no good for her and he never would be. He'd seen the contempt in the eyes of the trader, had known that the man thought Carrie no better than a whore for living with a half-breed. And it was all his fault. Carrie was young. She thought she was in love. And passion was a powerful incentive. It had taken only a few well-chosen words and she had melted in his arms, giving him everything she had to give. And he had taken it all, her virginity, her innocence, her trust. The fact that he loved her was no excuse. If the people in Ogallala found out she'd been living with him, she'd be ruined, all hope for a decent life forever forfeit. And all because he hadn't been able to control himself.

He pushed his horse harder, anxious to get Carolyn to her brother as soon as possible. The thought of being alone with her, sleeping under the stars, made him break out in a cold sweat. He'd promised himself that he wouldn't touch her again; and yet, he wanted her in his arms, wanted to drown himself in her sweetness and pretend that he was Rides a Dark Horse and she was truly his woman, for now and always.

He shook the thought from his mind and concentrated on the landscape. He had learned a lot in the few months they had spent with the Lakota, and he looked at his surroundings with new eyes now. Animal tracks were easily recognized, and he could tell the age of a track by its appearance. New tracks had sharp edges, older ones might be partly obscured by dust or rain. Of course, weather had a great influence on a track, and could make a fresh print look like an old one. Tracks that were widely spaced meant the animal was traveling at great speed; tightly spaced or wandering tracks usually meant an animal was grazing.

If only there were tracks to a woman's heart, he mused. If only she weren't so young, so rich. If she'd been born poor, perhaps her expectations wouldn't have been so high, and an out-of-work half-breed wouldn't have been so socially unacceptable.

He snorted softly. Socially unacceptable. That was an understatement. She'd been born to wealth and position, and he'd been born in the back room of a whorehouse. You couldn't get much more socially unacceptable than that!

Carolyn let out a sigh of relief when Morgan finally found a suitable place to spend the night. They'd ridden for hours without a break, and she groaned softly as she dismounted. Placing one hand against her aching back, she stretched, then groaned again. She hurt. Everywhere.

They quickly fell into their old routine, and in a short time the horses were brushed and hobbled, a small fire was burning, and coffee was warming on the coals. They ate in silence, carefully avoiding each other's eyes. Carolyn hardly tasted the roast rabbit, and could hardly swallow for the sob lodged in her throat. She had thought that Morgan loved her. The last few days had been wonderful. Why couldn't he believe that his being a half-breed didn't matter? What had happened to the warmth, the sense of belonging, that she'd felt in his embrace? She wanted to take him by the arm and shake him, make him talk to her, make him understand that she loved him, but the fierce look in his eye stilled her tongue.

Dinner was soon over and it was time for bed. She slid a glance at Morgan and quickly looked away. She didn't want to sleep alone. She'd told herself that she didn't care, that if he didn't want her, then she didn't want him, but it was all a lie. She wanted to be in his arms, tonight and always. But she couldn't bring herself to say the words, so she crawled into her cold, lonely bed, curled up in a ball, and closed her eyes.

But sleep would not come, and after a while she sat up, determined to make him talk to her, tell her what was wrong. "Morgan?"

"What?" He didn't look at her.

"Are you mad at me?"

"No."

"Then what is it? What's wrong?"

"Nothing."

"There is! You're mad because I threw myself at you, because I'm no better than ... than a ..." She couldn't say the word, not out loud.

He swung around to face her, his expression ominous in the light of the fire. "Don't even think of yourself like that," he growled. "You're not a whore. What happened was my fault, not yours. But it won't happen again. We'll be in Ogallala in a week or so, and you can put all this behind you."

"I don't want to. I love you."

"No, you don't." He took a deep breath, hating himself for what he was about to do, but knowing it was better to make a clean break now than let her think they could have a lasting relationship.

"I do love you!" she cried vehemently, shamelessly.

"Well, it doesn't matter. I don't love you. You're not my type."

"I'll change," she promised, her pride forgotten. "I'll be whatever you want. We can go back to White Eagle's village. I'll—"

"Stop it! What happened back there was a mistake. There's no sense in ruining your whole life over one stupid mistake. Now go to sleep."

She stared at him, silent tears streaming down her cheeks, the hurt in her luminous green eyes filling him with self-loathing.

Muttering an oath, he stalked into the shadows, quietly cursing himself for being the worst kind of heel. He stopped when he was out of sight, then hunkered down on his heels where he could keep an eye on Carolyn. He clenched and unclenched his fists as he watched her slip under the covers. He could see her shoulders shake as she wept, and it was all he could do to keep from going to her, from telling her he hadn't meant a thing he said, that he loved her more than his own life. But it was because he loved her that he stayed where he was until she was asleep.

Returning to the dwindling fire, he paced back and forth, his hands shoved into his pants pockets. Perhaps if he paced for an hour or two he'd be able to get some sleep. And perhaps if he didn't look at Carolyn he'd forget she was there.

And if he had the wings of an eagle he could fly.

Chapter 21

Ogallala was a rough-and-tumble town. The way of the gun was a way of life in a place inhabited by cowboys and drifters, gamblers and miners. Someone had nicknamed the town the Gomorrah of the Plains, and Morgan allowed as how the name might fit as they rode down the main street, which was lined with saloons and bawdy houses. A raven-haired girl dressed in a white chemise and flowing Chinese robe leaned over the balcony of a saloon, waving at him with a red silk scarf and inviting him to pay her a visit. Anytime.

Carolyn grimaced at the girl's indecent behavior and immodest attire. She couldn't help but wonder why Jordan had chosen such a dreadful place to live when he could live anywhere he pleased. Surely, if he felt the need to live in the West, there were other towns more civilized than this one.

She almost jumped out of the saddle at the sound of a gunshot, closely followed by two more in rapid succession. Glancing over her shoulder toward the sound, she saw a man stagger out of a saloon, his hand pressed to his chest. His shirt was covered with blood, and she watched in horror as he swayed unsteadily, then pitched headlong into the street.

She stared at Morgan, but he seemed unconcerned. "Do you know where your brother lives?" he asked.

"No."

Morgan glanced up and down the street, his gaze settling on a large white building on the far corner. "There's the bank. I reckon if he's not there, they'll know where to find him."

Carolyn nodded. "I guess so."

"I think I'd better leave you here. It won't look good, your being seen with me."

Carolyn stared at him, unable to believe he meant to leave her there in the middle of the street, alone. "You're going, just like that?"

"Just like that. What'd you wanna do, take me home and introduce me to the family?"

"Yes ... no ... I don't know."

"Believe me, it's better this way, Miss Chandler. The fewer people who see us together, the better."

Carolyn nodded, her heart breaking as Morgan touched his hat in a gesture of farewell and rode on down the street. She sat there, staring after him, unable to believe he could leave her just like that. He reined his horse to a halt in front of one of the saloons, dismounted, and made his way through the swinging doors. He never looked back. She felt the sting of tears as she urged her horse down the street and blinked them away. He wasn't shedding any tears over her, and she wasn't going to waste time weeping for him, either. She was here, in Ogallala, and she was going to start a new life for herself.

The Ogallala Bank and Trust was an impressive building. Made of brick, it took up almost half a block.

Dismounting, Carolyn brushed the trail dust from her dress and ran a hand over her hair. She had insisted on putting on her dress before they reached town, refusing to let anyone see her clad in pants. Her dress was terribly wrinkled from being folded up for so long, but at least it was clean and fashionable. Several men stared at her as she entered the bank.

She saw Jordan immediately. He was seated behind a huge walnut desk, looking just as handsome as ever. His hair was light brown, his eyes were blue. She saw him smile at one of the customers, and her eyes filled with tears of relief. Jordan was family. He would take care of her.

Wiping away the tears, she hurried toward him.

Jordan Chandler gazed at his sister in stunned disbelief. "Carolyn! Is it really you?" He stepped around the desk and wrapped her in his arms. "How'd you get here? Merciful heavens, girl, Father's been out of his mind."

"Oh, Jordan, it's so good to see you," Carolyn exclaimed breathlessly, and burst into tears.

Jordan glanced at his secretary. The very prim and proper Miss Leona Hines was staring at them, a look of disapproval on her pinched features. Several customers were also staring at them curiously.

"Carrie, hush," he admonished quietly. "You're causing a scene. Miss Hines, I'm going home early today. If Mr. Bradshaw comes in, tell him we'll sign those papers first thing tomorrow morning. Come on, Carrie, I'll take you home."

Carolyn nodded, her tears coming faster as she remembered how Morgan had called her Carrie the night they made love. No one had ever called her Carrie except Jordan, and she'd hated it. But the name had taken on a new meaning when Morgan whispered it in her ear.

"How'd you get here?" Jordan asked again when they were outside.

"I . . ." She realized abruptly that she couldn't tell him she'd come on horseback. If she did, she'd have to explain about Morgan and how she'd met him in a back alley, and that would lead to more questions, none of which she was prepared to answer. Down the street, she saw several people milling around a stagecoach that had apparently just arrived, and she pointed at the Concord. "I came by stage."

"Where's your baggage?"

"I didn't bring any."

"Yes, Father said you ran away in the middle of the night. Come along, my house isn't far."

Side by side, they walked down the street. Carolyn felt a twinge of regret as she walked past Whiskey, hoping that someone would take care of the mare. She slid a glance at Morgan's gray gelding as they passed the saloon, wondering what he was doing in such a place. He'd sworn to give up drinking. Had he changed his mind? She told herself it didn't matter, that she was well rid of him, but for a brief moment she was sorely tempted to run into the saloon just to see him one more time.

"When did you last hear from Father?" Carolyn asked as they approached a large white house trimmed in bright yellow. She was impressed by its beauty and simplicity, and surprised to see such an elegant residence in a place like Ogallala. It stood out like a daisy in a patch of weeds. "Is this yours?"

"Yes," Jordan replied, opening the front door. "And to answer your other question, the last time I heard from Father was this morning."

"This morning?" Carolyn echoed. She glanced around the parlor, impressed by its simple elegance. The furniture was of dark wood, covered with flowered chintz, the carpets were expensive, the lamps of cut crystal. There was a painting of a Paris street scene on one wall, and a large portrait of Jordan and Diana on another. "You heard from Father this morning?"

"Yes. At breakfast. He's here, Carolyn. He arrived day before yesterday."

"He's here," she said, her voice a high-pitched squeak. "In the house?"

"In the room."

Carolyn whirled around at the sound of her father's voice. Then he was striding toward her, a tall, austere man in a suit of black broadcloth that complemented his thick white hair and piercing blue eyes.

"Carolyn!" He pulled her into his arms and hugged her. "I've been so worried. Are you all right?" He drew away, his hands on her shoulders, while he examined her from head to heel. "You've lost weight."

"I'm fine, Father."

"How'd you get here?"

"On the stage. I just arrived."

Archibald Chandler nodded. She was here, alive and well. His relief at seeing her safe quickly turned to anger as he recalled how she'd run off in the middle of the night. "I've been worried sick!" he said curtly. "Dammit, daughter, if you ever do anything like that again, I'll—"

"You'll what, Archie?"

A cold hand clamped itself around Carolyn's heart as a short, stocky man in a bilious green suit entered the room.

Archibald Chandler grinned. "I'll leave it to you, Roger. After all, she'll soon be your worry, not mine."

Carolyn looked from her father to Roger Brockton and knew exactly how a fly felt when caught in a web. She was trapped, unable to escape.

"How are you, my dear?" Roger Brockton asked. Crossing the floor, he took her hand and kissed it. "We've been out of our minds with worry, Caro. It was most thoughtless of you to run off like that."

Carolyn nodded, unable to speak past the growing lump in her throat.

"I'm sure Carolyn's weary after her long journey," Jordan remarked. "Perhaps she'd like to go upstairs and freshen up."

229

"Yes, please." Carolyn threw her brother a grateful smile. "I'd like that."

"I'll show you the way," Jordan offered. "I'll send Diana up as soon as she gets home. She went to spend the day with one of her friends."

Carolyn nodded, anxious to get away from her father and Mr. Brockton. She could feel the room closing in on her, feel her freedom slipping from her grasp.

Wordlessly she followed Jordan up a long flight of stairs, then down a carpeted hallway. He opened a door for her at the end of the hall, then followed her inside.

The room was painted a pale rose. A four-poster bed was set against the west wall, white lace curtains hung at the windows, and a white spread covered the bed.

"It's lovely," Carolyn murmured unenthusiastically. "The loveliest prison I've ever seen."

Jordan frowned. "Prison? What are you talking about?"

"Oh, Jordan, I ran away because I didn't want to marry Roger Brockton, and now he's here, and Father's here, and . . ." She sighed heavily, wishing she'd never left the Lakota camp.

"Roger's not a bad sort, Carrie. I'm sure he'll do his best to make you happy."

"You're on their side," she accused bitterly.

"I'm not on any side. I just don't understand your reluctance to marry Roger. He's got position and money. He can give you a home, security, all the things a woman needs."

"What about love?" Carolyn asked bitterly.

"I'm sure he loves you."

"But I don't love him!"

"So that's what this is all about." Jordan paced the length of the room, and paused briefly to look out the window before he turned to face her again. "Are you in love with someone else? If you are, I'm sure Father would reconsider."

Carolyn sat down on the edge of the bed and stared at the braided rug beneath her feet. Dare she confide in him? She knew instinctively that Jordan would be appalled to learn his little sister had fallen in love with a man who earned his living working in a whorehouse, a man who had no family, no money, and no ambition.

"Carrie?"

"I just don't want to marry Mr. Brockton. He's too short. And he's old, Jordan, old enough to be my father."

"So in a few years you'll be a rich widow. I'm sorry, Carrie, I shouldn't have said that." Crossing to the bed, he patted her shoulder in big-brotherly fashion.

"He's not that old, Carrie. Is there something else?"

Carolyn hesitated a moment. She'd never put her true feelings for Roger Brockton into words. "I don't trust him, Jordan. There's something about him . . . I don't know what it is, exactly. But I feel like he's hiding something from us, that he's not really what he seems to be."

"I'm sure Father had Brockton's background checked out before he agreed to let him marry you. Maybe what you're feeling is just pre-wedding jitters. You are awfully young to be getting married, and you haven't had much experience with men."

Young, Carrie thought. That's what Morgan had said, and maybe he was right, maybe she was too young to get married. But she wasn't inexperienced, not anymore.

"Get some rest, Carrie. I'll have Diana bring you a change of clothing when she gets home."

"Thanks, Jordan."

He nodded, kissed her on the forehead, and left the room, closing the door behind him.

For a moment, Carolyn sat on the bed staring at the closed door. Then, rising to her feet, she removed her dress, shoes, and stockings and crawled under the covers, only to lie awake staring at the white-washed ceiling. She'd have to marry Mr. Brockton now. It was her father's wish, and she had no choice but to obey.

Once, in the Lakota camp, she had told herself it wouldn't be so bad being Mrs. Brockton. Morgan didn't want her, but Roger Brockton did, and he could give her everything she wanted or needed: fine clothes, expensive jewelry, a house of her own, a place in society, servants to wait on her. Everything she wanted, except Morgan.

Carolyn sat at the dinner table between Jordan and Diana, listening as her father and Mr. Brockton made elaborate plans for the wedding and the reception afterwards. It would be the biggest shindig Galveston had ever seen. Her father promised he would spare no expense, the champagne would flow like water, there would be tables full of food, a five-tiered wedding cake. Jordan would be best man, Diana would be the matron of honor.

Carolyn glanced up as she realized her father was speaking to her. "What?"

"The date, Carolyn. We need to set the date."

"The date?"

"For the wedding."

"Of course. I don't care, but I don't want to be married in Galveston. I want to be married here."

"Here? But all our friends are in Texas."

"I don't care. I want to be married here." She was being silly and she knew it, but she couldn't bring herself to leave Ogallala. Morgan was here, and as long as he was here, she wanted to be here, too.

Archibald Chandler looked at Brockton. "What do you think, Roger?"

Brockton shrugged. "If she wants to get married here, it's fine with me."

Archibald Chandler nodded. "It's settled then. You'll be married here, and we can have a reception when we get back to Galveston."

"After the honeymoon," Roger said, leering at Carolyn.

"Of course," said Archibald.

"You'll need a dress, Carolyn," Diana mused. "Ogallala doesn't have much in the way of wedding gowns, but we could order one from New York."

"Yes, that's a good idea," Carolyn said quickly. Sending to New York would take time. Perhaps in the interim she could find a way to change her father's mind about the wedding.

"I have a catalog," Diana said. "I'll look for it after supper."

Carolyn nodded, and the conversation turned to other things. Jordan mentioned that business at the bank was going well. Mr. Brockton remarked that he'd just bought a new fleet of ships and expected to make a small fortune from his investment.

Carolyn gazed thoughtfully at her father. He remained unusually quiet, and she wondered if something was bothering him. It wasn't like him to sit back and listen. He liked to be in the thick of things, bragging about how well he was doing, about how the bank was prospering due to his shrewd investments.

After supper, the men retired to the parlor while Diana and Carolyn browsed through a mail order catalog. The dresses in the catalog were beautiful, some elegantly simple, others frothy creations of lace and ruffles, and for a few minutes Carolyn pretended it was Morgan she was going to marry, Morgan who would be waiting for her at the altar. His eyes would glow with admiration as she walked toward him because, in one of these lovely gowns, she'd be beautiful for the first time in her life.

"Mr. Brockton seems like quite a nice man," Diana remarked, and Carolyn's fantasy vanished.

"I guess so."

"You're not in love with him, are you?"

Carolyn shook her head.

"Does your father know?"

"Of course he knows!" Carolyn exclaimed. "Why

do you think I ran away?"

"That's what I thought." Diana folded her hands in her lap. Carolyn was so young, perhaps too young to know what was best for her. "Your father only wants you to be happy, Carolyn. I'm sure Mr. Brockton will make you a fine husband. He has wealth and influence. You'll never want for anything."

"Money! You sound just like Jordan. Is that all anybody in this family thinks about, money? Is that why you married my brother, because he was rich?"

"Of course not," Diana retorted.

"Well, I don't want to marry for money, either. I want to marry the man I love."

Understanding dawned in Diana's eyes. "I see. There's someone else."

"No," Carolyn said quickly. She gazed at Diana, wondering how many proposals, proper or otherwise, her sister-in-law had received before she married Jordan. Diana was a beautiful woman. Her hair was dark blond, her eyes a beautiful sky blue, her skin unblemished. She had poise and sophistication, and Carolyn wished she knew the other woman better. It would be such a relief to be able to confide in someone.

But anything she told Diana would surely be repeated to Jordan. And Jordan would feel duty-bound to tell their father.

"Have you decided on a dress?" Diana asked.

Carolyn stared at the catalog in her lap. What difference did it make what she wore? Still, she was likely to be married only once. "This one, I think."

Diana nodded her approval. The gown was exquisite. Made of satin, it had long tapered sleeves, a round neck, and a flared skirt. The bodice was beaded at the neckline with seed pearls.

Diana turned down the page, then stood up. "I'll send the order first thing in the morning. Get some sleep now, Carolyn. Perhaps things will look better tomorrow."

"Thank you. Good night, Diana."

"Sleep well."

Carolyn undressed and slid into bed. The sheets smelled of soap and sunlight, the cotton was cool against her skin. Gazing out the open window, she thought of the nights she had spent under the stars with Morgan, of the first evening on the trail when he'd rubbed her back, his hands soothing and exciting. She missed him. She missed his sardonic smile, the sound of his voice, the touch of his hand. He had taken care of her, saved her life, made her feel desirable, if only for a little while.

A single tear slid down her cheek and she dashed it away. She would not cry for him. She had offered him her love and he had refused it. He hadn't refused to take her virginity, though, she reminded herself bitterly. Then she smiled. Maybe she'd tell Roger Brockton that she was no longer a virgin. He wouldn't want her then.

Her smile vanished like the sun before the rain. No one would ever want her if they knew what she'd done. Maybe Morgan had been right about that, too. She tried to imagine how her father and brother would react if she told them she had let an Indian make love to her. Her father would be shocked, hurt, outraged. He might even disown her. And Jordan ... he'd be ashamed, so ashamed.

She couldn't tell them; she could never tell anyone. And yet, if Morgan had loved her in return, she would have shouted it to the skies. She would have risked her father's wrath and her brother's shame; she would have followed Morgan to the ends of the earth just to be with him. But he didn't want her.

She put him out of her mind, refusing to think of him at all. She had made a mistake, but it didn't have to ruin her life. There were worse fates than being a wealthy young matron. She would ask Mr. Brockton to build her a new house in Galveston, one that would make everyone else green with envy. She'd have a new carriage and fashionable French gowns and give fabulous parties and everyone would say how lucky she was....

Perhaps, in time, she'd come to believe it herself.

Chapter 22

Morgan sat with his back to the wall, one foot resting on an empty chair, his right hand curled around a glass of whiskey. He'd been staring at the liquor for the past hour, but hadn't touched a drop.

He'd had every intention of getting drunk when he entered the saloon. He'd ordered a bottle of the best bourbon in the place, carried it to a table in a back corner, and sat down fully intending to get roaring drunk.

But he couldn't do it. He'd come in here every day for the past week, always determined to get drunk enough to blot her out of his mind, but he couldn't do it.

He'd thought about taking one of the saloon girls upstairs, too, but the thought of bedding a painted tart held no more appeal than the whiskey.

He didn't want booze, and he didn't want one of the scantily clad women prowling the saloon. He wanted Carrie.

A soft curse escaped his lips. She'd taken the pleasure out of drinking and killed his desire for other women, and he sat there feeling empty inside, hurting like he'd never hurt before. He told himself again that what he'd done had been for the best, that Carolyn deserved more out of life than he'd ever be able to give her, but it didn't ease the ache in his heart or lessen his sense of loss.

For all that she'd been spoiled rotten and about as ignorant of life as a newborn babe, he loved her. Loved her stubborn spirit, her sullen pouts, the way she'd looked at him after he rescued her from the Crow, as if he were a cross between a knight in shining armor and the hero in a two-bit novel.

She'd made him feel things he'd never felt, made him think maybe it didn't matter that he was a half-breed. That fact didn't seem to bother her, though it should have.

When they were in the Indian camp, she'd known how important it was for him to stay. He'd found his self-respect there. He'd learned that Indians weren't godless, inhuman savages, as his mother and others had told him. They were just people trying to survive in a harsh land, and they'd treated him better than anybody else he'd ever known, respected him for who he was, not what he was.

He drew circles on the table with the whiskey glass. Maybe he'd go back to White Eagle's village. Maybe he'd find a pretty little dark-eyed Lakota girl, get married and settle down. He could have a good life there.

Morgan closed his eyes, a deep sigh welling within him. Who was he trying to kid? He didn't want a Lakota wife. He wanted Carrie: Carrie lying beside him in the dark of the night, whispering that she loved him as he held her close, making him feel that he was the best thing that had ever happened to her. She was for damn sure the best thing that had ever happened to him.

Muttering an oath, he slammed the glass on the table and left the saloon.

Outside, he settled his hat on his head and glanced down the street, thinking maybe he'd go check on Whiskey and the gray and then go for a ride. He spent a lot of time with Carrie's horse, which just proved how far gone he really was.

He was heading for the livery barn when he saw her. She was wearing a dark green dress that complemented her complexion and flattered every delectable curve. Roughing it on the trail had done wonders for her figure, he noted appreciatively. Hard riding had trimmed her weight, hours in the sun had lent a healthy golden glow to her skin. She'd never looked lovelier, and he felt a sharp stab of jealousy as several men turned to stare at her.

He was staring himself, cursing the quick heat that suffused him as he watched her walk along the boardwalk, likely headed for the General Store. It was only when she drew closer that Morgan noticed she wasn't alone. The other woman was easy on the eyes, but it was Carrie who held his attention.

He knew the moment she saw him. Her eyes

widened in surprise, then glowed with pleasure, and she began to walk faster, heading right toward him.

Abruptly, he drew his gaze away and crossed the street.

Carolyn stared after Morgan, cut to the quick by his refusal to acknowledge her. Blinking back tears, she followed Diana into Dixon's General Store, wandering aimlessly up one aisle and down another while Diana took her list to the front to be filled.

"Carrie."

She whirled around at the sound of his voice, all her previous anger swept away at his nearness. She gazed up at him, so glad to see him again she couldn't think of anything to say.

"How are you, Carrie?" he asked quietly, conscious of the other people in the building.

"Fine. And you?"

He shrugged, the scent of her perfume tickling his nostrils. "All right, I guess."

She couldn't stop staring at him. He'd bought some new clothes, black whipcord britches and a dark gray shirt that emphasized his broad shoulders and matched his eyes.

"Was your brother surprised to see you?"

"Yes, very." Morgan hadn't shaved for several days, and she longed to run her hand over the coarse stubble on his jaw, to caress his cheek. Did he miss her at all?

Morgan gazed into her eyes, wondering why he couldn't say what he felt. They'd been through a lot together, good times and bad, yet he stood there

241

making small talk as if she'd never been more than a casual acquaintance.

"My father's here," Carolyn remarked.

"Oh?"

"And Mr. Brockton."

Brockton! A muscle twitched in Morgan's jaw and he clenched his hands into tight fists. Brockton. The man her father wanted her to marry, the man she'd run away from. "Carrie . . ."

"We can't talk here. Meet me tonight in the shed behind the house."

"Carolyn?" Diana's voice drifted toward them, and then she was walking down the aisle, her arms full of packages. "Are you ready to go home? I . . ."

Diana's voice trailed off as she realized Carrie had been talking to the man beside her. She studied the stranger intently for a moment, then looked at Carolyn more closely. Her sister-in-law's eyes were bright, her cheeks flushed. "Is this man bothering you?"

"No. He . . . I . . . He was just asking me where he could find—"

"I was asking the lady if she knew where the telegraph office was, ma'am," Morgan cut in.

"It's down the street, next to the barber shop," Diana replied, her voice cool and aloof.

Morgan touched the brim of his hat with his forefinger. "Obliged, ma'am." He sent a last, lingering look in Carolyn's direction, then turned and left the store.

"Is that all he wanted, Carolyn?" Diana queried. "Directions?"

"Of course," Carrie replied, not meeting Diana's curious gaze. "What else would he want?" She reached for one of the paper-wrapped parcels in Diana's arms. "Here, let me help you with those."

"What? Oh, yes, thank you." Diana stared at Carolyn, certain there had been more going on than appeared on the surface, but at a loss to know what it was. "Well, come along, Carolyn. Jordan will be home for dinner soon."

Carrie sat on the edge of her bed, listening to the downstairs clock strike the hour. It was eleven o'clock and the house had been quiet for over an hour.

Sitting there alone in the dark, she thought about Morgan, about the days and nights when they had made love in the dusky confines of a Lakota lodge. She remembered every kiss, every caress, every look.

Every word. *I don't love you*, he'd said, his voice as hard and cold as stone. *You're not my type.*

She couldn't believe that there'd been nothing more to his lovemaking than just the act itself, not when his kisses had thrilled her so, not when his touch had warmed her heart and made her feel cherished and desired. She'd been so sure that he'd grown to love her as she loved him.

She frowned, wondering if his words had been a lie, a way to keep her at arm's length so she'd be glad to leave him and marry the kind of man he thought was right for her.

That was it, she mused, her heart swelling with hope. That had to be it!

Rising, she hurriedly donned a pair of slippers, drew on a heavy quilted robe, and tiptoed out of her bedroom.

She paused at the head of the stairs. No lights showed below, and she glided silently down the carpeted staircase, her heart beating wildly. Would he be there, waiting?

Her feet hardly made a sound as she moved through the dark house to the kitchen and opened the back door.

Outside, it was as dark as ten feet down. Hazy clouds hid the moon and the stars, and she made her way carefully across the yard, uttering a low gasp when her foot struck a rock.

She could see the shed a few feet ahead, a darker shape silhouetted against the dark of the night. Was he there, waiting inside? What would she say to him if he was? A small smile curved her lips. Perhaps, if he felt as she did, no words would be necessary.

Happiness welled inside her, bubbling like a spring, as she thought of being with him again, of standing in his embrace, his arms tight around her.

The door squeaked as she eased it open, sounding dreadfully loud in the hushed stillness of the night.

Pausing in the doorway, she peered inside. "Morgan? Are you in there?"

She jumped as a hand closed over her arm.

"Shh, Carrie, it's me."

Gladness washed through her, warm and sweet as honeyed wine, as she whirled around to face him. "I didn't think you'd come."

"You asked me to." He gazed down at her, but it was too dark to see the expression in her eyes.

He drew a deep breath and her scent filled his nostrils, reminding him of the carefree days in the Lakota camp, of the nights they'd spent in each other's arms.

He ached with the need to hold her, and it was all he could do to keep from reaching for her. He longed to run his hands through her hair, taste the sweetness of her lips, bury himself in her softness.

He let out a long sigh as he fought down the desire raging within him, and then, feeling he must touch her or die, he traced the line of her cheek with his forefinger. "What do you want, Carrie?"

"I just wanted to see you," she said, her happiness shriveling at the coldness in his tone. "I . . . I missed you."

"I hear you're getting married."

"I don't want to. You know that, but my father doesn't care what I want. He thinks he knows what's best for me, and Jordan agrees with him."

"I hope you'll be very happy."

"Morgan, you know I don't want to marry him." She fought the urge to reach out to him, knowing that if he pulled away it would break her heart. "I want to marry *you*," she said quietly. "I *did* marry you, remember?"

He dragged his hand over his jaw, wondering why he had come to meet her. Nothing had changed. Hell, she was engaged to another man. A rich man with a pedigree that probably could be traced back to the *Mayflower*. The date had been set, and everyone in town was talking about the fancy wedding scheduled for the first of August. Coming here had been a mistake. He'd known it, but he hadn't been able to stay away.

"Remember?" she asked again, her voice soft and wistful. "You were Rides a Dark Horse, and I was your woman."

"I remember. And I remember I told you it wasn't a real marriage, that it was only good while we were with the Lakota."

"Then let's go back," she said, her voice softly pleading. "Please, Morgan. I don't care where we go so long as we're together."

It was tempting, so damn tempting, but nothing had changed. She was still a nice girl with her whole life ahead of her, too young to fully realize what she'd be getting into, and he was still a half-breed, almost broke, with no prospects in sight. What could he offer her? Life in a buffalo-hide lodge? A baby every year, and nothing but hard work and poverty? She'd age five years in one and end up hating him.

The moon broke through the clouds, shining down upon the yard with a ghostly white light, providing enough illumination for Carolyn to see Morgan's face.

Gazing into his deep gray eyes, she saw that he had closed his heart to her, that he believed she deserved a better life than the one he could give her.

She saw something else lurking in the depths of his eyes: sadness, she thought, or maybe regret, she could not be sure, and then it was gone.

"I'm sorry, Carrie," he said gruffly. "I . . . dammit, I'm sorry. Good night."

She longed to run after him, to throw herself at his feet and beg him to take her away, to tell him he was the most wonderful man she'd ever known, but she knew it wouldn't do any good. He'd never believe her, and she quietly cursed the mother who had raised him to believe he was no good even as she cursed every woman who had ever looked down on him because he was a half-breed, every man who had made him feel inferior because of his Navajo heritage.

Through eyes clouded with tears, she watched him walk away, her heart aching for what might have been. She'd never forget him, never.

She stared after him, her eyes committing to memory the way the hazy moonlight streaked his hair with silver, the graceful way he moved, his naturally long stride carrying him away from her until his dark silhouette was swallowed up in the shadows and he was gone from her sight.

Chapter 23

The next eight weeks were the longest and worst of Carolyn's life. People came and went constantly. All conversation in the house was centered around the wedding. Flowers were ordered. Diana spent hours with the cook, deciding on the menu, the cake, the wedding supper. The housekeeper and the maid worked overtime, cleaning and polishing until every wood surface gleamed, every mirror was spotless, and every piece of crystal sparkled like new.

Carolyn's wedding dress arrived, and when she tried it on, the skirt was three inches too long. Diana offered to shorten it and Carolyn agreed, not caring if the gown was too long or too short, not caring about anything. Over and over again, she replayed the scene outside the shed, wondering what she could have said to make Morgan change his mind, refusing to believe he didn't care. He *had* to care.

She went to town with Diana once a week, and

each time she saw Morgan standing outside the Dry Gulch Saloon, leaning negligently against the porch rail. He never smiled at her, never acknowledged that he knew her, but he was always there when she arrived, though he never followed her into Dixon's General Store again. She always browsed the shelves near the front window while waiting for Diana, her gaze forever drawn toward Morgan, her heart aching for him.

He stayed on the boardwalk until she left the store, and then he retreated into the saloon, effectively assuring that she could not follow him.

Two weeks before the wedding, Mr. Brockton took Carolyn aside and insisted on a private dinner, just the two of them. They dined in the formal dining room, sitting across from each other at the heavy oak table. The candlelight cast dancing shadows on the papered walls, reminding Carolyn of campfires beneath a starlit sky.

She ate what was placed before her, answered Mr. Brockton when an answer was required, and thought how awful it was going to be to spend the rest of her life with a man she didn't love.

Roger Brockton leaned forward, his elbows on the table, his chin resting on his clasped hands, as he studied the young woman sitting across from him. She was lovely, far more lovely than when he'd seen her last. She'd been a girl then; she was a woman now. He wondered idly what had wrought the change in her, then shrugged. He didn't really care. He wanted Carolyn Chandler for his wife, he had waited five years to have her, and in another week she would be his. The fact that she didn't want to marry him was of no consequence. He wanted her, and he always got what he wanted, one way or another. The fact that he'd had to lend Archibald Chandler a great deal of money in order to obtain his permission for the marriage was unimportant. Roger had plenty of money, more than he could spend in a lifetime.

He smiled fondly at his fiancée. "Where would you like to go for our honeymoon, Caro? Paris? London? New York, perhaps? You have but to name it, my dear."

"Anywhere you want to go is fine, Mr. Brockton."

"Don't you think you should call me Roger?" he chided softly. "After all, I shall be your husband in a matter of days."

"Wherever you like. Roger."

"That's better. I think you'd like Paris. It's a delightful city."

"Paris, then," Carolyn agreed without enthusiasm. Placing her napkin on the table, she stood up. "I'm tired. I think I'll go to bed now. Good night."

Roger Brockton stood up and moved quickly to Carolyn's side. He placed a possessive hand on her arm and pulled her toward him. "I think you might give me a good night kiss."

Carolyn stared down at him, unconsciously comparing him to Morgan. Roger Brockton was short and rotund, where Morgan was tall and lean. Roger repelled her, while Morgan had only to look at her to make her heart pound with excitement. But Roger would be her husband. How would she abide having him in her bed when the mere thought of a kiss turned her stomach?

"One kiss, Caro," Roger insisted, and drawing her head down, he covered her mouth with his. His lips were warm and moist, and his breath smelled of too much wine and tobacco. She felt his hand slide down her hip and wrenched out of his embrace, her cheeks scarlet.

"We are not married yet, Mr. Brockton," she said coldly. "Please remember that." Turning on her heel, she fled the dining room.

Running up the stairs to her room, she threw herself on the bed and scrubbed her mouth with a corner of the spread. She could not marry the man. Her father could not force her to say yes. Let them make all the plans they wanted, let her father and Mr. Brockton invite everyone in town, let them decorate the house and prepare tons of food and buy gallons of champagne. She would never say yes!

A week before the wedding, Carolyn decided to run away. She had done it before, and she would do it again. She made her plans carefully, packed a small valise, checked the departure days and times of the stagecoach. Each night when she went to bed, she vowed it would be the last night she would spend under Jordan's roof, but in the morning her determination was gone, swallowed up in the awful nausea that plagued her and by an overwhelming weariness that seemed to drain her of all energy.

It was stress, she thought, refusing to acknowledge the niggling fear that she might be pregnant.

She counted back, trying to remember the last time she'd had the curse and realized it had been over eight weeks. She knew very little about childbirth and conception, but she did know that women who were pregnant were spared the monthly curse.

But she couldn't be pregnant. It was impossible ... She felt her cheeks grow hot as she realized it was not impossible, not impossible at all considering the many times Morgan had made love to her.

Filled with panic, she went to Diana, shyly explaining that her mother had passed away before she could tell her what a bride might expect on her wedding night. Her cheeks burned with embarrassment as she asked numerous questions about the intimate relations between a man and a woman, gradually working her way to the real purpose of the conversation: how did a woman know when she was pregnant?

With growing alarm, Carolyn listened as Diana explained the symptoms: nausea in the morning, increased sleepiness, tenderness in her breasts, swelling in her ankles.

To her dismay, Carolyn realized she was experiencing all the symptoms. Dear Lord, she was going to have a baby, and Morgan was the father.

She would *have* to marry Roger Brockton now, she thought, her panic rising. Morgan didn't want her, but Mr. Brockton did. Perhaps she could pass the baby off as his. She thought of Roger, with his light brown hair and eyes, and prayed that her child would not have hair like black silk and copper-hued skin.

The next few days passed in a haze of fear and panic as she tried to hide her nausea from the family. She skipped breakfast, blaming her lack of appetite on pre-wedding jitters. She slept late and went to bed early, saying she needed lots of sleep so she'd be well rested for the big day.

The night before the wedding, she prayed that her dress would still fit, that she would not disgrace herself by being violently ill as she walked down the aisle, and that no one would ever find out that Roger Brockton was not the father of the child that would be born ten weeks too early.

August first bloomed bright and clear and warm. Morgan stood across the street from the whitewashed Methodist Church, his hands shoved in his pants pockets, his expression grim. Today was Carrie's wedding day.

He glanced at the sun, checking the time. Ten o'clock. In another hour, she'd be married to Roger Brockton. Just sixty minutes, and she'd be lost to him forever.

He started down the street toward the saloon, his palms damp as he contemplated a drink, then he turned on his heel and returned to his place on the corner. Whiskey wasn't the answer. It had never been the answer to anything.

People began arriving at the church about ten-thirty, people Morgan recognized as the elite of Ogallala: the marshal, looking uncomfortable in a dark brown suit and cravat; the newspaper editor, looking spry despite his sixty-odd years; the doctor and his family, looking healthy and prosperous; a number of the town's businessmen and their wives.

A few minutes later, he saw Carolyn's sister-in-law arrive with two men. He guessed the younger one was Carrie's brother, Jordan. But it was the older man who held his attention.

Roger Brockton was short and squat, with graying brown hair and light brown eyes. He was impeccably dressed in a black frock coat, crisp white shirt, and fashionable cravat complete with a diamond stickpin. Strutting like a game cock, he disappeared into the church.

Morgan frowned thoughtfully. Despite the expensive cut of his clothes and his citified manners, there was something about Roger Brockton that reminded Morgan of a wolf dressed up like a lamb. The thought of Carolyn sharing the man's bed made him sick to his stomach.

And then he saw Carolyn. She was riding in the back of an open carriage, her father beside her. Archibald Chandler was an imposing individual, with a mane of snow white hair and dark blue eyes. He sat tall and straight, like a general reviewing his troops.

Carolyn was a vision in white silk and lace, her hair covered with a gossamer veil, her face almost as pale as her gown.

Her father assisted her from the carriage, and for a moment father and daughter stood on the sidewalk facing each other, then Archibald Chandler took Carolyn firmly by the arm and escorted her into the chapel.

As if drawn by an invisible hand, Morgan

crossed the dusty street and stood just inside the door of the church. He could see Carolyn and her father standing a few feet ahead, and beyond them, waiting at the altar, stood Roger Brockton, Diana and Jordan, and the minister.

Morgan grimaced. The Chandler family had outdone themselves. The church was decorated with flowers, obviously imported, though from where he couldn't imagine. A long white runner covered the center aisle of the church, several pots of pale pink flowers decorated the altar. A shaft of morning sunlight streamed through the stained-glass window behind the altar.

Morgan clenched his hands into tight fists as the familiar strains of the Wedding March filled the air and Carolyn started down the aisle on her father's arm.

Carolyn looked up at her father as they walked slowly down the aisle. She'd thought herself resigned to this marriage. She'd told herself it was for the best, that it was the only way to avoid a scandal. But she couldn't go through with it.

"Please, Father," she whispered urgently. "Don't make me do this."

"We've been through all this a hundred times, Carolyn," Archibald Chandler said sternly.

"Please, I'll do anything else you ask of me, but please don't make me marry Mr. Brockton. Please."

"Be still," Archibald Chandler admonished as they reached the altar. "And for goodness sakes, smile!"

Morgan entered the chapel and took a seat in

the back row. In his mind's eye, he saw Carolyn
standing in his shack back in Galveston, scrubbing
the cast-iron stove, her hands covered with grime.
If she married Brockton, she'd never have to scrub
a stove again. Or wear pants. Or ride a horse.

"Who giveth this woman to be married to this
man?" the minister asked.

"I do," Archibald Chandler replied in a loud
voice. Placing Carolyn's hand firmly in Brockton's,
he took a step back and sat down in the front pew.

"If there be anyone here who knows why this
man and this woman should not be united in holy
matrimony, let him speak now or forever hold his
peace."

The minister looked over the congregation,
smiled, and opened his Bible. "Dearly beloved, we
are gathered here this day—"

"Wait!"

All heads turned toward the back of the church
as a tall, dark-haired man clad in black pants and
a blue shirt made his way down the aisle.

Roger Brockton's face turned an angry red as
Morgan reached the altar.

Jordan Chandler looked surprised; his wife
looked as though she might faint.

But Carolyn's face was radiant, her green eyes
glowing softly.

The minister cleared his throat. "Uh, young
man—"

"Hold on a minute, preacher," Morgan said. He
looked at Carrie, his dark eyes speaking volumes.
"Is this what you want?"

Carrie shook her head vigorously. "No."

"See here," Archibald Chandler said, rising to his feet. "What do you think you're doing?"

"Something I should have done a long time ago," Morgan replied, his gaze still on Carolyn's face.

"Jordan, do something," Archibald Chandler demanded angrily. He took a step forward, one arm outstretched.

"Keep out of this, old man," Morgan admonished curtly, and then, unable to believe what he was doing, Morgan grabbed Carolyn by the arm with one hand and drew his Colt with the other. "Back off, both of you." He slid a warning glance at the two Chandler men, then slipped his arm around Carrie's waist and hugged her to his side. "You make a beautiful bride, Carrie. Will you marry me?"

"Name the day."

"How about now?"

She felt like laughing, crying, shouting. Instead, she nodded solemnly.

"You heard the lady," Morgan said to the astonished minister. "We're getting married. Get on with it."

The minister glanced apologetically at Archibald Chandler, cleared his throat and croaked, "Dearly beloved—"

"Just skip on down to the end," Morgan said.

"Yes, sir," the minister replied, his gaze fastened on the gun in Morgan's hand. "Carolyn Chandler, do you take this man to be your lawfully wedded husband?"

"I do."

"Carolyn, you can't mean to do this!" her father protested.

"I told you to keep out of this, old man," Morgan warned. "Get on with it, preacher."

The minister ran a nervous finger around the inside of his clerical collar. "This is most unusual."

"It is that." Morgan agreed. "Now get on with it."

"Yes, sir. I . . . uh, I need your name."

"Morgan."

"Your full name."

"Slade. Morgan Slade."

Roger Brockton frowned.

Jordan Chandler looked stunned.

Carolyn looked at Morgan, wondering why his surname had affected Jordan so strangely.

"Morgan Slade, do you take this woman to be your lawfully wedded wife?"

"I do."

"Then by the power vested in me, I now pronounce you man and wife. You may, ah, kiss the bride."

Lifting Carolyn's veil, Morgan kissed her quickly on the cheek, not daring to take his eyes off her father, who was glowering at him. Surprisingly, Roger Brockton hadn't said a word the whole time.

"Let's go, Carrie," Morgan said. Taking her hand, they backed down the aisle and out into the street.

"What now?" she asked, laughter bubbling in her throat.

"I guess we'd better get out of town, pronto!"

"I'm ready."

"Good." He lifted her into the carriage, jumped onto the seat beside her, and took up the reins as Jordan Chandler ran out of the church, followed by Carolyn's father and Roger Brockton.

With a grin, Carolyn tossed her bouquet over her shoulder, then clutched her husband by the arm as the carriage lurched forward.

Unbelievable as it seemed, she was Mrs. Morgan Slade.

Chapter 24

Archibald Chandler waited until the wedding guests were gone before he turned on his son, his face red with anger. "What the hell was that all about?" he demanded. "And why didn't you do something to stop her?"

Jordan Chandler glared back at his father. "What did you expect me to do? The man had a gun."

Father and son glared at each other for a long moment, and then Jordan frowned. "Slade," he murmured. "You don't suppose he's related to Harrison Slade over in Cheyenne?"

"What difference does that make? He's taken Carolyn."

Jordan shrugged. "Slade's a powerful man in these parts. Owns the biggest cattle ranch in Wyoming." He glanced at Roger Brockton. "Got more money than just about anybody I know."

Archibald Chandler sighed impatiently. "So what?"

"So maybe Morgan Slade's related to Harrison. So maybe my little sister made herself quite a catch."

"Don't be silly," Roger Brockton admonished. "I don't know much about the Slade family, but this guy didn't look as if he had two bits to call his own."

Archibald Chandler frowned thoughtfully. Slade, Slade. Of course, he remembered now. "They never had any children, did they?"

"They had a daughter," Jordan remarked. "She caused a scandal of some kind, oh, maybe thirty years ago when they lived in New Mexico. She ran away. I don't think they ever heard from her again."

Roger Brockton made an impatient gesture. "So what?"

"So maybe this Morgan is the missing heir," Archibald Chandler mused aloud.

"What the hell difference does that make?" Brockton muttered crossly. "Carolyn's been kidnapped. Don't you think we should be going after her?"

"She hasn't exactly been kidnapped," Diana said dryly. "She's his wife now. And she seemed awfully glad to see him."

Brockton glared at Diana, then turned to Archie once more. "Are you just going to stand there, or are we going after her?"

"She's married, Roger," Jordan said. "Face it, she never wanted to marry you in the first place."

"Keep out of his, Jordan. This is between your father and me."

"I'd say it was between Carrie and Slade."

"You'd be wrong," Roger Brockton said tersely. "I gave your father ten thousand dollars to clear up a little mess at the bank on the condition that Carolyn would be mine."

"Ten thousand dollars," Jordan exclaimed, his gaze darting from Brockton's face to his father's. "For what?

"Nothing to worry yourself about," Archibald Chandler said quickly. "A little matter of a bad investment, that's all. I needed some cash right away and Roger loaned it to me, that's all."

"Why didn't you come to me?"

"There was no time," Archibald muttered, not meeting his son's eyes. "Anyway, I didn't want to worry you."

"You were using funds from the bank to further your own ambitions, weren't you?" Jordan accused. "I warned you about that."

"But it was a sure thing."

"Time's awasting, Archie," Roger Brockton said curtly. "I think we should go along to the marshal's office and inform him that Carolyn was kidnapped at gunpoint. I'll put up a five-thousand-dollar reward for her return, and another five for the man's capture."

"Forget it, Brockton," Jordan said. "My father may have been willing to sell his daughter, but I'm not willing to see my sister married to a weasel like you. If you come by the bank tomorrow, I'll settle my father's debt."

"Jordan—"

"Stay out of this, Father. You've made a mess of things all along."

Roger Brockton's face was the color of an overripe tomato. He glared at Archie Chandler and then, summoning as much dignity as possible, nodded at Jordan. "I'll be at the bank first thing in the morning. I'll want cash."

"You'll have it."

Brockton nodded. He still had every intention of putting up that reward poster. After all, Morgan Slade had stolen his horse and his carriage, and horse stealing was still a crime in these parts. And he'd use Jordan Chandler's money for the reward. The thought put a smile on his face.

Without another word, Brockton turned on his heel and left the church. He'd have his revenge and it would be sweet. Damn the girl! Marry another man, would she? Well, he thought, let's see how happy she'll be married to a jailbird!

Archibald Chandler stared after Brockton for a moment, then turned to face his son. "I'm sorry. I should have come to you."

Jordan nodded. "It doesn't matter now."

"I'll pay you back, I swear. Every cent."

"Don't worry about it."

Archibald Chandler nodded. He'd shamed himself forever in his son's eyes, and made his daughter hate him. His steps were slow and heavy as he walked out of the church.

"Go to him, Jordan," Diana urged. "He needs you."

Jordan shook his head. "Maybe later. Right now all I want to do is punch him in the nose. I can't believe he was willing to sell Carolyn to Roger just to hush things up at the bank. I knew Carrie didn't want to marry Roger, but I thought she was just being stubborn. I never thought Brockton was a bad sort, until now. He always seemed respectable and he certainly was well off.''

"Jordan, you sound just like your father!''

"I know, I know. Well, Father wanted her to have a rich husband. Maybe she got one after all. It's kind of funny, when you think of it.''

"Men! Did it ever occur to you that love is more important than money.''

"Now and then," Jordan said. He bent down to kiss his wife's cheek. "Where do you suppose Carrie met a man like Slade?''

"I can't imagine. He looks like a desperado.'' Diana frowned. "I have the feeling that I've seen him somewhere before.''

"Where?''

"I can't remember. But it's clear that Carolyn knew him very well.''

"Yeah.''

"When she told me she didn't want to marry Roger, I asked her if there was someone else, and she said no.''

"Apparently she was lying,'' Jordan muttered.

"Apparently.''

Jordan Chandler let out a long sigh. He'd pay off his father's debt, Roger would go back to Galveston, and eventually Carrie would forgive Archie for what he'd tried to do. For now, there was nothing he could do for his father or his sister but wait and see which one gave in first.

Lifting a lock of his wife's hair, Jordan kissed her neck. "Did I mention that you look awfully pretty today?"

"No," Diana said, concern for Carolyn retreating as Jordan's kiss warmed her skin and sent shivers down her spine. "Did I mention that we're going to have a baby?"

"A baby!" Jordan drew back, his face reflecting his astonishment. "After all this time?"

Diana nodded, her face radiant with joy. "I didn't want to say anything until I was certain."

"Diana, honey, that's wonderful news!" Picking her up in his arms, Jordan swung her around and around until she begged him to stop.

"I'm glad Carolyn married Slade," she mused. "She was smiling when she left, Jordy. It's the first time I've seen her smile since she got here."

Diana stared up at her husband, her eyes wide. "Now I know where I've seen Morgan Slade before!" she exclaimed. "He came into Dixon's one day while we were shopping. I saw him talking to Carolyn. She said he was just asking for directions."

"Well, it was obvious they weren't strangers."

"But where could she have met him?"

Jordan shook his head. "I don't know, but that girl's got a lot of explaining to do the next time I see her."

Chapter 25

Carolyn couldn't stop smiling. She gazed at her husband, admiring his profile, the cut of his jaw, the deep bronze of his skin. She was his now, truly his. She could hardly wait to tell him that he was going to be a father, but she wanted to wait until night when she was curled in his arms.

They drove until dusk, then stopped along the North Platte to spend the night.

Morgan grinned as he helped Carolyn from the carriage. "You're not exactly dressed for sleeping out, but you've never looked more beautiful."

She blushed prettily as he took her in his arms. It was wonderful to be with him again, to see his dark eyes shining with love. She lifted her face for his kiss, her heart beating with anticipation. Mrs. Morgan Slade.

"You're not sorry?" Morgan asked, drawing away a little so he could see her face.

"No."

"You'd probably have been better off with

Brockton, you know. I'm flat broke."

"I don't care. It's you I love."

"Carrie!" He swept her into his arms again, crushing her close as he removed her veil, then buried his face in her hair.

"Tell me," she murmured.

"What?"

"That you love me."

"I love you, Carrie," he said solemnly. "I've always loved you. I just want you to be happy."

"I am happy." She giggled as her stomach growled loudly. "And hungry. I haven't had breakfast and . . . oh!"

She turned away, fighting the urge to vomit, but to no avail. Doubling over, she began to retch.

"Carrie, what is it?" He rushed to her side and placed a supportive arm around her waist. "Carrie?"

"I'm all right."

"Like hell!" He handed her his kerchief. "What's wrong? Are you sick?"

"Not exactly." She wiped her mouth and eyes, then wadded his soiled kerchief into a ball. "I'm . . ."

"You're what?"

"I'm going to have a baby."

He stared at her as if he'd been kicked in the groin. "A baby? Whose? When?"

"Yours. In about six and a half months."

"Mine. How?"

"The usual way." Carrie gazed up at him, one arm curled protectively over her stomach. "Don't you want it?"

A baby. He had no job and no money, and she was having a baby. "Carrie, hey, don't cry." He pulled her into his arms and held her tight. "Of course I want it. It just takes some getting used to, that's all."

He led her to the carriage, pulled a blanket from under the seat, and spread it on a flat stretch of ground. "Here, sit down and rest awhile. I'll see if I can't catch us some dinner."

Carolyn watched as Morgan cut a slender branch from a nearby tree, sharpened one end, then waded into the river. In less than an hour, he had speared three fat fish and had them cooking over a bed of glowing coals.

Carolyn ate ravenously, not thinking about the future, not thinking about anything except Morgan and the night to come. Her wedding night.

Morgan winked at her as he gathered up the bones. "I'll go bury these," he said, "and then see to the horse. I won't be gone long."

Carolyn nodded. Sitting there in the quiet of the night, she thought about her father, grinning as she recalled the surprised look on his face when Morgan had charged down the aisle. He'd have to find someone else to marry Roger Brockton. Placing a hand over her stomach, she thought about her baby, and their future. She'd always taken money for granted, always had everything she ever wanted or needed. And she wanted that same kind of security for her child. She thought about Morgan. He didn't have any money. He didn't even have a job, unless he went back to work at the Grotto.

She grimaced as she imagined living in that awful shack in Galveston, raising her baby in a back alley, never having enough money to buy nice clothes and pretty things. She had a little money of her own, of course, but it wouldn't last long, and when it was gone, then what?

She heard footsteps and all her worries faded into the distance as she saw Morgan coming toward her. He knelt beside her, his hands cupping her face as he kissed her. Then he was turning her around, unfastening her gown, removing her satin slippers, her petticoats, her chemise and stockings.

He eased her down on the blanket and placed one hand over her stomach, a bemused expression in his eyes. Then he stripped off his own clothing and stretched out beside her.

"A baby," he murmured, nuzzling the slender curve of her neck. "I still can't believe it."

"You'll believe it soon enough, when I'm fat as a cow."

"You won't be fat," he corrected softly. "You'll be pregnant."

He kissed her then, his hands sliding over her back and thighs, cupping her breasts. He left little fires everywhere he touched, until she was smoldering with desire. She had never felt more beautiful than she did that night as Morgan slowly made love to her, his hands worshiping her, his eyes telling her more eloquently than words that he loved her.

Carolyn returned his caresses with all her heart, murmuring his name over and over as she stroked his hard-muscled flesh, delighting in the way they fit together, perfectly, completely. His skin was dark where hers was light, his hard where hers was soft, and yet she knew he had been made for her and no one else. He was Rides a Dark Horse, and she was his woman, content to be so for now and for always.

Later, lying sated in his arms, she gazed up at the stars and knew she'd never been happier in her life.

"So," she said, "where are we going to live?"

"I don't know. You got anyplace special in mind?"

"No. Do you want to go back to Texas?"

"Not really. But at least there's a job waiting for me there."

"And Red."

"Yeah, Red." Morgan dragged a hand over his jaw. He'd forgotten all about Red.

"Maybe we could live with my father," Carolyn suggested hesitantly. "He has a big house, and once he accepts the fact that we're married, he'll have no reason to object."

Morgan snorted softly. "Somehow, I don't think he's ever going to forgive me for bursting into the church and marrying you at gunpoint."

"Maybe not," Carolyn agreed. "But he is my father. I'm sure he won't turn us away if we ask for his help. Especially when he learns about the baby."

"I'm not asking for his help, Carrie, not now, not

ever, so put that thought out of your mind. I'll think of something." He paused for a moment, then asked, "How would you feel about going back to the Lakota?"

"Is that what you want?"

"I don't know. I'm asking what you want?"

"I'd rather not. I want to be near a doctor when the baby comes."

Morgan nodded. "We'll go back to Texas, then. I'll go back to work for Danny. He pays good, and now that I'm off the booze, we should be able to save some dough. Maybe we can buy a little place in town."

"Oh, I'd like that," Carolyn exclaimed. "A place of our own. Oh, Morgan, I'll make you happy, you'll see."

"You already make me happy, Carrie. I just hope I don't let you down."

"You won't."

He nodded, but inwardly he wasn't so sure. A wife, a baby...it was more responsibility than he'd ever dreamed of, certainly more than he was used to.

"Why did Jordan look so surprised when you said your name was Slade?"

"Harrison Slade is my grandfather."

"Is he famous or something?"

"He's rich."

"He is?"

Morgan grinned faintly. "Yeah. He had a big ranch down in New Mexico. He sold it nine or ten years ago and moved to Wyoming. I hear he's got a big spread about thirty miles outside of Cheyenne. Raises beef for the Army."

"Why did he move to Wyoming?"

"How the hell should I know? I've never met the man." The old bitterness welled up inside him as he thought of his mother dying in a brothel. But for Harrison Slade, she could have lived in luxury and comfort.

"But he's your grandfather."

"He treated my mother like dirt when she needed him the most," Morgan replied flatly. "I wouldn't pour water on him if he was on fire."

Morgan lay awake long after Carolyn was asleep, wondering if he'd done the right thing in marrying her, wondering if he had it in him to be a husband, a father. Carrie had so much faith in him, maybe it was time he had a little faith in himself.

They stopped in the first town they came to for supplies. People stood on the street and stared at them as they passed by: a young woman in a rumpled wedding dress and a tall half-breed clad in whipcord britches, a blue cotton shirt, and hard-soled moccasins.

Carolyn sent a wire to the bank in Galveston, only to discover that her father had closed the account the day after she ran away.

"Forget it," Morgan said.

"I will not! It was my money, left to me by my mother. How could he take it?"

"Maybe he was hoping you'd run back home

when you found out you didn't have any money to fall back on."

"Maybe." Carrie stared down at her wedding dress speculatively, then pursed her lips and headed for the mercantile store. "Come on, I've got an idea."

Morgan remained in the background while Carolyn haggled with the proprietor. In the end, she sold her wedding gown for enough to buy herself a gingham dress, a pair of pants and a shirt, boots, and a flat-brimmed hat. She also purchased a warm jacket for each of them, as well as provisions for the trail, and still managed to have money left over. Following her lead, Morgan went to the livery barn and traded the horse and carriage for two saddlehorses complete with saddles and bedrolls.

It was a nice little town, and after taking care of their business, they went to the restaurant and ordered a big breakfast. Lingering over a second cup of coffee, they talked about names for the baby until Carolyn suggested she should get a job.

"A job!" Morgan exclaimed with a grin. "Doing what?"

"I can make moccasins and tan a hide with the best of them," Carolyn retorted, grinning back at him. "And I do needlepoint very nicely."

He burst out laughing as he recalled the first time she had said that. She'd been a spoiled brat then, incapable of looking after herself, but she'd grown up a lot since then.

"My wife isn't going to work," he said sternly.

"She's going to stay home and have a dozen kids."

"I'll do my best," Carolyn promised.

Morgan spotted the Wanted poster when they stepped out of the restaurant. "Damn," he muttered. "I should have known."

Carrie frowned as she recognized the pen-and-ink sketch on the poster.

MORGAN SLADE
BLACK HAIR, GRAY EYES, OVER 6' TALL
MID-TO-LATE 20's, NO VISIBLE SCARS
WANTED FOR KIDNAPPING AND
HORSE STEALING
LAST SEEN IN OGALLALA,
NEBRASKA TERRITORY
$10,000.00 REWARD FOR HIS CAPTURE
CONTACT ROGER L. BROCKTON,
GALVESTON, TEXAS

"Kidnapping!" Carolyn exclaimed. "I wasn't kidnapped!"

"I doubt if anyone will care when they see the size of that reward," Morgan remarked dryly. "And horse stealing is a serious offense in this part of the country."

"What does he hope to gain by having you arrested for horse stealing?" Carrie wondered. "It doesn't make sense."

"Maybe he figures if he can't have you, neither will I."

Carrie's expression grew solemn as she realized what Morgan was saying. Then another thought occurred to her. "We can't go back to Galveston now, can we? What are we going to do?"

"Get the hell out of town before somebody recognizes me," Morgan said.

He lifted Carrie onto the back of her horse, a rangy piebald gelding, then swung into the saddle of his own mount. "Come on, let's get out of here."

Chapter 26

Archibald Chandler drummed his fingers on the dining room table. "Well, what are we going to do?"

Jordan shrugged, his expression grim as he studied the Wanted poster. "I don't know what you can do. Morgan took Roger's horse, sure enough. I suppose we could send out flyers stating Carrie wasn't kidnapped, but I doubt if that would do much good. That ten-thousand-dollar reward is gonna draw more attention than a whore at a prayer meeting."

"Damned spiteful man," Archibald muttered.

"What about Carolyn?" Diana said, taking a seat at the table. "What will happen to her if someone captures Morgan?"

Archibald Chandler shook his head. "I don't know. Maybe we could offer an alternate reward for information leading to their whereabouts."

"We'd have to match Brockton's offer," Jordan remarked, "and I don't know how we'd do that.

I'm out of cash just now."

A red flush crept up the back of Archibald Chandler's neck. They all knew why Jordan was out of funds.

"Maybe we're worrying for nothing," Diana suggested hopefully. "Surely Morgan's seen that poster, too. I'm certain he's smart enough to lay low until Brockton cools off and rescinds his offer."

"I hope so," Archibald said quietly. He stared at his hands, the burden of what he'd done weighing heavily on his shoulders. Promising Carolyn to Roger Brockton had seemed like such an easy solution to his dilemma. Carolyn would get a husband who had money, power, and position in the community, and he'd be spared the embarrassment of being caught with his hand in the vault. It had all seemed so easy at the time, but now all that had changed. Carolyn had run off with a man they knew nothing about, and there was a king's ransom posted for her husband's capture.

Archibald Chandler shook his head, his expression bleak as he remembered the gun in Morgan's hand. Slade was sure to resist being taken in. There could be violence, gun play, and Carolyn would likely be there, caught in the middle. If anything happened to her, it would be all his fault.

"I hope she comes home," he murmured. "Please, God, just let her come home."

Chapter 27

They rode steadily for the next four days. Morgan changed directions, heading west instead of south, hoping to throw Brockton off the trail. They couldn't return to Texas, not now. He was too well known there. Then, too, Kiley might still be hanging around. Morgan frowned at the thought of the man who'd stabbed him outside the Grotto. He'd forgotten about Lou Kiley until now.

They reached Sidney the fifth day, and Morgan knew they'd gone as far as they were going to go, at least for a while. The constant riding wasn't doing Carolyn any good. She continued to be sick in the morning, unable to keep anything in her stomach. Once, she'd fallen asleep in the saddle and he'd caught her just before she fell.

Carolyn insisted they go on, but Morgan was adamant. They were stopping.

Sidney was a hell of a town, Morgan thought as they rode down the main street. It seemed to consist of little more than gambling houses, saloons, and dance halls. Just riding down the street, he counted twenty-three saloons. The town was filled with prospectors headed for the Black Hills, hoping to strike it rich in spite of the fact that the Hills belonged to the Sioux.

Morgan drew rein at the first hotel he came to. He didn't miss Carrie's look of relief as he lifted her from her horse. She hadn't complained about the long hours on the trail. She'd cooked their meals, beaming when he remarked that her biscuits were much improved, but her outward cheerfulness hadn't fooled him a bit. She was nauseous in the morning, and sometimes in the evening, and it seemed to him that everything she ate came back up again. She needed rest, and he intended to see she got it.

He settled Carolyn in a room at the hotel, left their horses at the livery, and went to the nearest saloon to see if he could find a job. As luck would have it, they needed a faro dealer, and when Morgan left the saloon twenty minutes later, the job was his.

Carolyn was less than enthusiastic about Morgan working nights in a saloon, but he assured her it was only temporary, and that as soon as she was feeling better, they'd move on, perhaps to California. Wouldn't she like to see the ocean?

Carolyn agreed because she was too tired to argue. It seemed she was tired all the time, and when she wasn't sleeping, she was throwing up. Diana had told her that being sick in the morning and being tired all the time would likely pass after the first few months. Until then, it was best just to rest while her body adjusted to its new burden.

Their life quickly settled into a routine. Because the saloons never closed, Morgan was able to work days, much to Carolyn's relief. It wasn't so bad, spending her days alone. She wasn't sure she could have stood being alone at night in a strange town. Shootings were daily events, and gunfire was as common as the sound of bawling cattle.

Morgan came home one evening after work and told her there'd been a fight in one of the dance halls that turned into a shooting and a man was killed. Rather than stop the dance, the corpse had been propped up in a corner and the dancing continued. Later, another man was killed, and his body had been placed next to that of the first. It wasn't until a third body joined the first two that someone decided the party was getting too rowdy and everyone went home.

Lynchings were also frequent. She'd once heard her father remark that the Union Pacific railroad warned its passengers not to leave the train during any stopovers in Sidney if they wanted to leave town alive. She'd thought he was exaggerating at the time; now she knew better.

But, in spite of shootings and lynchings, Carrie was happier than she'd ever been. She bought material and began sewing a new dress to accommodate her expanding girth, as well as tiny baby gowns and blankets for the child she carried beneath her heart. She had newspapers to read, and plenty of time to sleep. And best of all, Morgan came home to her each evening, his dark eyes shining with love as he took her in his arms.

With his first paycheck he took her shopping, and she bought a day dress of blue muslin, a straw hat, pins for her hair, and a bar of sweet-smelling soap. Morgan bought a black silk shirt, black trousers, a brocade vest, a new hat, and a pair of boots. Clad in his new clothes, he looked every inch the gambler. He also bought a deadly-looking derringer, and insisted she learn how to shoot it.

At first, Carolyn refused to even touch it, but Morgan explained he'd feel better about leaving her alone knowing she had it, just in case. And once Carrie learned to handle the derringer, she felt better, too.

She never ventured out of the hotel room alone, content to sit by the open window and watch the people come and go. She'd never seen such an assortment of humanity, from bewhiskered prospectors to women whose heavily painted faces and scantily clad bodies clearly proclaimed them to be saloon girls. She saw men staggering down the street, dead drunk, in the broad light of day, and a flame-haired tart strolling down the road clad in little more than black net stockings and a corset.

She was sitting by the window three weeks later, wondering why Morgan was so late getting home, when she heard the now-familiar sound of gunfire. Leaning out the window, she glanced down the street and saw two men dragging a third out of the saloon where Morgan worked.

As they turned the corner into the alley behind the saloon, Carolyn gasped aloud. The third man was Morgan! A riot of emotions whirled through her mind: He'd been killed, he was being arrested, he'd been caught cheating at cards and his captors were going to take him into the alley and beat him up. He was in danger.

Impulsively, she grabbed her derringer, checked to make sure it was loaded, then ran out of the hotel, down the stairs, and out into the street.

"Hey, girlie, what's your hurry?"

Carolyn squealed as a man's hand closed on her arm. "Leave me alone!" she cried.

"Hey, settle down, missy. I ain't gonna hurt ya."

She didn't answer. Instead, she kicked him in the groin, hard.

Several passersby laughed as the man grabbed his injured manhood and dropped heavily to the ground, his face the color of chalk.

Feeling a glimmer of satisfaction, Carolyn continued down the street. She stopped when she reached the alley, and cautiously peered around the corner.

She saw Morgan first. He was mounted on a big black horse. Blood was running down his left arm, and there was a bruise on his right cheek. His hands were tied behind his back. The two men who had dragged him out of the saloon were standing beside his horse, grinning as they passed a piece of paper back and forth.

"I told you it was him," she heard one of the men exclaim. "He fits the description perfectly. Ten grand!"

It was now or never, Carolyn thought, before what little courage she had deserted her altogether.

Lifting the deadly little derringer, she began

walking down the alley. The two men still had their heads together, talking excitedly about what they could do with ten thousand dollars.

They looked up when she was about a yard away. She almost laughed at the look of astonishment on their faces.

"What is this?" the man called Quint asked. "A hold-up?"

"Untie him," Carolyn said, nodding at Morgan.

"Untie him? Why?"

"Because I said so."

The second man shook his head. " 'Fraid not, lady. He's a wanted man, and we're taking him in."

" 'Fraid not," Carolyn retorted.

"She ain't gonna hit nothing with that little pop gun, Roy," Quint said smugly. "Let's take her with us."

"All right by me," Roy remarked, and the two men started toward her, grinning impudently.

Taking a deep breath, Carolyn sighted down the barrel and gently squeezed the trigger, just as Morgan had taught her. The bullet hit right where she'd intended, and Quint howled and dropped to the ground, his hands cradling his right leg. Roy came to an abrupt halt, his eyes worried.

"Untie him," Carolyn said again.

"Yes, ma'am," Roy said.

Morgan was grinning as he swung out of the saddle, then relieved the two men of their guns. Using their kerchiefs, he tied their hands behind their backs.

"Carrie, go back to the hotel and get our things.

I'll keep an eye on these two while you're gone."

"You're bleeding."

"It's nothing. Hurry along now, Carrie."

It was dusk before Morgan agreed to stop for the night. Dismounting, Carolyn insisted on tending the wound in his arm. As he'd said, it wasn't serious, just a shallow crease in his upper arm, but she washed it thoroughly before bandaging the wound.

After dinner, she asked him what had happened.

Morgan shrugged. "I was dealing poker at one of the back tables, filling in for Parker while he took a break, when those two men sat down. We played a couple of hands and then the one calling himself Quint excused himself and went to the bar.

"When he came back, they drew on me. I wasn't expecting it, and when I tried to draw, Roy took a shot at me."

"You could have been killed."

"Maybe." He drew her to his side and kissed her cheek. "Listen, Carrie, I know you want a doctor close by when the baby comes, but I think maybe we'd best hole up with the Lakota for a while. At least until things cool off. No one will look for us there."

Carrie bit down on her lip. What Morgan said made sense, but the thought of being far from a doctor when the baby came frightened her. But not half as much as the thought of Morgan being killed.

Forcing a smile, she nodded. "If you think that's best."

"I'm sorry, Carrie."

"It's all right. I'll be fine." She forced a smile. "After all, women have babies every day."

Morgan nodded. She was afraid, though she tried to hide it. "I could take you home," he said. "You'd be safe there."

"No! It's too dangerous for you. I'll be fine, honest."

"It'll be winter soon. We could spend the winter with the Lakota and then head out for California when the snow breaks. Who knows, maybe by then Brockton will have called in those damn posters."

Later, sitting side by side under the stars, they talked about the baby, wondering if it would be a boy or a girl, if it would have Morgan's black hair and Carrie's green eyes.

"I'd like to call it Morgan if it's a boy," Carrie mused, but Morgan shook his head.

"One Morgan Slade in the family's enough. Think of something else."

Carrie looked pensive. "Well, how about Zedekiah or Vladimir?"

Morgan nodded thoughtfully. "Or maybe Cuthbert, or Alphonse."

"And if it's a girl?" Carrie asked, trying to keep a straight face.

"I've always liked Brunhilde."

Carrie giggled. "Or maybe Bathsheba."

"Bathsheba," Morgan said. "Yes, Bathsheba for a girl, and Vladimir for a boy."

Carrie was laughing now. "Vladimir Alphonse Slade. Yes, it has a nice ring to it."

"A ring," Morgan muttered. "Hell, I never even

gave you a wedding ring."

"It doesn't matter," Carrie said quickly, not wanting his good mood to end.

"It matters to me."

"We're together, Morgan," Carrie said quietly. "That's all that matters to me."

But later, with Carrie sleeping peacefully beside him, Morgan gazed up at the stars and prayed that Carrie would never be sorry she'd married him.

Chapter 28

Morgan felt a sense of homecoming as they rode into the Lakota camp. White-Eagle-That-Soars-in-the-Sky made them welcome, then escorted them to the lodge they had shared before.

Morgan glanced around, surprised to find the floor newly swept and the bedrolls aired and waiting. Wood was stacked in the firepit, and the scent of sweet sage filled the lodge. Sunrise Woman smiled at Morgan and told him that Keeper-of-the-Wind had known they were on their way back to the Lakota. The old medicine man had seen their return in a vision.

New clothes awaited them, a doeskin tunic with a blue yoke and fringed sleeves for Carolyn, a clout, leggings, and sleeveless vest for Morgan.

Changing into her new clothes immediately, Carolyn was surprised at how familiar the dress seemed, how much more comfortable it was than her usual clothes, especially now when she couldn't stand to wear anything snug around her middle.

She watched Morgan change into his clout and moccasins and felt her breath catch in her throat. How handsome he was in his Indian attire. She stared at the single eagle feather tied in his long black hair, remembering that he had killed a man because of her.

Overcome with love and tenderness, she placed her hand on his arm, raised up on tiptoe, and kissed him. "I love you," she murmured.

"Carrie..." His throat was thick with words he could not speak, emotions he did not completely understand. He had lived his life alone for so long, sometimes the hold she had on his heart frightened him. If he ever lost her...

He put the thought away from him. She had healed all his old hurts, banished all his fears, and he wouldn't waste time dwelling on something that might never happen.

In a few days, it was as if Morgan and Carolyn had never gone away. Quickly and easily they slipped back into the life of the village.

When they had lived with the Lakota before, Carolyn had known it would only be temporary. But now the village was to be her home, perhaps for a few months, perhaps for years. She pestered Morgan to teach her the language. *Higna* meant husband, *mitawicu* meant my wife, *sunkawakan* was the word for horse. She tried hard to fit in, to learn and obey the laws and customs of the tribe. She went out of her way to make friends with the other women, and learned a remarkable thing: White Eagle's wife, Sunrise Woman, had gone on a war party before they were married.

When Carolyn mentioned this extraordinary fact to Morgan, he shrugged. "The whole Lakota society revolves around war, Carrie. Even though women are barred from participating in war games, they sometimes sneak out of the village after the men have gone and follow the war party. Old Mak'awin, the storyteller, once had a dream that told her she should go to battle to seek vengeance for her brother, who was killed by the Crow."

For the next few days, Carolyn studied the women in the village, trying to guess which ones had gone to war, but she couldn't imagine any of the women going to battle. They were all so happy, such good wives and mothers, it was hard to picture any of them taking a life. And yet ... Carrie pressed a hand over her belly, thinking that she would fight to the death to protect Morgan's child. Vladimir Alphonse Slade. Carrie giggled out loud, thinking their son would have to do a lot of fighting himself if they didn't come up with a better name than that.

Carolyn gained a new appreciation for her home as the days went by. The door faced the east so that each morning the lodge was blessed by the rising sun. The tipi shed wind and water; it was warm and well ventilated. The lining kept out drafts, provided insulation against the summer sun, and added color to the interior. Nights, while Carolyn sewed tiny baby things, Morgan sketched a warrior riding a dark horse on the tipi lining.

His holster hung from one of the lodge poles; their extra clothing, neatly folded in a rawhide bag, hung from another. It was her home now, the first home that was truly her own, and she took pride in it. Morgan had made a pair of willow backrests, Sunrise Woman had given them several baskets and cook pots, and other women had given her robes and utensils, much as white women gave gifts to friends who were newly married.

Morgan was pleased to see how eagerly Carolyn took to the Lakota way of life. Her youth and innocence and her willingness to learn quickly made her a favorite with the People, and he thought maybe everything would work out for the best after all. But as the days passed, he noticed a change in the mood of the warriors, and he knew it had to do with the increasing number of whites crossing the plains, and the decreasing number of buffalo. Like the Sioux, Morgan knew that if the buffalo disappeared, the Indian would soon follow.

Of course, the whites had been killing the buffalo for years, though the real slaughter began in 1870 when the American leather industry realized there was money to be made from the hides.

By 1872, the railroad lines leading into the plains were swarming with would-be hunters from the East. Hides were selling for $3.75 a piece, and the hunters went out by rail, wagon, and horseback, thrilled at the prospect of participating in a buffalo hunt and getting rich in the bargain.

In 1873, several hunting outfits operating out of Dodge City had crossed into the northern panhandle of Texas in violation of the Medicine Lodge

Treaty. They had established a trading post at Adobe Walls, which quickly had the Comanche riding the warpath again.

Morgan knew it was just a matter of time until the buffalo would be gone, and the Indians would be forced to live on the reservation and accept the white man's charity.

But he refused to dwell on that now.

They'd been in the village about a week when they were invited to Zitakala-zi's lodge. Carolyn sat beside Sunrise Woman, smiling as old Mak'awin began to tell the legend of the rainbow.

"It was long ago, on a bright summer day. All the flowers were outside. Some were playing. Some were nodding their heads in the breeze. Some were scattering their bright colors through the grass.

"The Great Spirit heard one of the older flowers say, 'We are happy now, but I wonder what will happen to us when winter comes and we must go. I wish it could be different.'

"'Yes,' said another. 'We do our share to make Mother Earth beautiful. I think we should have a happy hunting ground of our own so that we could go there when we leave the earth.'

"The Great Spirit thought about this and he decided that when winter came, the flowers wouldn't disappear completely. When he told the flowers of his plan, they were happy.

"Now, after the rain, when you look up into the sky, you can see the flowers of the past year making a colorful rainbow across the sky."

The Indian men and women clapped their hands

in delight and begged for another story.

Mak'awin nodded, pleased by their approval. "For thousands of years," she said, her voice quickly mesmerizing her listeners, "an old woman has been sitting in the moonlight decorating a large bag with porcupine quills.

"Near her, a fire burns brightly, and a kettle boils. A small black dog sits watching her. When the old woman puts her work down to stir the herbs in the kettle, or to add more wood to her fire, the little dog quickly unravels her quill work. As fast as she sews and decorates, the little dog unfastens it."

Mak'awin paused dramatically, her sunken black eyes twinkling as she gazed around the circle. "If the old woman ever completes her work, the world will come to an end, because she will put the world in her bag and carry it away."

Carolyn grinned at Morgan, charmed by the old woman's tale.

Later, walking hand in hand toward their own lodge, Carolyn was filled with a sense of happiness and peace. She had little in the way of worldly possessions; indeed, all she owned could be counted on the fingers of one hand, and yet she had never been happier. She had food to eat and a soft robe to sleep on. She had a roof of sorts over her head, and a husband who loved her.

She smiled up at Morgan, her heart swelling in her breast. He was happy, too, she could see it in his eyes, hear it in his voice. He belonged here, with her, and she belonged here, with him.

Inside their lodge, they undressed for bed, sliding naked beneath the buffalo robes to lie close in each other's arms. Morgan placed his hand over Carrie's abdomen, grinning as he imagined how she'd look in a few months with her belly sticking out, proof to all the world that she was his woman.

"You weren't sick this morning," he remarked.

"No. Maybe it's finally passed."

"I hope so." It had been hard, watching her suffer, knowing there was nothing he could do to help. *It is the way of women*, White Eagle had told him, but that hadn't made it any easier to bear.

Carolyn covered Morgan's hand with hers. "Will you be disappointed if it's a girl?" she asked.

"No."

"But you'd rather have a son."

Morgan shrugged. "I guess every man wants a son, but a daughter will be fine. Especially if she looks like you."

His words filled her with joy and she lifted his hand to her lips and kissed his palm, wishing she had words enough to express how much she loved him.

"Carrie." He took her face in his hands and kissed her gently, tenderly.

They had not made love in a long while and the spark between them quickly ignited, engulfing them in passion's flame. His hands moved in her hair, releasing it from the heavy braid until it flowed over his hands like silk.

He caressed her thighs, marveling at the warmth of her skin, then nuzzled her breasts, imagining what they would be like when they were heavy with milk to feed his son.

His fingertips slid down her arms, the arms that would cradle his child, the arms that had cradled him when he was sick and alone and afraid. She was woman and wife, mother and sister, all the women he had ever wanted, ever needed, and he vowed he would never let her go, never let her be sorry that she had chosen him for her husband, for the father of her child.

Carolyn held Morgan close, her hands rejoicing as she caressed his hard-muscled back and shoulders. Waves of tenderness crested and broke over her as his arms tightened around her, and she heard his voice whispering that he loved her.

She rained kisses on his cheek, his neck, the hollow of his shoulder, while her hands roamed over his arms and torso. A mat of fine black hair covered his chest and her fingers played there for a moment, running along his ribcage, following the narrow line of curly black hair that led down, down ...

She smiled at Morgan's quick intake of breath as her hand moved lower. He whispered her name, his voice like rough velvet, as he rose over her, the ardor in his dark gray eyes making her toes curl with anticipation.

He was her husband, the father of her child, and she sighed with pleasure as his flesh joined hers, two hearts and two souls now made one, forever united by the new life she carried beneath her heart.

Chapter 29

Morgan stood alone near the end of the village, his arms upraised, his head back as he gazed at the rising sun, watching in awe as a new day was born amid a blood-red sky.

Until he had come to live with the Lakota, he had never paid much attention to sunrises or sunsets, had never taken the time to enjoy the beauty that came at the beginning of a new day, or given much heed to the way the setting sun went down in a riotous display of red and gold and orange.

He'd never been much of a praying man, either, but Lakota men prayed to Wakan Tanka each morning, and in the quiet hours of dawn, Morgan had found his faith and himself, as well as a keen appreciation for the sacredness of life. The Lakota embraced and revered all of nature, all of life, from birth to death. No man owned the land; it was a gift from the Great Spirit, to be used by all his children. No one owned the trees or the rivers or the mountains or the animals. A man took only what he needed to survive. All people were respected, the old, the helpless, the young, the sick. Children were a gift from Wakan Tanka and were cherished and protected.

Children. He thought of the child he had created with Carrie and felt a rush of love for their unborn child, and for the woman who carried it.

"Le anpetu waste. Aneptu mitawa kon letu nenwe," he murmured. "This day is good. May this be the day I consider mine."

He stood there a moment more, filled with a sense of peace and well-being, before he lowered his arms and walked back to his lodge.

Inside, he took Carolyn into his arms. He held her for a long moment, breathing in the scent of her hair, enjoying the way she fit in his embrace, and then he kissed her gently. "Morning."

"Morning." Carolyn looked at him curiously. "Is something wrong?"

"No. Are you happy here?"

"Yes. Why do you ask?"

"I don't think I ever want to leave this place."

"Never?"

"Never."

"You belong here," Carolyn said. She brushed a lock of hair from his forehead, then let her fingertips slide down his cheek. "And I belong with you."

"Carrie, you make me feel like . . ." He shrugged, hoping she understood what he couldn't seem to say.

"I know." She smiled up at him, so filled with love it was almost painful. "Are you hungry?"

"Not for food."

Laughter bubbled in her throat as he kissed her neck, then turned away to secure the lodge flap. When he turned to face her again, she had slipped out of her tunic and was waiting for him on the buffalo robes, her arms outstretched.

He quickly shed his clout and moccasins and stretched out beside her, eager to make love to her, but she straddled his thighs, her long brown hair brushing his chest as she leaned forward and began to kiss him, first his forehead, then his eyes, his nose, his cheeks, his jaw. She pressed against him, her breasts warm against his chest, laughing softly as she felt his immediate response. She began to kiss him again, her tongue sliding playfully across his lips, when he put his hands on her shoulders and held her at arm's length.

"What is it?" she asked, puzzled by his sudden rejection.

"Listen!"

"I don't hear anything."

"Shh." He sat up, one arm around her waist, a frown furrowing his brow. Then he heard it again, the sound of rapid hoofbeats.

Putting Carolyn from him, he stood up, pulled on his clout, and reached for his rifle. "Stay here," he said curtly, and left the lodge.

The village was eerily quiet. In the distance, a dog whined low in its throat. There was the sound of a baby's cry being muffled. And then, seemingly without reason, warriors were running from their lodges, vaulting onto the backs of the war horses that were kept tethered near their tipis.

He saw the lookout on the ridge beyond the village rein his horse in a tight circle, heard the hoofbeats again, louder this time, and then the clear ringing notes of a bugle.

They were being attacked!

He swung onto the back of his own horse and rode after White Eagle, his heart pounding as a dark blue tide swept into the valley, rifles cracking loudly.

Morgan thought briefly of Carolyn, and then there was no time for thought as a soldier lifted a rifle in his direction. Morgan raised his own weapon and fired, and the soldier went limp and slid out of the saddle.

Around him he heard the sounds of battle: the harsh grunts of men in combat, the almost human scream of an injured horse, the low rumble of gunfire. He saw men locked in mortal combat, and saw Sunrise Woman drive a butcher knife into the back of a trooper who was about to shoot Keeper-of-the-Wind in the head.

He saw other women, armed with knives and war clubs, standing outside their lodges, ready to fight to the death to defend their homes and children.

The air was thick with dust and powder smoke, with the curses of injured men, the shrieks of frightened children.

But it was all a blur as he fired his rifle again and again, killing another trooper, wounding two more. He heard a dozen voices utter the shrill ululating war cry of the Lakota, *"Hoka hey! Hoka hey!"*

White Eagle rode into the melee, his voice rising above the others: *"Hlihe'iciya!"* he shouted, waving his lance high over his head. "Take courage!"

The warriors rallied around White Eagle, the Lakota kill cry rising on the wind, *"Huhn! Huhn! Huhn!"*

But the Indians were badly outnumbered. Women and children ran from burning lodges and raced toward the river, seeking shelter in the brush and trees, while the men stayed behind, firing at the soldiers to give the women and children time to get away. Morgan saw a warrior throw himself in front of a woman who was half-dragging, half-carrying a wounded child toward the river. He saw White Eagle ride out of the midst of the warriors, his chest covered with blood, a war cry on his lips as he hurled himself at a soldier grappling with a Lakota brave.

Morgan called White Eagle's name as he fired at the soldier and missed. He froze in horror as another soldier drove his bayonet into White Eagle's back. For a single instant of eternity, Morgan's gaze held White Eagle's. He saw the Lakota warrior mouth the words "Good journey, my brother" before death took him home.

Swiftly Morgan fired a deadly shot at the man who had killed White Eagle, then turned to fire at a trooper riding up on his left. As he did so, he saw old Mak'awin hobble from her lodge and start toward the river. He heard a triumphant shout as a trooper ran her through with his saber.

They were killing the women, too. Rage boiled through Morgan as he fired at the man who had killed the old storyteller. Then he broke away from the others, no longer a part of the whole, but a man who had only one thought in mind, to get to Carolyn before the troopers did.

He rode wildly through the village, trampling a soldier, and smashing his rifle butt into the face of a blue-clad trooper who tried to pull him from his horse. He heard a bullet whine past his ear, and felt a sudden white-hot pain as a chunk of lead slammed into his right thigh.

He reined his horse to a rearing halt when he reached his lodge. He couldn't help the other women, but if he hurried, there might be a chance to get Carrie out of danger.

Sliding to the ground, he hurried inside.

Carolyn was standing on the far side of the fire-pit, a long-bladed skinning knife in her hand.

There was no time to talk, no time to explain. He took the knife from her hand, slashed an opening in the back of the tipi, and pushed her through it. Before following her, he grabbed a buffalo robe, a sack of pemmican, and a waterskin.

Ducking outside, he took her hand and ran for the cover of the trees behind their lodge.

Carolyn ran blindly after Morgan, her ears ringing with the frightened cries of women and children, the hoarse shrieks of men in pain. She stumbled once, skinning her knee on a rock, but Morgan yanked her to her feet and forced her to keep running, uphill, into the cover of trees. Her side ached, her lungs felt as though they would burst, and still he forced her to go on, until the sounds of the battle could only be heard in her mind.

She was gasping for breath when he finally stopped. Dragging her down behind a huge boulder, he gathered her into his arms and held her tight. She could feel his heart pounding beneath her cheek, feel the cold sweat under her hand. Gradually she became aware of a damp warmth beneath her, and when she looked down, she saw his thigh was dark with blood.

"You've been shot!"

"I'm all right. Be still."

"Morgan—"

"Shhh. Look."

She looked over his shoulder. Below, she could see that the battle was over. A thin haze of blue-gray smoke hung over the village. Bodies littered the ground. Soldiers moved among them, wrapping their own dead in blankets, stripping the Indian dead of whatever caught their fancy: a beaded arm band, a medicine pouch, a breastplate made of porcupine quills.

The survivors stood in a forlorn group in the middle of the camp, surrounded by armed troopers. She could see other soldiers rounding up the Indian ponies, and others going from lodge to lodge, emerging with blankets and robes, feathered lances and ceremonial shields, cradleboards and moccasins.

"What will happen to them?" she asked, her throat clogged with tears.

"They'll be taken to the reservation."

"But their homes . . . their belongings. . . ."

"Spoils of war," Morgan said bitterly. "I thought we'd be safe here for a while, but I was wrong. Treaties won't keep the whites out of Indian land, not when there's rumors of gold in the Black Hills, not when there's talk of land and grass free for the taking. If you don't mind taking it from the people who're already here."

Carolyn stared at the scene below, her heart sinking as she realized the truth of what he said. Back home in Galveston, she had heard stories of gold being discovered on Indian land, but she had never paid them any mind. She had heard rumors of Indian unrest, and of treaties being ignored, but it hadn't meant anything then. She hadn't known any Indians, and had never expected to leave Texas.

But now she was here watching while people she had grown to know and love were being forced from their homes, robbed of their goods, stripped of their pride. It wasn't fair. White Eagle and his people deserved to live here. It was their land, after all.

The soldiers had finished looting the tipis. The Army dead had been gathered, the Indian ponies had been rounded up, and now the march began. Carolyn wept quietly as she saw Sunrise Woman, Keeper-of-the Wind, and others she knew being forced to walk behind the soldiers' horses. It was a strangely quiet group. No babies cried. No dogs barked. No one spoke. They just walked quietly, their heads bowed, as they were driven away from the only life they'd ever known.

Her eyes searched for White Eagle, but she

couldn't see him among the survivors. She glanced at Morgan and was about to ask, "Where is White—" but the question died in her throat. One look at his face told her that White Eagle was dead.

She was still staring at the village when Morgan grabbed her by the shoulder and pulled her down behind the rock again. She stared at him, eyes wide and frightened, as she heard voices coming their way. Then she saw them, two soldiers riding up the hill, sabers drawn, as they searched the underbrush for runaways.

Morgan stood up, putting Carolyn behind him as the two soldiers turned in their direction. Slamming his rifle against his shoulder, Morgan fired at the man on the right, and grinned with cold satisfaction as the soldier toppled from his horse. He squeezed the trigger again, and swore softly when he realized the rifle was empty.

With a cry, he sprang at the second trooper, dodging the man's saber as he grabbed the man around the waist and dragged him out of the saddle.

Carolyn choked back a scream as Morgan and the soldier struggled for the saber. She heard the soldier curse, then he rolled to one side and lashed out with both feet, one booted foot striking Morgan's injured leg.

Morgan groaned, the color draining from his face as a sharp pain ripped through his right thigh.

With a triumphant grin, the soldier rolled nimbly to his feet, the saber clutched in his hand.

Morgan also gained his feet, but his movements were slow and awkward and he stood with most of his weight balanced on his left leg.

The trooper smirked at Carolyn. "Well, well," he drawled, his dark eyes traveling leisurely over her face and figure. "Howdy, ma'am. You and me'll get acquainted just as soon as I dispose of this here buck."

His words sent a wave of revulsion through Carolyn. She stared at him in horror as he began to walk forward, the saber raised and ready to strike.

Morgan took a step backward, swearing softly as he searched the ground for a weapon.

The sound of a gunshot pierced his ears. The soldier staggered backward, the saber falling from his grasp as he clutched at his shirt front.

Morgan whirled around to see Carolyn standing behind him, an Army-issue revolver clutched in both hands. Her face was as white as paste, her eyes wide with horror and disbelief.

"I had to," she whispered, her voice filled with anguish. "He was going to kill you. I had to do it."

She looked at Morgan, her eyes haunted and pleading for understanding. "I had to do it. I didn't want to." She shook her head as tears welled in her eyes. "I had to do it. I had to."

"It's all right, Carrie," Morgan said quietly. Hobbling to her side, he took the gun from her hand and shoved it into the waistband of his clout. "We've got to go, Carrie, before someone else comes."

"I had to do it." She stared at the body of the man she had killed. "I'm sorry," she murmured. "I'm so dreadfully sorry."

Moving as quickly as possible on his injured leg,

Morgan gathered their gear together. He stripped the uniform off the first trooper, who was about his size, tied the dead man's kerchief over the angry wound in his thigh, then boosted Carrie into the saddle of the nearest horse, a long-legged gray gelding with a U.S. Cavalry brand on its right hip.

"You all right?" he asked as he adjusted the stirrups.

"I had to do it," she said, staring down at him.

Morgan nodded. "I know. It's all right, Carrie. Don't think about it right now."

Taking up the reins of the second horse, he pulled himself into the saddle. They had to get away from here, now, before somebody came looking for the two dead men.

Ignoring the growing pain in his leg, he urged the big buckskin up the hill. Behind him, he could hear Carrie sobbing quietly. He wanted to hold her, to comfort her, but there was no time now. They had to get away from here, find a place to hole up for the night. He pressed a hand to his thigh. The bleeding had finally stopped. He'd have to dig the bullet out sooner or later, but first he had to get Carrie out of danger.

Morgan sat beside Carolyn, his eyes dark with worry. She had withdrawn into herself again, hiding where the pain and guilt of what she'd done couldn't find her. And neither could he. She obeyed his commands, eating and drinking when he told her to, but there was no life in her eyes. Now, she slept by the fire, the buffalo robe drawn up to her chin. She'd been crying in her sleep; there were tears drying on her cheeks. Once, he'd heard her whimper, "I had to do it. I had to."

A sharp twinge drew his attention from Carrie and he stared at his blood-caked thigh. He had put it off long enough, he thought bleakly. The bullet had to come out, and Carrie was in no condition to do it.

He found a thin-bladed Spanish dagger in the buckskin's saddlebags and held it over the flames, staring at the blade as it changed from glowing red to shimmering white.

He cursed softly as he waited for the blade to cool; then, biting down on a stick, he drew a deep breath and began to probe for the bullet embedded in his thigh. Sweat beaded across his brow as he worked the blade deeper, fighting the nausea rising in his throat as he concentrated on removing the bullet before he passed out.

He bit the stick in half as he dislodged the slug from his thigh and tossed it into the fire. Spitting the wood from his mouth, he pressed a handful of dirt over the jagged wound to stop the bleeding before he surrendered to the darkness that hovered around him, promising relief from the pain.

He woke to the soft sound of crying. Rolling over, he drew Carrie into his arms, his hand lightly stroking her hair.

"It's all right, Carrie," he said soothingly. "Don't cry."

"I killed a man."

"Would you rather he'd killed me?"

"No!" She wrapped her arms around him and

held on tight. "You've killed men," she said quietly, remembering the Crow warrior he had killed because of her. "How do you live with it?"

"I guess I don't think about it much. Usually it's a matter of self-defense. I'm not saying that makes it right, but it makes it easier to live with."

Carrie gazed at Morgan. She loved him desperately, loved him so much she would have killed a dozen men to save him.

"How're you feeling this morning?" she asked.

"My leg's a little sore."

Carolyn sat up, tossing the buffalo robe aside so she could examine Morgan's thigh. She looked at him in alarm when she saw the dirt spread over the wound. "What happened?"

"It was the best way I could think to stop the bleeding."

"I wasn't much help, was I?"

"You had a lot on your mind. Taking a life is never easy, especially the first time. I was afraid . . . afraid maybe I'd lost you."

"Lost me?"

"You were so withdrawn last night. I thought maybe you were blaming me, that maybe you wouldn't be able to accept what you'd done. I knew a man once who witnessed a killing and retreated into himself like that and never came out."

Carrie traced a heart on Morgan's chest with her forefinger. "I'd never leave you, don't you know that?"

He nodded as he lifted her hand to his lips and kissed her palm, his tongue moving in lazy circles against her skin. His touch sent shivers of delight down her spine, and she sat up, bracing herself on one elbow as she leaned forward and kissed his forehead.

She drew back abruptly, her eyes wide with alarm. "You've got a fever!"

Morgan shrugged. "It's nothing."

"Are you sure?" she asked dubiously.

"I'm fine, Carrie. Don't worry."

She wanted to believe him, but was afraid he was lying to keep her from worrying. She knew that a fever, however slight, was cause for concern.

"I think we should go," she said, standing up. "You need a doctor."

"Have you forgotten about those Wanted posters Brockton's got out?"

"No."

She moved to the fire and stirred the embers, then added some dry leaves and fresh wood. She withdrew a roll of pemmican from a saddlebag and sliced a piece for herself and one for Morgan. "Eat that, and then we're going."

"Yes, ma'am," he said, amused by her commanding tone.

In less than twenty minutes, they were on the trail, heading west. Carrie insisted that Morgan drink as much water as he could hold. At noon, they ate Army hardtack while they rested the horses. She watched Morgan constantly all day, checking his temperature every couple of hours, asking him how he felt. He assured her that he was fine, but he knew it was a lie. His thigh throbbed mercilessly, and it was all he could do to remain in the saddle.

At dusk, they made camp in the lee of a sandstone bluff. Ignoring Morgan's protests, Carolyn insisted on examining his wound. She washed the dirt from his thigh as best she could with water from one of the canteens, and bit down on her lip when she saw how red and swollen it was.

Worried now, she hovered over Morgan, wishing they had some of Yellow Sage's magical salve, wishing there was a town nearby.

"Stop worrying, Carrie, I'll be all right."

"You've got a fever and an infection," she exclaimed, concern making her voice sharp. "You need a doctor."

"Yeah."

The fact that he admitted he needed help worried her more than anything else.

"Wish I had a drink," he muttered. "Purely for medicinal purposes, Mrs. Slade," he assured her with a wry grin.

"I wish I had some to give you," Carrie replied solemnly. She'd have given him a gallon of the stuff to erase the pain that flickered in the depths of his eyes. "Do you feel like riding?" she asked.

"Tonight?"

"I think we should keep moving. There must be a town nearby."

Morgan hesitated. "Cheyenne's not far."

"How far?"

"Couple of days." Cheyenne. He'd never been there, never even been to Wyoming because he was afraid of running into his grandfather. But he was too sick to worry about that now.

Carrie nodded. She would get him to Cheyenne,

and then she would wire her father and ask him to send her a couple of train tickets home. She did not discuss it with Morgan, because she knew he wouldn't like it. She insisted he put on the cavalry uniform for warmth, then packed their gear. When she started to help him mount, he shook his head.

"I can do it," he said. The look of pain that crossed his face as he pulled himself into the saddle made her more certain than ever that wiring her father for help was the right thing to do.

They rode all night. Morgan dozed in the saddle, waking now and then to make sure they were headed in the right direction.

Carrie found it frightening, riding through the dark with only the stars for light. Her imagination conjured up all sorts of horrible monsters lurking in the underbrush. She jumped at every sound, and no matter how often she told herself she was being silly, she couldn't relax.

At dawn, she helped Morgan from the saddle. He didn't object to her help this time. They had nothing to eat but pemmican, and only water to wash it down with.

"Should we rest awhile?" she asked, laying her hand on Morgan's brow.

"If you want."

Carolyn shook her head. "I'd rather go on if you feel up to it."

They let the horses rest a few minutes, then Morgan climbed back in the saddle. His thigh was a constant throbbing pain and he knew it was badly infected, knew he had to get Carrie to a safe haven while he could still think clearly.

His jaw set against the pain, he rode steadily onward, aware of Carrie's anxious glances in his direction. At noon, he drew rein along a shallow creek. Easing from the saddle, he dropped to his knees and, after burying his face in the cold water, drank deeply.

When he sat up, he saw Carrie watching him again, her face drawn with concern.

"The wound's infected," he said tersely. "I'm gonna try and drain some of the poison out and see if that helps. Get me that knife, will you?"

Wordlessly, she went in search of the dagger he had used to remove the slug from his thigh. She stared at it for a moment, resigning herself to what had to be done, and then walked back to Morgan and knelt beside him.

"You probably won't want to watch this," he said, taking the knife from her hand. "Why don't you see if you can find some moss?"

"Moss?"

"To stop the bleeding."

"I'll lance the wound for you."

"I can do it, Carrie."

"I know."

He stared at her for a moment; then, with a nod, he unfastened his trousers, grimacing as she tugged them over his hips to expose the wound in his thigh.

Carrie stared at the jagged wound. It was red and swollen, and the thought of piercing Morgan's flesh with the dagger made her sick to her stomach. But it had to be done.

"I'll be as careful as I can," she promised, and

taking a deep breath, she lanced the wound. A thick stream of dark red blood and yellow pus flowed in the wake of the blade.

Morgan swore softly as Carrie applied pressure to the wound, expelling more pus, more blood, until only bright red blood flowed from the wound. Cutting a strip of cloth from her skirt, she pressed it over the wound.

"Hold that in place," she told him. "I'll see if I can find some moss."

Morgan nodded. Closing his eyes, he tried to relax, tried to pretend that the pain belonged to someone else.

Carrie returned in a few minutes with a handful of damp tree moss. Carefully she placed it over the wound, then bound his thigh in a length of doeskin cut from her skirt.

"You keep hacking pieces from that dress and you'll be naked soon," Morgan muttered. "And I'll be too weak to care."

"You'll never be that weak," Carrie retorted, but inwardly she was afraid, terribly afraid, that he was going to die. "Do you think you can ride now?"

"Yeah."

Blinking back tears, she helped him to his feet, and then into the saddle. Mounting her own horse, she rode up beside him, smiling encouragingly.

"How are you feeling?" he asked, glancing pointedly at her stomach.

"Fine. Don't worry about me."

"You're a hell of a woman, Mrs. Slade. A few months ago you couldn't boil water, and now you're doctorin' my worthless hide."

"You're not worthless! Don't ever say that again."

"Spunky, too. I always liked that about you."

"You can ply me with compliments later. Let's go."

With a nod, he reined his horse westward. He'd get Carrie to safety, and then he'd find a place to lie down and he'd never get up again.

Chapter 30

Lou Kylie sat hunched over a back table in the Golden Grotto, the drink in his hand forgotten as he stared at the faded Wanted poster spread in front of him. Morgan was supposed to be dead, but that was his likeness, sure enough.

Kylie grunted softly. He remembered the night he'd finally found Morgan alone, in the alley behind the Grotto. The breed had been pretty well liquored up and hadn't even heard Wylie approach until he was on top of him. *This is for Jim*, Wylie had said, and driven his knife into Morgan. He'd been certain he'd killed him. But before he could make sure, he'd heard footsteps in the alley and had run away. When he went back, there was nothing but a bloodstain.

Kylie grimaced as he read the amount of the reward. Ten thousand dollars. Hell, he knew men who would turn in their own mothers for that much money.

"Last seen in Ogallala," Kylie murmured to

himself. "Looks like I'll be takin' a little trip."

Kylie frowned. Morgan Slade. Slade. No, it couldn't be. If Morgan was related to Harrison Slade, he wouldn't have been working for Danny Monroe. Harrison Slade was a rich man. Still . . .

He looked up as the red-haired tart who had assured him Morgan was dead passed his table. She'd lied to him. He ought to teach her a lesson for that, but he'd never been much for hitting women, even when they deserved it.

He grabbed her skirt when she passed by his table again, pointing at the Wanted flyer with his finger.

"Seen this?" he asked.

Red hesitated, then nodded. She didn't like Lou Kylie, and not only because he'd tried to kill Morgan. There was something about him that wasn't quite right, an odd look in his light brown eyes that scared her.

"He ain't dead," Kylie said, his voice angry. "You told me he was dead. Remember? I came by here the night after it happened and you told me he was dead."

"I thought he was," Red replied innocently. She looked Kylie straight in the eye. "I stopped by the undertaker's in the morning and told him to pick up the body, and when I got back to Morgan's place that afternoon, he was gone."

"You're lyin'."

"No," Red said. "Maybe it's not him."

Kylie swore under his breath. "Not him? Look at that picture!"

Red nodded. "Well, it does look like him. But

what would he be doing in Ogallala?"

"I don't know," Kylie snapped. "Has he got kin there?"

"No."

"How about in Cheyenne?

Red shook her head. "He never had any kin but his ma, and she died a long time ago."

"You're lyin', dammit!" Kylie pounded his fist on the Wanted poster. "I'm gonna find him if it's the last thing I do, and this time he's gonna stay dead!"

Chapter 31

It was late afternoon when they reached Cheyenne. For Morgan, it was just in time. It was an effort to stay in the saddle, an effort to keep his eyes open.

Reining his horse to a halt at the edge of town, he stared down the street. Cheyenne was a young town that had grown up fast, spawned by the tracks of the Union Pacific railroad pushing their way west back in 1867. General Grenville Dodge had established his first camp on Crow Creek. With the coming of the railroad and the supplies needed in Army camps, a depot was necessary, and Cheyenne had been born. Soldiers from Fort Russell had provided protection from the Indians for the growing community and for the railroad workers.

Cattle barons and cowboys mingled with stagecoach drivers and outlaws, mule skinners and soldiers, railroad men and city dudes.

Morgan saw a boardinghouse a little ways down the street and rode toward it. Carrie followed him, more worried than she'd ever been in her life. He looked pale, so pale. He needed a doctor immediately.

When they reached the boardinghouse, Carrie quickly slid out of the saddle and hurried up the steps. She rapped on the door, praying there was a vacancy, and a doctor nearby.

A middle-aged woman wearing a plain brown dress and a white apron opened the door. She looked at Carrie suspiciously, and Carrie was suddenly aware of how disreputable she must look in her travel-worn doeskin dress and Cheyenne moccasins. And Morgan looked just as bad. His uniform was stained with blood and covered with trail dust.

"Good afternoon," Carrie said, forcing what she hoped was a cheerful smile. "We need a room."

"He drunk?" the woman asked, waving a hand in Morgan's direction. "I don't allow no liquor in my place." She stared at Morgan with blatant disapproval. "Don't allow no Injuns, either, even if they're Army scouts."

"He's not drunk, he's sick," Carrie said urgently.

"What ails him?"

"He was wounded and it's become infected. We need a room, please. And a doctor."

"Why don't the Army look after him?"

"Please, couldn't we discuss it later?" Carrie pleaded. "He's lost a lot of blood."

"Are you married?" the woman asked suspiciously. "I don't allow no shilly-shallying in my place."

"Yes, this is my husband, Mr. Slade. My name's Carolyn."

The woman stared at Carolyn for a long moment, and Carrie felt her heart sink. What if the woman refused to let them stay? She had to get Morgan to a doctor, and soon. He'd lost so much blood.

"I'm Martha Galway," the woman said. "Bring your man inside. I'll send my boy for the doctor while you get your mister into bed. Take the first room down the hall on the left."

"Thank you," Carrie said gratefully. Hurrying down the stairs, she helped Morgan dismount. He leaned heavily on her shoulder as they climbed the stairs and entered the house, making their way through a large parlor, then down a narrow hall.

The room was clean and spacious, dominated by a big brass bed covered by a pink and blue quilted spread. Blue muslin curtains fluttered in the faint breeze. A ladderback chair and a small mahogany desk occupied one corner of the room. A four-drawer chest stood against one wall, and a watercolor of a Paris street scene hung above the chest.

Morgan sat down on the bed, oblivious to his surroundings as Carrie removed his shirt, pants, and moccasins, then drew back the covers and helped him into bed.

His skin was burning hot to her touch. There was water in the pitcher on the commode, and after giving him a drink, Carrie quickly soaked a washcloth and placed it on Morgan's forehead. That done, she sat on the edge of the bed holding his hand in hers. It was like holding a small fire.

She looked at him, wondering if he was asleep, wondering if he was in much pain. His face was pale, there were dark shadows under his eyes, and it seemed to be an effort for him to breathe. It occurred to her, not for the first time, that he might die.

She shook her head, fighting back tears. He couldn't die, not now. She hadn't known him long, not long at all, and yet he had become the most important person in her life.

He didn't stir when she placed her hand on his brow, and she fought down a rising tide of fear. He'd be all right. He had to be all right. She refused to think otherwise.

Tapping her foot impatiently, she stared at the door. Where was that doctor?

A low groan returned her attention to Morgan. He began to murmur incoherently, thrashing about on the bed as though in the throes of a nightmare. He groaned softly, his voice filled with pain and anguish as he whispered, "Lily, no!"

"Morgan." Carrie shook his shoulder gently, worried by the fine sheen of sweat on his brow, by the sudden tensing of his muscles.

"Lily," he mumbled. "Dammit, Lily, I didn't mean it." His hand crushed hers. "Don't leave me," he begged, his voice thick with unshed tears. "Don't . . ."

He woke abruptly, his eyes filled with misery as he stared up at her.

"It's all right," Carrie said, squeezing his hand. "You were dreaming."

"Yeah. Stop worrying, Carrie. I'll be all right."

She nodded, praying he was right.

"I just need some sleep." He frowned, wondering at the strange expression on her face.

"Who's Lily?" It was the wrong time to ask, the wrong thing to ask, but she had to know.

A wry smile tugged at Morgan's lips. "You jealous?"

"Of course not," Carrie said, knowing it was quite possibly the biggest lie she'd ever told.

"Another hope crushed," Morgan replied, and then the smile faded. "You don't have anything to be jealous of, Carrie. She was my mother."

Before she could think of anything to say, there was a knock at the door and Mrs. Galway peered into the room. "Doctor Aames is here."

"Thank you," Carrie said. "Please show him in."

Doctor Aames proved to be a tall, gray-haired man with sharp brown eyes and a grizzled goatee. He nodded politely in Carrie's direction. "What seems to be the trouble here?"

"It's my husband. He was hurt and the wound is infected."

"When did it happen?"

"Four days ago."

"Where's the wound?"

"In his right thigh."

The doctor grunted softly, then crossed the floor to the bed. He laid the back of his hand against Morgan's cheek, and checked his heartbeat and pulse. Drawing back the covers, he removed the bandage from Morgan's thigh, then peeled away the moss.

Madeline Baker

"Good idea," Aames remarked. He put on a pair of wire-rimmed spectacles pulled from his coat pocket, then bent down to examine the wound. The edges were ragged, crusted with blood.

"Is he going to be all right?" Carrie asked anxiously.

"I think so." Aames gently prodded the wound with the tip of his finger, and grunted softly as a thin stream of yellow pus oozed from the ragged hole. "I'll leave you something for the fever, and a poultice to draw the poison from the wound."

"Thanks, doc," Morgan said, offering his hand.

"Quite all right," Aames said, shaking Morgan's hand. Taking a piece of paper from his coat pocket, he wrote down the instructions for the poultice, then withdrew several small white packets from his bag and handed them to Carrie. "Dissolve these in warm water. Give him one now, and one every four hours. If his fever doesn't break by morning, let me know. I'll check back tomorrow evening to see how he's doing."

"Thank you," Carrie said fervently.

The doctor smiled at her. "He's going to be fine, just fine." His gaze swept over her in a long professional assessment. "How far along are you?"

"About three and a half months."

Aames nodded. "Frettin' over your husband won't do that baby any good. You see that you get plenty of sleep. Eat proper. Take a walk now and then, but don't overdo it." He smiled as he glanced at Morgan, who was already asleep. "I reckon your husband will mend a lot quicker if he's not worrying about you and that young'un."

Carrie nodded. She liked Doctor Aames, liked his forthright attitude and kindly smile.

"That powder should ease the pain in your husband's leg. Likely make him sleep for quite a spell. I think you should take a little nap, too."

"I will."

"Good day to you, then," the doctor said, and taking up his satchel, he left the room.

A few minutes later, Martha Galway knocked at the door. "I thought you might like a change of clothing," she said, thrusting a dark green dress and a pile of petticoats into Carolyn's hands. "I've gained some weight and can't wear it no more. I don't have no shoes that'll fit you."

"Thank you," Carrie said. "You've been very kind."

"Ain't got nothing to do with kindness," Martha Galway said in her usual brusque tone. "I can't have folks thinking I'm taking in Injuns and no-accounts." Martha put one hand on her hip and studied Carolyn for a moment. "When did you eat last, missy?"

"Yesterday."

"Dinner's in an hour, but I don't reckon it'd be too much trouble to fix you something now."

Carrie nodded her appreciation, smiling to herself as Martha Galway left the room and closed the door behind her. Not kind, indeed! The woman's manner might be curt, her voice might be as rough as a whetstone, but Martha Galway had a heart of gold.

Chapter 32

Lucius Aames sat at his desk, his fingers drumming lightly on the arm of his chair, while his visitor paced the floor, his weathered face lined with disbelief.

"Are you sure, Lucius?"

Aames pulled the Wanted poster from his pocket and tossed it on the desk top. "There's his picture. See for yourself. He looks just like you, Harry."

Harrison Slade picked up the poster and stared at the pen and ink drawing intently. "Morgan Slade," he muttered, and shook his head. "I can't believe it." But there was no doubt in his mind that he was looking at a likeness of his grandson. He'd been at home when he received the doc's message. He hadn't bothered to change out of his range clothes; he'd just kissed his wife goodbye and rode hellbent for town, afraid to hope, afraid to believe. But the proof was there, in his hands.

"Those flyers are posted all over town," Aames remarked. "I thought you'd want to know he was here before some hothead tries to take him in. That reward's gonna draw every bounty hunter in the territory."

"Yeah."

"Did you tell Elizabeth?"

"No. I wanted to be sure." Harrison Slade began pacing the floor again, the flyer clutched in his hand.

"So, what are you going to do now?"

"I don't know." Slade ran a hand through his hair, his dark gray eyes troubled. "How can I face him, Lucius? What can I say?" He stopped in front of the window and stared out into the street. "When Beth told me Lily was pregnant, I went a little crazy. I couldn't believe she had let that Navajo cowboy touch her. I was hurt and angry. I had such plans for her, such hopes. She was so young, and so beautiful. She could have had any man she wanted. And she wanted a damned redskin!"

Lucius grunted softly. Everyone knew of Harrison Slade's hatred for Indians. They'd killed his younger brother, scalped his parents, and left him for dead. It had been a miracle he survived, but he'd been bull-headed even then and too damned stubborn to die.

Slade crumpled the paper in his hand. "I said some terrible things that night. I . . . I called her a slut, threatened to send her to a convent. Hell, I didn't mean it, we're not even Catholic, but I couldn't let her marry that Indian."

Slade looked away, unable to face the man he'd

called friend for the last ten years. "I had a couple of my men rough him up, and then they took him for a ride and left him out on the prairie. I told Lily that her so-called lover had run away rather than marry her. Later that night, after I'd cooled off some, I knew I'd done a terrible thing, but I thought she'd get over it, that she'd thank me for it later. But the next night she was gone. I looked for her everywhere."

He shook his head. "Beth never forgave me. Lily was our only child, and I drove her away. She knew how I felt about Indians. Now I understand why she never came home, why she never wrote. She was afraid I wouldn't accept a boy with mixed blood. Hell, she was probably right. And now this..."

Slade turned around, his dark eyes filled with pain and self-reproach. "I looked for her for five years, hoping I could find her, that somehow I could make everything right, but it was as if she'd disappeared off the face of the earth. And now her son's here. How can I face him?"

Harrison made a gesture of despair. "How do I know I can even accept him? Dammit, Lucius, he's a half-breed! Every time I look at him I'll see his father's face, see the accusation in his eyes."

"I didn't say it would be easy, but I think you owe it to him, and to yourself." Lucius paused. "And to Lily."

Harrison Slade nodded. The doc was right. He had a responsibility to Lily's boy. He'd done Lily a terrible wrong, but maybe, in some small way, he could ease his conscience by looking after Lily's son.

"Send your boy down to the livery barn and have him hire me a rig. Tell him to drive it to over to Martha's and hitch it out back." Harrison let out a long breath. "Are you sure my ... my grandson is strong enough to make the trip?"

"He'll make it. You just be sure he stays off that leg for at least two weeks, and off a horse for two more. I'll ride out in a couple of days to see how he's doing."

Harrison Slade nodded. Shoving the crumpled Wanted poster into his pants pocket, he left the doctor's office.

Lily's son was here, in Cheyenne. His steps slowed as doubts crowded in on him. He hadn't changed his opinion of Indians. How could he accept a half-breed grandson? And what about the boy, Morgan? How much did he know about his mother's past? Did Lily's son hate him for what he'd done?

Harrison Slade squared his shoulders. He'd always been a man of action, one to face things head on. Lily's son was here. He quickened his step, eager to get this first meeting over with, eager to hear about his daughter. Lily. Where had she been all these years? He wondered if she'd married, if she'd had other children, if she was happy.

He swallowed hard, hoping that it wasn't too late to make things right, and that she'd forgive him for behaving like a fool.

He pulled the Wanted poster out of his pocket,

straightened it, and stared at the black-and-white drawing. Perhaps when he brought his grandson home the light would shine in Beth's eyes again and she'd forgive him for the horrible mistake he'd made all those years ago.

Perhaps he'd even be able to forgive himself.

Chapter 33

Carrie stared at the man who claimed to be Morgan's grandfather, astonished as much by the man's resemblance to her husband as by his unexpected appearance at her door.

"May I come in?" Harrison Slade asked. His voice was deep and gruff, yet polite.

"Yes, please." Carrie stepped backward, allowing the man into the room.

Closing the door, she took a deep breath, and when she turned around, Harrison Slade was standing beside the bed. He was a big man, almost as broad and tall as Morgan. His hair was black, graying at the temples. His eyes were as gray as a winter sky.

Carrie studied him surreptitiously as he gazed at Morgan, who was sleeping soundly, thanks to one of Lucius Aames' powders. She was confused by the conflicting emotions she read in Slade's face: contempt, guilt, disbelief.

She felt her own throat swell with emotion as a

single tear rolled down Harrison Slade's cheek.

"I can't believe it," Slade said, his voice thick with unshed tears. "Lily's son, after all these years."

"Won't you sit down?" Carrie asked, indicating the room's only chair.

"No, there's no time for that now."

"I beg your pardon?"

"We're leaving." He spoke with the authority of a man who had made up his mind, a man who was accustomed to giving orders and having them obeyed without question. "I've got a carriage waiting out back."

"Leaving? For where?"

"My ranch." Slade pulled the Wanted poster from his pocket and handed it to Carrie. "Aames tells me these are posted all over town. We've got to get him out of Cheyenne. He'll be safe at the Double S."

Carrie frowned. "I don't know . . ."

"I know. You collect his gear, and yours, too. I'll carry him outside."

"But he may not want to go with you."

"He's going. You can come or not, that's up to you. But he's going with me."

It didn't take long to get their meager belongings together. They had little more than a change of clothing. Filled with trepidation, Carrie followed Harrison Slade down the hall and out the back door.

Martha Galway was waiting for them outside. She had spread a pallet in the back of a wagon, and Harrison Slade placed Morgan on it and covered him with a heavy quilt.

"You want to sit up front with me?" Slade asked.

"I'd rather sit back here, with Morgan."

Slade nodded, then lifted Carrie into the back of the wagon and fastened the tailgate.

"Thanks, Martha," Slade said, patting the woman on the shoulder. "I'd appreciate it if you didn't tell anyone about this."

"I ain't no gossip. Are you sure you wouldn't rather leave first thing in the morning?"

"I'm sure."

Martha Galway grunted softly. "That's what I figured. There's a basket under the seat. Thought you might like something to eat along the way."

Slade nodded. "Thanks, again."

"Give my regards to your missus."

"I'll do that," Slade promised. "Send me a bill for the room."

Carrie waved goodbye to Martha Galway, then settled down beside Morgan, wondering how he'd react when he woke up and found himself in the company of the man he held responsible for his mother's wasted life.

Morgan squinted against a bright sun, grimaced as he opened his eyes, then muttered, "What the hell ..." as he realized he was lying in the back of a wagon, and that the wagon was moving. Carrie was lying beside him, her head pillowed on her arm.

Ignoring the pain in his thigh, Morgan struggled to a sitting position, his gaze moving toward the front of the wagon. A man was driving, a man with

331

a broad back and wide shoulders. He wore a heavy sheepskin jacket and a broad-brimmed black hat.

Morgan scowled blackly. He was buck naked under the blanket, but that didn't bother him half as much as being unarmed in the back of a wagon driven by a man he didn't know.

He took hold of Carrie's shoulder and shook it gently. "Carrie, wake up."

She stretched and made sleepy sounds before opening her eyes. Then she smiled up at him. "Hi. How are you feeling?"

"Where the hell are we? Who's driving this wagon? And where's he taking us?"

"You're on the Double S Ranch, son," boomed a voice as big as Texas. "Harrison Slade is driving the wagon, and I'm taking you home."

Carrie sat up, her eyes widening in alarm as she watched the play of emotions across Morgan's face. Disbelief came first, and then anger as dark as the grave.

Morgan glared at Carrie. "What the hell's going on?"

The wagon came to an abrupt halt as Harrison Slade gave a sharp jerk on the reins, secured the lines around the brake, then turned on the seat to face his grandson.

"Don't blame your wife, son. This wasn't her idea."

"Who the hell are you?" Morgan demanded.

"Harrison Slade, like I said. Lily was my daughter."

Morgan stared at his grandfather. This was the man who had caused his mother to run away from home, who had been so disgusted by the thought of a half-breed grandson that he'd threatened to send his daughter to a convent when what she'd needed was her father's love and support.

His mother's image sprang quickly to mind; he saw her as he had seen her last, dying in his arms. Always, when he thought of her, he saw her covered with blood, heard her voice cursing the day he'd been born, lamenting the man and the good life she had lost because of him.

"You bastard," Morgan growled, and scrambled to his feet, his hands reaching for the man who had wronged his mother. He swore under his breath as pain exploded in his thigh. He heard Carrie's anxious cry as he dropped to his knees, his head hanging limply as he fought to control his rage.

"That was a damn fool thing to do, son," Harrison Slade remarked. "You all right?"

"Go to hell," Morgan said, gasping for air. "And don't call me son."

Slade looked at Carrie. "Is he all right?"

"I don't know. He's bleeding again."

"Do you need any help?"

"We don't need anything from you," Morgan said curtly.

"Morgan, he's just trying to help," Carrie said, laying a restraining hand on his arm. "Sit back now so I can check the bleeding."

He rested his head on the side of the wagon and closed his eyes, willing the pain to stop, not wanting to believe that the man calling himself Harrison Slade was his grandfather. And yet he knew it was true. Looking at Slade was like looking at himself forty years down the road.

Morgan's hands curled into tight fists as all the hatred he felt for the man came boiling up. But there was nothing he could do now but sit in silent rage as Carrie tended to his wound.

"All set?" Harrison asked a few minutes later.

"Yes," Carrie replied.

Slade nodded. "Here," he said, handing Carrie a canteen. "He should drink plenty of water. Aames says he lost a lot of blood."

Carrie offered Morgan a drink, but he knocked the canteen aside, his face dark with impotent anger. "I don't want anything from him."

"He's right, Morgan," Carrie said patiently. "The doctor said you should drink a lot of water."

Morgan scowled at Carrie. He didn't want to take anything from Harrison Slade, but his mouth was as dry as dust and the thought of a drink, just one drink, was more than he could resist.

"Please, Morgan?" Carrie said quietly. "For me."

He grabbed the canteen and took a long drink, salvaging his pride by telling himself he was doing it for Carrie. It was a lie that made him hate Slade all the more.

"We'll be at the ranch house soon," Slade said. Taking up the reins, he clucked to the horses and the wagon lurched into motion.

Morgan stared at the passing countryside. Miles of grassland spread as far as the eye could see. A narrow ribbon of blue bordered by a stand of tall timber marked a river. *Harrison Slade*. Even the name left a bad taste in his mouth.

"Where's my gun?"

"He has it, up front, under the seat."

"My clothes?"

"Over there." She gestured to a neatly wrapped bundle in a corner of the wagon.

Morgan grimaced, wondering what the doctor had given him the night before. Whatever it was, he'd slept like the dead. Like Lily ...

A fresh spasm of pain twisted in his gut. He'd thought he'd put all the hurt, all the pain of her death behind him, but he'd been wrong. It was back, as raw and soul-shattering as the day she died.

Carrie was hovering beside him, anxious to say or do something that would ease his pain, but he was in no mood to be coddled, and in no mood for conversation. He was hurting deep inside and he didn't think he'd ever be free of the pain.

They reached the Double S two hours later. The main house sprawled across a flat-topped rise, looking like a great white bird poised to take off. A whitewashed three-rail fence separated the house from the big red and white barn and the other outbuildings. Several horses stood dozing in a corral alongside the house. A hen and a half-dozen yellow chicks scratched in the dirt beneath a lodgepole pine. A big black dog slept in the shade of the veranda. He could see hundreds of cattle grazing in the distance.

Morgan looked at the land, the house, and all the other buildings, and all he saw was money and the ease it could buy. He thought of his mother, never having a place of her own, never having enough money to buy the things she wanted, frivolous things like a lace parasol or the figurine of a bluebird she'd seen in a store window.

The Double S, the servants, the security of a good name—it should have belonged to Lily, he thought bitterly. Instead, she'd lived in a dreary room above a noisy saloon, barely making enough to support the two of them, and all the while her father had been living here, making more money than he could spend in a lifetime.

Morgan stared at his grandfather's back. The old man's hat and boots probably cost more than his mother had made in a month.

He remembered how Lily had been, before drink and discouragement got hold of her. She'd been young then, more beautiful than any woman he'd ever seen. Her smile had been soft and warm, her eyes filled with hope for the future.

It's only for a little while, she'd promised him time and again. *Only for a little while, and then we'll go away and never look back.* But it never happened. The days and the weeks ran together and became months and years, and he watched her smile fade, saw the hope die in her eyes, saw her beauty decline as she looked for happiness in a bottle.

His helplessness ate at him. She was his mother and despite his youth, he felt responsible for her, but there was nothing he could do. The older he got, the less time she had for him, and by the time he was ten, they were more like strangers than mother and son. She cursed him as she cursed all men, hating herself for what she'd become, hating him because he'd been born.

Morgan closed his eyes. Each jolt of the wagon

sent slivers of pain darting along his injured thigh, but the physical pain was as nothing compared to the rage he felt each time he looked at Harrison Slade's back. If he'd had a gun, he would have killed the old man without a qualm. It wasn't fair, he thought, choking down his rage. It just wasn't fair. His mother had lost her youth and whatever hope she'd had for happiness while Harrison Slade had lived in luxury, eating three meals a day, every day, sleeping on clean white sheets, riding blooded horses, wearing expensive clothes ...

He opened his eyes as the wagon came to a halt, felt the tremor in Carrie's hand as she touched his arm.

"This is it," Slade remarked as he reined the team to a halt at the front gate. He jumped lightly to the ground and opened the gate, then vaulted onto the seat and drove the wagon up to the house.

The dog trotted down to meet Slade, wagging its tail as its master hitched the team to the rail. Slade scratched the dog's ears, then made his way to the back of the wagon. Unhooking the tailgate, he put his arms around Carrie's waist and lifted her to the ground.

"I don't need your help," Morgan said, waving away Slade's hand.

"Suit yourself, son."

"I told you not to call me that."

A dark shadow flickered in Slade's eyes. "Yeah."

Gritting his teeth, Morgan scooted to the end of the wagon, then swung his legs over the side. For a moment he sat there, catching his breath as he tried to decide how he was going to get out of the wagon without losing hold of the blanket wrapped around his hips.

Carrie came to the rescue. She slid her arm around his waist, supporting him while he dropped to the ground.

Slade walked up the steps and opened the massive front door, his craggy face showing no emotion as he watched Carrie help Morgan up the stairs.

"Follow me," Slade said. He led them down a wide hall paneled in mahogany and into a large, sunlit bedroom. "I think you'll be comfortable in here."

"It's lovely," Carrie said. She helped Morgan get into bed.

"I'll send Margarita in with some hot water and towels. I reckon you'd both like to clean up a little. Dinner will be ready at six. You're welcome to join us, or I can have Marda fix you a tray if you'd rather eat in here."

"I think I'll eat in here if you don't mind," Carrie said.

Slade glanced at Morgan. "I understand. Make yourself at home."

"Thank you, Mr. Slade."

"It's nothing," Slade said quickly. He glanced at Morgan again, nodded at Carrie, and left the room.

"Nothing is right," Morgan muttered. "How the hell did he find me?"

"Doctor Aames sent him a message and told him about the reward posters. Your grandfather felt you'd be safer here than in town."

"Dammit, Carrie, I don't want to be here."

"You need to rest. The doctor said you're to stay in bed for at least two weeks, and that you weren't to ride for two more."

"I feel all right."

Carrie stared at him, not saying a word, but her silence was very loud.

"Okay, so I've felt better. But as soon as I can travel, we're getting out of here."

"If that's what you want."

"It is." His expression softened as he looked at her. "How are *you* feeling, Carrie?"

"Fine. A little tired. A little worried."

"About me?"

"Yes. I overheard the doctor talking to Mrs. Galway. He said that reward would probably draw a lot of attention from bounty hunters."

"I can take care of myself."

"I know, but..."

Morgan held out his hand and Carrie went to him. Sitting on the edge of the bed, she laid her head on his shoulder and closed her eyes. She was almost asleep when she heard a knock at the door.

"Come in," Carrie called, sitting up.

The door swung open and a small dark-haired woman entered carrying a pitcher of hot water and several large bath towels. She smiled at Morgan and Carrie, her full skirts swishing as she crossed the room and placed the pitcher and towels on the table beside the bed.

"Do you wish anything else, señora?"

"No, thank you."

"Señor Slade, he says to tell you that after you have washed up, you may help yourself to the clothes in the armoire. They belong to Señora Slade's sister."

"Thank you."

Margarita nodded. "Young Señor Slade will have new clothes waiting for him when he is able to get out of bed. Do you wish anything else?"

"No, thank you."

"Wait," Morgan called. "Bring me a bottle of Scotch."

"*Sí*, señor."

"No whiskey, Margarita," Carolyn said firmly. "Thank you for the towels."

Margarita glanced at Morgan, shrugged, and left the room.

"I want a drink, Carrie."

"I thought you didn't want anything from your grandfather."

"Just one drink."

"No."

Morgan grinned wryly. "All right, you win."

"Would you like a sponge bath?"

"Yes, ma'am."

It was the best bath he'd ever had. She soaped her hands and washed him from head to toe, lingering here and there, until the ache in his thigh and his desire for a drink to ease the pain were nothing but ashes compared to the fire that burned in his loins. She didn't resist when he reached for her and dragged her down on the bed beside him, his hand sliding under her skirt and petticoats to caress her thighs.

"No drawers?" he murmured as his hand moved higher.

"Mrs. Galway didn't have any extras."

"I'm glad. Makes everything so much easier . . ."

She was drowning in pleasure when Morgan withdrew his hand from her thigh. She felt his body tense and realized, to her embarrassment, that they were no longer alone in the room.

Cheeks flaming, she jerked her skirt down over her legs and glanced toward the door. A woman stood there, a frail gray-haired woman with skin as pale as alabaster and sad brown eyes.

The woman stared at Carolyn intently. "Lily?"

Carrie shook her head, her heart aching for the faint note of hope in the woman's voice. "I'm Carolyn. And this is my husband, Morgan."

The woman looked at Morgan, and the shadow of a smile lingered on her lips. "Lily's son. Harrison told me you'd come home. I'm your grandmother, Elizabeth." She moved toward the bed and drew Morgan's head to her breast, holding him close for a moment before she stepped back, her eyes searching his face. "Where's your mother? Where's my Lily?"

Morgan gazed up at his grandmother, then looked away. How could he tell this woman that her daughter had died in the back room of a brothel trying to rid herself of another unwanted child?

"Elizabeth! I told you not to come in here."

A muscle twitched in Morgan's jaw as he heard Harrison Slade's voice.

"Come along, Beth. Morgan needs to rest for a

few days. You can talk to him then."

"But I want to know about Lily. Please, Harrison, I've waited so long."

Harrison Slade looked at Morgan, his eyes asking the question he'd been too big a coward to put into words.

Slowly, Morgan shook his head.

"Let's go, Beth," Slade said heavily. "We'll talk about it in the morning."

"Where's Lily?" Elizabeth Slade cried. She clutched at Morgan's arm as tears rolled down her cheeks. "Where's my daughter? Is she all right? Why won't she come home?"

"We've got to go, Beth." Harrison pried her hand from Morgan's arm and led her out of the room. "We'll talk to him tomorrow, honey. He needs to rest now, and so do you."

Morgan stared after his grandparents, his thoughts chaotic. He yearned to hurt his grandfather, to tell him in vivid detail every lurid moment of Lily's life, to watch his face as he told him how Lily had died, bleeding to death as she cursed her own son. He wanted to hurt the man as he'd been hurt. But he felt only pity and compassion for the fragile woman who was his grandmother.

"Are you going to tell them about your mother?" Carrie asked. "The truth, I mean?"

"I don't know." Morgan put his arm around Carrie and drew her down beside him. "I'd like to see him burn in hell."

"But not her."

"No, not her."

Chapter 34

Harrison Slade rubbed his wife's back, his big, callused hands gentle as they moved across her shoulders. She submitted to his touch as she submitted to everything else, with cool detachment and a total lack of passion. He knew her gaze was fixed on the faded portrait of Lily that stood atop the dresser on the far wall. He could feel the tension in her shoulders and neck, feel the quiet hatred she'd carried for him all these years.

In public, she was gracious and polite, allowing him to take her arm, to escort her to church and other social affairs, but privately she rarely spoke to him. Privately, she was heartbroken and soul-sick, and nothing he'd done in the last twenty-eight years had been able to bridge the gulf between them, a gulf formed by one night of unbridled rage. And yet, he'd had a right to his anger.

Even now, after all these years, he couldn't forget how he'd felt the night Beth came in to tell him that Lily, his precious Lily, was pregnant, and that the father was the Navajo horse wrangler they called Jonnie because no one could pronounce his Indian name. Harrison had been younger then, with a temper as hot as the chili peppers that old Marda served. He'd flown into a rage, threatening to shoot Jonnie on the spot, and to send Lily to a convent where she could never shame him again. He'd never expected Lily to take him seriously. He'd loved her, cherished her. He'd dreamed of the day when she would marry. He'd looked forward to giving her the biggest wedding New Mexico had ever seen, along with a thousand acres of land. And then she'd turned up pregnant and his whole world had turned upside down. Lily had run away. And Beth had never forgiven him. But then, he'd never forgiven himself.

He stared at his hands resting on Beth's shoulders, big, capable hands that had never been raised against Lily in anger, hands that had cradled her, hands that had patted her back when she cried and swung her high in the air to make her laugh.

Beth shifted her weight on the bed. "Thank you, Harrison," she said, her tone one of dismissal, and he stood up so she could get under the covers. She let him kiss her cheek, and then she closed her eyes, shutting him out.

With a sigh, Slade left her bedroom and went into the parlor. It was a big room. A massive stone fireplace took up all of one wall.

Crossing the floor, he sank into his favorite chair. Hands braced on his knees, he stared into the fireplace, his thoughts filling with memories of his daughter. She'd been a pretty baby, a beautiful little girl, an enchanting young woman. Her hair had been long and black, her eyes brown, her skin like smooth cream. He'd been so proud of her.

A muscle worked in his jaw as he imagined her sneaking around to meet Jonnie, lying in his arms. Had she really expected him to react any differently? What father wouldn't have been shocked to learn his daughter was lifting her skirts for the hired help. If she'd only waited until his outrage passed, until his anger cooled, he would have forgiven her. He'd even have let her marry Jonnie if that was what she wanted, though the thought of a Navajo son-in-law would have been a bitter humiliation in a town where Indians were viewed with mistrust and disdain.

How many times in the last twenty-eight years had he reviled himself for the things he'd said, for yelling at her when he should have taken her in his arms? One brief fit of anger and he'd lost everything he held dear.

But his grandson was here now. Perhaps Morgan could tell him where Lily was. Perhaps there was still a chance to regain his wife's affection, to repair the damage he had done.

He thought of his grandson, his feelings ambivalent. The boy hated him. There was no doubt of that. But then, who could blame him.

Tomorrow he'd talk to Morgan, try to make him understand how it had been.

Tomorrow he'd try to explain his sense of betrayal, of outrage, of disappointment.

Tomorrow.

Chapter 35

Beth Slade opened the door and entered the room where Morgan and his wife lay sleeping. Her slippered feet made no sound as she crossed the room and stood beside the bed, looking down at her grandson. Lily's boy. How handsome he was! Tall and muscular, with hair as black as Lily's had been.

And skin the color of his father's. Jonnie had been a handsome young man, perhaps twenty years old, with smooth copper-hued skin, beautiful black eyes, and a smile that could break your heart. He'd been a quiet man, more at ease with horses than with people. She had grown fond of him in the few short years he had worked at the ranch. She'd been the one to convince Harrison to give him a chance. She regretted it now, of course, but how could she have foreseen what the future would hold? Who would have guessed that Lily would fall in love with Jonnie? Though Beth didn't share her husband's hatred of Indians, she had been astonished to discover that her daughter had fallen in love with the Navajo cowboy.

Beth stood there for a long while, gazing at Morgan, remembering the night Lily had told her she was pregnant, remembering how shocked she had been to think her little girl had let a man, any man, touch her "that way." But of course Lily hadn't been a little girl. She'd been sixteen and very mature for her age.

Perhaps, Beth thought, it had been her own fault her daughter had grown up so fast. But Lily had been such an intelligent child, walking and talking far earlier than other children. And she had matured so fast, changing overnight from a slender girl with coltish legs into an amply endowed young woman.

All the men from the surrounding ranches had come to call on her, courting her with flowers and candy, serenading her. Harrison had been so proud of Lily. She could have had her pick of any of a dozen young men from well-to-do families. Who'd have thought she'd fall in love with Jonnie, that she'd let him get her with child?

Beth would never forget the night Lily had told her she was pregnant. Lily hadn't meant to confide in her mother, of course, but once she started, the words had poured out of her like water. Jonnie was waiting for her in the barn, she'd said, and they were going to face Harrison together and ask for his permission to get married. Beth had talked Lily out of that notion, certain it would be better if she and Lily confronted Harrison alone. She had never forgotten how Harrison had reacted. He'd flown into a rage, screaming at Lily, saying terrible things, making awful threats. Beth had been afraid of her husband for the first time in her life, afraid he might actually send Lily away, afraid he'd kill Jonnie with his bare hands.

When she realized Harrison wasn't going to listen to reason, she sent Lily to bed and bore the brunt of Harrison's wrath alone. In the morning she'd been horrified to learn that Harrison had sent a couple of his men to beat Jonnie, and even more distressed to learn that he had lied to Lily and told her that Jonnie had run away rather than marry her. And the next night, Lily was gone. At first, Harrison thought Lily had found out what had happened to Jonnie. They'd hoped she had gone after her lover. Harrison had tracked Jonnie down without much trouble, but the boy hadn't seen Lily and didn't know where she'd gone.

They'd spent five long years looking for Lily, but to no avail.

Beth smiled as Morgan stirred and then opened his eyes. "Good morning, son," she said, her voice warm with affection.

Morgan stared at Elizabeth for a moment, startled to find her standing at his bedside. "Morning ...ma'am."

"So formal. Couldn't you call me Grandmother?"

"If you like."

"How are you feeling?"

"Better." He gazed up at her, looking for a resemblance between his mother and his grandmother, but there was none. Lily had taken after Harrison, just as he did.

Unable to keep from touching him, Elizabeth laid a hand on Morgan's shoulder. "Are you hungry? Breakfast will be ready soon."

"Yeah, thanks." He wished she wouldn't keep staring at him like that, her dark brown eyes filled with adoration. It made him uncomfortable because he was afraid he couldn't measure up to what she was expecting from him, but, worse than that, he was afraid of hurting her.

She smiled at him, then glanced at Carolyn, who was still sleeping soundly. "She's lovely. Have you been married long?"

"No. Just a few months. We're expecting a baby."

"A baby!" Beth clasped her hands to her breast, her eyes glowing with delight. "Oh, to have a baby in the house again."

"I don't think we'll still be here when the baby's born."

"You can't leave, not now! Please, Morgan, you can't go, not until I've seen my great-grandchild."

Carolyn was awake now and Beth sent an imploring look in her direction. "Please, make him stay."

"It isn't up to my wife," Morgan said, and then, seeing the light fade in Beth Slade's eyes, he relented. "We'll talk about it later, all right?"

Beth nodded. Drawing the rocker up to the bed, she sat down, her hands folded in her lap. "Tell me about my daughter," she said, her gaze focused on Morgan's face. "Tell me about Lily. Is she all right?"

"I'm sorry, Grandmother," Morgan said as gently as he could. "Lily passed on about five years ago."

Beth Slade nodded. "I knew it," she murmured. "I guess I knew it all along. Did she have a good life? Was she happy?"

Morgan felt Carrie's hand on his arm, felt his insides knot up as he thought of telling this gentle woman the truth about her only child, and knew he couldn't do it. He would tell her a lie, tell her what she wanted to hear, because he couldn't bear to tell her anything else.

"Yeah. She married a fine man name of Flint. He was good to her, gave her everything she ever wanted."

Beth smiled. "And was he good to you?"

Morgan nodded. "He treated me like I was his own son."

"How did my Lily . . . was she sick? Did she suffer?"

"No, ma'am. She passed on in her sleep, real peaceful."

"Is he still alive, her husband?"

"I don't know. I left home after Lily passed on. I sort of lost touch with Flint."

"And she never had any other children?"

A muscle worked in Morgan's jaw. "No." Glancing up, he saw Harrison Slade standing in the doorway. There was a faint look of hope in Slade's eyes, and Morgan knew the old man wanted to believe every word he'd heard. But there were doubts lingering behind Slade's gray eyes, too, doubts and an ever-present weight of guilt.

Beth leaned forward and took Morgan's hand in hers. "Thank you, dear. You've taken a load from my mind and my heart." She gave his hand a squeeze, then stood up. "I'll have Margarita bring your breakfast in as soon as it's ready."

Beth left the room, and Harrison followed her.

Rising, Carolyn closed the door. "That was kind of you," she said. "The truth would have broken her heart."

"I couldn't hurt her." He ran a hand through his hair, then swung his legs over the side of the bed and sat up. "I can't stay here, Carrie. Every time I look at that old man, I want to kill him."

"You're in no condition to travel. Doctor Aames said you shouldn't ride for another month. You shouldn't even be getting out of bed."

"I've laid around long enough. If I don't get out of this room, I'll go crazy."

There was no arguing with him. Carrie went to the wardrobe and opened the door. Inside were a dozen shirts, a dozen pairs of trousers, several belts, two Stetsons, one black, one gray, and a pair of boots.

"Dammit, I told that old man I didn't want anything from him," Morgan muttered as Carrie tossed a pair of black trousers and a wine-red shirt on the bed.

"Well, I suppose you could wear what's left of that Army uniform," Carrie replied, pulling a pair of socks from the dresser drawer, "or perhaps you could just parade around in your clout and moccasins." She smiled at him serenely.

Ten minutes later, he was dressed and limping out the door. Carrie hurried after him, offering him her shoulder to lean on.

They found Harrison and Beth seated at a long table laid with linen and silver.

"Morgan, Carolyn, I'm so pleased you could join us," Beth said. "Come, sit here by me."

Beth kept up a constant stream of chatter through breakfast, making plans for the baby, promising to let Carolyn use one of the spare bedrooms for a nursery, assuring her she could redecorate it any way she pleased.

Morgan said little. Though he refused to look at his grandfather, he was aware of Harrison Slade's eyes watching him, judging him.

After breakfast, Beth took Carrie on a tour of the house. Morgan declined to go. He needed to get out of the house, to be alone. He knew how much his grandmother wanted him to stay, and it was mighty tempting. They'd be safe here. Carrie would be well cared for.

He walked slowly toward a shallow stream bordered by a stand of timber and sat down, favoring his wounded leg. Leaning back against one of the trees, he closed his eyes.

He was almost asleep when he heard footsteps. "What do you want, old man?" Morgan asked curtly.

"The truth. I want to know about Lily."

"You heard what I told Beth."

"I heard it. Now I want the truth."

"No, you don't."

Slade hunkered down on his heels, his gaze level with Morgan's. "Dammit, boy, she was my daughter! I've got a right to know what happened to her."

"You've got no rights at all. She deserved better than you gave her."

"I know that! Don't you think I know that? Don't you think I've spent every day of the last twenty-eight years wishing I'd done things differently?"

Slade raked both hands through his hair. His eyes were filled with a deep inner torment, his voice cracking with pain as he said, "I loved her. I never meant to hurt her. You've got to believe that. I spent five years looking for her, night and day." Slade let out a long sigh. "I haven't had a moment's peace since the night she ran away."

"If you're looking for sympathy, go somewhere else. I've got none to give."

"I'm not looking for sympathy," Slade retorted angrily. "I'm looking for the truth."

"You want the truth? The truth is, she died in the back room of a whorehouse. Is that what you want to hear?"

All the color drained from Harrison Slade's face. "No." He shook his head, his face dark with anguish. "No."

"Yes. She died in my arms, cursing the day I was born. She blamed me for everything, old man. She said it was my fault Jonnie left her, my fault you'd turned on her, my fault for the way she had to live." Morgan laughed bitterly. "She never blamed you. Not once."

Harrison Slade rose slowly to his feet. "I'm

sorry, Morgan. I wish there was something I could do, something I could say, to make it up to you."

Slade stared into the water, and Morgan thought the man looked as if he'd aged ten years in the last ten minutes.

"I wish you and your wife would stay on," Slade said. "It would mean a lot to Beth to have you here." *And it would mean a lot to me.* The words hung, unspoken, in the air between them.

Morgan looked at his grandfather's profile and felt a sudden wave of unwanted sympathy for the old man, and with it, a rush of guilt. What purpose had it served to tell his grandfather the truth? Nothing had changed. Lily was still dead, and there was still a Wanted poster with his name on it.

"I'll beg, if that's what you want," Slade said. "If that's not enough, I'll give you the deed to the Double S. It'll be yours when I'm gone anyway."

"I don't want it," Morgan said quickly. "I don't want anything from you. I never did."

"It's yours," Slade insisted. He swung around to face Morgan. "I changed my will the day Lucius told me you were here. I got no other kin."

Morgan struggled to his feet. "Dammit, old man, you can't buy me."

"I'm not trying to buy you, son. If you don't want the ranch, you can sell it, or burn it to the ground. It's yours whether you stay or not, but I'm asking you again to stay, for Beth's sake. She's happy with you here. She hasn't been happy in a long time."

Morgan clenched his hands into tight fists. He wanted to smash something, hit something until his hands hurt and the rage had been burned out of him, but he couldn't hit the old man. Hell, he couldn't even hate him anymore.

Slade saw the hesitation in his grandson's eyes and played his ace in the hole. "If you won't consider staying for your grandmother's sake, you might give some thought to your wife's well-being. I know there's a flyer out on you. I won't ask you why, that's your business, but ten thousand dollars is a lot of money. It's sure to draw every bounty hunter west of the Missouri."

Morgan glared at his grandfather. The man was right on all counts, but he didn't have to like it. "I'll stay," Morgan said curtly. "Until the baby's born. And then I'm leaving."

Harrison Slade nodded. He'd won, if only temporarily, but he had the good grace not to gloat. "You won't be sorry."

"Hell," Morgan muttered as he turned away and started toward the house. "I'm already sorry."

Chapter 36

Morgan and his grandfather reached an uneasy truce in the days that followed. They took their meals together in the dining room, spoke when necessary, and avoided each other as much as possible the rest of the time.

In spite of the way Morgan felt about his grandfather, Carolyn and Beth quickly became friends. For Carrie, Beth was the mother she'd lost, the mother she'd longed for. It was good to have another woman to confide in, someone she could talk to about her fears of childbirth, her doubts about her ability to be a good mother. Beth understood. She sympathized with Carrie's fears, assuring her that childbirth was normal and natural and that, while it was indeed painful and strenuous, it was worth every minute of it to hold a new life in your arms.

In the days that followed, Beth's whole attitude and demeanor changed. She doted on Carrie, making sure she had enough to eat and plenty of rest.

She took her into Cheyenne and bought her a whole new wardrobe, dresses and hats and shoes, parasols and gloves, lace-trimmed petticoats and nightgowns. They bought yards and yards of soft muslin and spent a part of each afternoon sewing things for the baby.

On Sundays, Beth and Harrison went to church. They tried to get Morgan to go, but he refused. He had never been to church in his life, and saw no need to start now. He did, however, insist that Carrie go along with them. They'd never talked much about religion, but he knew somehow that attending church was important to Carrie, that she found strength and comfort there.

They'd been at the ranch almost four weeks the day Lucius Aames came to call. He'd been by on several occasions to check on Morgan, but this wasn't a professional call. He'd come to warn Morgan that the Wanted posters were creating a stir in Cheyenne.

"Of course no one knows for sure you were ever there, except for Martha Galway, and she won't say anything." Lucius shook his head. "But you don't have to be a college professor to look at that flyer and see the resemblance between you and Harry. Sooner or later, people will wonder if you're related. I wouldn't advise you to go into town any time soon."

"I won't," Morgan said. "Thanks, doc."

Aames made a gesture of dismissal with his hand. "Now that I've said what I came to say, I'd like to have a look at your missus."

"Something wrong?"

"No, no, I just thought I'd examine her while I'm here. Nothing to worry about."

Thirty minutes later, Aames declared Carolyn to be in excellent condition. The baby was due in late February, and the doctor advised her not to do any heavy lifting, not to ride, and to take a nap every afternoon.

"Well," Lucius said, swinging into the saddle, "give my regards to Beth and Harry. I'm sorry I missed them."

"They'll be sorry they missed you," Carolyn replied. She smiled at the doctor, then stared down the road. "That looks like Beth's carriage coming now."

"Yeah," Morgan muttered. "She's driving like the devil's at her heels."

Lucius Aames vaulted to the ground as the carriage came thundering up to the front of the house.

"Oh, doc, thank God you're here!" Beth called as she reined the team to a halt. "It's Harrison! He's unconscious."

"Help me get him into the house," Aames said, and Morgan helped the doctor lift Slade from the carriage and carry him into the big bedroom at the end of the hall.

Beth turned down the covers, then hovered nearby while Aames examined her husband.

Morgan and Carrie waited in the hallway. The minutes passed like hours, but finally Lucius Aames left the bedroom, closing the door behind him.

"It's his heart," the doctor said. "He's had a bad attack. I've been warning him for years to slow down, but he's a hardheaded cuss and wouldn't listen." Aames shook his head ruefully. "By golly, he'll listen to me this time, or he'll be singing with the angels."

"How's Beth?" Carolyn asked.

"She's fine. I expected her to go to pieces on me, but she's doing just fine. I left some medication for Harry. What he needs now is rest and lots of it. He won't make a good patient, and the minute he feels better, he's gonna want to get up. Don't let him out of that bed for anything."

Carrie nodded. "We'll take care of him."

"I know you will," Lucius said. He fixed his gaze on Morgan. "You know anything about running a cattle ranch?"

"No."

"Maybe it's time you learned."

"I don't intend to be around that long."

"Maybe, maybe not. But Harry's gonna need someone to look after the place until he gets back on his feet."

"He's got a foreman."

Aames nodded. "That's right, and Yates is a good man, but he's just help. And he's shorthanded right now. One of his men quit about a month ago, and another one's laid up with a broken leg."

Morgan swore under his breath. He had the feeling that fate was conspiring against him, backing him into a corner, and he didn't like it.

"Maybe you don't think you can handle it," Lucius remarked candidly. "Maybe you're not man enough to fill the old man's shoes."

"I can handle it," Morgan snapped. "Don't

worry about the ranch. You just get that old man back on his feet as soon as you can."

"I'll do my best," Lucius promised, and then he let out a long sigh. "I've known Harrison Slade since he came to Cheyenne. He's a good man, a strong man, but I don't know if he's gonna come out of this. If he doesn't, Beth's gonna need somebody to take care of her."

"I'll look out for her," Morgan said. "You don't have to worry about that."

It was touch and go for the next few days. Harrison Slade slipped in and out of consciousness, sometimes calling for Beth, sometimes calling for Lily. Beth stayed at her husband's side, refusing to leave him, begging him to get well, begging him to forgive her for the way she had treated him, vowing that she loved him, had always loved him.

It tore at Carrie's heart, listening to Beth's heart-rending sobs. How awful to have wasted twenty-eight years blaming your husband for something that couldn't be changed, only to realize, perhaps too late, that you had been wrong.

She could understand Harrison's outrage when he'd found out what Lily had done. She could understand Beth's hurt when Lily left home and her initial anger with Harrison. She could readily understand what had driven Lily away. But she could not understand how two people who obviously loved each other could have lived together for twenty-eight years, both of them too proud, and too stubborn, to say I'm sorry.

When she mentioned it to Morgan, he just shrugged.

"Don't get involved with their problems, Carrie," he warned. "We're only staying here until the baby's born, and then we're leaving."

But Carrie didn't want to leave. She liked it on the Double S. She liked Harrison; she loved Beth. But she didn't tell Morgan that. Hopefully, as time passed, his feelings for his grandfather would change. Until then, she'd bide her time and try to make him as happy as possible.

Lucius Aames came out to check on Harrison every day, and at the end of three weeks, he declared his patient was out of danger and allowed that he could get up for a short time each afternoon, gradually extending his time out of bed. But he wasn't to do any work of any kind until he had the doctor's approval, and he wasn't to get upset over anything.

"Over anything," Lucius repeated. "Understand, Harry?"

Harrison Slade's gaze rested on his grandson's face for several moments before he said, "Yeah, Lucius, I understand."

"Good. I'll be back to check on you in a couple of days." Aames took Beth's hand in his and smiled at her. "He's gonna be fine, Elizabeth. Stop worrying and get some rest, or I'll be coming out here to check on *you*."

"I'm fine, Lucius."

"I know. See that you stay that way." Lucius shook hands with Morgan and gave Carrie a hug, then picked up his black bag and left the house, whistling softly.

Harrison Slade scowled at the three people standing around his bed. "Well, are you gonna stare at me all day, or help me out of bed?"

"Do you think you should get up?" Beth asked.

"Aames said it was all right," Harrison snapped. "If I have to lie here much longer I'll go crazy."

"He's well enough," Carolyn said, grinning. "Morgan, help him up while Beth and I go fix him a place on the sofa."

Before Morgan could object, the two women grabbed the pillows and an extra blanket from the bed and left the room.

"C'mon, old man," Morgan said, and taking his grandfather's arm, he helped him to his feet and down the hall into the parlor.

Harrison was smiling as he settled himself on the long black leather sofa. "For a while there, I was afraid I'd never see this room again."

"You're going to be fine, Harrison," Beth assured him. She sat on the edge of the sofa and took his hand in hers. "You heard what Lucius said."

"I know, but I don't mind telling you I was damn scared. I was afraid I might not live to see my great-grandchild. Afraid I'd never see you smiling at me again."

"Oh, Harrison, can you ever forgive me for the way I've treated you?"

"Beth, Beth, there's nothing to forgive."

Harrison put his arms around Elizabeth and they held each other close.

Carolyn took Morgan by the hand and gave it a

tug. "Come on," she whispered. "Let's leave them alone."

Morgan nodded. He didn't want to get involved in the lives of his grandparents. He'd carried his hate too long to let it be swept away by one touching scene of reconciliation. Nothing had changed. He'd still been born on the wrong side of the blanket, and his mother was still dead.

And it was all Harrison Slade's fault.

Chapter 37

Morgan hadn't realized what he was getting into when he agreed to help out on the ranch. The morning after the doctor pronounced his grandfather out of danger, Morgan went in search of Yates.

He found the Double S foreman doctoring a cut on the hind leg of a bawling red and white calf. R.J. Yates was whipcord lean, tough as horsehide. His skin, as brown as a walnut, was lined by years of squinting into the sun. He looked exactly the way Easterners expected cowboys to look, from his high-crowned black Stetson to his high-heeled boots. His hair was gray, his eyes blue and penetrating. Morgan knew instinctively that Yates was a man to ride the river with.

When he finished with the calf, Yates wiped his hands on his Levi's. Rising to his feet, he acknowledged Morgan's presence with a curt nod.

"You'd be the old man's grandson, I reckon," Yates remarked.

Morgan nodded. "I'll be handling things for Slade until he's back on his feet."

Yates assessed Morgan in a quick glance. He heard the underlying resentment in Morgan's voice and wondered why there was bad blood between the boss and his grandson. But he didn't dwell on it. His business was running the ranch, nothing more. "You know anything about cattle?"

"Not a damn thing. That's why I came looking for you."

Yates grunted softly and launched into a quick and concise rundown of the Double S, his voice edged with pride.

It was a big spread, over ten thousand acres, more like a small community than a ranch. Besides the main house, there were two bunkhouses and a cook shack where the men took their meals. A small blacksmith shop was located behind the smokehouse. There was a barn big enough to hold a dozen horses and several tons of hay. In addition, there were a half-dozen holding pens, a tack room, a root cellar, and a couple of small sheds.

"So," Yates said, eying Morgan speculatively. "Exactly what are you planning to do?"

"I'm not taking over your job, if that's what's worrying you," Morgan assured him. "Just put me to work."

"You ever worked cattle?"

"No."

"Well, there ain't much time to teach you, what with winter coming on. I suppose you can fill Early's place."

"Fine."

"Maybe you shouldn't agree quite so fast. Early was the last man to hire on, so most of the dirty jobs fell to him."

Morgan raised one brow. "Like what?"

"Mucking the stalls. Currying the horses. Chopping the wood, stuff like that."

"That doesn't sound like the kind of thing cowboys generally take care of."

"Early wasn't a cowboy, just a drifter looking for work."

"He didn't break his leg mucking stalls."

"No. He was patching a hole in the roof of the main house, and he fell off." Yates shoved his hat back on his head and regarded Morgan thoughtfully. "You don't have to do it. I can always pull one of the hands in off the range. You're the boss's grandson. That should be good for something."

"I'll do it," Morgan said curtly. He didn't want any favors from Yates, or from the old man.

"You'll find a shovel and a wheelbarrow in the shed alongside the barn."

"Right. Did anybody fix the roof?"

"Not yet."

"I'll take care of it."

Mucking stalls didn't turn out to be as bad as he thought it would be. The barn smelled of hay and horses, of neatsfoot oil and leather. And manure. Surprisingly, he enjoyed the work, though he thought it was rather amazing the amount of manure that one horse could produce out of a few pounds of fragrant hay. But he didn't mind the work, and he liked being around the horses.

And it gave him time to think. Cleaning the stalls, currying the horses, he couldn't help remembering that his grandfather had said the ranch would be his. But did he want it? Maybe he couldn't handle it, maybe he'd never be anything more than what he was. Maybe marrying Carrie had been a mistake.

He shook his head as he scooped up a shovelful of fresh manure and dumped it in the wheelbarrow. Marrying Carrie hadn't been a mistake; hell, it was the smartest thing he'd ever done.

But he had to admit that the responsibility of caring for her and the baby scared him right down to his socks. He'd never had to look out for anyone but himself, never had to worry about what other people thought of him because he'd never given a damn. But Carrie had changed all that, just as she'd changed everything else.

He looked up at the sound of footsteps, and grinned as he saw her picking her way toward him.

"Something wrong?" He left the rake in the stall and stepped out to meet her.

"No, I just wanted to see you." She grinned back at him. He'd removed his shirt, and his chest was covered with sweat and dust and bits of straw.

Morgan held out his arms and shrugged. "Well, do you like what you see?"

"Oh, yes," she said, wrinkling her nose as he walked toward her. "But not what I smell."

"Sorry." Bending, he kissed the tip of her nose. "Seven down, only five to go."

"Do you like doing this?"

"Strangely enough, I do."

"But you still don't want to stay?"

"No."

She'd known what his answer would be, but she was disappointed just the same. Daily, she was more aware of the child growing under her heart, of the need to have a place of her own, a home of her own. She felt a fierce protectiveness for her unborn child, a driving need to put down roots, to know there was a place where she belonged.

She folded her hands over her belly and took a deep breath before she asked, "What do you want to do?"

"I don't know."

"We need to decide where we're going to live after the baby's born. One of us will have to get a job."

"I know that, Carrie. Don't you think I know that?"

"Please, Morgan, don't be angry. But I need to know what the future holds. We haven't talked about it. I want a home of my own some day, and security for our child."

He raked a hand through his hair, angry with himself, and with her, and angry because of it. Carrie was right. It was time he gave some serious thought to the future. They couldn't just drift from town to town dragging a baby behind them. And he couldn't go back to Galveston and expect Carrie to live in that shack behind the Grotto. He'd have to get a job, save some money, find a decent place for them to live.

And it was all here for the taking, everything he

needed to provide for Carrie and their child, everything Carrie wanted.

And that made him more angry than anything else.

"Lunch is ready when you are," Carrie said.

"Carrie . . ."

"I love you, Morgan. I'll go wherever you want."

He swore under his breath as he brushed the dirt from his chest, then pulled Carrie into his arms. He had intended to kiss her gently, to tell her he loved her more than life itself, that he wouldn't let her down, but she felt so good in his arms, and her lips were so soft, so inviting, that he swung her into his arms and carried her into one of the stalls and there, on a pile of sweet-smelling straw, he made love to her, drowning in her sweetness, in the husky sound of her voice as she whispered his name, declaring that she loved him, would always love him, that she'd follow him wherever he wanted to go.

And that was his undoing. She was so willing to do what he wanted, go where he wanted, how could he do less? He didn't say the words aloud. He refused to even let them form in the back of his mind, but he knew then and there that he couldn't ask Carrie to leave the Double S, that he'd stay here as long as she wanted, even if it meant spending the rest of his life with his grandfather.

Morgan was cutting firewood the day that two of the cowhands brought in a big paint stallion. It was obvious the horse wasn't a mustang. It was too tall, its head too finely shaped, and its legs too long to be a range-bred horse. But it was as wild as a Wyoming winter.

Morgan took one look at the animal and decided to keep it. The paint had beautiful conformation; it stood close to sixteen hands high, and had a long black mane and tail.

He judged it to be about three years old, and the first time he tried to throw a saddle over its back, he knew it had never been ridden.

He worked the horse first thing in the morning, and again later in the afternoon after he'd cleaned the stalls and curried the other horses. There were a lot of ways to break a bronc. One method was to blindfold the horse, throw a saddle on, and ride out the storm. But Morgan didn't care much for that. Too often, the horse's spirit was broken. He wanted to win the stallion's trust, and so he took his time, offering the horse a carrot or an apple, gentling the animal to the sound of his voice, the touch of his hand. He tied the horse to a snubbing post and let it learn for itself that it could fight the rope but it couldn't win. Later, he took a light-weight blanket and rubbed it over the horse. Starting at the stallion's neck, he drew the blanket over its back, under its belly, and down its legs until the horse realized there was nothing to be afraid of. The saddle came next. He put it in place and cinched it loosely, gradually snugging the girth tighter and tighter until the stallion accepted the saddle's weight without complaint.

And then came the hard part.

It was on a cold gray morning when Morgan stepped into the saddle for the first time. He expected the stallion to buck, and he wasn't disappointed. The horse exploded beneath him like ten pounds of dynamite, bucking and rearing for all it was worth for about twenty minutes.

It was the wildest ride of Morgan's life. When it was over, he was surprised he was still in the saddle.

Dismounting, he offered the stallion a carrot, scratched the horse behind its ears, then stepped into the saddle again. But the horse just stood there, ears flicking back and forth, and Morgan knew he'd won the battle, if not the war.

His grandfather was at the dinner table that night. Beth had dressed with care, and the cook had prepared all Harrison's favorite foods in honor of his recovery. Morgan was surprised the table didn't collapse under the weight as Marda piled on platters of roast beef and fried chicken, mashed potatoes, corn on the cob, green beans, fresh-baked biscuits and cornbread.

"There's enough food here to feed an army," Harrison remarked.

"She's just glad you're feeling better," Beth said, smiling. "We all are."

Harrison glanced at Morgan and felt a keen disappointment. Not everyone was glad he had recovered, he mused bleakly.

"So tell me," Carrie said brightly, "how's the stallion coming along?"

"Stallion?" Harrison said. "What stallion?"

Carrie started to answer, but Harrison was looking at Morgan.

"A couple of the hands brought a big paint stud

371

in off the range. I've been breaking him."

Harrison shook his head. "I've got no use for those range-bred broomtails."

"He's not a mustang," Morgan replied curtly.

"He looks like a thoroughbred, Harrison," Beth said, laying her hand over her husband's arm, "and he's a beauty, Wait until you see him."

"How's he working out?" Slade asked gruffly.

"Fine," Morgan replied. "I rode him for the first time this morning."

"And?"

"He bucked like a rodeo bronc."

Harrison grunted. "I wouldn't give you two bits for one that didn't."

Morgan nodded. On that, at least, they agreed. "Has Yates started moving the cattle in from the south range?"

"Yeah."

"Any losses?"

"Fifteen, maybe twenty head."

Harrison nodded. That was to be expected, what with wolves and Indians always on the prowl.

There was silence for a few minutes as they filled their plates. Carrie ate ravenously, then blushed under Morgan's amused grin. Lately it seemed she was always hungry. She'd even taken to raiding the pantry in the middle of the night, sometimes craving something sweet, sometimes craving foods she didn't even like.

"If you keep eating like that, you'll be round as a watermelon," Morgan remarked.

"She's eating for two now," Beth reminded him. "Leave her alone."

"She's eating enough for two, all right. Two horses."

Carrie stuck her tongue out at him as she reached for another biscuit.

Harrison sat back in his chair, his gaze on Carrie, his expression wistful. Would it have been like this with Lily if he hadn't acted like a damned fool? He'd missed his chance to share in his daughter's life, and he had no one to blame but himself. It was good to hear laughter at the dinner table again, to see the love in Carolyn's eyes when she looked at Morgan, to see Beth smile with pleasure.

Furtively, he watched Morgan. What would it take to win his grandson's affection? How could he persuade Morgan to stay on after the baby was born?

After dinner, Harrison and Beth went into the parlor, but Morgan took Carrie by the hand and led her outside where he drew her into his arms and held her close, drawing her length against his. He grinned as he felt the gentle swell of her abdomen. It was hard to believe there was a baby growing there.

Tilting her face up, he gazed into her eyes, marveling that she could create a new life, that she was happy to be carrying his child.

He wished he could tell her what it meant to him, but the words sounded silly. How could he tell her she'd given him all the things he'd ever longed for? The funny thing was, until Carrie came into his life, he hadn't even known he wanted a home or a family. He hadn't realized how unhappy he'd been, living in that tar paper shack, working for Danny at the Grotto, taking his pleasure in tawdry rooms. Then Carrie had come along and given him a reason for living, and he knew he'd live and die for her. But he didn't think he could give her the one thing she really wanted, and that was to stay here on the Double S.

"What is it?" Carrie asked. Lifting her hand, she let her fingertips caress his cheek. "Is something wrong?"

"No. I . . ." He shrugged and then, unable to say the words he wanted to say, kissed her instead.

Carrie moaned softly and pressed herself against him at the first touch of his lips on hers. What sweet magic did he possess that he had only to touch her to bring all her senses to life? A little spark warmed her belly as his hands slid down her ribcage, a small flame wrapped around her heart as he whispered he loved her, a tiny inferno began to blaze deep in the core of her being as his kiss deepened and his hands found her breasts.

"Carrie . . ." His tongue dipped into her mouth, tasting butter and honey. He drew in a deep breath, and his nostrils filled with the scent of freshly washed hair and the faint fragrance of rose-water. His hands moved over her breasts, and his body responded instantly to the touch of sweet womanly flesh. Her eyes, as deep and green as a high mountain lake, were brimming with love and desire as he swept her into his arms and carried her away from the ranch, not stopping until he came to a small pond awash in moonlight.

Putting her on her feet, he cupped her cheek in his palm, his fingers threading through the hair at her temple, his thumb teasing the corner of her lips, until she turned her face into his hand and slid her tongue over his palm.

"Carrie, Carrie," he murmured, "do you know what you do to me?"

"Show me," she whispered.

Slowly, reverently, he undressed her, his eyes as warm as a midnight fire as he placed his hand over the gentle mound of her belly, then bent to kiss the place that cradled his child. He had never loved her more, he thought, or desired her as much.

When he started to undress, she stopped him and then slowly began to unbutton his shirt. He was trembling with eagerness by the time she'd removed his trousers. Too late, he realized how cold the grass would be for her. To spare her, he rolled her on top of him, smiling at her bemused expression. Her hair fell over her shoulders like a dark curtain, and her eyes were luminous in the moonlight as she leaned toward him, the tips of her breasts brushing against his chest. She kissed him and caressed him, making love to him with such ardor that he never felt the cold at all.

Chapter 38

Lou Kylie sat back in his chair, one hand curled around a glass of good Kentucky whiskey. The saloon was full at this time of night; the bar was crowded with cowboys, drifters, and easy women. A couple of businessmen sat at a far table playing penny-ante poker.

But it was the cowboy standing alone at the end of the bar who held Kylie's attention. He was a tall young man wearing stovepipe chaps and a Texas hat. His face was clean-shaven, innocent, except for his eyes. They were as cold as a Montana winter. His clothes were well-worn, his boots run down at the heel. He looked like a man down on his luck, a man in need of a little hard cash.

Kylie nodded to himself. Here was the man he needed to carry out his plan. He wanted revenge, and he wouldn't rest until his brother had been avenged. There were some who allowed that the fight between Morgan and Jim had been fair, that Morgan had killed Jim in self-defense, but Lou refused to believe it. Jim was all the family he'd had in the world, and now Jim was gone and Lou was alone. He didn't like being alone.

Kylie smiled to himself. Most folks thought he was a little crazy, and maybe he was. But he was certain there was a connection between the drifter he'd known simply as Morgan and the territory's wealthiest rancher, Harrison Slade. He couldn't just ride onto the Slade place and gun Morgan down though. First he had to find someone who could go to the Double S and determine whether Morgan was there. Once his whereabouts had been established, there might be a way to make Morgan come to him.

Kylie stood up and walked toward the tall cowboy, hoping the bankroll in his back pocket would be enough to buy the information he needed.

Chapter 39

Yates had hired on a new man. Morgan met him for the first time on a cool Saturday morning when he went out to the barn to check on the paint stallion.

The newcomer had a mild face, dark brown hair, and eyes as cold as any Morgan had ever seen. He wore a dark blue cotton shirt, faded Levi's, stovepipe chaps, a big Texas hat with a snakeskin band, and boots that were run down at the heel. He introduced himself as Brody.

"Been here long?" Morgan asked.

"Just a couple of days."

"Where'd you work last?"

"The Bar J over in Montana."

Morgan saw a lot of Brody in the following week. It seemed like every time he went into the barn, the cowboy was there. He always had a good reason: his horse had thrown a shoe, he was picking up a load of hay for Yates, he'd been sent to ask Slade about moving the cattle down from the north range. But there was something about Brody that set Morgan's teeth on edge.

He was thinking about Brody the next day while he curried the stallion. Maybe he was being overly cautious, but it occurred to him it might be a good idea to send a wire to the Bar J and see what they had to say about Brody. A man with a ten-thousand-dollar reward on his head couldn't be too careful. Like most Western men, Brody was pretty close-mouthed about his past. It could be just his way, and it could be he was hiding something.

Morgan let out a sigh as he smoothed a blanket over the stud's back, then swung the saddle in place. Hell, he could understand a man wanting to keep his past quiet. His own was nothing to brag about. But checking on Brody seemed like a smart move. He'd have Yates send one of the men into town tomorrow. He rolled his slicker into a tight cylinder and tied it behind the cantle, checked to make sure his canteen was full, then stuffed a couple tins of meat and peaches into his saddlebags along with a dozen strips of jerky.

Stepping into the saddle, he reined the horse out of the yard. Yates had told him to ride out and see how far south the cattle had drifted. It would take a day, maybe two.

Morgan grinned wryly, remembering how Carolyn had teased him the first time Yates had sent him out on the range, saying he was being promoted from stable boy to cowhand.

She was quite a woman, his wife. He hadn't told her yet that he intended to stay on at the Double

S. Hell, he hadn't told anyone because, once he put the thought into words, there'd be no going back. Once he told Carrie they were staying, he'd have to stay. But he wasn't ready to commit himself yet. Coward that he was, he wanted to make sure he could still ride out if he changed his mind before the baby was born...

Morgan shook his head. Who was he trying to kid. He wasn't going anywhere. Lily's grandchild deserved to grow up here, to have the kind of life that Lily should have had. Hell, maybe he deserved it himself.

He urged the stud into a trot, admitting for the first time that he was happy at the Double S. The main cause of his happiness was Carrie. She'd gone into town with Beth to look for curtain material and to pick up the mail, and he smiled as he imagined her wandering from store to store, buying yarn and bunting, laughing with Beth as they planned for the baby. He smiled some himself as he thought of the child that would be born. A son that he could teach to ride and hunt and fish. Or a daughter with Carrie's beautiful green eyes...

He gigged the stallion into a lope. The sooner he checked on those cattle, the sooner he could go home, to Carrie.

Carolyn stood in the back of the dry goods store, trying to decide whether to do the baby's room in pink or blue, or maybe yellow. She knew it was a waste of time and money to decorate a bedroom for the baby. Once the child was born, they'd be leaving the ranch. But Beth had insisted on converting one of the bedrooms into a nursery, arguing that it would be at least a week or two after the baby was born before Carrie would feel like traveling, and the baby would need a room of its own until then. Carolyn had expected Morgan to argue that the baby didn't need a room of its own, that they didn't need anything from Harrison, but he'd been strangely silent on the matter.

Carrie smiled as she ran her hand over a length of light blue fabric. She supposed he'd held his tongue because he loved his grandmother. Morgan tried not to show it, but it was something he couldn't hide, not completely. The only thing he continued to refuse Beth was the one thing she wanted most—for Morgan and Carrie to stay on at the ranch.

Carrie had resigned herself to the fact that they'd have to leave once the baby was born. She knew it irked Morgan to be there. Even though he worked hard, cleaning the barn, repairing the corrals, patching the roof, looking after the horses, and doing the hundred other things that needed to be done to keep the ranch in good repair, he felt beholden to his grandfather for the food they ate and the roof over their head. She knew it galled him, being forced to remain on the ranch against his will. He couldn't even ride into town with her because there were still a couple of bounty hunters hanging out in Cheyenne on the off chance that he might show up.

Leaving the yard goods store, Carolyn walked down the street toward the post office where Beth had gone to pick up the mail.

She was about to cross the street when a man stepped out of the barber shop and fell into step beside her.

"Mrs. Slade?"

"Yes."

"I'd like to talk to you for a few minutes if you don't mind."

Carolyn took a step backward, wondering at her sudden apprehension. There was nothing in the man's looks to provoke it. He was of medium height, with sandy blond hair and light brown eyes. He wore a gun, but then, most men did.

"Excuse me," she said, "I'm meeting someone."

"Please, ma'am, this is important."

Carolyn's gaze swept the street, but it was virtually empty. "How can I help you?" she asked, taking another step back.

"I want you to come with me. No," he admonished sharply, "don't cry out! It won't do you any good, or that half-breed, either."

She went suddenly still as she recognized the underlying threat in the man's voice. "What do you mean?"

"I mean that your husband's life is in my hands, and unless you wanna see him dead, you'll do exactly as I say."

"You're lying. Morgan's back at the Double S."

"Is he?"

Carolyn felt cold all over as the man drew his gun. "Get in that buggy," he ordered softly, pointing to a small black rig parked behind her.

Wordlessly, she did as she was told, her mind

racing. She thought of yelling for help, thought of grabbing the reins and driving out of town, but before she could act, the man was on the seat beside her, and then they were out of shouting distance.

A fine sliver of fear pricked her heart. "Where are we going?" she asked, trying to keep her rising apprehension out of her voice. "Where's my husband?"

"All in good time, Mrs. Slade."

"Are you a bounty hunter? My father-in-law will pay you twice the reward to let my husband go."

"I don't care about the money!" the man said, his face livid with anger.

"I'm sorry," Carolyn said. "I didn't mean to upset you." She folded her hands in her lap, her knuckles white with the strain. "Who are you?"

"Lou Kylie," he said curtly. He slid a glance at Carolyn. "I don't mean you no harm, ma'am. I'm sorry you got to be drawn into this, but I want Morgan Slade, and you're the bait for the trap."

"You're going to kill him, aren't you?"

Kylie didn't answer, but she saw his hand tighten on the butt of the gun he held in his lap.

"Why? What has he done?"

"He killed my little brother," Kylie answered, his voice thick with rage. "He killed Jim."

Carolyn bit down on her lower lip. "I'm sure it was an accident."

"Like hell! They was gambling when Morgan accused Jimmy of cheating. But it was a lie. Jim wouldn't do no such thing. They had words, and then there was a fight, and when it was over, Jimmy was dead."

"But it was self-defense. Surely you can see that?"

"No!"

"Mr. Kylie, please—"

"Shut up, ma'am," Kylie warned, his voice hard. "Just shut the hell up."

They were far from town now, riding along a narrow path that led away from Cheyenne, away from the Double S. *Poor Beth*, Carrie thought, *she'll be at her wit's end when she can't find me*.

But she couldn't worry about Beth now. She wasn't even worried about herself. It was Morgan who was in danger.

They rode for several hours. Kylie refused to tell her where they were going. There were no ranches to be seen, no signs of civilization at all, only tall grass and gently rolling hills. And with each mile that passed, Carrie grew more and more afraid.

The sun was setting when Kylie stopped the buggy alongside a river. Jumping to the ground, he looped the reins around a cottonwood tree, then helped Carrie out of the buggy.

"We'll wait here," Kylie said. Reaching into the back of the buggy, he pulled out a blanket and a covered basket. "There's some fried chicken and biscuits," he said, and after handing the basket to Carrie, he spread the blanket on the ground. "Eat if you want. We might be here awhile."

Carrie sat down, but for once she wasn't hungry. Worry for Morgan dulled her appetite and left her on edge. She played with the hem of her skirt, twisting it back and forth in her hands.

Kylie stood against a tree, his arms folded over his chest, his expression placid.

"What are we waiting for?" Carolyn asked after a while.

"Your husband. He should be here soon, and then you can go home."

"Please, Mr. Kylie, killing Morgan won't solve anything. It won't bring your brother back." She cringed at the anger she saw in his face. A muscle twitched in his jaw, and his eyes narrowed ominously as he drew his gun and began to wipe the barrel with his handkerchief, his touch gentle, almost a caress. It occurred to her that Lou Kylie might be mentally unhinged, and that frightened her more than anything.

"He'll be here soon," Kylie mused, staring into the distance. "And then Jimmy can rest in peace."

Chapter 40

Morgan reined Sunkawakan to a halt and patted the horse's neck. The stallion had proved to be everything he'd hoped for and more. The stud was fast, seemingly tireless, and quick to learn. They'd covered a lot of miles since morning, and Morgan thought the stud could probably go another twenty, but he was ready to call it quits.

Morgan stared with distaste at the line shack where he was to spend the night. Shack was a perfect description. Built of weathered wood with a tin roof, it looked as if it might collapse at any moment.

Dismounting, he pulled the rigging from the paint, then turned the horse loose in the small corral beside the shack. Hefting his saddle to his shoulder, he opened the sagging front door and stepped inside.

The interior looked even worse than the outside, if that was possible. A thick layer of gray dust covered the stove, the floor, and the two cots. He found an assortment of tinned meat, vegetables, and a can of Arbuckles coffee. An armload of firewood was stacked in a crate beside the stove.

Closing the door, he struck a match and lit the lamp. There was no way he was going to sleep in here, he thought ruefully. He'd fix some chow, then spread his blankets outside.

He ate beans and jerky for dinner, washed it down with hot black coffee, then took up his bedroll and spread it under the stars alongside the corral. Arms crossed behind his head, he stared up at the sky, wishing Carrie was lying there beside him.

He'd waited a long time to fall in love, he thought with a grin. And now he had it bad. He'd thought of her all day, wondering what she was doing, what color material she'd finally settled on, how she'd spent the day when she got back to the ranch. He imagined her sitting on the sofa with Beth, talking about booties and blankets, frowning as they tried to decide on a name for the baby. Lately that had been the main topic at the dinner table. Carrie wanted to name the baby Morgan if it was a boy, Deborah Elizabeth after her mother and Beth if it was a girl. Beth was pleased beyond words that they were considering naming their first child after her. Harrison hadn't expressed an opinion.

Morgan didn't care one way or another. With every passing day, he grew a little more apprehensive, a little more worried about Carrie. Women died in childbirth. He'd seen it happen in the brothels, and he couldn't forget that was how his own mother had died, although she'd died trying to get rid of a child, not bring one into the world. No, he didn't care what they called the baby, so long as the mother and the child survived the ordeal.

Morgan shook his head, then let out a long sigh. Having a woman in his life had turned it upside down, and he'd never been happier. For the first time in his life, he had a reason for living. Though he hated to admit it, he was even starting to take an interest in the ranch. In time, he thought he might even get to like the idea of being a cowboy. Of course, the cattle were about the stupidest creatures he'd ever seen, but working outdoors was a lot better than working in a smelly saloon. He liked spending the day in the saddle, rounding up strays, checking the waterholes, even riding the line. He loved Carrie, felt a deep and abiding affection for the gentle woman who was his grandmother. And he figured he could learn to tolerate Harrison Slade if he had to.

He was almost asleep when he heard the stallion blow softly, then heard a soft whicker in reply. Motionless, he glanced to the left, then the right.

The man was tall, his face shadowed in the moonlight, but there was no mistaking that big Texas hat.

Frowning, Morgan watched as Brody made his way to the shack, put his hand on the latch, drew his gun, and slowly opened the door.

Moving quickly and silently, Morgan rolled out of his blankets and stepped into the shadows beside the shack, his gun in his hand.

There was no sound from inside for several long moments, then Morgan heard a muffled curse.

He grinned as he realized Brody had just discovered that the lump on the cot was a pile of blankets. He waited patiently, wondering what Brody's next move would be. Would the cowboy sit tight, waiting for Morgan to return, or ride on and make his move another time?

He heard the whisper of a boot heel crossing the wooden floor, and saw Brody's faint silhouette as he approached the door and peered cautiously outside.

Morgan waited, tense as a cat, waiting for Brody to make up his mind. Brody stood just inside the door for several moments; then, apparently convinced that Morgan wasn't in the vicinity, he moved noiselessly through the doorway, his gun cocked and ready as his gaze swung right and left. He nodded as he spied Morgan's bedroll spread alongside the corral; his steps were quick and purposeful as he stealthily approached his quarry.

"I'm over here," Morgan said, and stepped out of the shadows.

Brody whirled around, his gun tracking the sound of Morgan's voice as effortlessly as a wolf on the scent of blood.

Two gunshots echoed into the night, the twin reports sounding like one long rolling crash of thunder.

Morgan swore softly as Brody's bullet whistled past his ear, then grinned as his own bullet slammed Brody to the ground.

The stallion snorted and shied away, spooked by the muzzle blast and the acrid scent of gunpowder.

"It's all right, Sunkawakan," Morgan murmured to the stud. Then, in a louder voice, he said. "Throw your gun away easy like, Brody."

Brody hesitated a moment, and then, hearing Morgan cock his revolver, did as he was told.

Leaving the cover of the shack, Morgan crossed the short distance between himself and the gunman.

"You're a long way from the ranch, cowboy," Morgan drawled.

"Go to hell," Brody rasped. Glaring up at Morgan, he pressed his hand over the wound in his side.

"I guess you were looking to collect that ten grand," Morgan mused.

"Why not? It was more than that idiot Kylie was willing to pay."

Morgan's eyes narrowed. "Lou Kylie?"

Brody nodded.

"Did he offer you a reward to kill me?"

"No, he just wanted to know if you were at the ranch."

"And then what?"

"Go to hell."

A feral gleam burned in Morgan's eye as he took a step forward and placed his foot on the bloody wound in Brody's side. The cowboy turned bounty hunter screamed as Morgan ground his heel into the wound.

"And then what?" Morgan repeated.

"Once he knew you were here, he was gonna nab

your wife and use her for bait."

"When?"

"The next time she went into Cheyenne."

Morgan frowned. "Carrie went to town today."

"I know."

"Are you saying that Kylie's got Carrie?"

"Yeah." Brody grinned though the pain. "I was supposed to tell you where he's holding her, but I decided to go after the ten grand myself."

"Where is she?"

"What's in it for me if I tell you?"

"You'll tell me, Brody, one way or another." Morgan grabbed the rope from his saddle horn and lashed Brody's hands behind his back, then spread his legs apart, tying his left ankle to one end of the hitching post and his right ankle to the other.

"What the hell's going on?" Brody demanded. He pulled against the rope, fear making its presence known as Morgan gathered a handful of dry leaves and brush and piled it between his legs.

Morgan didn't answer. Instead, he pulled a box of matches from his shirt pocket and struck one on his thumbnail. Squatting on his heels, he held the burning match over the little pile of kindling. "Where is she?"

Brody arched his back as he tried to pull away from the brush piled next to his crotch. "Are you crazy!"

Morgan nodded as he touched the match to the little pile of brush. "Could be."

"Kylie's waiting for you about twenty miles west of the Double S, near the river crossing." Brody shrieked as the heat from the fire penetrated his jeans. "Cut me loose!"

"All in good time."

"You dirty half-breed, cut me loose!"

Morgan stood up, his expression hard as he watched the tiny flames lick at Brody's crotch. There were tears running down the man's cheeks.

Morgan swore under his breath as he kicked the pile of brush aside.

Kylie had Carrie.

Going into the shack, he collected his gear, then went out to saddle the paint.

Kylie had Carrie.

Chapter 41

Harrison Slade looked up at his wife in disbelief. "What do you mean, you couldn't find her?"

"Just what I said. Carolyn was supposed to meet me at the post office. I waited for half an hour, Harrison, and then I went into every store and shop in town. She wasn't there, and no one had seen her. It was like she just disappeared."

Beth sat down on the sofa beside her husband. "Where do you suppose she is?"

"I don't know, but I'm sure she's fine."

"Where's Morgan?"

"Riding the line. He won't be back until tonight, or maybe tomorrow."

"You don't think something's happened to her?"

"I don't know." Harrison dragged the back of his hand across his jaw. Suppose Beth was right. Suppose Carolyn was missing. Where would she go? He didn't think she'd leave town without telling anyone. It was possible that Morgan had decided to leave and, rather than put up with a lot of tears and goodbyes, had simply gone into town to get Carolyn and jumped on the first train out of Cheyenne.

Harrison shook his head. That didn't make sense. Morgan wouldn't risk putting Carolyn's life in danger, and if he had any sense, he wouldn't ride into Cheyenne knowing there were bounty hunters there just waiting to take him in.

Harrison frowned. If Carolyn was really missing, and she hadn't left town on her own, then who . . .

He stood up and began pacing the floor. Carolyn had run away from home. Was it possible that her father had learned of her whereabouts and come after her?

Beth watched her husband, alarmed by the expression on his face. "Harrison, what is it? Are you all right?"

"I'm fine. Let's suppose Carolyn left Cheyenne. If someone had taken her by force, she'd have made a scene. Surely someone would have noticed. But suppose she left with someone she knew."

"Who?"

"Her father."

"You think Archibald Chandler found out she was here?"

"Have you got a better idea?"

Beth shook her head. It made as much sense as anything else. "What are we going to do? How will we find her?"

"We'll find her," Harrison said firmly. He kissed Beth on the cheek. "Don't worry."

" 'What are you going to do?"

"I'm going after Morgan."

"Harrison, no! Lucius said you weren't to leave the house for another two weeks."

"I'm fine. Pack me some food for the trail, will you? And find my poncho. It looks like rain."

"Harrison, please let Yates go after Morgan."

"Yates is out rounding up strays with the rest of the men. They won't be back for a couple of days. We can't wait until then."

"Harrison, please don't go," Beth pleaded, but he'd already left the room.

Thirty minutes later he was ready to go.

"You be careful," Beth said. "Promise me."

"I'll be careful. Don't worry, we'll find her."

Blinking back her tears, Beth kissed Harrison goodbye. Standing in the doorway, she watched him ride away, grieving for the years they had wasted, for the days and nights they could have shared that were forever lost.

She watched her husband until he was swallowed up in the darkness. Then she went into her bedroom, closed the door, and dropped to her knees, praying that her husband would find Morgan, and that together the two men would find Carrie, and maybe at the same time find a way to heal the breach between them.

Chapter 42

Carolyn woke with a start. She'd been dreaming of Morgan, dreaming that he had come for her. She'd run to him, flying into his arms to cover his face with kisses, her hands threading through his hair. And then Kylie had stepped between them, his eyes filled with an unholy light. She had screamed when Kylie pulled a gun, and it had been the echo of her own scream that had wakened her.

Pressing her hand over her wildly beating heart, Carrie gazed around the room, breathing a sigh of relief when she saw Kylie sleeping on the floor on the far side of the room, his head pillowed on his arm.

They'd stayed by the river for several hours the day before, waiting for Morgan to arrive. Lou Kylie had grown more and more uneasy as the hours passed. Looking confused, he'd paced restlessly up and down the riverbank. At dusk, he decided that something had gone wrong, but he couldn't seem to decide what to do next. To make matters worse, it began to rain. Ordering Carolyn into the buggy, he'd driven downstream until they came to an abandoned line shack cut into the side of a hill about a mile away. It was more like a cave than a building. The floor was hard-packed dirt overlaid with planks. There was no furniture of any kind, nothing but an old pot-bellied stove.

Moving as quietly as possible, Carolyn sat up. She stared at Kylie for a moment, then her gaze moved toward the door. If she could get past Kylie, she could sneak out of the cave, take the horse, and ride for home.

Holding her breath, she stood up and took a step toward the doorway, and then another.

"Going somewhere?"

Kylie's voice stopped Carolyn in her tracks. "I was just going to put some more wood in the stove. I'm cold."

"I'll do it." Rising, he grabbed a piece of firewood and tossed it on the flames. Then, settling his hat on his head, he went to the door and looked out. "Still raining," he muttered and peered up at the sky. "But I don't think it will last much longer," he said, as if to reassure himself, "and then he'll come."

"Maybe he doesn't know we're here," Carolyn said, keeping her voice calm. "Maybe he won't come."

"He'll come," Kylie said. "Brody will tell him I've got you, and Morgan won't stop searching until he finds us."

"Brody! What does he have to do with this?"

Lou Kylie looked suddenly pleased with himself.

"Brody works for me," he said, thumping himself on the chest. "Are you hungry? There's some bread left in the basket, and a couple of apples."

She wasn't hungry; food was the last thing on her mind, but she knew she should eat for the baby's sake. "Yes, thank you."

Still looking pleased with himself, Kylie handed her a hunk of dry brown bread and an apple.

Carolyn took a bite of the bread, chewing slowly as she tried to figure it all out. Morgan had killed Kylie's brother. No doubt Kylie had hired Brody to find out if Morgan was on the ranch, and when he'd found out that Morgan was indeed on the Double S, Kylie had decided to kidnap her to use her as bait. It was all so simple. But surely Morgan wouldn't come alone. Or would he? Maybe Brody would bring him at gunpoint and Kylie would shoot Morgan down in cold blood. The thought was too horrible to contemplate. And then another thought occurred to her. Maybe Brody hadn't found Morgan. Maybe Morgan had gone back to the ranch and Beth had told him she'd disappeared from town. Maybe he didn't know anything about Kylie. He would come looking for her and ride into a trap.

She cocked her head to the side, listening to the rain drumming on the ground. The storm would wash out their tracks. Even Morgan couldn't track her through the mud. And it might rain for days. Winter was late this year, but Harrison had said that once it started, it was likely to be severe.

She refused to let herself become discouraged. Somehow, she'd find a way to warn Morgan. He'd always managed to take care of her in the past. He'd bested Comancheros and Indians; surely he could outmaneuver one crazed man.

Morgan rode hard, quietly cursing the rain that slowed his progress. Thunder and lightning chased themselves across the sky as he urged the paint on, praying that Carrie was all right. If Lou Kylie had dared to lay a hand on her, the man would regret it for the rest of his life, as short as that would be.

He reined the stallion to a halt, peering into the darkness. What the hell? For the space of a heartbeat, a dazzling bolt of lightning turned the night to day, and Morgan saw a rider headed his way.

Drawing his gun, he watched the rider approach. "What the hell," he muttered in disbelief. "What are you doing out here?"

"Looking for you," Harrison Slade replied curtly. "Carolyn's missing."

"I know."

"You know? How?"

"I'll tell you about it later. I know who's got her, and I aim to get her back."

"Where is she?"

"Near the river crossing down by Grass Ridge. Go on home. We're wasting time."

"I'm going with you."

"Don't be ridiculous. Go on home where you belong before you catch pneumonia."

"I'm going with you. Anybody that messes with any of my kin messes with me." Harrison caressed the Winchester rifle cradled in his arm. "I'm a damn good shot, and you might need someone to watch your back."

"Oh, hell, do whatever you want, old man. I don't have time to argue with you."

"Let's go then."

Morgan rode back and forth along the river crossing, rage building within him. She was gone, and the rain had washed out her tracks.

Where would Kylie take her? Back to Cheyenne? No, he wouldn't risk taking Carolyn there. Too many people knew her. "Damn!"

"It's been raining since last night," Harrison remarked. "Assuming he didn't take her back to Cheyenne, he'd likely have looked for a place to hole up until the weather cleared."

"Tell me something I don't know."

Harrison dragged a hand across his jaw. "The only shelter he's likely to find out here would be one of the line shacks."

Morgan nodded, cursing as it began to snow.

"Might as well start with the closest one," Harrison said, pointing to a hillside about a mile downriver.

Morgan slid a glance at his grandfather. Harrison was warm and dry, all bundled up in an oiled yellow slicker. Despite his age, he rode like a man born in the saddle. Unaccountably, Morgan was suddenly glad to have the old man along.

"There!" Harrison exclaimed. "Isn't that a horse? Over there, just beyond that stand of timber."

Morgan peered into the darkness, eyes straining, and then he saw it, a single horse standing with its back to the wind. Lifting his head, Morgan caught the faint scent of smoke.

"Let's go slow," Morgan said. "He might not be alone."

"I'll cover you," Harrison said, holding his rifle at the ready.

Morgan nodded, then urged the paint forward. He could see the line shack now. It wasn't much, just a hole cut in the side of a cave. The door was made of wood fastened to an uneven frame that had been built inside the opening.

About six yards from the shack, Morgan dismounted, slogging as quietly as he could through the slush. The horse tethered in the trees whinnied softly, but the sound was swallowed up in the wail of the wind.

Drawing his Colt, Morgan pressed his ear against the door, frowning when he didn't hear anything but the faint crackle of flames.

He took a step back, trying to see through the narrow crack between the door and the frame, when the door eased open and he saw Carrie outlined in the faint light cast by the stove.

Morgan took another step back, waiting until she had closed the door behind her before he placed his hand over her mouth and dragged her into the trees.

"Shh, Carrie, it's me," he whispered as she began to claw at the hand that covered her mouth.

"Morgan! Oh, Morgan!" Twisting in his grasp, she threw her arms around his neck. "I knew you'd come."

He kissed her quickly. "Who's in there, Carrie?"

"Kylie. He fell asleep. Let's get out of here."

"Not yet."

"Morgan, no."

"I'll be all right."

"I'm not leaving you. If you're going back in there, so am I."

"Dammit, Carrie—"

"Please, let's just leave him."

Morgan looked down into her face and then nodded. He'd take her to Harrison and ask the old man to see that she got home, and when they were out of sight, he'd go back and settle up with Lou Kylie.

He had just taken Carrie by the arm to help her cross the slippery ground when the door to the line shack swung open and Kylie stepped outside, gun in hand.

Morgan blinked against the light, his hand tightening on Carrie's arm as Kylie hollered his name. He swore softly as the muzzle of Kylie's gun swung in his direction, and swore again as he realized that Carrie was positioned between himself and Kylie.

Then the door slammed shut behind Kylie and he was swallowed up in the darkness.

"Drop your gun, Morgan," Kylie said. "Drop it, or I might have to hurt your missus."

"Take it easy, Lou. Think about what you're saying."

"You killed Jim. You killed my little brother, and you've got to pay for it." Kylie eared back the hammer of his Smith and Wesson. "Drop the gun."

Morgan hesitated only a moment. He heard the

steel in Kylie's voice, the implacable determination. Kylie wouldn't rest until Morgan was dead, and he might not be too particular about who got caught in the crossfire.

Wordlessly, Morgan dropped his gun.

"Get out of the way, Mrs. Slade," Kylie said, never taking his eyes from Morgan. "I don't want to hurt you if I don't have to."

"Do as he says, Carrie," Morgan murmured.

She threw a desperate glance at Morgan, afraid to leave his side, hoping that somehow her presence would keep him safe.

"Do it, Carrie. I'll be all right."

Kylie laughed softly as Carrie took a few steps away. There was a look of triumph in his eyes. "Now," he mused, "would Jim want me to kill you quickly, or let you suffer awhile?"

"Mr. Kylie, please," Carolyn begged. "Let him go."

But Kylie didn't hear her. "A bullet in the gut makes for slow dyin'," he drawled, apparently savoring every moment.

"Just do it and get it over with," Morgan snapped.

"Yeah," Kylie said, his revolver pointing like an accusing finger at Morgan's chest. "Maybe that's the best way. Maybe—"

The rest of Kylie's words were cut off by the high-pitched whine of a rifle.

Lou Kylie yelped with pain as the bullet plowed into his arm, forcing him to drop his gun.

"About time, old man," Morgan muttered as he picked up Kylie's gun and shoved it into the waistband of his pants, then fished his own weapon out of the mud.

Carrie looked up in surprise as Harrison Slade rode into view.

"Harrison, what are you doing here?" Carrie exclaimed, thinking she'd never been so glad to see anyone in her life.

"Just watching the back door, so to speak," Slade replied with a grin. He glanced at Morgan. "Well, what now?"

"You two go on back to the ranch. I'll take Kylie into town and see about filing charges for attempted murder."

"Will you be all right?"

"I'll be fine. Take Carrie home. It's colder than hell out here."

"Morgan—"

"I'll be fine, Carrie." He laid a hand over her stomach. "Go on home and take care of my son."

She smiled, leaning forward for his kiss.

Lou Kylie mumbled his brother's name as he shoved his hands into his pants pockets. Face impassive, the fingers of his right hand closed around the little derringer that had belonged to his brother.

Harrison saw the furtive move and shouted, "Morgan, look out!" as Kylie drew the weapon.

Instinctively, Morgan pushed Carrie to the ground, then in a single fluid movement he dropped to one knee, raised his Colt, turned, and fired. The roar of the .44 blended with the report of Slade's Winchester, and Lou Kylie staggered backward, slamming into the door of the line shack before he fell face down in the mud.

Morgan took Carrie by the hand and helped her to her feet. "Are you all right?"

She nodded, too stunned to speak.

Morgan looked up at his grandfather. "I guess you saved my life. Twice."

"My pleasure."

Morgan gazed down at Carrie. Her face was pale and she was shivering, whether from the cold or the turn of events, he couldn't say. Putting his arm around her shoulders, he drew her against him. "Let's go inside where it's warm. You coming, old man?"

"I'll be along in a minute. I'll see to the horses."

Morgan nodded. Opening the door, he helped Carrie inside, then took her in his arms and held her tight.

"Did you really kill his brother?" she asked when her heartbeat had returned to normal.

"Yeah, but it was an accident. We'd been playing poker. He was cheating, and when I called him on it he drew a knife and lunged at me across the table. We struggled a while and when it was over, he was dead. Landed on his own knife. There was a trial and I was acquitted, but Lou was convinced I'd killed his brother in cold blood."

Carrie snuggled against him, grateful to be in his arms again, grateful that the nightmare was over.

Chapter 43

Morgan opened his eyes slowly, wondering what had roused him. Carrie lay on her side, one hand tucked beneath her cheek, the other resting on his chest.

He gazed at her fondly, thinking how beautiful she looked with her hair spilling over her shoulders and her lips slightly parted. She smiled faintly, and he wondered what she was dreaming about, and then he heard it again, a low groan filled with pain.

Sitting up, he glanced across the shack to where his grandfather had made his bed. The old man was tossing fitfully. His face was pale and sheened with sweat.

Rising, Morgan went to his grandfather and knelt beside him.

Slade smiled weakly. "I guess Beth was right. I should have stayed home."

"Yeah."

"Tell her I love her."

"Tell her yourself."

"I'm done for, son."

"I thought I told you not to call me that," Morgan said, but there was no anger in his voice.

"You're never going to forgive me for what I did, are you?"

Morgan glanced across the room to Carrie still sleeping peacefully. If Slade hadn't been on hand last night, things would have turned out differently. "I forgive you."

"Take good care of your grandmother, Morgan. Don't let her grieve too long."

"What the hell kind of talk is that? You're not gonna die. You're too damned ornery. Besides, you wanna see your great-grandchild, don't you? Who's gonna teach him about ranchin' and ropin' and brandin' and all that cowboy stuff if you're not around? Dammit, old man, don't you dare die on me now."

A faint smile tugged at Slade's lips. "You really have forgiven me, haven't you?" he murmured, his voice filled with wonder. "Why?"

"I don't know. Maybe because you were there last night when I needed you. Maybe because hating you just got to be too damn hard."

Morgan let out a long sigh as he faced a truth he'd been avoiding most of his life. "Maybe I hated you so I wouldn't have time to hate myself. I should have taken Lily away from that kind of life whether she wanted to go or not. Maybe, deep down, that's what she wanted me to do all along and I let her down. Hell, maybe that's why she hated me."

"It's all over and done with now, son. We can't do anything about the past except learn to live with it."

But there was one more thing Morgan had to know before he could put the past behind him. "My father," he said slowly. "What was he like?"

"Do we have to talk about it now?"

"Right now."

"He was a good-lookin' kid," Slade said grudgingly. "Tall for a Navajo, with long black hair and skin a little darker than yours."

"What was his name? My mother would never tell me."

"Bahahzhoni, but that was too big a mouthful for most of us, so we called him Jonnie. He was a good man. Quiet. Kept pretty much to himself when he wasn't working." Harrison paused a moment before adding, "He was the best wrangler I ever had."

"Did he have any kin?"

"I don't know. He never mentioned anybody." Slade eyed his grandson for a moment. "You put me in mind of him the way you sit that big stud horse of yours."

"You liked him, didn't you?" Morgan asked, his surprise evident in the tone of his voice. "In spite of everything."

Slade nodded. "Your grandmother convinced me to hire him. I guess he was about seventeen at the time. Never gave me a minute's trouble until ..."

"Until he fell in love with my mother."

"Yeah. Funny, I never saw it coming."

"Would you have let them get married if he'd been white?"

"I don't know. I admit I wasn't crazy about having an Indian for a son-in-law, but if they'd given me a chance to cool off, I might have learned to live with it."

Slade raked a hand through his hair. "It was knowing Lily was pregnant that set me off. I had the devil's own temper back then, and I'd have gone after any other man the same way." He sighed heavily. "I found him, but I couldn't find Lily."

"She went by another name for a while. Called herself by some fancy French name she'd read in a book."

Morgan gazed at Carrie, thinking of the lives that had been ruined. If only his mother hadn't run away, if only she'd stayed and faced her father's anger, how different all their lives would have been. And yet, if things had been different, he never would have met Carrie.

"What happened to my father?" Morgan asked after a while.

Slade took a deep breath. "I had a couple of my men beat him up. He was a proud man. He knew what was coming, but he never uttered a sound. I felt justified at the time, but now I feel bad about the way I treated him."

"I guess you know I'm planning to stay on after the baby's born?"

Harrison smiled faintly. "I thought you might."

"Come spring, I want to drive a couple hundred head of cattle to the Lakota reservation."

Slade started to protest, then shrugged. "I told you the place was yours. Do whatever you want."

Morgan nodded as he laid an affectionate hand on his grandfather's shoulder and gave it a squeeze. "Get some rest, Harry. I'm going out to rig up a travois, and then we're going home."

"Home," Slade murmured, and closed his eyes.

They reached the Double S shortly after dusk. It had been slow going, with Morgan walking beside the travois-laden stallion while Carrie rode Slade's big Tennessee walker and led Kylie's horse. Kiley's body, wrapped in a blanket, was draped across the saddle. Harrison had slept most of the day, his face gray beneath his tan, his breathing labored.

Beth ran out of the house and down the front steps as they rode into the yard, falling to her knees beside her husband. "Harrison, oh, Harrison." Her voice rose hysterically as she clutched his hand to her breast.

"I'm gonna be all right, Beth," Slade said, his voice weak. "Don't you go worrying about me. My grandson says I'm too ornery to die. Ain't that right, son?"

"That's right, Harry."

Beth glanced at Morgan, wondering what miracle had bridged the gulf between her husband and her grandson, but there was no time to dwell on that now. Harrison's breathing was shallow and labored, his skin cold and clammy.

Morgan lifted Carrie from Slade's horse and placed her gently on the ground. After giving her a quick hug and a kiss, he picked up his grandfather and carried him into the house.

Beth ran ahead to turn down the bed covers. She looked at Morgan, anxiety reflected in the depths of her eyes, but he only shrugged. Right now, it was anybody's guess whether Slade would survive the night.

Leaving Beth to look after his grandfather, Morgan went into the parlor to talk to Carrie.

"I'm gonna take Kylie's body into town and then swing by and pick up Lucius," he said, taking both of Carrie's hands in his. "Will you be all right?"

"Yes." She gazed up at him, her eyes filled with love. "Be careful."

"I will, don't worry." He caressed her cheek with the back of his hand, wishing he had time to tell her how much he loved her. "I'll be back as soon as I can."

He kissed her, hard and quick, and then left the house, striding through the snow to the barn where he threw a saddle on a big blood bay gelding.

Yates entered the barn as Morgan was leaving. "You seen Brody?" the foreman asked.

"Yeah, I've seen him," Morgan said, swinging into the saddle. "I left my stallion up at the house. Look after him, will you, and the old man's horse, too. And then stick around in case Elizabeth needs you. The old man's sick and I'm going after the doc."

Yates nodded. "Don't worry, I'll look after things here."

It was near ten o'clock when Morgan rode into

town. His first stop was at the undertaker's parlor, and after making arrangements for Kylie, he remounted and rode on down the street toward the doctor's house, which was dark and quiet.

Dismounting, Morgan pounded on the door, figuring the sawbones had gone to bed. "Come on, doc," he muttered impatiently.

When there was no answer, he decided Aames was probably out on a call or bending his elbow at one of the saloons.

Tossing the bay's reins over the fence, Morgan headed back down the street, poking his head into the first saloon he came to, then moving on to the next, and the next.

Impatiently he crossed the street and glanced into the Hog's Breath Saloon, and breathed a sigh of relief when he saw Lucius Aames seated at a back table playing poker.

Entering, Morgan crossed the floor to stand behind Aames, noting absently that Lucius was holding a full house, kings over sevens. "Doc, we need you out at the ranch right away."

"Somebody sick?" Aames asked, tossing a silver dollar into the pot.

"Harrison. I think he may have had another attack."

Aames tossed his cards into the center of the table and reached for the black bag at his feet. "Let's go."

"Not so fast." One of the men at the table stood up, a .45 clutched in his hand. "You're Morgan Slade, ain't ya?"

Morgan swore under his breath. "Maybe."

The man nodded and licked his lips. "Looks like this is my lucky night after all. Put your hands up."

"Listen, Harper, we don't have time for this right now," Aames said placatingly. "So put the gun away. We've got to be going."

"Keep out of this, doc," Harper warned. He thumbed back the hammer on the .45. "The flyer I got says he's worth ten grand. It didn't say dead or alive, and it makes no difference to me."

"Get going, Lucius," Morgan said urgently. "Take my horse. I left him at your place. He's saddled and ready to go."

"Morgan—"

"There's no time to argue. The old man wasn't looking so good when I left."

Lucius nodded. There was nothing he could do here. Anyway, for all his talk of dead or alive, Harper was a family man and Lucius didn't think he'd kill Morgan out of hand, and he was pretty certain Morgan wouldn't give Harper any reason to pull the trigger.

Grabbing his bag, the doctor hurried out of the saloon.

Harper gestured toward the swinging doors with his gun. "Let's go, pal."

Hands up, Morgan walked to the door and stepped outside. Turning left, he headed for the sheriff's office, which was located toward the end of the block next to the Cheyenne Telegraph Office. He thought briefly of making a run for it, but the chance of outrunning a bullet was mighty slim, and he had too much to live for.

Madeline Baker

Five minutes later, he wasn't sure he'd made the right decision. He shuddered as the cell door slammed shut behind him, and grimaced as the sheriff turned the key in the lock.

"Well, sheriff, there's Morgan," Harper declared. Holstering his weapon, he withdrew a grease-stained Wanted poster from his back pocket and tossed it on the sheriff's desk. "Where's my money?"

"Well, it for sure ain't here," Sheriff Lansky replied. "I'll have to wire Galveston and inform Brockton that his man's been caught. And then we'll need someone to make a positive identification before I can release the reward."

"That could take days!" Harper complained.

"Weeks," the sheriff remarked indifferently. He tossed his keys on the desk, removed his hat, and ran a hand through his hair. "Now go along, get out of here."

Muttering under his breath, Harper stomped out of the sheriff's office.

Lansky studied the Wanted poster, then stared at Morgan through narrowed brown eyes. "Kidnapping and horse stealing," he mused. "You could be hanged for that."

Morgan scowled at the lawman. "I didn't kidnap anybody."

"And the horse?"

"Let's just say I borrowed it under dire circumstances."

"I've never yet met a thief who admitted he was guilty," Lansky said, chuckling. "You might as

414

well make yourself comfortable. You'll likely be here quite a while."

"I need to get home."

Lansky shrugged. "Sorry."

"My grandfather's sick. Harrison Slade. You've heard of him?"

"I've heard of him. What's your point?"

"I need to be with him."

"Yeah, well, there's lots of places I'd rather be than here, myself. But here we are."

"Dammit, sheriff, I give you my word I'll come back as soon as he's out of danger."

Lansky grinned wryly. "Son, I don't know who the hell you are, but you got a lot of brass. And until I find out who you are, you're not goin' anywhere."

Carrie glared at Lucius Aames. "And you just left him there?"

"He seemed to think it was more important for me to get out here as fast as I could," Aames said, drying his hands on a damp towel. "And I'd say he was right. If I'd gotten here thirty minutes later . . ." He shrugged. "As it is, it'll be touch and go, but I think Harrison will pull through." The doctor glanced at Carrie's belly and smiled. "He's got a lot to live for."

"Thank you, Lucius," Beth said fervently.

"Get some rest, Beth. You, too, Carolyn. There's nothing either one of you can do now, except pray."

Settling his old felt hat on his head, Aames picked up his bag and headed for the front door.

"Lucius, why don't you stay the night?" Beth called, following him out of the room.

Aames grinned. "It's near dawn," he said, "and I always sleep better in my own bed."

Yawning, he opened the door and found himself staring at a world swathed in white. Huge snowflakes swirled through the air, driven by a harsh wind.

Closing the door, he smiled at Beth. "Guess I will stay the night," he said. "And tomorrow, too."

Carrie stood at her bedroom window staring out at the snow that continued to fall in huge white flakes, piling high around the fence posts, drifting against the sides of the barn and the house.

When would it stop? Would it ever stop? She had to get to town to see Morgan and make sure he was all right.

She pressed her head against the window frame, trying to remember what the Wanted poster said, but all she could recall was the amount of the reward. Ten thousand dollars. It wasn't a reward, it was a ransom.

She had to get to Cheyenne. She had to send a wire to her father and ask him, beg him, to convince Roger Brockton to withdraw the reward.

She pressed her hand to her belly and smiled as Morgan's child gave a lusty kick. It was hard to imagine she was carrying a living being, that there was a tiny human form growing within her, nurtured by her blood, created by her love for Morgan.

Sitting on the window seat, she rested her head against the wall and closed her eyes. Was it a boy or a girl? It didn't really matter, as long as it was healthy. She grinned as she recalled the day she and Morgan had discussed names for the baby. Bathsheba, indeed!

With a sigh, Carrie wrapped her arms around her body, wishing Morgan was there to hold her. She needed to feel his strength, wanted him to be there in case Harrison got worse. Beth would need Morgan if anything happened. But surely the Lord wouldn't take Harrison Slade now, not when Morgan's attitude toward his grandfather had changed so drastically, not before Harrison had a chance to see his first great-grandchild.

"Oh, Morgan." Just saying his name made her feel better. Lucius had assured her that Pete Harper wasn't a bounty hunter, just a local man who thought he'd found a way to get rich quick. As soon as the snow stopped, they'd go into town and straighten everything out.

She murmured Morgan's name again, praying that he was all right, hoping that even now he was on his way home.

Chapter 44

Morgan paced the narrow cell restlessly, pausing now and then to stare out the small, iron-barred window at the snow-covered street.

He'd been a fool to come into town, he knew that now. He should have sent Yates or one of the men, but it hadn't occurred to him at the time. He'd been worried about his grandfather, too worried to sit around waiting and wondering if the doctor had been found, if he was on his way. So he'd gone himself, and now he was paying the price.

It had stormed for the last five days. He knew that was why Carrie hadn't come to see him. He knew that was why Lucius Aames hadn't returned to town. But he couldn't completely smother the sense of panic that threatened to engulf him as he stared out the window.

The storm had passed during the night and the sun was shining bright in a clear blue sky. People were on the street for the first time in five days.

He could see the owner of Dixon's shoveling snow in front of the mercantile store. Further down the street, a handful of boys were throwing snowballs. He could hear the steady drip, drip of melting snow falling from the roof.

He cursed Roger Brockton as he paced back and forth. Damn the man for putting up that reward, for being mean-spirited enough to press charges because he'd stolen his horse. Hell, Brockton had enough money to buy a whole herd of horses.

Morgan drove a hand through his hair. Horse stealing was a serious crime. There'd be a trial. If he was found guilty, he could be looking at a long jail sentence. Or a noose!

He rested his forehead against the cold stone wall of his cell. He'd been here five days, and it seemed like five years.

Damn! He had to get out of here. He'd been in jail once before and had hated it, hated being locked up, hated the cramped cell, the loss of his freedom, the knowledge that his life was no longer his own.

But it was worse now. Much worse. There were people who needed him, people who loved him. People he loved. He wondered how Carrie was feeling, how his grandmother was holding up, if his grandfather was still alive.

Damn, the old man couldn't die on him now. They had a lot of catching up to do.

He was lying on the hard, narrow cot the following afternoon, one arm flung over his face, when he heard footsteps. Rising, he went to the door of his cell and saw Archibald Chandler walking toward him, followed by Sheriff Lansky.

Carrie's father looked older than he had the last time Morgan had seen him. There were dark shadows under his eyes, deep lines etched near his mouth. His steps were slow and heavy, his shoulders sagging as though burdened down by a great weight.

Chandler stopped at the cell door and shoved his hands into the pockets of his heavy sheepskin jacket. "Where's Carolyn?" he demanded without preamble.

Morgan frowned, irritated by the man's surly attitude. "Go to hell."

"Dammit, Slade, where's my daughter?"

With a shrug, Morgan turned and walked toward the back of the cell.

"Please, Morgan," Chandler said. "Tell me where she is?"

"No."

"Is she all right? At least tell me if she's all right."

Morgan turned to face Chandler. "She was fine the last time I saw her. What the hell are you doing here anyway?"

"Roger got a wire from the sheriff saying you were in custody, and he forwarded it to me."

"And you came arunnin' so you could take Carrie back to Galveston? Well, forget it. She's my wife now, and she's staying here, with me."

Chandler made a gesture that encompassed the cell block. "Is this the kind of life you want for Carolyn? Do you expect her to sit around and wait while you rot in jail?"

"You could get me out of here quick enough."

"Why should I?"

"You want to see Carrie, don't you?"

"Yeah. Sheriff, turn this man loose. The charges against him have been dropped."

"Dropped?" Morgan stared at Chandler. "What do you mean, dropped?"

"Roger got married last month." Chandler reached into his pocket and pulled out a sheet of paper. "He sent me a letter stating that all charges against you had been dropped. I've notified the authorities." Archie grinned wryly. "He said you could keep the horse and buggy as a wedding gift."

"You took your own sweet time telling me about it."

"I know. I guess I just wanted to see you squirm a little. Can you blame me? I've been worried sick about Carolyn. You might at least have let me know where she was."

"She was afraid you'd try to take her back to Texas."

"I guess I can understand that." Chandler handed Roger's statement to Lansky, then backed away from the cell so the sheriff could unlock the door.

Half an hour later they were riding out of town on a couple of rented horses, unaware of the dark-skinned man who followed them.

They rode in silence until Chandler cleared his throat and asked the question uppermost in his mind. "Is Carrie happy?"

Morgan nodded. "She's happy. And pregnant."

"Pregnant! My little girl?"

Morgan nodded again. "The baby's due sometime in February."

"A baby," Chandler murmured. "In February."

Morgan grinned. "It took me a while to get used to the idea, too."

"So what are your plans? Are you coming back to Texas?"

"No. We're gonna stay here, on the Double S. Carrie likes it here, and my grandfather needs me."

"Oh." Chandler didn't try to hide his disappointment.

"I'm sure we could find room for you if you want to stay awhile," Morgan offered.

"I'd like that."

"It's settled then." Life was mighty strange, Morgan thought with a wry grin. For a man who'd never had any family other than his mother, he was rounding up kinfolk faster than a hen gathering chicks before a storm. It wasn't a bad feeling.

They rode into the Double S shortly after dark to find Carrie and Beth fixing supper in the kitchen. Lucius was in the bedroom with Slade playing draw poker.

For a few minutes, there was considerable talking and hugging and hand-shaking as Carrie was reunited with Morgan and her father, and Archibald Chandler was introduced to Beth and Harrison and Doctor Aames.

They ate in the bedroom to keep Harrison company. Chandler didn't say much. He seemed to be concentrating on the plate in his lap, but he saw every look and touch that passed between Carrie and Morgan and he realized his daughter was indeed happy. There was a glow in her eyes that had never been there before, a softness in her expression that told him better than words that she had no regrets.

Chandler watched Morgan carefully in the next few days, noting the adoration in young Slade's eyes when he looked at Carrie, the love he expressed for his grandmother, his respect for his grandfather. Archie knew he'd never have chosen a half-breed for a son-in-law, and yet he could find no fault in Carrie's husband. Morgan Slade seemed to be a good man. He took his responsibilities seriously, deferred to his grandfather with regard to ranch decisions, and treated his father-in-law with as much good grace as possible under the circumstances. And he loved Carrie. A blind man could have seen that.

Lucius Aames left for home on the first clear day, declaring that he'd taken advantage of Beth's hospitality long enough and that Harrison was out of danger.

Once on the road to recovery, Harrison recuperated quickly. Carrie's belly grew big as a barrel. Beth smiled all the time, and Archie Chandler continued to stay on at the Double S, reluctant to leave Carolyn.

Morgan was just beginning to feel that everything was going to turn out for the best when Yates came knocking at the back door, a worried expression on his face.

"We need to talk," Yates said. He glanced over

Morgan's shoulder, nodded briefly at Carolyn, who was sitting at the kitchen table sipping a cup of coffee. "Alone."

"Sure." Stepping outside, Morgan closed the back door. "What's wrong?"

"I'm not sure, maybe nothing, but some of the hands have seen a stranger prowling around at odd times of the day."

"Any idea who it is?"

"No. Charlie said he thinks it's an Indian."

"Probably just looking for a stray to take home," Morgan mused.

"Probably. But—"

"But it might be a bounty hunter who hasn't heard the reward was canceled," Morgan said, finishing the foreman's thought.

"Yeah. I thought you ought to know."

"Thanks. Don't say anything to the family. I don't want to worry Carrie or the old man."

"Right."

Morgan stood outside for a long while after Yates had gone back to the bunkhouse. A stranger, prowling around the ranch. He felt the short hairs prickle along the back of his neck. Who could it be? Kylie was dead, and no one else was out to get him that he knew of. It could be a bounty hunter, but it seemed unlikely at this late date.

Carrie knew that something was wrong the minute he stepped into the kitchen. "What is it?" she asked anxiously.

"Nothing, Carrie."

"Don't lie to me, Morgan. Something's wrong."

"Carrie—"

"It isn't good for pregnant women to worry, you know."

Walking up behind her chair, he placed his hands on her shoulders, then bent down and kissed the top of her head. "There's nothing for you to worry about. Everything's fine. Come on, let's go have breakfast."

Two days later, Morgan rode out to check on a small herd of cattle that had been spotted north of the ranch. It was slow going, riding through the deep drifts, but he was glad to be outdoors. As much as he loved Carrie, as much as he'd come to love his grandparents, there were times when he needed to be out of the house, alone with his thoughts.

He'd ridden about five miles when he had the oddest feeling that he was no longer alone. Reining his horse to a halt, he scanned the snow-covered hills. He felt a sudden chill creep down his spine, a chill that had nothing to do with the wind or the weather.

His hand dropped to his rifle and then he shook his head. He was imagining things. There was no one there. He'd be shooting at shadows next.

He'd convinced himself that he was acting like a fool when he rounded a bend in the trail and came face to face with a man he'd never seen before.

He reached for his rifle, intending to shoot first and ask questions later, when the man raised his hands over his head.

"Do not shoot. I mean you no harm."

Morgan's eyes narrowed as he studied the stranger. He was an Indian, as Charlie had suspected. His hair was long and black and tinged with gray, his skin the color of dark mahogany, lined with years of hard living. He wore a heavy wool coat over a red flannel shirt, canvas pants, and thick winter moccasins. A bright blue kerchief was knotted at his throat.

"What do you want here?" Morgan asked, his hand still resting on his rifle.

"I am looking for someone," the Indian said. His voice was soft and low. His eyes, black as night, were filled with a deep sadness. "I have been looking for him for many years."

"Does this person have a name?"

"Yes. His name is Morgan Slade."

"You've found him, but if you're looking to collect that bounty, forget it. It's been withdrawn."

"I am not looking for a reward," the man said quietly. "I am looking for my son."

For a moment, Morgan couldn't speak. The words "my son" echoed and reechoed in his mind. "What?"

"I am looking for my son."

"Bahahzhoni," Morgan murmured.

The Indian nodded. "I have searched for you for many years."

"The Wanted poster..."

A faint smile lit up the older man's eyes. "Yes. I saw it in New Mexico."

"Why didn't you come to the house?"

Bahahzhoni laughed softly, bitterly. "Do you think Slade would have welcomed me?"

Morgan nodded. "Yes."

"Then he has changed since I saw him last."

"It was wrong, what he did, but he's sorry for it now."

Bahahzhoni grunted softly, as if it no longer mattered. "You look as I imagined you would," he murmured. "Tell me, what happened to your mother?"

"She died a long time ago."

"I tried to find her, as I tried to find you. A lifetime," he said without regret. "I've spent a lifetime looking for the two of you. Are you happy?"

"Yes. I have a beautiful wife and we're expecting a child in the spring. I want you to meet her."

"No. I wanted only to see your face."

"You can't go, not now. I've . . ." The words stuck in Morgan's throat. He hadn't felt so scared, so tongue-tied, since he was a child. He'd wondered about this man his whole life. He swung out of the saddle and crossed the short distance between them. Placing a hand on his father's thigh, he said, "Please don't go."

"I must. No good will come of my being here."

"This is my ranch. I say who stays and who goes. I'm asking you, begging you, to stay."

"You know I did not leave your mother because I wanted to."

"I know."

Bahahzhoni let out a deep sigh, as if releasing all the old hurts and sorrows of the past, and then, sliding from the back of his horse, he embraced his son, unashamed of the tears that filled his eyes.

* * *

Harrison Slade frowned as Morgan entered the parlor followed by an old man who looked disturbingly familiar, and then he swore under his breath. Bahahzhoni!

Beth pressed a hand to her heart and then, rising from the sofa, hurried toward their guest, her arms outstretched. "Bahahzhoni, welcome," she said, and hugged him.

Harrison waited until Beth ran out of steam, and then he stood up and walked toward Morgan's father. For a moment, the two men stared at each other, a world of pain and loss between them, and then Harrison put out his hand.

"I'm sorry," he said gruffly. "I was wrong."

Bahahzhoni hesitated only a moment, and then shook Slade's hand.

Carrie, sitting in the big overstuffed chair by the fireplace, was quick to realize who the Indian was. She had only to see the guilt in Harrison's face, and the quiet happiness in her husband's eyes, to know that this was Morgan's father.

Later, when the excitement was past, Bahahzhoni told of his life, of how he'd spent the years looking for Lily and his son, stopping to work as a wrangler whenever he ran out of money. He had kept track of Harrison Slade, always hoping that Lily would go home. Strangely, he did not hate the man who had ruined his life.

"How could I hate him?" Bahahzhoni asked with a slight shrug of his shoulders. "He had taken Lily away from me, but in doing so, he too had lost her. I could not hate the man who shared my loss, even though he had caused it, for I understood his suffering and his grief."

Morgan stared at his father, touched by the aching sadness in his voice. How differently his own life might have turned out if Bahahzhoni had found Lily. He might have grown up in a home filled with love and security. His mother might still be alive. His father wouldn't have spent his life looking for a woman who ceased to exist long before she passed away. And he would never have met Carrie.

"It's late," Bahahzhoni said, rising. "I must go."

"No," Morgan said. "We still have a lot to talk about. I'll have Margarita prepare a room for you."

"I would rather sleep outside."

"You'll be here in the morning?"

"Yes."

"I'll, walk you out."

Bahahzhoni said good night to the rest of the family, then followed Morgan outside. For a moment, they stood on the porch, the emotion between them too strong for words. Morgan looked at the man who was his father and thought of all the wasted years, and then he thanked God that they still had time to get to know each other.

"Your Carrie is very beautiful," Bahahzhoni said after a while. "I think she will give you many fine sons."

"I want you to stay," Morgan said. "I want you to make your home here, with us."

Happiness swelled in Bahahzhoni's heart, filling him with a warm sweet pain. He had been alone most of his life. He had loved Lily, but that love had been denied him and he had never looked for another. But he was no longer alone. He had a fine son and a beautiful daughter-in-law. And soon he would have a grandchild.

A wistful smile played at the corners of his mouth as he pictured himself surrounded by grandchildren, telling them the old stories of First Man and First Woman and how they made the sacred mountains in the land of the Navajo.

"You will stay, won't you?" Morgan asked.

"I will stay, if that is your wish."

"It is. I don't want you to be a stranger to my children, or to me." Morgan smiled. "Perhaps you will teach me the ways of the Dineh, and together we can teach my children."

Bahahzhoni nodded, unable to speak past the lump in his throat. Lily was gone, but their son was here. At long last, he had found the home he had been looking for.

Chapter 45

Morgan felt a new happiness in the days that followed. Bahahzhoni insisted that he be allowed to earn his keep, so Morgan put him in charge of the horses. It didn't entail much work other than grooming and feeding, but his father seemed content and the horses had never looked better.

The most surprising thing was the friendship that developed between Bahahzhoni and Harrison. They passed many a snowy night hunched over a checkerboard. Morgan had a sneaking suspicion they spent a lot of time talking about Lily, and an equal amount planning for the baby.

Christmas was a joyous occasion, marked by brightly wrapped gifts and enough food to feed a small army. There were presents for everyone, but the one that touched Morgan's heart and brought tears to Carrie's eyes was the delicately carved cradleboard his father made for the baby.

Later, sitting in front of the fire with his arm around Carrie, Morgan realized it was the first really happy Christmas he'd ever had. They'd celebrated Christmas at Mozelle's, of course. The girls all took the day off to exchange presents and drink champagne, and they'd had a big dinner in the afternoon, but after dark, it was back to business as usual.

Morgan smiled as Carrie placed his hand over her belly and felt the baby move. Sometimes he wondered that it didn't hurt her, the way their child tossed and turned.

Looking up, he saw that his father was watching him, that Beth and Harrison were smiling in his direction, and he was filled with such a sense of belonging and love that it was almost painful. Somehow, someday, he would find the words to tell Carrie how grateful he was that she had stumbled down that dark alley and into his life. But for her, he'd still be swilling whiskey in that tar paper shack in Galveston.

Thoughts of Texas brought Red to mind, and he wondered what she was doing, and if Trey Corrigan still came calling at the Grotto. But then Archie stood up to make a toast, and Beth started playing "Silent Night" on the piano, and he forgot all about Red as Carrie put her arm around his waist and urged him to sing.

It snowed on New Year's Day, keeping everyone inside around the fire. Then, almost overnight, it was February and Carrie became the center of attention. Marda began preparing special drinks for her in the afternoon, Beth and Archie hovered over her, insisting that she rest and keep her feet up. Harrison didn't say much, and Bahahzhoni said even less, but the two of them looked worried most of the time and Harrison talked about sending for Lucius to come and stay at the ranch until the baby was born.

On a cloudy morning in late February Carrie begged Morgan to take her outside for a walk.

"I can't stand it anymore," she complained. "Everybody staring at me all the time. Please, Morgan, let's go down by the lake."

"Carrie, it's cold outside."

"I don't care."

He started to refuse, and then, unable to resist the look in her eyes, he said, "All right, I'll get your coat."

They left the house a few minutes later. Morgan wore a heavy sheepskin jacket and leather gloves. Carrie wore a long wool coat over a long-sleeved dress. A hat protected her head, there were boots on her feet, fur-lined gloves on her hands, and a scarf at her throat.

"I can hardly move," she lamented.

"I can't have you freezing to death," Morgan retorted, although it wasn't nearly as cold as he'd feared. The sun broke through the clouds, and he drew a deep breath as he took Carrie's arm. "I never heard of anything so silly, wandering off for a walk when it's likely to rain any minute," he muttered, and then he grinned. "I guess a little rain never hurt anybody."

"Except Noah," Carrie said, and grinned up at him. She loved him more with every passing day.

He was never angry with her, never impatient with her moods. And, goodness, she'd grown moody in the past few months, but she couldn't seem to help it. She felt cranky and ugly and fat, but he constantly assured her that she was beautiful, and that he loved her. He rubbed her feet, massaged her back when it ached, got up in the middle of the night to find her something to eat. Once, he'd ridden all the way into Cheyenne because she had a craving for a peppermint stick.

They were near the lake when she felt the first contraction.

Morgan felt Carrie stiffen, heard her gasp with pain. "What is it?"

Carrie shook her head. "I'm not sure. Nothing, I guess."

"Let's go back."

"In a minute." She spied a log and sat down.

"Are you all right?" Morgan asked, frowning.

"Yes." Carrie looked up as the sky grew suddenly dark. A gust of wind shook the trees.

Morgan reached for Carrie's arm. "C'mon, let's get back to the house. There's a storm coming."

Nodding, Carrie reached for Morgan's hand, then groaned softly as a contraction knifed through her. Frightened, she stared up at Morgan.

"The baby?" he asked.

"I think so."

He helped her to her feet and put his arm around her as they started walking toward the house. Damn, he'd been a fool to let her talk him into going for a walk.

It began to rain, gently at first, then harder and

with more force. "I guess Noah knew what he was doing when he built that Ark," Morgan muttered.

Carrie moaned softly and Morgan felt her tense with the pain, then gasp as a sudden gush of warm water trickled down her legs.

Swinging her into his arms, Morgan walked as fast as he could. She was shivering now, and he stopped long enough to wrap her in his jacket, ignoring her protests that he'd soon be soaked to the skin. That was the least of his worries. He had to get Carrie home.

He peered into the distance, offering a silent prayer of thanks when he saw the house.

Beth hurried to meet them, clucking worriedly when she saw the pain etched in Carrie's face, the worry in Morgan's. She followed them up the stairs, turning down the covers on the bed, helping Carrie out of her coat and dress and underthings while Morgan removed her shoes and then lit a fire in the fireplace.

"Morgan, go down and heat some water," Beth said, lifting the hat from Carrie's head.

"No," Carrie cried, reaching for Morgan's hand. "I want him here. Just him."

"Carrie, Beth knows more about this than I do."

"I don't care. I want you here, beside me. Please."

Morgan looked up at his grandmother and saw the faint hurt in her eyes. Then she smiled. "I'll be downstairs if you need me." She patted Morgan on the arm. "There's nothing to it, really."

With a last reassuring smile, she left the room and closed the door behind her.

Sitting on the edge of the bed, Morgan took Carrie's hand in his. The pains were coming harder now and her nails dug into his palms with surprising force. Perspiration beaded her forehead as she writhed on the bed, her beautiful green eyes filled with fear.

"Try to relax," he said quietly. "Don't fight the pain."

"It hurts so bad," she said, panting heavily. "Oh, God, it hurts."

"I know. Let me go get Beth."

"No." She shook her head, afraid to let him out of her sight.

Morgan rubbed Carrie's back as the pains grew more intense, and grimaced as she clung to his hands, her fingernails digging into his skin. He stared at the tiny drops of red blood dripping from his hands and remembered the blood that had stained his mother's thighs as she tried to rid her body of an unwanted child. He vowed then and there that this child, his child, would never know what it was like to feel unwanted or unloved. His child would grow up secure in the knowledge that he had been conceived in love, that his birth had been a cause for joy and celebration, that his life was precious to those who loved him.

When the pains were so close together they seemed like one long contraction, Morgan lifted her out of bed and made her kneel before him.

"The Lakota women don't have their babies lying down," he said, wincing as Carrie's nails dug into his shoulder. "They claim this is easier."

Carrie nodded. Right now, she was willing to try

standing on her head if it would help.

"Look at me, Carrie. Try not to think of the pain. Think about how much I love you." He smiled as he caressed her cheek. "I am Rides a Dark Horse, and you are my woman. Think of Mak'awin and the stories she told. Remember the tale of the old woman who kept the world from coming to an end?"

Carrie nodded, but it was impossible to think of anything but the pains that threatened to tear her in half.

She screamed as the worst contraction of all took hold of her, bearing down harder, harder. As from a great distance she heard Morgan urging her to push. Her fingers dug into his arms as she closed her eyes and pushed. For a moment, she was swallowed up by blackness, and then she heard a baby cry, and Morgan was helping her to lie down, whispering softly that it was over, and that he loved her.

Morgan gazed at the tiny infant lying between Carrie's thighs. A son. He had a son. Awkwardly he lifted the baby and cradled it in his arms, smiling as the boy's lusty wails filled the room with the sweet sound of new life.

"He's perfect, Carrie," Morgan murmured as he cut the cord and placed the baby on Carrie's stomach. "Ten fingers and toes. Just perfect."

Moving carefully, he wrapped the baby in a sheet pulled from the bed, then, placing the child in Carrie's arms, he lifted the two of them and put them on the bed, covering Carrie with a blanket.

Her face was radiant as she gazed at their son.

Gently she stroked the curve of his cheek, outlined a tiny shell-like ear with her fingertip, kissed his nose. Slipping her hand under the sheet, she counted his dimpled fingers and toes, marveling at how small they were, how perfectly formed. His skin was as soft as down, his hair like fine black silk. Her heart swelled with love as a tiny hand curled around her finger.

"He's beautiful, Carrie," Morgan murmured, his voice thick with emotion as he stroked her cheek with the back of his hand. "Just like you."

"Like you," Carrie said, and fell asleep with their son cradled in her arms.

Morgan sat beside her for a long while before he went downstairs. Beth, Harrison, Archie, and Bahahzhoni were waiting for him at the foot of the stairs, their faces filled with joy.

"It's a boy," Morgan said. "Carrie's asleep." He looked at Beth. "You might want to look after the baby, clean him up a little."

"Of course," Beth said, and hurried up the stairs, anxious to see her great-grandson.

In the parlor, Harrison poured drinks while Archie and Bahahzhoni slapped each other on the back. Morgan accepted their congratulations and then, murmuring his apologies, went outside.

It had stopped raining and the air smelled fresh and clean and new. In the distance he could see a rainbow. It arched over the Double S like a benediction from the Almighty.

The rainbow signifies that which you desire. The words of Keeper-of-the-Wind echoed in the back of Morgan's mind. *Your medicine will be powerful so long as you do not stray from the path of the warrior on the dark horse.*

A sense of peace engulfed Morgan as he lifted his arms.

"Wakan Tanka, I thank you for my son," he murmured. "Bless him with courage and a strong heart. Help me to guide him toward the true path, the warrior's path . . ."

Morgan's gaze settled on the rainbow, and he heard the medicine man's words again: *The rainbow signifies that which you desire.*

And will I obtain that which I desire? he asked, and Keeper-of-the-Wind nodded. *If you are worthy, then yes, it shall be yours.*

Bowing his head in gratitude, Morgan returned to Carrie's side. His vision had indeed been a true one, he mused as he reached out to touch the baby sleeping in its mothers arms.

Everything he desired was within reach of his hand.

Chapter 46

Beth gazed down into the face of her great-grandson, tears shining in her eyes. "What have you decided to name him?"

Carrie looked at Morgan and smiled impishly. "Vladimir Alphonse Slade."

Beth blinked several times. "Vladimir?"

"Alphonse Slade," Morgan finished for her. He grinned at Carrie, then looked at Beth innocently. "Don't you like it?"

"Well, I'm sure they're very nice names, but ... I mean, don't you think something a little more ... uh ..."

Carrie and Morgan burst into laughter. "Don't worry, Grandma," Morgan said, "we're not serious." He took Carrie's hand in his and gave it a squeeze. "His name's Chandler Bahahzhoni Slade, but I think we'll just call him Johnnie for a while."

Carrie pressed Morgan's hand to her heart as she gazed around the room. Beth and Harrison were cooing over the baby, stroking his downy black hair and marveling at his tiny fingers and toes as they tried to decide whether he looked more like his grandfather or his grandmother. Her father was sipping a glass of bourbon, while Bahahzhoni was smoking an enormous cigar, both men looking as proud as only first-time grandfathers could look.

Happiness swelled in Carrie's breast as she smiled up at her husband. Everything she had ever wanted was right here in this room, she thought happily. Her father had finally given his blessing on her marriage, Morgan had found his father and made peace with his grandfather, and she had a beautiful son. And in a few days Jordan and Diana would be here with their new baby, born only a few weeks earlier.

How funny life was, Carrie mused. Only a short while ago she had run away from home, never dreaming that her decision to turn down a dark alley would lead her to the man who would fulfill her every dream, a man who had hair as black as night and eyes as warm as a midnight fire.

Morgan smiled as Beth placed Johnnie in the cradle beside the bed, then followed Harrison, Bahahzhoni, and Archie out of the room.

It was hard to believe he was a father, he mused as he gazed into his son's dark blue eyes. Hard to believe that he had sired such a tiny perfect being.

He sat on the edge of the bed and gazed at Carrie, loving her as never before. She was a miracle, he thought; nothing less.

"Let's have a girl next time," Carrie remarked.

"Next time," Morgan agreed.

"And then a boy."

Morgan raised one thick black brow. "How many kids do you wanna have?"

"Dozens," she answered. "Handsome boys with black hair and gray eyes, and beautiful girls."

"With green eyes."

Carrie nodded. "Dozens of children so we can name them Bathsheba and Cuthbert."

"And Delilah and Xavier," Morgan agreed solemnly.

"And Mortimer," Carrie said, choking back a giggle.

"And Rowena," Morgan said. He was laughing now, his heart full as he bent down to kiss her.

She was a miracle, all right. She'd brought love and laughter into his life, and he planned to spend the rest of his days showing her how grateful he was, and how much he loved her.

Dozens of kids, Morgan thought as he blew out the lamp. Undressing, he slid into bed beside Carrie. Dozens of kids. That could take a while, he mused as he drew Carrie into his arms, but he wouldn't mind.

He wouldn't mind at all.

Epilogue

Carrie stood across the table from Morgan, her eyes radiant as she watched him blow out the candles on a huge frosted birthday cake. A ton of presents were piled on the table, and smiling faces wished him well.

She had been shocked to learn that Morgan had never had a birthday party. In the past year, birthday parties had been given for everyone in the family, and when she asked Morgan his date of birth, he shrugged and said he didn't know. His mother had never considered the day of his birth a cause for celebration, and so she had ignored it year after year. The truly sad thing, the thing that made Carrie furious, was that Morgan himself didn't know the date of his birth, only the year. So Carrie had picked a day—July 3—to celebrate her husband's birthday.

Even now, she could hardly comprehend it. Imagine, Morgan was thirty years old, and this was his first party. She had planned it with Beth and Diana for weeks, but all the preparation, all the secrecy, all the hours of cooking and baking had been worth it just for the look on Morgan's face.

Happiness welled in her heart as she gazed around the room. Beth and Harrison sat holding hands on the sofa, their faces warm with love as they watched Morgan cut the cake. Her father sat beside the fireplace, trying to keep Jordan Jr. from grabbing the cigar out of his pocket, while Morgan's father held Johnnie, who was sleeping peacefully in spite of the noise.

Jordan and Diana were laughing together. They had moved to Cheyenne the year before, and Archie had soon followed. And now all Carrie's family was together at last.

She smiled at Morgan as he came up beside her and slipped his arm around her waist, patting her belly which was just beginning to swell with their second child. So far, it was a secret only the two of them shared.

"A girl this time, remember?" Carrie whispered.

"Bathsheba," Morgan whispered back, his eyes aglow as he grinned at the remarkable woman who was his wife, and then he let his gaze wander around the room.

Everyone he knew was there: Margarita and Marda, Lucius, his grandparents, Jordan and Diana, Archie, Yates and the Double S cowhands, Martha Galway, even Sheriff Lansky and Pete Harper.

And Red.

Morgan shook his head as she sashayed up to him.

"Hi, cowboy," she drawled, her brown eyes still glowing with merriment. "Get over the shock yet?"

"I'm working on it," he replied, winking at her. It had been a hell of a surprise, seeing Red at the Double S, and even more of a surprise to learn that Carrie had invited her.

Red laughed softly, and Morgan noticed for the first time that, without all the garish paint and powder, she was a lovely young woman. Her long-sleeved green dress complemented her hair and her figure.

"I'm glad you could make it, Annie," Carrie said. She threw an amused look in Morgan's direction. "I didn't get much of a chance to say hello when you first arrived."

"Wouldn't have missed it," Red replied. It had made the whole trip worthwhile, seeing the look on Morgan's face when she walked into the house on Danny's arm. She looked up at the tall, dark-haired man at her side and gave him a dazzling smile. "When I got your letter, I told Danny it was time I took a vacation from the Grotto, and for once he agreed with me."

Danny Monroe chuckled softly as he draped his arm around Red's shoulder. "Honey, I always agree with you."

Morgan grinned and shook his head as the two of them walked to the dining room table where Marda was serving cake and punch. Red and Danny! He still couldn't believe it. But he was happy for Red, happy that she'd finally found someone to love, and someone to love her. Danny had demanded she give up her job, insisting that she stay home and behave like a proper wife, and she seemed content to do so. He wished her all the happiness in the world.

Taking Carrie by the hand, he led her outside. Slipping her arm through his, he walked into the twilight, away from the lights and the noise. She was *his* happiness, his life, his past and his future, all rolled into one.

He drew her into the circle of his arms, resting his chin on the top of her head as he gazed at the ranch. Maybe it had been Fate that brought him here, the same Fate that had taken him to the Lakota. Because of White-Eagle-That-Soars-in-the-Sky, he had become a warrior, and he had repaid White Eagle the best way he knew how, by providing the Lakota Agency with beef and supplies so that the Indians had food and clothing.

He missed the Lakota people, missed their way of life, but the Double S was home now and his roots ran deep into the earth here, roots that bound him to the land, to his grandparents, to his son, and most of all, to the enchanting creature in his arms.

Leaning back, he gazed into the face of the woman he loved, wishing he had the words to tell her how much he adored her, how important she was to him.

And then he saw Carrie smile, her beautiful green eyes shining with love, and he knew he didn't need to say the words out loud. Carrie could read them in his eyes, feel them in his arms, taste them in his kisses.

So he kissed her with all the love in his soul and trusted Carrie to hear the words with her heart.

And she did.